MIRRORS BENEATH THE EARTH

Short Fiction
by Chicano Writers

Edited by Ray González

CURBSTONE PRESS

FIRST EDITION, 1992
Introduction copyright © 1992 by RAY GONZALEZ
ALL RIGHTS RESERVED

Cover image: detail from a mural in L.A. by Luis J. Rodriguez
Cover design by Stone Graphics
Printed in the U.S. by BookCrafters

Curbstone Press is a 501(c)(3) nonprofit literary arts
organization whose operations are supported in part
by private donations and by grants from the ADCO
Foundation, the J. Walton Bissell Foundation, the
Connecticut Commission on the Arts, the LEF Foundation,
the Lila Wallace-Reader's Digest Literary Publishers
Marketing Development Program, administered by the
Council of Literary Magazines and Presses, the Andrew
W. Mellon Foundation, the National Endowment for the
Arts, and the Plumsock Fund.

Library of Congress Cataloging-in-Publication Data

Mirrors beneath the earth: short fiction by Chicano
    writers/edited by Ray Gonzalez. — 1st ed.
        p.   cm.
      ISBN 1-880684-02-0: $13.95
      1. Short stories, American—Mexican American
    authors. 2. Mexican Americans—Fiction. I.
    Gonzalez, Ray.
    PS647.M49M56   1992
    813'.010886872—dc20   92-27664

distributed in the U.S. by
InBook
Box 120261
East Haven, CT 06512

CURBSTONE PRESS
321 Jackson Street
Willimantic, CT 06226

ACKNOWLEDGEMENTS

ALCALA, "Mrs. Vargas and the Dead Naturalist," from *Mrs. Vargas and the Dead Naturalist*, Calyx Books. Copyright ©1992 by Kathleen Alcalá and Calyx Books. Printed by permission of the author.

ANAYA, "The Man Who Found a Pistol," Copyright ©1992 by Rudolfo Anaya. Printed by permission of the author.

BACA, "Brown Hair," Copyright ©1992 by Ana Baca. Printed by permission of the author.

BLANCO, "Rosario Magdaleno," Copyright ©1992 by Patricia Blanco. Printed by permission of the author.

BURCIAGA, "La Puerta," Copyright ©1992 by José Antonio Burciaga. Printed by permission of the author.

CANDELARIA, "Family Thanksgiving," Copyright ©1992 by Nash Candelaria. Printed by permission of the author.

CASTILLO, "Subtitles," Copyright ©1992 by Ana Castillo. Reprinted by permission of Susan Bergholz Literary Services, New York.

CHAVEZ, "Saints," from *Face of an Angel*, a novel by Denise Chávez. Copyright ©1992 by Denise Chávez. Reprinted by permission of Susan Bergholz Literary Services, New York.

CISNEROS, "Tepeyac," from *Woman Hollering Creek*, Copyright© 1991, Sandra Cisneros. Published in the United States by Vintage Books, a division of Random House, Canada, Limited, Toronto. Originally published in hard cover by Random House, Inc., New York in 1991. Reprinted by permission of Susan Bergholz Literary Services, New York.

CORPI, "Insidious Disease," from *Eulogy for a Brown Angel*, Arte Publico Press, 1992. Copyright ©1992 by Lucha Corpi. Printed by permission of the author.

FERNANDEZ, "Esmerelda," Copyright ©1990 by Roberta Fernández and Arte Publico Press. Excerpted from *Intaglio: A Novel in Six Stories*. (Arte Publico Press, 1990). Printed by permission of the author.

GASPAR DE ALBA, "The Last Rite," Copyright ©1992 Bilingual Press/Editorial Bilingüe. From *The Mystery of Survival and Other Stories*.(Bilingual Press, Arizona State University). Reprinted by permission of the author and Bilingual Press.

GILB, "The Death Mask of Pancho Villa," Copyright ©1992 by Dagoberto Gilb. Published in *American Short Fiction (1)* in spring 1991. Reprinted by permission of the author.

GONZALEZ, "Of Color and Light," Copyright ©1992 by Rafael Jesús González. Printed by permission of the author.

GONZALEZ, "The Ghost of John Wayne," Copyright ©1992 by Ray González. Printed by permission of the author.

HEINEMANN, "Salvation," Copyright ©1992 by Alexanna Padilla Heinemann. Printed by permission of the author.

HERRERA, "Days of Invasion," Copyright ©1992 by Juan Felipe Herrera. Previously unpublished. Printed by permission of the author.

LOPEZ, "La Luz," Copyright ©1992 by Jack Lopez. Reprinted with permission by the author.

Table of Contents

INTRODUCTION by Ray González   9

Dagoberto Gilb
THE DEATH MASK OF PANCHO VILLA   13

Patricia Blanco
ROSARIO MAGDALENO   22

Alberto Alvaro Ríos
WALTZ OF THE FAT MAN   28

Denise Chávez
SAINTS   38

Sandra Cisneros
TEPEYAC   52

Alma Luz Villanueva
PEOPLE OF THE DOG   55

Leroy V. Quintana
THE ROSARY   59

Luis J. Rodriguez
SOMETIMES YOU DANCE WITH A WATERMELON   67

Lucha Corpi
INSIDIOUS DISEASE   76

Ray González
THE GHOST OF JOHN WAYNE   83

Juan Felipe Herrera
DAYS OF INVASION   99

Benjamin Alire Sáenz
ALLIGATOR PARK   113

Mary Helen Ponce
THE MARIJUANA PARTY   140

Victoriano Martinez
THE BLACKBIRD   157

Ana Castillo
SUBTITLES   166

Jack Lopez
LA LUZ   176

Rafael Jesús González
OF COLOR AND LIGHT   191

Ricardo Means Ybarra
Chapter One from THE PINK ROSARY   194

Rich Yañez
AGUA BENDITA (HOLY WATER)   220

Roberta Fernández
ESMERALDA   226

Danny Romero
FIREWORKS   243

José Antonio Burciaga
LA PUERTA   250

Ana Baca
BROWN HAIR   256

Nash Candelaria
FAMILY THANKSGIVING   262

Natalia Treviño
CARDINAL RED   269

Rudolfo Anaya
THE MAN WHO FOUND A PISTOL   280

Alexanna Padilla Heinemann
SALVATION   288

Kathleen Alcalá
MRS. VARGAS AND THE DEAD NATURALIST   293

Luis Alberto Urrea
MR. MENDOZA'S PAINTBRUSH   301

Alicia Gaspar de Alba
THE LAST RITE   312

Alejandro Murguía
A SUBTLE PLAGUE   321

BIOGRAPHICAL NOTES   327

INTRODUCTION

by Ray González

Mirrors Beneath the Earth celebrates the art of Chicano short fiction, perhaps the strongest genre in Chicano literature today. Short story writers have been largely responsible for the growing audience for multicultural writing and the national attention Chicano authors have gained in recent years. While poets led the way in the sixties and seventies, writers like Sandra Cisneros, Benjamin Sáenz, and Ana Castillo have brought new life and vision to fiction in the nineties. They join the experienced voices of Alberto Ríos, Roberta Fernández, and Juan Felipe Herrera in welcoming a talented group of younger Chicano fiction writers, many of them gathered in this book for the first time.

The title for this collection evokes how Chicano short fiction is always rising out of the earth, a natural and cultural writing which encompasses the power of landscape, autobiographical experience, and the political realities of the environments in which these writers first gained their need to create and speak out. As we uncover each story, we find two crucial aspects of Chicano fiction — real knowledge of the world and wild, imaginary adventures grounded in family myth, superstition, and traditional values. The result is some of the most magical and unpredictable contemporary fiction.

The short story received a great deal of attention in the previous decade. Its renaissance in the eighties has made it one of the most effective genres in capturing the spirit of the Americas as the turn of the century approaches. A key to understanding the state of the country is acknowledging how much political and artistic power so many cultures and people have gained in the United States. The result is a multicultural nation whose writers are deeply involved in preserving their unique experiences, but also writing to encompass the universality of living in the same country.

Chicano fiction writers know this is a time of rich creativity and cultural prosperity, so they are in the thick of all these changes. They are also realistic enough to see there are still too many political and racial barriers impacting on their people and their evolution as artists. By using the form of the short story to respond, these writers have made Chicano literature one of the most important areas of American arts and letters — a truly ground breaking element of the current boom in multicultural writing.

The stories in *Mirrors Beneath the Earth* reflect on how the Chicano experience belongs to us all because the action of its characters and its fictitious worlds are part of the daily evolution of all people, not only sharing the immediate earth of family, but also seeing themselves throughout the entire continent.

July, 1992

MIRRORS BENEATH THE EARTH

Short Fiction by Chicano Writers

THE DEATH MASK
OF PANCHO VILLA

Dagoberto Gilb

It's late, very late. I've been in bed since eleven o'clock, for almost four hours, trying to get some sleep. I haven't been going to bed this early, but it's Sunday night and there's nothing on television. Not that I really like to watch television late at night the rest of the days. I do it too much because I don't know what else to do with myself. Probably I could listen to music on the radio. That's not true, I almost forgot. There's nothing on on the radio anymore, and around here, whether it's El Paso *tejano* or Juárez *ranchera*, pop from Mexico City, hard or soft American rock, it's all boring, and anyway there's commercial after commercial, just as irritating, maybe even more so, as the ones on late-night television. Okay, so maybe it's me.

Really it's not late, it's early, early morning, and one other reason I need to get some sleep is that I have to be somewhere at eight. I've arranged, finally, to see about getting some work. I've been treating it pretty easy for a while, telling myself I was sick of doing physical labor and trying hard to blame my age for feeling that way. Unsuccessfully. So I've been sitting around, not doing as much as I probably should, getting soft. Doing too much television, I'll tell you the truth. I have to admit, that isn't what I consider having a great time, but it can't be called suffering either. Our bills might be getting paid, my kids might be running around laughing and breaking things, my wife might finally keep a job for a while, but we're not getting rich. Not

13

that I ever really lived my life trying to get rich. Which is why I've been feeling guilty about my working situation, my lack of it. It's gotten me jumpy and nervous, worried about something really bad happening to us while I'm doing nothing about a paycheck. Which might help explain why I think the worst when I hear that pounding at the door. For a few seconds I don't realize what it is, and my wife is so sound asleep I can't wake her up enough to get her opinion.

What I do is pick up my son's aluminum baseball bat. I even think of putting on my boots. I guess that's some deal I have, not wanting to get into late-night violence shoeless. Why do I think it might be something violent? Good question. I guess it shows how I'm thinking, even if it doesn't make much sense — violent criminals aren't going to be knocking on the door, ringing the bell to wake me up. I'm just asleep and not reasoning too clearly. Also there's been a lot of talk in the papers about thieves breaking in. Desperate young punks from the other side of the river disobeying all the rules of thief etiquette.

But when I finally get the door open it's just a friend and some other guy I don't know. One of my oldest, best friends in all the world, a guy I started hanging out with in high school, then after that worked a few construction jobs with. We shared a lot of girlfriends, a lot of bottles and cans, and traveled together often when we did...well, outlaw business, years ago. All to say that I've had some of the best times I've ever had with the guy. We're still friends, but time has passed. We both ended up married — him first! — and we both had kids, and our wives talk to each other more than we do. Which is how I heard he was having some home troubles. First he got suspended from his job at the railroad. Then he got caught, or accused of, being bad with another woman, and Dora, his wife, threw him out of the house. She did the whole routine — threw his clothes out onto the driveway with an empty suitcase and locked all the doors and windows.

"You whore," I tell him after I turn on the yellow outdoor light. Gabe's wearing a tight, too-small, white T-shirt and still looks in good shape, particularly for a man in his late thirties. It

14

makes me feel bad that there he is, like always, a beer in his hand, a glaze in his eyes, somehow being healthier than me, drunk and whatever else. The only thing not like him is that the T-shirt and jeans are a little dirty and wrinkled, and his hair, which when he worked steady he didn't keep so long, looks like it just got off a pillow, same as mine. Stuff his wife, it would seem at this moment, has been taking care of for a long time.

I go ahead and open the screen door too, and go onto the front porch with my socks on. "Everybody in the house is asleep," I say, an explanation for why I'm not offering them the indoor accommodations. We shake hands, then wrap arms around one another for a long-time-no-see *abrazo*. "I've been wondering about you. Hear about you having too much fun."

"Gotta have fun sometimes. You know that." Gabe's grin is almost exuberant.

"I heard about the clothes on the driveway too."

"Which ones?" he says, still smiling.

"Whadaya mean?"

"There were two sets of them."

I don't understand, and I don't say anything.

"A day or two after the old lady handed me a suitcase, that other bitch came over and threw a pile she had on the driveway too," he tells me, and we laugh pretty good. "You know what I said when Dora called me about that? 'She didn't hit the grease spot, did she?' When she hung up on me my fucking ear hurt."

We're both laughing while Gabe's friend keeps this steady smile throughout. "This is Ortíz," Gabe says, finally introducing us. "Román Ortíz." I shake his friend's hand. Despite the smile, the man's gauntness, for me, translates into something I can't quite put a name on, and my first impression is that his loose, western-style clothes don't seem to suit his character.

It gets too quiet for a moment. Not a dog, not even the shuffle of a breeze. It looks very dark beyond the yellow porch, and cold, though it isn't.

"You wanna beer?" Gabe asks me, plucking off a can from the vine of three he'd carried to the porch.

"No. It's kinda late for me. Or early."

Gabe looks at me disappointed and the other guy looks at Gabe, though still with that smile. Gabe breaks the tab from the can he'd offered me.

I feel bad, immediately, for saying no. Somehow I've done something to spoil the visit, I've brought things down a notch. "So how you been really?" I ask.

"All right," he tells me, uneffusive. He takes a couple swallows of beer.

"What about that job?" I ask. "You gonna get back there?" Working at the railroad, you have to understand, is one of the best-paying jobs in the city.

Gabe makes a sour face and leans against the porch railing. "A bunch of suckass *culeros*. I'll find something better."

Very few people could. Very few people would want to leave that job. Gabe can do both. I believe it as much as he does. I used to feel the same way about myself, though not anymore. I try to blame that on El Paso or the times or my age. But I'm only a year older than Gabe. It's another thing I admire about him and dislike about me.

Ortíz hasn't so much as moved except to sip on the beer he has. "You mind if I piss over there?" he asks, indicating beyond the porch.

"Of course not," I say. "I do it all the time." I don't all the time, but once in a while, just to keep in practice.

Gabe and I don't say anything until we hear Ortíz's stream hitting the hard dirt that is my front yard.

"So what's up?" I finally ask.

"This guy has something I thought you'd want to see," Gabe says. "Remember that time we were in Mexico and that old dude said he had pictures of him with Pancho Villa?"

I was into collecting Pancho Villa stuff years ago because he was my hero. More than that really. Anyway, I'd found letters he'd written, bought a holster and pistol that was supposed to be his, and in our front room I still have a framed document Villa'd signed for my great-uncle saying what an honor it'd been to fight together during the Revolution. It has been a while since I've thought about any of this though. I guess because I had children and got married. And worked a lot. And because I got older. I've got all kinds of excuses if I let myself think about it.

"So he has photographs?" I say, trying to sound interested. I'm not at all.

"A mask," says Gabe.

Ortíz is stepping back up onto the porch. "His death mask."

"I've never heard of such a thing," I say.

"There were three of them made," Ortíz says. Same smile. "A Hollywood producer has one and a senator has the other." Ortíz opens another can of beer. No change in the smile, but the face around it seems prouder now.

My first impression isn't improving. I'm pretty sure Gabe's just met the guy in a bar, and in my humble opinion...well, I'd call it bar talk.

Gabe lights a joint. I'm wishing I were back in bed, the door locked. Which makes me feel bad again. What's happened to me? I don't think anything's wrong with marijuana, and I like smoking it the same as I always have. That's what I say anyway. The only thing is I don't smoke it very often anymore. I even have about two or three joints' worth in a bag that was given to me almost a year ago. I guess I never want to smoke it by myself, and I'd be embarrassed now to use it with anyone else because it's so dried out. I should throw it away. I will throw it away.

I go ahead and smoke some because I don't know how to say no to this too, though the truth is that's what I feel like saying. I don't know why we're not talking. I think it has something to do with me, with me standing in my socks, not inviting them in, not saying let's go. Though maybe it's Gabe. He's too quiet, and it can't be only that he's unhappy because I don't feel like drinking beer. Maybe it's something between him and Ortíz. When we used to hang out together a lot, it was usually Gabe who met the guys like this in the first place. Gabe was the one who'd listen and believe, while I was the one who was skeptical. Gabe'd get all the information, I'd put it together, then we'd both come up with a conclusion, a decision — you know, we'd solve another little human-oddball mystery, and sometimes actually do something with the person. Either buy or sell. Is this guy trying to sell Gabe something? Or trade? Or is Gabe thinking of a sale to him? But why would he need me after all these years? And if he does, why doesn't he just say something straight out? Then maybe he thinks I'd want to buy this mask. But why right now? It's about three A.M., or later, and I can't think.

"So are you selling this thing or what?" I ask Ortíz.

"Absolutely not."

He stares at me with that smile. I look for some kind of indication from Gabe, but there's none. We're finishing off the joint.

"Then what are you doing with it?"

"He's got it at his place," Gabe says. "Let's go see it."

"You haven't seen it?" I ask him.

"Sure. I want you to see it." He looks down at my feet. "All you gotta do is get some shoes." He drops the roach and grinds it out with the sole of his boot. Then he pops another can of beer. He stops leaning on the wrought-iron railing around the porch, and stands like he's ready to get going.

Gabe's push isn't out of exuberance now, but it's along those lines, some excess of something, and I can't figure it out. I start thinking about the problems he's having. No job, being away from his kids. Except that's not Gabe at all. I know him too well. He'll get back together with Dora whether she thinks she never wants to see him again or not, he'll get his job back or a better one, and I know he believes that too, and even if it doesn't turn out that way a few years from now, I know he wouldn't think it wouldn't. So it's not that, it's not like he needs me, needs a friend or some TV emotion like that. And somehow it doesn't seem like he really wants me to hang out either. He wants me to go with him, but it doesn't seem personal, it doesn't seem to me like he's asking. It's more like he's telling me to go with them. Like it's for my own good or something.

"I can't go tonight," I say, thinking it's not tonight but this morning.

"How come?" Gabe asks. He's disappointed again.

"I gotta do things. In a few hours as a matter of fact. Normal shit."

All of a sudden a cop car cruises by. Not slow and not fast, just on a routine pass through the neighborhood, except from behind us, from the dirt alley where we wouldn't have expected that blue-and-white to come from, and a dog starts barking at it because a dispatcher talks over the police radio and the window on the driver's side is down.

"Normal shit?" says Gabe. "Since when did you worry about normal shit?"

That stings because he's right. Or used to be. "Why don't I just see it tomorrow? You taking it out of town or something?" I'm feeling a little defensive now. "Somebody buying it?" I look at Gabe. He's not looking back at me.

"I'm giving it away," says Ortíz. "There are only three of them, and I'm sending mine to Moscow." His smile is the same but it's fading.

"Moscow?" I look at Gabe once more and feel stoned. He hits on his beer.

"In Russia," says Ortíz.

"I know where it is," I tell him. "Why there?"

"Because that's where John Reed is buried," Ortíz says. "John Reed wrote about the Mexican Revolution, then went to Russia and wrote about the Russian Revolution."

A smile starts to come on me because now the cop car is cruising by again, only this time in front of us, and it seems so ridiculous, especially because we're about to talk about communism or something at three or so in the morning and I don't have shoes on. Then another cop car goes by. We know it has to be another one because it's coming from another street, toward us, too soon after the last one. It turns right, opposite the direction the first one did. And now more dogs are barking in the neighborhood.

"I better turn off the light," I say. I open the screen door, then the other and reach inside to turn off the yellow porch light. A cop car passes a second later. "You guys better not leave for a while."

"I don't need a DWI," says Ortíz.

Ortíz's car, I notice for the first time, is faded green, or blue, I can't be positive in this dark, with a peeling vinyl roof.

"So how'd you get this mask?" I ask.

"I just did," Ortíz says, finishing his beer.

"How do you know it's Villa?"

"People have seen it. Warren Beatty saw it and wanted it." Warren Beatty, the actor. Now I am smiling the most. Dogs are barking all over the neighborhood and another cop car passes us. I swear it's a third one. I'm sure we can't be seen without that porch light on.

"Why not just keep it right here, right here in El Paso?" I suggest. "Probably a lot of people would like to see it. It'd be a great contribution. It seems to me anyway."

Ortíz turns his head away from me and my naïveté. "People here wouldn't respect it enough, and it's fragile. Over there they care about things more than they do here. All of Europe is like that too. They have museums to take care of important cultural things. In Germany there are probably thirty opera houses to every one here." The speech erases Ortíz's smile, and he steps over and reaches down to get the last can of beer.

"So you've been to Europe, to Germany?" I ask.

"No," Ortíz says, humorless.

It's that I've stolen his smile. I'm looking for cop cars and watching lights go on in the house across the street where a dog is barking the loudest and steadiest. "Moscow, huh?"

Ortíz gathers himself after a big swallow of beer. "The Mexican Revolution was the first in this century, and the Bolsheviks used it as an example of common people rising up. John Reed was there for both revolutions and was buried at the Kremlin as a hero. They'll put the mask near him as a memorial."

I'm still smiling, but not because I'm unconvinced or skeptical. More that the cops have quit driving by and the dog across the street won't stop barking, which is probably why another dog barks farther down the street. I'm smiling just thinking about how we're having this conversation about Russians and death masks in the dark and quiet on my El Paso porch with the light out, all while I'm in my socks.

"I'd really like to see it sometime," I say.

Neither of them say anything.

"I guess I should probably get a couple hours in," I say.

Gabe looks a little disappointed again. Or maybe apologetic. I don't want him to feel bad for coming by, for banging on my door. I haven't done anything for weeks but watch stupid television.

"You guys better look around to see if the police are waiting for you to pull away," I say. I wish I knew how to say more.

Gabe just shrugs off my worry. He never did care about things like that and, maybe because he didn't, never had to.

They both stop and piss before they get into Ortíz's car. It starts with a cheap gas and old motor sound, and finally rolls away without headlights for a few yards.

I lock the door and climb back in bed. I'm thinking that I probably can wait on seeing about this job, and I'm thinking how nice it feels being stoned and sleepy. My wife asks me who it was and I say it was Gabe and wait for her to ask me some more. She doesn't, but in my head I start asking questions for her and answering them. Or asking for myself: He wanted me to go out with him. To go see something this guy he knows had. No, I don't really know why I didn't go. No, I really don't know why he wanted me to. Maybe he thought because of Pancho Villa. Or maybe because he thought I'd have a good time. Which I haven't had in a long time. No, I don't know why I didn't go, I don't know why it didn't seem like I should. I used to not think about it, I used to just go. Gabe and I used to do things together. Things just like this.

I'm on my back in bed and my wife, after I've been lying there all this time, finally asks me what Gabe wanted. Nothing, I tell her, except he wanted me to go look at Pancho Villa's death mask. That makes me smile all over again. At what? she asks. Don't think about it, I say. But what time is it? she asks What's the difference? I say.

ROSARIO MAGDALENO

Patricia Blanco

I

So when I came to Phoenix in 1945, I stayed with my cousins on Maricopa Street and shared a bed with my cousin Kika. The son Chepe had TB and I took one look at him and knew he was going to die. And you know they were terrible cooks. All they ever ate was beans and *tortillas* for breakfast and *avena* and coffee. And then the same thing for lunch. Then for supper maybe a little meat or *sopa*. So one day I said, "Why don't we make a salad?" and my Aunt Ricarda said, "Oh I don't like salads," and I said, "Well maybe Chepe would." And so she asked him and he said, "Yes, I would." So after that I started making things. I made salads and pot roasts and *mole* and *enchiladas*. And then I would make pies. My mother and father used to make pies out of dried fruit because at that time it was cheaper than fresh. I told Kika, "I think I'll make some pies," and she said, "Out of what?" So I made so many pies — apricot and apple and others. And I made fudge and *jamoncillo*. Oh, Chepe loved my fudge. He would tell Kika, "Why don't you ask Chayo to make some fudge," and so I'd make some for him. It was such a hot summer and fall. He'd sit out on the screened porch with his cane — just sit and look out all day long, come in to eat, and go back out again. Sometimes my Aunt would sit there and talk to him.

I always did love to bake since I was a little girl. On Sundays I would bake them muffins or this *pan batido* that Nana used to make. Then one night my Aunt came into the bedroom and said, "*Está muriendo Chepe*." My cousin Mary and I ran down to the church and knocked and knocked. Finally the priest came to the door and we told him and he said, "*Sí, ahorita voy*." That was the first time I'd noticed the nights were getting cooler. It was such a beautiful night. I remember there was a harvest moon. Then we ran back to the house and by the time we got there he had died. His brother was already loading the truck with his cane and clothes and mattress. He took them out to the dump that night and burned them.

II

You know, my cousin Mary was so spoiled. She never did any work around the house and she was always complaining about something, always wanting something that the other girls had. I used to tell her, "Go to school. You can't do anything without a high school education." So she finally decided to go. One Saturday we took the streetcar down to the Salvation Army and we bought an old Smith Corona typewriter for her for fifteen dollars — one of those big, heavy black steel kind. She wrote a letter on it to her brother who was stationed in Germany just after the war. He wrote her back saying he was so proud of her that she was in school. I remember he told her, "I'll help you. I'll send you money."

But she wasn't serious. She didn't even last the month.

III

Once when my father was walking home from work, he found a dime on the sidewalk. So he went to Don Pedro's store and bought a loaf of bread and that night we ate those slices of bread as if they were cake. They tasted so good to us. We never had bread, only the corn *tortillas* my mother made. And at school it was considered a sign of prosperity to have bread to make sandwiches. At school we were ashamed of our *burritos* and we would try to hide them in our hands as we ate our lunch.

But you know there were times when we had more to eat during the Depression than we did before or afterwards because the government gave us surplus food. The welfare department set up an office in Miami and all the unemployed miners put in for welfare. At first they wouldn't give anything to people from Mexico and if you said anything they would tell you, "Go back to Mexico; we'll give you $250 to go back." Finally, one of the better-educated *mexicanos*, Mr. Baroldy, spoke to the higher-ups in Phoenix, and they said they could not deny aid to *mexicanos* since their children were born here. So they gave us half-rations. And later on after more interventions, they gave us full rations.

Oh, it was so nice when our order would come through. They would give us one quarter gunny sack-full of carrots, turnips, beets; one pound each of meat and one pound of butter. It was years before I could eat beets after that. I ate so many during the Depression.

But before then, before those programs, sometimes we just didn't have enough. I remember one afternoon my sister and I were so hungry and my mother had just made some *tortillas*, but there were only enough for dinner. I wanted one so bad, so Carmen and I each took one. We went outside and played on the tire swing my father had made for us. It was a very cold day and there we were swinging and laughing, eating those *tortillas* still warm and I was so hungry. My dad happened to come home just then, and he asked us what we were eating. We told him we were eating the *tortillas* my mother had made for dinner. He only looked at us with a very serious face and said, "Why are you doing that? Don't you know that if you eat those now we won't have enough for everyone?" Oh, he had tears in his eyes he felt so bad. He hated saying that to us because he knew we were hungry. I'll never forget how he asked us that question. And I didn't know what to answer.

IV

My father used to say, "There's no more excess baggage than an orphan. They'll always point to you and tell you, 'You're too lazy. You eat too much.'"

Well you know, his father died when he was two and his mother when he was thirteen. At first, after he was orphaned, he went to live with his brother Lúcio, but I guess he was never very happy there. He had so much pride; if someone would ask him, "Are you hungry?" he'd say no. "I'd just tighten my belt one more notch," he used to tell us. He never wanted to beg. I remember him saying to my mother, "*Cómo pasé hambres.*" *Pobrecito. Sufrió mucho.* Later, his brother Nicolás took him in. And his sister-in-law never begrudged him. They were good to him. His brother told him, "I want you to finish school," so Nicolás sent him to school and he finished the sixth grade, which for Mexico at that time was an accomplishment. He was always grateful for that.

In Miami, on cloudy days, he would go to bed — just go to bed and stay there for hours, because they reminded him of the day his mother died.

V

Mijita, now that you've asked me how my father died, I'm going to tell you once and then I don't want you to ever ask me again. He died in the Claypool mines, in a mining accident. I was a junior in high school and someone came to our classroom with a message. When my teacher looked straight at me and motioned me into the hall, I just prayed, "Please don't let it be my mother." I knew it was one of them and I knew it would be better if we didn't lose my mother, with all those little children to take care of. Can you imagine — ten children and some still in diapers, without a mother?

Oh, that was a black day. So terribly sad. And the house that night — all of us crying and crying. Our dog, Otelo, howled all night. He knew, somehow. Every evening he used to listen for my father's footsteps coming up the *cañón*. He could recognize them from far away. When he'd hear my father coming, he'd cock up one ear and then run to the top of the hill and watch to see him coming. Then he'd run down to meet him and he'd be so happy. For months after my father died, he'd still wait at the top of the hill in the afternoons, watching for him to come walking home.

VI

Sometimes I'll ask Joe or Carmen about something from our childhood in Grover's Canyon, and they won't remember. Even though they're older than me and they lived there longer, they don't remember things the way I do. Like one time I was asking my brother Joe, "Remember that family that lived on the other side of the *cañón*, what was their name?" "I don't remember." "Of course you do; they had two boys that were friends with you." "No, I don't remember them."

But I remember that family so well. They had this little girl, Lydia, and we were friends. Oh, we used to play by the hour, jumping rope, sewing clothes for our dolls — we had dolls then, before the Depression. And Lydia gave me this metal box with a lid on it, a real cute little box, to keep my doll clothes in. One day my father saw it and said, "Oh, that would make a good box to keep my tools in." So I gave it to him; I was glad to give him something that he needed. And then when he died, my brother Cuco took the box and the tools and I told him one day, "That box should be mine. I gave it to my father because he wanted it, but it was mine; my friend Lydia gave it to me." But he never did give it back.

I have so many memories, things I remember seeing that are as clear as if they were right here before me. There was this *cañón* next to ours called Warrior Canyon and the *mexicanos* lived on the top half and the *gringos* lived on the bottom. There was this old woman that lived up at the top. You know in those days all old women wore black and she looked so old. Every day she would take a walk along the top of the *cañón*. That is one of my first memories — seeing her walking up there, talking to herself, gesturing. She was a little retarded, actually. Or maybe she was crazy; I don't know. But she wasn't all there. There she would be on the top of the hill, holding conversations with herself, shaking her finger. Sometimes we would wave and she would wave back. And sometimes her grandchildren would be looking for her and start calling to her. Something must have happened to her, to make her go crazy. But we were used to things like that. And we never asked why.

WALTZ OF THE FAT MAN

Alberto Alvaro Ríos

Noé's house trim was painted blue, good blue, deep and neat, with particular attention to the front door, that it should stand against spirits. He kept the house in repair, and hired a gardener in the three seasons, spring and summer, a little in autumn. In this place it was a gray wind after that, a time for planting things in the ground to save them, or to hide them.

His personal appearance suffered nothing from the attentions to his house, as Noé kept on himself a trim mustache and a clean face, neat clothes for which he thanked Mrs. Martínez, patronizing her for a quarter of a century. From ironing his clothing, she knew the shape of his body more than he did, and for her consequent attention to detail in that regard he was appreciative — just the right fold in the collars, a crease moving a little to the left along his right leg, the minor irregularities and embarrassments. And he was doubly thankful as she never said a word to him about it.

His was a body full of slow bones, after all, and Noé moved as if long fish swam in a small place.

He did not think himself fat, but he felt himself heavy, in a manner he could not explain to anyone. His body to be sure was overweight, but he did not feel it to be something of the stomach or thighs; rather, it was a heaviness that came from the inside out, manifesting itself to the world as the body of a fat man.

On his best days, Noé could make that weight look like muscles. On his best days he could make his stomach go into his chest and his shoulders, and people would believe anything he had to say.

Noé had a business as a butcher, but it was too much for him, a sadness cutting the meats. He had become a butcher, after all, purely for social reasons. It was a civic service, and he wanted to do good things. But it was not a good choice, given what he desired, which was simply to be part of the town.

To be sure, people patronized his shop, and took him up on his offer of extra services and niceties, but they did not finally stay very long to talk, not in the way they stayed for coffee and to warm themselves at the baker's. He could see them in there, with their mouths open and their eyes rolling along a line of laughter.

He could not say why the townspeople were like this, exactly. Perhaps it was his full size, or something about his looks, or about being the butcher in a town and being too good at his trade. But, the whole of his life was that no one cared much for him, or even spoke to him very much, and when he attended wakes, which he did because he was a courteous man, he left indentations in the kitchen linoleum which would not go away.

Noé knew that, though he tried not to be, in the people's minds he was simply an irritation.

In whatever part of the town he walked, people spoke behind their hands, and pointed when they didn't think Noé could see them. But his eyes were fat as well, and because of that he could see more.

§ § §

When Noé danced, he wore a blue suit, and was always alone, always at the same place outside of town, by the river reeds.

He danced with the wind, which was also cruel like the women of the town, but the wind at least did not have a face. He locked the trunks of his arms with the branch arms of the black walnut trees, which also like the women of the town did not bend around to hold him, did not invite him to another, softer room.

But neither could these arms of a tree leave Noé so easily. They could not so quickly give him over cruelly to the half-hot tongues of the weeds so that they might talk about him, and make their disapproving sounds.

When he danced this dance he let out with a small noise his thin girl, which he kept inside himself. This is what had made him look fat, the holding in, the keeping in of the noise inside himself, his desire to freely speak his needs as a human being in the company of other human beings. This was his thin girl.

And Noé would let her out and they would dance the dance of weddings into the night.

§ § §

Noé took to wearing his blue suit to the shop, because he thought he looked better. He did this in case someone would look at him, and think the better of him, think him something of a fine man after all.

Then his plan of the blue suit grew into a great deal more, taking as he did the wearing of his suit as some small license. It was the license, he thought, of a regular man. And he tried what he imagined to be the secret work of a regular man in the company of a regular woman.

When he shook the hands of women, he did so vigorously, hoping to see movement on their bodies, some small adventure to take his breath, some nodding yes, some quiet dance of the upper body. This first adventure of a man.

His was a modest plan, and worked a little. The shaking of the hand was, however, the most Noé did. It gave him so much, and he thought the intimate movements of a woman to be so loud, there in front of everybody, that he could go no further.

But it is why Noé attended wakes so faithfully as well, sometimes as if they were the whole of his social life: how in comforting a bereaved wife he could — properly and in front of everyone so that there was no question of propriety — kiss her on the cheek.

Even then, after the hour of praying for the deceased and thinking about what he would do, by the time his moment was at hand, his attempt at kissing was a dizzied missing of the mark. His lips to the cheek were so clumsy and so fast that the kiss was more of something else, something not quite anything, something in keeping with his life after all.

§ § §

The butcher shop through the slow years began to change, as did Noé himself. He had taken up in his house the collection and caring of clocks, because, he said to himself, they had hands, and in so many clocks was a kind of heaven, a dream of sounds to make the hours pass in a manner that would allow him to open up shop again the next day.

His nighttime dream became a daytime dream as well. He did not keep them, could not keep the clocks, finally, only at home. Along with Noé in his blue suit, the shop also began to find itself dressed differently, hung with clocks, first one, a plain dark wood, and then two, and then a hundred. Each of them with two hands for him.

There was a blue clock. Cuckoos and 28-day, anniversary clocks to the side of the scale, large-faced numbers where once there had been letters in the sections of an illustrated cow.

What Noé knew and did not say was that here was the anniversary Mariquita, the schoolhouse Mariette, Marina the singular blue, Caras with her bird tongue. Armida had hands that sometimes rose outstretched to the two and ten like the blessing arms of Christ, and sometimes lowered to the five and seven of desire, one hand shorter, in the act of beckoning him, *a come here, Noé. A come here, I've got something to tell you, Noé, come on, don't be afraid.*

This was no butcher shop, the townspeople would say to themselves, not with clocks. One or two clocks maybe, but not so many as this. It would not have been so bad, except that he was the only butcher in town, and people had to make use of his services. An unofficial inquiry was opened as to whether or not there was perhaps a law, some ordinance, prohibiting such abuses of the known world, but no one could find any reference that applied to the walls of a butcher shop, other than cleanliness. And of that, there could be no discussion. Noé did not neglect the clocks, and therefore did not neglect the white-sheeted bed of his walls.

§ § §

One evening in winter as Noé was closing up his shop, having wound the clocks for the night and having left just enough heat in the stove that they would not suffer, he heard the blue clock falter. So much like a heartbeat had the sounds of the clocks come to be for him, that he was alarmed and stumbled in his quickness to reach the clock, though it could not move and was not falling. It called to him nonetheless as a wife in pain might call to her husband: *honey*, it said, *please*.

He reached it too late, he thought, though it was simply a clock, and he laughed at himself.

He tried winding the clock again, thinking the unthinkable, that perhaps he had missed its turn in his haste to leave. But that was not it: the spring was taut, and there was no play.

He took it down from its nail, and looked at it from different angles in his hands, but he could see nothing extraordinary. There was no obvious damage, no one had dropped it without telling him and rehung it, no insect had been boring into its side. Its blue was still blue, without blemish.

He took it to the counter and measured out some butcher's paper in which to wrap it, deciding that he would take it home to see to its difficulty. He put string around it and made a good blanket of the paper, which should comfort, he always said, what was inside. As he picked it up he could hear the workings move, and he resolved to be wary of its delicacy.

He need not have done it, but he warned himself, as if he were his own mother. He put the clock in the crook of his arm, closed and locked his door, took a deep breath in the cold air, hunched his shoulders and began his walk toward home.

He had errands, but they could wait. And he was, in any event, the last of the merchants to close for the evening, so he would have been out of luck anyway. Save for the clock, this was how his evenings most often came to an end, the closing of the door and the walk toward home.

An occasional voice greeted him, and he returned the hello, but it was the conversation of single words, friendly enough, and that was all.

§ § §

Some theorized later it was the soldiers who were common in those days and who hung around with nothing better to do, that it was they who had been paid, because they never did anything for nothing, but would do anything for something, those soldiers from that kind of army.

There was nothing tragic, of course, nothing for which any charges could be drawn, in much the same manner that nothing could be legally said about what Noé had done to his butcher's shop. You get back what you give, someone was later reported as having said, someone but not anyone in particular. That's how it was told to the captain of the police.

Noé was walking home with his package, which no one could have known was the blue clock. No one but perhaps the soldiers, and only then if they had been nosy enough to have been watching through his window, which had been recently broken and was full of cardboard patches, easy enough to hide behind.

The package's aspect was of a ham or a roast of some sort, a good rabbit, something simple and natural in the arm of a big man walking home to dinner.

Darkness had set and the moon was new. He cast no shadow and made his way quickly as he left the last of the downtown buildings. The ground was neither muddy nor dry, resembling something closer to a woody mulch, and through him passed a moment of gardens from sometime in his life, gardens he had passed through, or that his mother had kept. It was a simple feeling, and brought a prickling to his skin.

He next passed by the stand of walnut trees and wild oleander which was white-flowered in the summer.

The oleander called to him, *Noé*.

At first it was so quiet he said to himself he did not hear it, *Noé*.

Noé the oleanders said, louder this time, and he stopped to look. Though it was dark and the moon was hidden, he was not afraid.

His size was such that he had never been made to be afraid, not at a moment like this. It was, if one could read his face, a curiosity, this sound which was reminiscent of his name. It was like the mulch and his mother's garden, and it gave him a prickling of the skin once more.

Noé. He heard it again, and stopped, and turned to it, saying who was there, what did they want, that perhaps he could be of some service.

No one answered, so he reached his free hand into the leaves and moved them around. He heard the sound and then saw what seemed like, in the dimness, a rabbit, running into the underbrush.

Ha, he said, and let it go. He turned again to walk, pulling his coat back up onto his neck.

Noé. It was a whisper, this time he was sure. Not a voice, but more of a breath. A half-breath, but unmistakable in its enunciation.

As a child, Noé might have crossed himself, and as he was sometimes his own mother, he had the impulse, but he just stood there, once more.

He put down the clock in order to enter the oleander more fully, and see what was what, but he found nothing, only branches and the small noises of startled birds and lizards.

When he came out he could not find his package, though he concentrated with his eyes and with his hands. It was not there.

A voice whispered once more, *Noé. You know me*, it said, *you know who I am.*

Noé no longer moved around. He listened, and he waited.

Noé. He did know the whisper. He had in fact heard it many times. He knew the whisper more than the voice of his neighbor, whom he had seen a thousand times.

He would not have believed any of it had this not been the blue clock. Marina his blue, who had made so many places for herself in his life. Not big places, but so many, her hair color on the trim of his house, the color of her eyes in his suit, and so on. She was the blueness inside him, the color of his appetite, the color both of what filled him and what he needed more of.

Marina, he said.

Noé.

He stood there and waited.

Do you love me?

Noé did not answer.

You can love me if you love me like a horse, said the whisper. *Can you be a horse. Noé? Can you show me how you are a horse?*

Noé stood there, quietly.

He stamped his foot, gingerly at first, unsure and sure at the same time.

Is that it, Noé, is that all the horse you are?

Noé stamped his foot harder, and made a noise with his nose, and partway through his mouth.

Yes Noé. And are you more of a horse still?

If this were anything but his blue clock, Marina, he would have gone, and given the moment up as the ghosts of this place. Or children, or who knew what. But he could not.

And then he heard the laughter of the soldiers as they could no longer contain themselves camouflaged so well otherwise in the oleanders. He heard the laughter, but did not bother with it. He turned and went home, without the clock.

§ § §

He had gone away from home once before, from his family. He had to. One thing and another, right or wrong, these things didn't matter. It was simply too much to stay.

He had in some manner become an exponent to a regular number. He was ordinary times ten or times twenty, always too much. And his desire carried an exponent as well. He wanted everything to be nice, to be only the Golden Rule, but times ten, and that is too much. He had no sense of himself, and yet he was everything. In that sea of mathematics he had drowned a sailor's death.

And now he had to go away again. The tide had come up, and caught him once more. He sold what was left of his business at a loss finally to Mr. Molina, who had a scarred face and who wanted to do the work. There was an art in the cutting, and it took Noé, because he was a courteous man, the afternoon to teach the profession's immediate intricacies to Mr. Molina, who had had no idea there was so much.

And that same night Noé bought a brown horse and rode it as far into the following days and weeks, as far into the future as he could because he could not wait to see what was there. He arrived at the circus, and in it he made his life again.

But he almost did not make it. A man and a sparrow — each puts a shoulder to the wind, each to his own intention: a sparrow to fly, a man to run. Noé on this night was in between, and even with his weight he felt himself lifted, as if he were in league with angels at the edge of heaven, not quite deserving, but sneaking in with some help through a back door, hoping to go unnoticed again, as he had felt when he had come to this town. But it was not heaven, these places.

He stopped because the circus people were the first to wave him down, all of them standing near the road, as if this were the place, and they knew him, and they had been waiting, and what took him so long, had he not heard them calling into the night for him.

But they had called him without telegraph or telephone. Something stronger.

His mustache curled up from the wind and his body, which had sometimes seemed fat, was hardened, tense in that moment from the cold which had made him hold his breath and flex his muscles for the whole distance of the ride.

He arrived as a beast, almost, something crazed and unshaven, out of breath.

Or as a beast on top of a man, as if the horse itself were more human, and asking for help.

His was a body full of slow bones still, but if it had taken his lifetime up to now to be slow, now the other foot was coming down, and it was fast.

It was the other half of himself now, for the rest of his years.

This was, after all, the place. And in that moment of dust kicked up and of noise, he began his real career, this life with a whole company of half-size men, two-bodied women, and all the rest of the animals who danced.

SAINTS

Denise Chávez

I have always identified with saints.

St. Dymphna, particularly, patroness of the mentally ill.

I also identify with martyrs, young women who chose Christ as their sole spouse, women who would rather have their breasts ripped off than betray their chastity.

I identify most especially with María Goretti, the Italian girl who chose to die rather than succumb to the concupiscence of the flesh. María lived on a farm in Italy, with her parents, brothers, sisters, and a hired hand, a young man. Drawn to the flesh, he hid magazines of naked women under his bed that he reveled in lasciviously.

One day, while all the family was out working, the young man stayed behind. For some reason, Maria was in the house as well.

The young man cornered María with evil intent. She cried out, but no one could hear her. She tried to escape. He chased her, insisting she give in to him, that it would be all right. She resisted, praying to God to save her. Throwing her down, he beat her, raped her, and then killed her.

When the family returned later that day they found María dead. The young man had escaped. He was hunted down, captured, and put on trial. He repented, calling upon the Holy Father, his Holiness the Pope, to forgive him. Interceding in a way not known before, the Pope took the fellow into his residence, where he was assigned the role of gardener. For many years the man, quietly and repentantly, cared for the Pope's roses.

This is the story as I remember it from the little book on María Goretti that I used to read in school. There was a series of small books for children, *Lives of the Saints*, that were kept on the window ledge library of the sixth grade class of Holy Angel Elementary School. The book on Saint María Goretti was one of the most popular. She was a contemporary saint, that is what struck us as unusual, not some by-gone Roman virgin thrown into a pit of lions. Her story was all the more potent because it was set in modern times. St. Maria Goretti was not some removed, far-flung virgin, she was someone who lived in the present.

I myself checked this book out three or four times. It was a mysterious book to me, for it hinted at a unknown world of vice and degradation so evil it could barely be imagined.

I was removed from that world. I could not conceive of it at all. Just as I could not understand the number 69 or the word FUCK seen on the walls on my walks home from school, I had no knowledge of the violent creation sexuality had become, always was to some.

I knew María Goretti was violated, but how?

This book, then, was our introduction to passion. Unbridled, unrestrained, demoniac. The book was checked out by everyone that passed through Holy Angel, because it dealt with the secret, unapproachable world of sex, and crimes against the very core of one's self.

Recently, someone tried to correct my version of the Goretti tale. The Pope part was supposedly not true, not to mention all the gardener business. But I do remember reading an article and seeing photographs of the gardener.

To me, it was more just and wonderful that the young man, slave to his baser nature, had found peace and rest in the sweet, cleansing aroma of the roses. To think of him there made me cry. I want to believe that he is the Pope's gardener. It's more tolerable to imagine he repented in the beauty of the roses, in the sunlight, under the shade of cool trees than in a prison cell, cut off from all redemption.

Saints come in all shapes, sizes and moods.

I think of St. Sebastian, showered with arrows and bound by rope to a tree, his magnificent body slumped in death. His beautiful male form stands there, in perfect stillness, beyond all further mutilation, a bloodied male flower in sunlight.

The Little Flower, St. Theresa of Lisieux, is the saint of the child in all of us. She is a pure, simple, unaffected child of God. Saints are different to children than they are to adults. When you are a child, saints have more of a sweet reality. Adult saints and the saints adults revere are more desperate, like St. Jude, patron of impossible cases, or St. Anthony, who spends all his time looking for lost glasses or shoes. They are gimme gimme something saints, help me saints, incurable last stand saints, lost and found saints.

Saints are also culturally rooted, like San Martin de Porres. He is the first black man I ever knew about. He is very handsome and always seems happy. He is a saint for all displaced people; himself an outcast by color. He is somehow very dear to all Mexicanos. He once worked with lepers and the poor. He is so nice! We embrace him like a brother and admire his thick curly hair, not unlike our own. He is a saint for all Latinos, a get-ahead saint, who is loved and accepted by all the *viejitas*, who would never allow their daughters (¡Ni lo mande Dios!) to marry Black. Proudly these old women display large, glass-covered framed images of San Martín in his brown habit over their antique bureaus in their darkened, private bedrooms, bedrooms unvisited by men for over thirty years.

Then there is the Santo Niño de Atocha, who goes out regularly with his worn shoes to help the poor and the defenseless late at night. Returning in the early morning hours, before anyone is awake, he settles into his tiny niche, his shoes splattered with mud.

San Isidro helps the farmers and blesses their animals.

Juan Bosco always draws a crowd of young people to his side, mostly young boys, because all the good women saints are usually ex-whores or breathless virgins, or old women widowed for many years.

St. Christopher, brawny, fearless, ferries travelers across strange shores.

St. Joseph is the surrogate father of Jesus, so all male-related cases fall to him: errant and lazy husbands, sex-starved, shiftless *pelados*, men with small and/or ineffectual penises, troubled male children who lock themselves too long in the bathroom, incorrigible fathers and bachelors. Mothers who are looking for a husband for their daughters also pray to him, as do young and old women who want to either find or lose a husband.

St. Anne is prayed to by old women and future mothers, those concerned about their wombs in one form or another.

St. Francis is the saint for everyone, even non-Catholics. What is more universal than birds and animals, and marauding wolves to be tamed? St. Francis is also the saint of the once rich and now poor, or the poor and the spiritually rich and the not rich not poor who would like to give themselves up to nature and the spirit of brotherhood inherent in all men, if only they could. St. Francis is definitely male and in the upper echelon of male saints. One rarely hears about his counterpart, St. Claire her work. But then again, most saints are male, except the unfortunate heretofore mentioned limbless, sightless, wombless, or sexless.

For years I wore scapulars, blue, brown, green, white. I carried wood from Jerusalem in my bra, blessed myself with Holy Water, ate sacred bread and touched wondrous dirt. I carried relics of splintered bone or tiny locks of hair or nails in my wallet and purse, pinned them to my undergarments and wore sacred wood around my neck and wrists. I said countless ejaculations, short prayers that rolled off the tongue like a litany of breath. My mother my confidence. My mother my confidence. *Dulce corazón de María sálvame. Dulce corazón de María sálvame.*

I always prayed to the Holy Mother, the Virgin Mary. She was Our Lady of Fatima, Our Lady of Guadalupe, the Black Virgin and Our Lady of Lourdes all rolled into one. She was the spirit mother that held me, small child against her breast.

But always I come back to St. Dymphna, saint of the insane. I don't remember when I first encountered her. Definitely after St. Francis, the childhood saint of our purer nature, and St. Theresa, and the Goretti. To me, St. Dymphna is as crazy as her name. She comes after St. Mary Magdalene, the supreme woman saint, ultra-whore, no cloying virgin, the top sinner among all the saints, except St. Augustine. The Magdalene is almost as popular as the Goretti, except she's older, more jaded. She is the saint of hussies, fallen women, and mistresses, something I imagined as a child I would never become. She is the patron saint of Luardo's woman with the gold lamé shoes.

I identify with the Goretti. Mary M. is older, more used up. St. Anne is the Mother of God's mother, and she, too, is old and shriveled up, despite the fecundity of her womb. It was only through divine intervention that her woman juices still flowed. St. Rose of Lima is beautiful, and young, one of the many virgins who clump together in my mind, her saintly life not tossed about by the anxious aches and yearnings of other women.

There is St. Joan of Arc, but she is French, and hears voices. I can't really trust her, somehow. She looks like a man and that makes me nervous. I am more comfortable with the passive lay-down-their-life-and-die-rather-than-screw virgins. St. Joan is too aggressive for me. I was indoctrinated into believing that having rounded ample breasts and living in constant fear of having them ripped off was the only way.

John the Baptist is a wild man, not your usual saint. It's always a relief to hear about him at the river. God really loves him, so wildness is okay, if you are a man, or look like a man. You can't be wild and a woman. Look what might happen to you. Burned to death on a spit like a witch.

Having breasts has always had its curses. Throughout history men would rip them out, burn them away or throw themselves upon them in a crazed frenzy of lust, the smell of roses never attainable, as faraway as Rome.

The Good Thief is probably my favorite male saint. On Good Friday I take out my missalette and read the Passion to myself, beginning with the part about the thieves, the cynical one and the repentant one. Over and over I read how the Good Thief feels the Lord was unjustly punished. He asks to be remembered in God's kingdom. I long to be with him in Paradise as well. He is a last minute dark horse saint, a God-will-save-your-soul-if-you-really-love-there's-hope-after-all-if-your-heart-is-pure kinda saint. During the elevation of the host I am filled with great longing as my nostrils fill with the unforgettably sweet and intoxicating smell of incense.

I mouth with The Good Thief the words: *Lord, remember me when you come to your Kingdom.*

Love-filled music instantaneously floats back to me from that holy body wracked in pain: *This night thou shalt be with me in Paradise.* I am seared, wrenched, and burned further into that ecstatic essence that is my soul.

I like the Good Thief because his story moves and excites me, but to live on that feverish plane is something I could never do for long. Someone like Mother Cabrini is good to cool the blood and settle the heart. Mother Cabrini has a nice face, but I always feel she is a bit stodgy. She looks like a spider in her black dress and dark veil.

Lastly, there is my Guardian Angel, a saint, no doubt, but faceless, as all angels are. Male or female? Decidedly, glorifiedly female. Or female with the best of male. For years I depend on her, talk to her and bless her. Then years go by and I ignore her, forget to talk to her. When I apologize off we go again. She never gets mad at me, not like Dolores or Luardo or Hector or even Mara, she is even-tempered, and very kind. No dramatics, no theatrics, just your everyday, dependable variety of saint. Sweet and loving, no fanfare, no trumpets, just old reliable love. A comfortable spiritual old sock. The best. A buddy. A pal.

And then there is me, for after all, this is about me. Little Soveida, wanting to *be*, not *become* a saint. Everybody has their chance at sainthood, what will be mine? *What* cause will be thrust upon me, what unspoken affliction? And *when* will it begin?

My grandmother, Mamá Lupita, wants me to become a nun. She often takes me aside and talks to me.

"Priests in the family are a dime a dozen, Soveida. Everybody knows they're *jotos* and *maricones* or lusty goats in search of skirts. What this family needs is a nun. Women's prayers, everyone knows, are more powerful. Any man can give up sex for four years, especially if they get him before he knows what to do with that thing between his skirts. Cassocks, that's what they call them. After that, you know what happens. When a woman gives up sex, it's final. Try and sneak sex on a woman, see what happens. Nine months later there's everlasting hell to pay. No *m'ija*, you are the one, Soveida. You are going to be a nun, someday, one day, may I live to see it, and if I don't you'll never rest until it's done or you're done or I'm done. One way or another. One time or another. Every woman wishes she could become a nun. You don't know what I mean yet, *m'ija*, may the Blessed Mother, she was a woman too, don't forget that, so she knows what I'm talking about, may she spare you a drunken man late at night smelling of *chicharrones* and *tequila*, worse yet, of *frijoles* and beer. ¡*Dios mío el gas*! Worse yet a man in the middle of the afternoon, *en Agosto*, when you're roasting *chile*, *hasta al copete en chile*, and he comes in from the farm, smelling of sweat and dirt, and carrying on, as if it wasn't hot enough already! I want to spare you this, *m'ija*, look at me, listen to me. You need to think about it, now before it's too late! You like to read. Nuns read all the time and no one bothers them. They can be quiet. They don't have no one belching and scratching and making *pedos*, you know, farts, on the way to the you-know-what, *el escusado*. *Escusado*, bathroom, a word like that, it sounds like an excuse. Well, that's what sex is, but in a different way. But let's no talk about it now. We'll talk about it later. I want to spare you the details, *m'ija*. And once in the *escusado, Dios mío de mi vida*, the noises and later the smell. I keep matches in there, but your grandfather, Profesito, he don't use them. Men cannot be trained. They're wild bulls or *changos*, monkeys, I don't know which. And that's not all. They shed. I could never keep a clean bathtub. *Pelitos por donde quiera*. Little hairs all over the place. But I want to spare you the details. Think about the Divine Service. I know what Father Escondido thinks marriage is, but remember, *m'ija*, all priests are men, just men, what do they know? I'd like to see *el padrecito* take three rounds *con mi viejo*, let's see what he says. Maybe someday women will become priests, *ay*, I won't live to see it, may you live to see it, and if you don't, well then, may other women live to see it. Me, I never wanted to become a nun. A priest, that's what I wanted to be! May the Blessed Mother support me in this, she knows I would have been a good priest. Ay, we do what we can. So think about it, I mean, becoming **at least** a nun. Your mother's childhood friend, Estella Fuentes, became a nun. She's now Sister Mary Margaret Marie of the Holy Magdalenes. She don't have no wrinkles. Her face is as smooth as a baby's *nalgas*. Look at Dolores' eyes. A road map. Texas. Luardo did it to her, and he's my son. With him, priesthood was out of the question from the very beginning. He was always pulling on his *cosita*, his little thing; there was no way he was ever going to be consecrated. ¡*Ni lo mande Dios!* It's as if some children are born with an invisible sign on their foreheads: Priest. Married Man. *Pendejo*. Yes, I knew. The man was oversexed from the day he was born, no way he could have ever been ordained. *La Cosita*, the thing, *it* would have stuck out between the skirts. Cassocks, that's what they call them. *It*, it should have been, you know, right then and there, but he was my last boy, for all the shame *it* brought this family, all the trouble it caused your Mamá, not to mention the others, *putas sin vergüenzas desgraciadas pintadas chorreadas. En el nombre del Padre, del Hijo, y del Espíritu Santo....* He may be your Daddy, but he's half man, half goat. Which half the goat, you'll have to guess. But let's not talk about that now. *Testudo como un chivo*, stubborn as an old goat, that's what I say, he thought with his

45

cosita, not with his head. Look at your Mamá. That road map near her eyes. California. All on account of you can imagine. *La cosita!* She didn't have no chance. *It* had a will of it's own. *Como chile colorado.* Think about *it, m'ija*, think about the Divine Service. Just promise me you'll think about it. IT, not *it*. We'll talk more later, eh, *con mas tiempo*.... You like to read...."

Mamá Lupita and I get up early and go to the 6:30 a.m. Mass every morning. We walk because she likes to walk and is too old to drive a car. I am only six years old. When we go to Church I am convinced I am going to become a nun. In the air of sanctity that surrounds me there, it is the only place I felt saved.

For family gatherings, Mamá Lupita prods me and then I will proudly announce that I am consecrated to God. I am going to become a nun. I myself believe this with all my heart. When, I don't know. Perhaps after high school, after a few years of dating. I want to see the world before I leave it. And what harm can there be, really? All the seminarians I've ever known dated during the summer vacations, and a few of them eventually became priests.

Mamá Lupita thinks I should join an order right after high school, the sooner the better. As soon as possible. She knows a few of those same seminarians and has her doubts about waiting too long and having too many distractions. St. Theresa of the Child Jesus had a Papal dispensation, she'd gone all the way to Rome to beg the Holy Father to admit her to the Holy Life, why can't I?

The only problem is that when I started school, I saw Manny Ordóñez, and fell in love.

But before, there was my brief year of grace, my one experience of saintliness.

Mamá Lupita was so proud of me that short year. All her friends, the old men and women of the six-thirty mass admired me, she told me so. They couldn't imagine a six year old child getting up so early every day to go to Mass. "It's unheard of!"

one old lady said. Dominga Fierro is her name. She is Mamá Lupita's best friend. Her only friend other than her old maid, Oralia, who has been with her for over sixty years. Dominga is Mamá's *comadre*. She baptized Tenecia, or Teeney, as she was nicknamed, Mamá's oldest girl, when she was small.

"Imagine that! Must have been a long time ago, it's hard to imagine three hundred pound Teeney, a small baby, incredible!"

Dominga is fat and wears the waist of her dress over her stomach. She looks pregnant, about to give birth to something. The only child she carries, Mamá says, is Death herself. She has cancer. And she knows it. That false fertility she has ignored for so long will finally kill her, giving her life in the only kingdom that, to her, really matters, Mamá says.

When she dies, part of Mamá Lupita will die as well. Dominga is her best friend, her last friend, besides Oralia. But what lady admits to the fact that your maid is your best friend? Not Mamá Lupita. So when I ask her if she has friends, she replies dryly, "I have one friend, but she's dying."

On our walks to church every day we swing by Dominga's house, a small adobe near the large intersection that leads to Our Lady of Grace Catholic Church and the altar where I once again renew my eternal vow to become a nun.

Each day I dip my hand in the Holy Water font, cross myself Mexican style, one small fast cross on the forehead, small fast cross on the chin, small fast cross on the breast, one big salute to the forehead, breast, left shoulder, right shoulder, and one final tap to the chin, or if you are more pious, which I am, one last prayerful gathering of the fingers to the lips with a small sacred kiss. I would then genuflect, full knees to the cold, hard floor, and walk up the aisle, repeating the Crossing Ritual, crossing myself again, eyes to the altar, where I see the monstrance gleaming gold in the early morning light.

Later, I kneel at the wooden communion rail, shyly, like a gently submissive bride, lacing my fingers through the dark metal that surrounds the wood, afraid that if I displease my God the host will burn my tongue out like acid, or that the unfortunate priest will stop in front of me, refusing to give me the host, knowing by some innate sense an evil demon lurks above my head, taunting me in front of the Divine Presence, the Paraclete. I imagine all kinds of last minute punishments and torments for a sinful mind and a blackened soul. The priest might drop dead in front of me, or worse yet, I might drop dead in front of him, falling downward into the open flames that are always just below the floor of the church, a burning facade for the fires of a never-ending hell.

Nothing like this ever happened. The most dramatic occurrence is when the host occasionally gets stuck to my palate; it's not uncommon. If this happens, I have to cluck down the host. My eyes downcast, trying to remain calm, my tongue works feverishly to rid myself of the strange, inhibiting feeling of stuck host. Hosts are so sticky, and Hell seems so close. Just around the corner. Under the floor.

I am always fighting off temptations, worrying myself sick about my eternal soul, not realizing I am too concerned about myself, forgetting all others.

Mamá Lupita looks around to me as she comes back from the communion rail. Her black mantilla falls around her shoulders. Through the spidery delicate lace she winks at me, then nods her chin as she sits down. She strokes several long white chin hairs, her eyes closed, as she rests in deep thanksgiving. She doesn't notice I am still clucking. An unusually difficult host is causing me much panic. I look around. All her friends are so proud of me. Sister Soveida. Almost a saint.

Whenever I look at her *mantilla*, with its large black bobby pin holding it in place, it reminds me of a story she told me. A nun friend of hers had told it to her. This was in the years when she still had friends. It concerns a young nun who had just been received into the order. In those days, all the nuns wore black, thick, habits, not like today. Today nuns look like librarians or teachers. But then, nuns were nun-ish, with long, full robes and a headpiece that fell about the shoulders.

On the very first day of the nun's induction, she was being dressed by an older nun with bad eyesight. The old nun accidentally jabbed the long straight pin that held the young nun's habit in place, catching some of the skin on the top of her head. It hurt! But what was the young nun to do? It is God's will! Praise the Lord for his love! If that is what he asks of me each day, I will obey!

The next day the young nun arose, put on her habit, arranged her head cloth, sticking the pin directly in the center of her head, piercing her scalp. The pain grew worse. Blood appeared. What was she to do? This went on some time, until one day another older nun noticed the blood.

"Sister, what is it?" she said. "Let me see."

"Sister," the younger nun replied, "it is nothing but The Cross."

"What are you talking about, Sister? For God's sake!"

"But it is for God's sake, Sister," the young nun answered.

Crying, laughing, the older nun shook her head, and exclaimed, "Sister, Sister! God's will for us is a merciful thing, full of love, not pain. How long have you been doing this?"

"Since the day I became the Bride of Jesus," the young nun replied. "Since the day I joined the order. Since the day I took my vows of obedience and poverty and chastity. Since the day Mother Elizabeth caught my skin. Oh, but Sister, while I did not question God's will, I didn't know how much it would bleed!"

Mamá Lupita knew many nuns. They told her stories like these. There were other stories as well, about nuns who lost their hair from lack of air underneath those starched habits, of nuns who had skin diseases as well, other stories, too, about other parts of that never-seen body, the body of Christ. I am the vine and you are the branches.

"They are holy women, Soveida. And yet they know what the world is, they know the ways of men. Many of them have been married. And others have brothers. Some of my best friends were nuns. Their prayers, m'ija, are *very* strong. They have dedicated their lives to God, and he is grateful. Little by little the nuns are making God a nicer man."

Mamá Lupita smiles. When she speaks, I listen. When she is silent, I am silent. We have no need to speak to each other. It's she who gave me my first shot at sainthood, and I am grateful.

That year came and went. Another year followed. I'm still trying to recapture the glow of the bright, burning candles. I inhale the incense and Mamá Lupita comes to mind. I see her peering sideways at me through semi-transparent black lace. She was a friend to so many nuns. She was never a nun, knew she could never become one. It was only much later I found out she never really wanted to become a nun. She should have become a priest, but when her mother looked at her she'd seen the invisible words written on her forehead: Woman. Wife. Mother. Martyr.

Together she and I charted and plotted my sainthood, together we cried and beat our breasts, *mea culpa, mea culpa, mea culpa*-ing ourselves into a fever.

Mamá Lupita was a small hunchbacked old lady who was always trying to straighten herself up, long after her back was doubled over in grief. I was a short little girl who was always trying to reach the light switch, calling out in my childish way, "Open the light, open the light." Both of us were people trying to become taller, something we were not.

Mamá Lupita lifted me up to kiss the outstretched hand of the statue of the Blessed Mother. The left hand was rubbed clean of paint already. The holy fingers were gritty from so much daily contact with the world. Mamá Lupita set me down after a short while, and off we went, back home. Her to her Blue House, me to the brown house right next door to hers. Dominga puffed alongside of us, panting and rubbing her belly, talking to it as if she were talking to a child. "Ay, *ay ay 'stá, amorcito....*"

I felt the movement of early morning houses coming alive. Mamá Lupita kissed me and went inside her Blue House, which looked so lovely in the morning light. I saw her pass the large blue window that gave the house its name. Once the house was painted white, but after many years it too was painted blue, in

honor of the famous window. I skipped up the small cement
walkway between our houses, closing the door softly behind me.
Quietly, I made my way to my room closing the door gently. I
took down my nun doll from her spot on the chest of drawers
and played with her. Mamá Lupita had given her to me for my
last birthday. Knees bent in prayer, Sister Mary Dominica Jane
Agnes Monessa Gabriella Danielle Doll crossed her tiny pink
plastic hands in prayer and then arose. Her day had just begun.
Sainthood was a hard road and she had better get started.

TEPEYAC

Sandra Cisneros

When the sky of Tepeyac opens its first thin stars and the dark comes down in an ink of Japanese blue above the bell towers of La Basílica de Nuestra Señora, above the plaza photographers and their souvenir backdrops of La Virgen de Guadalupe, above the balloon vendors and their balloons wearing paper hats, above the red-canopied thrones of the shoeshine stands, above the wooden booths of the women frying lunch in vats of oil, above the *tlapalería* on the corner of Misterios and Cinco de Mayo, when the photographers have toted up their tripods and big box cameras, have rolled away the wooden ponies I don't know where, when the balloon men have sold all but the ugliest balloons and herded these last few home, when the shoeshine men have grown tired of squatting on their little wooden boxes, and the women frying lunch have finished packing dishes, tablecloth, pots, in the big straw basket in which they came, then Abuelito tells the boy with dusty hair, *Arturo, we are closed*, and in crooked shoes and purple elbows Arturo pulls down with a pole the corrugated metal curtains — first the one on Misterios, then the other on Cinco de Mayo — like an eyelid over each door, before Abuelito tells him he can go.

This is when I arrive, one shoe and then the next, over the sagging door stone, worn smooth in the middle from the *huaraches* of those who have come for tins of glue and to have their scissors sharpened, who have asked for candles and cans of boot polish, a half-kilo sack of nails, turpentine, blue-specked spoons, paintbrushes, photographic paper, a spool of picture wire, lamp oil, and string.

Abuelito under a bald light bulb, under a ceiling dusty with flies, puffs his cigar and counts money soft and wrinkled as old Kleenex, money earned by the plaza women serving lunch on flat tin plates, by the souvenir photographers and their canvas Recuerdo de Tepeyac backdrops, by the shoeshine men sheltered beneath their fringed and canopied kingdoms, by the blessed vendors of the holy cards, rosaries, scapulars, little plastic altars, by the good sisters who live in the convent across the street, counts and recounts in a whisper and puts the money in a paper sack we carry home.

I take Abuelito's hand, fat and dimpled in the center like a valentine, and we walk past the basilica, where each Sunday the Abuela lights the candles for the soul of Abuelito. Past the very same spot where long ago Juan Diego brought down from the *cerro* the miracle that has drawn everyone, except my Abuelito, on their knees, down the avenue one block past the bright lights of the *sastrería* of Señor Guzmán who is still at work at his sewing machine, past the candy store where I buy my milk-and-raisin gelatins, past La Providencia *tortillería* where every afternoon Luz María and I are sent for the basket of lunchtime *tortillas*, past the house of the widow Márquez whose husband died last winter of a tumor the size of her little white fist, past La Muñeca's mother watering her famous dahlias with a pink rubber hose and a skinny string of water to the house on La Fortuna, number 12, that has always been our house. Green iron gates that arabesque and scroll like the initials of my name, familiar whine and clang, familiar lacework of ivy growing over and between except for one small clean square for the hand of the postman whose face I have never seen, up the twenty-two steps we count out loud together — uno, dos, tres — to the supper of *sopa de fideo* and *carne guisada* — cuatro, cinco, seis — the glass of *café con leche* — siete, ocho, nueve — shut the door against the mad parrot voice of the Abuela — diez, once, doce — fall asleep as we always do, with the television mumbling — trece, catorce, quince — the Abuelito snoring — dieciséis, *diecisiete, dieciocho* — the grandchild, the one who will leave soon for that borrowed country — *diecinueve, veinte, veintiuno* — the one he will not remember, the one he is least familiar with — *veintidós, veintitrés, veinticuatro* — years later when the house on La Fortuna, number 12, is sold, when the *tlapalería*, corner of Misterios and Cinco de Mayo, changes owners, when the courtyard gate of arabesques and scrolls is taken off its hinges and replaced with a corrugated sheet metal door instead, when the widow Márquez and La Muñeca's mother move away, when Abuelito falls asleep one last time — *Veinticinco, veintiséis, veintisiete* — years afterward when I return to the shop on the corner of Misterios and Cinco de Mayo, repainted and redone as a pharmacy, to the basilica that is crumbling and closed, to the plaza photographers, the balloon vendors and shoeshine thrones, the women whose faces I do not recognize serving lunch in the wooden booths, to the house on La Fortuna, number 12, smaller and darker than when we lived there, with the rooms boarded shut and rented to strangers, the street suddenly dizzy with automobiles and diesel fumes, the house fronts scuffed and the gardens frayed, the children who played kickball all grown and moved away.

Who would've guessed, after all this time, it is me who will remember when everything else is forgotten, you who took with you to your stone bed something irretrievable, without a name.

PEOPLE OF THE DOG

Alma Luz Villanueva

To the children of Mexico City

The young man, with the wind god clinging to his back, runs ahead of me. His entire body is tattooed with snakes, birds and circles. They are strangely wonderful. Beautiful. They crawl, fly and spin up his powerful legs, to his groin, to his chest and back, and the wind god is strapped to his back like a baby. Is he his mother, I wonder, chasing him, knowing I will never catch him. I laugh, thinking of how a wind god would be born from a man: a fart. Why would a god want to be a baby? Why does he choose the young man with the beautiful tattoos? Maybe he's safer with a man, I think. Women are weak. My mother was weak. She could no longer feed me, protect me from the new man who fed us all. When he took my food, she cried. When he hit me with his fists till I bled, she cried. When he threatened to kill me, she cried. Go to the city, you'll survive there, my mother said, so I came. I'm almost a man, I'm almost ten. I sleep with four other boys, two younger. The older boys torment us, raped the youngest, made him whimper all night, now he's shy and will not speak.

The young man, with the wind god clinging to his back, climbs into a boat and, kneeling, begins to paddle. I feel the water at my feet and smile at the freshness. I haven't bathed since my mother's house. The baby wind god smiles at me, upside-down, his head thrown back. It must be uncomfortable and stupid to be a baby and have someone take you wherever they want to go, however they want to take you. But the wind god does look happy, like he trusts the young man, like he wants him to be his mother and carry him everywhere, so I jump into a boat and begin to paddle, following the smile of the baby wind god.

The young man never looks at me, as though he doesn't even know I'm chasing him. Just the baby wind god knows I'm chasing him. I paddle so hard and fast, changing sides of the boat to make me go straight, that I'm covered with the sweet lake water. I'm not tired at all. If I was ever hungry, I don't remember. If I was ever thirsty, I don't remember. If I was ever hurt, I don't remember. If I was ever afraid, I don't remember. The young man's tattoos begin to crawl, fly and spin faster and faster, his skin seems to be dancing and the baby wind god looks at me and laughs. A fart, a fart, he says in baby talk, but all I smell is the sweet lake water. If I was ever afraid, I don't remember.

The young man, with the wind god clinging to his back, glides under a half-circle rainbow and when I follow him I'm covered with all the colors, only I have no tattoos, but it's better to be lots of colors than just naked with nothing on. His snakes, birds and circles dance with color, but the baby wind god, even though he has hands and feet and a head, is beginning to look like a cloud. When he opens his mouth a small jagged piece of lightning shoots out and drops into the water. It sizzles and turns into a glowing shell. I grab it and put it into my mouth, it tastes like light, I laugh out loud. If I ever felt pain, I don't remember.

The young man, with the wind god clinging to his back, raises the paddle over his head and yells with joy like a song. There's land and a beautiful city. There are strong and fearless Indians everywhere and their women smile, bathing their children and washing their own long, black hair in the morning sun without fear or shame. They look at the young man — his dancing snakes of red and purple, his birds of blue and green, his spinning circles of yellow and orange — and lower their eyes with respect. I look at the beautiful city and it feels familiar, like Mexico City, when I first saw it, before I entered it, before it ate me up. But this city feels like a long time ago when there were Indians everywhere, people that looked like me and my mother, not the Mexican who wants to kill me. I look at the baby wind god and ask, "Is this Mexico City long ago?" The baby wind god opens his mouth and an eagle flies out and lands on a cactus, stretching his huge wings and turns his head from side to side and shits. I want to laugh, but the young man turns, for the first time, and looks at me. Only his face is naked, except for one small tattoo on his forehead that looks like the moon or sun. Sometimes it's the moon, sometimes it's the sun. One side of his face is gentle, the other side is fierce. He turns away from me and steps onto the shore. The young man holds his fingers in a circle, his hand high in the air. There are drums beating and the sounds of women crying, as though someone has died. The men gash their arms and legs so that blood runs out. The cactus that the eagle rests on blooms, full of soft, feathery flowers, and a snake sleeps under the cactus in the warm sun. The snakes and birds on the young man's body are still, so are the circles. He looks like stone. Then the baby wind god becomes a thin, white cloud and passes through the young man's circled fingers. The thin, white cloud comes to me and I breathe him in. If I am dead, I don't remember. Quickly, I leap from my boat and I know what I must do. I leap and cling onto Quetzalcoatl's back and I remember peace, a clear, wide peace as big as the sky, as far as I can see and even farther. Now I know we will go together to look for her, she who isn't weak, she who feeds and protects us. I will remember Quetzalcoatl, I will remember the wind god clinging to his back, I will remember the baby wind god.

I will remember birth.

§ § §

The woman bends over the child's body, pushing his thick, black hair from his forehead. The blankets that cover him are filthy. She notes that his shoes are still on, stuffed with rags against the cold. A tube of glue lies next to him, uncapped. There is no sign of blood, no sign of struggle. His face looks innocent, terrible with peace and the stillness of death. His face is without pain and she imagines a kind of light surrounding him, but she straightens herself immediately. The woman is Mexican, but the Indian in her blood has claimed her features.

The boy who'd come to her office was one of the boys they fed and clothed when they came to the shelter, when the funds were there. He'd asked her to come with him because his friend wouldn't wake up. He said his friend had gone with a man and he'd paid his friend with money and some pills. He tells her a younger boy is missing and that he thinks the older boys have killed him.

Sometimes, the woman sighs, I think the dead ones are better off than the living. The sigh is a mixture of sadness and anger. There are no parents to contact, no relatives, no one to mourn this child, and the next one and the next. Now, I'll go call the police and they'll come and take the body and dispose of it like a dog.

The woman doesn't know that the ancient one, Quetzalcoatl, came from a clan called the Chichimecs. People of the Dog.

The boy quickly probes the dead boy's pockets and takes the remaining pesos. The woman sees it but says nothing. Like a dog, she thinks, covering the dead boy's face with the filthy blanket. The seven-month fetus within her moves, with a leap, making her sigh loudly, disturbing the room with her sudden wind.

THE ROSARY

Leroy V. Quintana

It was on the last evening of Doña Matilda's *novena* to St. Jude, the Patron Saint of the Impossible, that Pepe saw the burning rosary on the wall and ran out of the house, stark raving naked, all the way across San Luis and burst into the church shouting "¡Milagro! ¡Milagro! ¡Milagro!" claiming he would never taste another drop of wine again as several women fainted in the middle of a "*Padre Nuestro*" and Father Schmidt, who had survived such *milagros* as the face of Jesus scorched on a *tortilla*, the face of Jesus illuminated on the south wall of the church at sunset and the face of Jesus among the wanted posters (between two thieves, Tranquilino Sanchez, who robbed banks, and his brother, Salvador, who worked for the government) at the post office in The Emporium, began running alongside Pepe, trying desperately to cover his front, his back, his front with his small prayerbook, screaming "¡Ave Maria Purisima! ¡Ave Maria Purisima! ¡Ave Maria Purisima!" dismissing the faithful with a haphazard sign of the cross as he shoved Pepe into the confessional and Pepe, not wanting to be disrespectful, immediately made the sign of the cross and began "Bless me, father, I had just undressed, I've been meaning to fix that switch, I was going to take a bath, a terrible day, absolutely, you have to turn the light OFF to turn it ON so I turned it OFF and all I see is *chispas* flying everywhere and so I turned it ON to turn it OFF and when I turned it OFF again the lights wouldn't come on and that's when I saw it, a rosary burning on the wall, '¡Milagro! ¡Milagro!'" and when Father Schmidt inquired "Have

59

you been drinking, my son?" Pepe admitted, sheepishly, "Well, yes, father, one little *tragito*, only one, absolutely, you see I made a *promesa*, absolutely...."

§ § §

But I should begin at the beginning, that morning when Pepe realized he had put off — like he had the lawn, the fence, the kitchen faucet, the blinkers, the roof, painting, pruning, ("*Una desgracia,*" Matilda said every morning, and she was right, she was absolutely right), the electric sockets — getting his driver's license renewed and now he had to take the driving test and that meant being ordered around by Sheriff Sapo Sanchez for an hour.

After calling and informing Chango Vasquez, the foreman at the mine, that he would not be in, and after agreeing that this was happening a little too regularly and reassuring him that this was not going to happen again, and after agreeing with Matilda that this was happening a little too regularly, and after reassuring her it was not going to happen again, and after promising "None, no, absolutely no drinking, yes, I promise, *absolutamente nada,*" Pepe drove downtown, all the way absolutely convinced that the perfect way to begin a day, that was going to begin with Sheriff Sapo Sanchez, was with a chilled swallow, just a little *tragito* of Wild Irish Rose, or Mogen David down at La Golondrina with Botas Meadas and Dupo, but a promise was a promise was a promise. Absolutely.

"Your blinkers," Sapo said immediately, indicating there was no need to proceed any further than the first item on his safety checklist. "Two sixty-five point one of the State Code. No driver's examination to be conducted until vehicle has passed all safety checks. Period." What the Town of San Luis did not need was another Caruso Zamora.

All the way to Caruso's garage Pepe was more than absolutely convinced that the perfect way to begin a day that began with Sheriff Sapo Sanchez would be to stop off at La

Golondrina...*pero no, no*, absolutely no drinking, *absolutamente nada*. A promise was a promise was a promise. Absolutely.

Caruso was under a jeep accompanying himself with a ball peen hammer. "*Besame, besame muchooo!*" No he couldn't get to the blinkers right now. "*Besame muchoooo*...fifteen minutes."

Fifteen minutes and Caruso, the undisputed champion of the demolition derby Saturday night after Saturday night, as well as the proud owner of more traffic citations for speeding than anybody in all of San Luis, revved up his tow truck and sped off for parts. "Your cheatin' heeaaaaart...."

"Your brights," snapped Sapo immediately. No use proceeding beyond the second item. "Two sixty-five point one...."

The best way absolutely to begin to save a morning that led from Sapo to Caruso back to Sapo back to Caruso was to stop at La Golondrina, just one chilled *tragito* of Wild Irish Rose or Mogen David, but just one, after all, a *promesa*....

"*Acuerdate d'Acapulco*...." Caruso was bent over the heart of a Coupe de Ville pounding a large screwdriver into the defenseless carburetor. "Not right now...fifteen minutes. *Maria bonita, Maria del almaaaaaaaaa.*"

"Back in fifteen. My Rooose, my Rooose of San Antooone...." Fifteen turned into twenty. Caruso rocketed back into his parking space, the tow truck lurching to a stop as he jumped down from his seat. "All the way! She sent it to her lover who was Airborne all the waaay!" He was sorry for the delay. *El cabron del Sapo* and his speeding tickets, the same boring lecture over and over. "Yeah, I know which law I'm breaking. Three Seventy-One point Three. *Espeeding. ¿Y Que?* Now blue ain't the word for the way that I feeeeel...."

"Los wipers," snorted Sapo, removing his drill sergeant hat to wipe his fat brow with his cuff. All this work was making him hungry, mighty hungry. He flipped up his dark sunglasses to check his wristwatch. Coffee break in thirty minutes. Hungry. Mighty hungry.

The best way absolutely was to stop off...a *tragito*, one, a *promesa* was absolutely....

"Mis wipers," Pepe intoned.

Caruso put down the crescent wrench he had been hammering with. "From a jack to a queen! Not now, fifteen minutes. From loneliness to a wedding riiing."

"Coffee break," barked Sapo. "Come back in fifteen minutes. State regulations say an employee is entitled to one fifteen-minute break in the a.m. and one in the p.m. Period."

How could two bowls of *menudo*, a half dozen *tortillas*, two *tamales*, a slice of apple pie (a la mode) and two cups of coffee...a coffee break? *Absolutamente* a *promesa* was a *promesa* and stop off at La Golondrina, no, none, *absolutamente nada*, coffee break.

"O.K.," snapped Sapo, "let's roll," his chins trembling, fresh grease stains down his shirt and official black tie.

Now first was second and...no, no. Second was first and third was second, reverse was third. Absolutely. Or was it first was reverse. Second was first, third was second, reverse third...no, no. A third *tragito* had been absolutely out of the question, absolutely. Good thing, otherwise.... "I'm citing you for a Two Eighty-Nine point Three, Pepe, operating an unsafe vehicle." After all, a promise. *Absolutamente*.

"My transmission, Caruso."

"*Hoy no*," replied Caruso, the sledge hammer high over his head, then burst into song on the downswing: "*¡Aaaaaiiiee que laureles tan verdeees! Si piensas abandonarme, mejor quitarme la vidaaaaaa....*"

What was absolutely necessary, absolutely, was a new car, or better yet, the image that goes along with a new car. A quick stop at La Golondrina before driving down to Martinez's car lot. A quick *tragito* (or two), chilled....

But why buy a car when, after wrestling with figures with Maxie Baca (a greedy man and, naturally, the mayor's brother-in-law) for an hour and a half, you could take it out for a test (!) drive, buy on a deferred payment plan, a good deal, absolutely.

"Lunchtime!" bellowed Sapo. Hungry. Mighty hungry. "State regulations...."

Lunch? An *enchilada* special (extra sour cream and avocado), a side order of *menudo*, a *tamale*.... Time enough to return the car, haggle, haggle with Maxie over the price, get another to test drive, stop off behind La Golondrina for a *tragito*, just one by the time Sapo slurped up the last of his apple pie (a la mode) and his third cup of coffee.

"Weren't you operating a green car a while ago, Pepe?"
"Traded it in."
"Maxie give you a good deal?"
"Damn good deal."
"Let's roll." Chins trembling, fresh grease stains.

"I will be asking you to execute various maneuvers such as parking, backing up, proper signaling, proper lane changes...."
"¿Que?"
"I said I will be asking you...ummmhhh, let's begin by backing out, place your left hand at twelve o'clock and your right arm over the seat, checking continuously for approaching vehicles, checking your blind spot...."
"¿Que?"
"...accelerating slowly. SLOWLY!"

"Proceed in an easterly direction for two blocks, then execute a right after coming to a proper stop...No honking to greet other motorists...Keeping both hands on the steering wheel, eyes on the road at all times, constantly scanning...No smoking during testing...All mirrors should be adjusted prior to testing...No loud music that might prevent you from hearing approaching traffic...."

Hijo de la chingada. One more *tragito*, absolutely, just one, and this would be as easy...but a *promesa*. Ninety nine per cent of all accidents (with the exception of Caruso, of course) in San Luis have to occur while taking a driving test, people going suddenly insane, driving full speed into a block wall, *como los kamakazis*.

"Pay no attention to motorists who blow their horn — as long as you're observing the speed limit...."
"It's Caruso, he's trying to pass...."
"I'm gonna throw the book at that son of a bitch! That's a Two Seventy-One point Nine, following too close. Stop this car."

"Follow that tow truck, Pepe! I'm throwing the book at that son of a bitch! Crossing the yellow line, a Two Thirty-Four point Seven, speeding, that's a...."
"*¿Que?*"

"Follow that truck...that's a Three Seventy-One point... go, go! Accelerate, *hombre*, accelerate."
"*¿Que?*"
"Step on it, *pendejo*! I'm throwing the book...."

"Turn, Pepe, turn!"
"But it's against the law."
"Make a U-Turn, goddammit! I'm nailing him for a Two Twenty-Two point Two...."
"But it's a one way...."
"I don't give a shit. Follow that son of a bitch! That's a Two Nineteen point Three!"

"He's coming back this way!"
"Turn, *pendejo*, turn!"

"*Chingao*, it happened so fast. First the mailbox and then the picket fence and Sapo yelling 'Stop! Stop!' and then slamming on the brakes, sideswiping the giant cottonwood and skidding in slow motion towards the swimming pool, *como los kamakazis*, or like the fighter jets when they miss the aircraft carrier and coming to a stop, half the car over the water, the back half on dry land, sweet dry land, and then Sapo opening the door, thinking he could inch his way out I guess, and the car dipping, beginning to plunge *como un submarine, o como el Titanic* and Sapo hollering that he didn't know how to swim, 'Help! Help!' as if I could help him, I don't know how either, and then Maria Manteca, (Mrs. Mayor) came out shrieking because we've splashed water all over the papers on the table where the mayor was working only a couple of minutes before, 'The budget! The audit!' all the figures he had been up all night manipulating smeared all to hell and now they didn't know how they were going to bullshit their way past the government agent, and 'My begonias! My greenhouse!' *chingao*, I hadn't realized we had plowed right through it, and then she's screaming for the mayor to call the sheriff and Sapo is clinging to the mayor trying to tell her that the sheriff has already arrived and I'm clinging to Sapo until finally Maria Manteca flipped us the lifesaver and the mayor manages to cling on to it while Maria Manteca fishes Sapo (and me) out by hooking that long aluminum pole under his gun belt and tugging like a harpooner and then giving Sapo mouth to mouth (me and the mayor are barely walking the road of the living) and suddenly she's throwing up because Sapo has coughed up the *enchilada* special (with extra sour cream and avocado), the *menudo, tamale* and the apple pie (a la mode), and half a hour or so later Caruso's yanking the car out of the pool and Sapo's explaining to the mayor why he was going the wrong way on a one way street and the mayor is shouting right in his face 'You don't break the law to enforce the law, *pendejo*, I'm taking all of this out of your budget' and all Sapo can say is 'Yes, sir, Yes sir, Yes sir' and when the mayor is through with him he squeezes in behind the

65

wheel of his official car that Raton Montoya (his peacock, puff of a brother-in-law, and faithful deputy) came driving up in, siren blaring, lights flashing like Maxie's Car Lot at night and yells at me to get in, asks me where I want to go and I tell him to Maxie's where I explain the whole thing to Maxie and he begins punching *figuras* on his adding machine, double checks them and then hands me the contract, and I sign on the dotted line, deferred payment plan, absolutely the worst day, worse than yesterday with the tax auditor, and to top it all off, *p'acabarlo de chingar*, I flunked the driving exam, O.K., but just one little *tragito*, after all, a *promesa* is a *promesa*, you know."

§ § §

Except for Matilda and her family the entire town gathered around Pepe's house within half an hour. The faithful (including the women who had fainted in church) knelt, holding candles, praying rosary after rosary. The skeptics, of course, congregated in the rear, argued, placed bets.

At two A.M. Father Schmidt arrived (finally) with Monsignor Chavez, who had driven the sixty miles from Albuquerque in a time that made Caruso shudder with envy, only to see the newest miracle of modern science: a luminous rosary Matilda had purchased earlier that day and hung on the wall that evening before walking to church to pray to St. Jude, who, perhaps on this, the last evening of her *novena*....

SOMETIMES YOU DANCE
WITH A WATERMELON

Luis J. Rodriguez

muylo

"Ayyyyyy."

A man's voice. Then the tumbling of a body, like a sack of potatoes, down a flight of stairs.

"*Pinchi cabron, hijo de la....*"

A woman's voice.

"*¡Borracho!* Get out of my house!"

Next door to the commotion, Susana tossed and turned — her fragile mirror of dreams split into fragments.

"You dog! Get out of here!" the woman continued outside the bedroom window. A raspy stammering tried to push through the woman's shrieks.

"But, *muñeca*," the man slurred. "Give me a chance, *querida*. Let me in, *por favor*."

"This house is not for *sin verguenzas* like you," the woman wailed.

Then a loud rustling sound reached over the window as the man toppled back onto a row of shrubbery. Whimpers of small children followed the man's moans.

Susana painstakingly opened her eyes. Early morning sunlight slipped into the darkened bedroom through small holes in aluminum foil which covered the window. The foil kept the daylight out so Susana's husband Pete could sleep. Susana turned away from the heavy figure next to her, which was curled up in a fetal position.

Pete worked the graveyard shift at a foundry near their East L.A. home. He slept during the day and labored at night until, managing his way home from the heat and din of the blast furnaces, Pete clambered onto the mattress, propped up by cinder blocks, to the comfort of Susana's warm body.

As the noise outside subsided into the deception of quiet, Susana felt the urge to go someplace. Anyplace. She arose from under the heavy covers and grabbed a dirty pink bathrobe with strands hanging from the hem. She tiptoed to the door and peered backward toward the bed while opening it to a frustrating medley of creaky hinges. The bump beneath the covers rolled into another position, and then lay motionless.

Susana entered the living room and stepped over bodies stretched out on mattresses across the floor. Among them lay her daughter Chela; her sister Sybil; her sister's three children; and Sybil's no-good, always-out-of-work husband, Stony.

Susana worked her way to the kitchen and opened a cupboard. Several cockroaches of various sizes scurried to darker confines. The near-empty shelves could not answer the calls from her near-empty stomach. Those days were filled with non-fat powdered milk for breakfast, _tortillas_ and butter for lunch and corn flakes for dinner — most of which her sister got on food stamps.

"This life is draining the life out of me," Susana whispered, as she stared at the vacant cupboards in front of her.

Susana then thought about the 10 years which had passed since she first came across the border from Nayarit, Mexico. It was about the time her daughter Chela was born. Susana was 16 years old then.

She recalled the nights in downtown's dingy apartments among the homeless and winos, with small child, no husband or livable skills. She recalled how she endured being cast off into a strange world of neon and noise, of the people on city buses who never say anything to you unless they happen to be crazy or drunk.

"*Chingao,* there's never anything to eat," Susana grumbled.

She didn't mind the adults not eating, but the children had to eat. She was prepared to starve so the children could eat.

But Susana didn't have the same concern for Sybil or Stony. Certainly, she believed, they were into drugs or other illicit enterprises.

Why Sybil would end up with an ex-convict like Stony was beyond her. When the two were children in Nayarit, Sybil had been the more restrained of the girls. But ever since Susana helped Sybil sneak across *la frontera,* assisting her through the tumble of city life, her sister began to frequent the night clubs off Spanish Broadway and on Brooklyn Avenue. Sybil brought home many a strange character, one of whom gave her the three children she bore — only to leave for Chicago with another woman.

Susana, who thought her sister may have learned something from the experience, felt somewhat betrayed one day when Sybil brought Stony home. At first glance, Stony seemed nice. But as soon as he smiled, his missing front teeth and constantly shifting eyes gave off an ominous look — the kind Susana noticed in many Chicanos just out of the joint...let alone that he never worked but, when pushed, would somehow come up with beer money. Susana figured Stony sold food stamps to buy booze.

Susana's hunger intensified. She closed the cupboard doors and walked toward the kitchen window which overlooked an alley behind their home, strewn with burnt mattresses, threadless tires and furniture parts.

Susana leaned against the streaked glass, her hair like spider webs across her face. She looked over the Los Angeles sky, a haze of smog emerging out of the red tinge of a quickly rising sun. Children played and chattered in broken English, half-Spanish and a language all their own.

What a strange place this Los Angeles, Susana thought. So much noise: factory whistles at varying intervals of day; a deafening pounding of machinery, with cars and trucks in a sick symphony of horns blasting, tires screeching and engines backfiring. Susana sensed a thick tension, like a huge rubber band, hanging over the streets, ready to snap at any moment.

Two *winitos* staggered by just then. They sat down on the curb's edge, one of them taking out a half-empty bottle of Muscatel wine from a brown paper bag. Across the way a young woman pushed a market cart down the street; three small children were crowded inside.

Family quarrels became battlegrounds with children running out screaming from houses and police cars sharply turning around corners.

Susana thought of the Third Street gang: tough, tattooed *calo*-speaking young men and women with their strange clothes and mannerisms. How they were always fighting somebody — rival *barrios*, police officers and themselves.

Although life in Susana's village in Nayarit may have been full of want, it was not as complicated as the world she ended up in. But she mulled that over a while and accepted the fact: She could never go back.

This was her life now. In Boyle Heights. East L.A. With Pete and Chela — sharing whatever she had with Sybil, Stony and her nephews and nieces. No, she could never go back.

But often she dreamed. She recreated worlds back in Nayarit. And she resolved: When I die, let me die in Mexico. Bury me deep in Nayarit soil. In my red hills. In the cactus fields. Bury me in long braids. In a *huipilli*. Bury me among the ancients — among the brave, strong and wise ones; in the wet earth of my birth, taking with me the fingers which have shifted new ground, eyes that have gazed on new worlds — remembering I lived in North America.

And she thought about Pete, slaving a life away. A good man, she almost said out loud. Pete was so different than the men Sybil always seemed to be stuck with. In Susana's eyes, Pete was truly decent. Working nights, double shifts: Tapping a heat with a large vertical jack hammer and then opening up metal-plugged *tuyeres* with long iron bars. All for Susana. And she knew it.

§ § §

Susana needed to get away. The morning beckoned her to get out and do something. Anything.

She sat on the kitchen table — dirty dishes still there with bits of hardened *tortillas* from the night before — and worked on a scheme.

Susana could take Stony's dented Ford pickup and visit the old furniture stores and used clothes shops along Whittier Boulevard. Or she could go throughout the Eastside, gathering newspapers, cardboard boxes, aluminum cans or whatever to turn in for extra money — she did this so many times that the men at the county dump site looked forward to Susana's visits, to her bright face and brash approach and the way she mixed up the words in Spanish and English.

Susana dressed quickly, and gathered money and faded coupons into an old leather purse. She then meandered around the bodies on the floor to where Chela was sound asleep. Susana looked at the child's closed eyelids and fingered her small hand.

"*Ama*," Chela moaned as she awoke. "*¿Qué páso?*"

"Come, *mija*, I need you to help me."

It took a moment before Chela made out her mother's face in the dimness of the room. Oh no, she thought, Mama wants me to help steal old beaten-up lamps and chairs from the back of Goodwill trucks again.

"Oh, *ama*. I'm tired."

"*Mira nomas* — you're tired, eh? You ain't done nothing yet. Now get dressed and come with me."

Susana stalked into the kitchen. Chela grumbled, then tossed a blanket off, unmindful of the other children next to her, and rolled off the mattress. Mama is stubborn, she thought, there's no moving her at all.

Chela pushed herself into the bathroom while her mother prepared a couple of tacos from left-over meat in the refrigerator for later.

"What are we going to do, *ama?*" Chela asked as she attempted to brush her hair into some kind of shape. She had grown feisty at her age and, unlike Susana, refused to wear braids — just long hair, wavy and free-flowing on her head.

"*Adio — a donde quiera dios.* Wherever God desires," Susana said. "What's it to you?"

"Gee, I was just asking!"

Susana hurried outside to check the truck. An empty kitchen cupboard was a sharp contrast to the driveway deluged with oily engine parts, boxes of yellowed newspapers and rain-soaked cartons. She managed to reach the truck and maneuver herself inside. She turned the ignition and the truck began to gripe, but it eventually turned over with smoke filling the cluttered driveway.

"Let's go, *mija,*" she yelled for Chela over the truck's engine roar. "*A la volada!*"

By then other members of the family had awakened. Stony was the first to pop his head through a window.

"Hey, man, quit gunning that thing — you'll break something."

Susana pressed the accelerator even more as the smoke thickened behind the truck.

No sleepy-eyed, ex-con and drunk of a brother-in-law was going to ruin her beautiful day, she thought. A day which begged her to do something. Anything.

Chela flew out of the house, banging the torn screen door behind her. Susana backed the truck out while Chela hollered for her to slow down as she leapt into the passenger side. The truck clamored out of the driveway.

The pickup continued down the street; smoke trailed from behind as Stony cursed from out of the window.

"*¡La loca mendiga!*"

The Ford roared through Eastside streets and avenues, toward Alameda Street where old Mexicanos sold fruit on the roadside while factory hands gathered in front of a chain-link fence waiting for employers to arrive in trucks to pick them out for work. Susana decided to go to *el centro* — downtown Los Angeles.

Through skid row, the blocks of warehouses and garment plants, Susana pulled into the congestion of cars and people on Spanish Broadway as gray-haired black preachers sermoned from the sidewalks with dog-eared bibles in their hands.

Shoe-shine men and newspaper vendors on a number of corners studied the people who wandered by to scan the latest news in Mexican publications — including the cut-up bodies and close-up shots of dead people in the crime and murder magazines.

"How about a shine...shoe shine," exclaimed a half-blind man. "*Para zapatos brillosos.*"

The streets bristled with families, indigents and single mothers shopping. Hundreds gathered in front of a Spanish theater with the names of Mexican actors and actresses and movie titles like *Mexicano Hasta Las Cachas.* The broken pieces

Norteño and *Salsa* music poured out of record shops.

A drunk stumbled out from a *tejano* bar, followed by another man. The second man knocked the first one to the ground and repeatedly punched him in the face. Nobody stopped or did anything.

Another man pulled a little boy from the crowd and had the boy pee in the gutter.

Susana and Chela cruised further up Broadway and its peopled intersections: *Cholos* stood inside brick alcoves, ancient women walked along cautiously with heavy bags, winos lay in fresh vomit — the stubby-faced homeless pushed shopping carts filled with belongings. There were the rapid-fire Spanish voices, workers unloading merchandise out of trucks, and foul-smelling buses loading people.

Susana noticed an empty parking spot and swiftly moved into it. On the sidewalk was a sign that read: NO PARKING, TOW ZONE. But she left the pickup there anyway.

"*Ama*, the sign says...." Chela tried to say, but she saw it didn't matter. Susana walked off as if by ignoring it, the sign would go away.

"Damn her," Chela muttered and ran up behind her mother.

The day bubbled and churned. The walks became tortuous as Susana browsed and bartered over items, most of which she had no intention of buying.

"It's so hot," Susana conceded. "How about a watermelon, *mija?*"

"Sure, I'd like that."

They stopped at a Grand Central Market fruit stand. Laid out in front of them, with a crash of colors like works of art, were papayas, mangoes, apples, bananas and oranges. Susana picked out a sizable dark-green and speckled watermelon. She argued with a man on the price, but finally she assembled her change and paid for it.

"Here Chela, carry this."

Suddenly to Chela the watermelon looked at least a quarter her size. And soon the weight of the watermelon, the cluster of people, the heat and hubbub became unbearable.

They stopped to rest at a bus-stop bench.

Chela looked at her mother and said: "I'm tired, *ama*. The watermelon is too heavy."

Susana stood up, looked at her daughter — sweat beading on her nose — and pondered a way to ease her burden. At that moment, her thoughts turned to Nayarit, to a time when she was a little girl, to when Sybil and she carried bundles and baskets of clothes or food on their heads. With the pressure of these thoughts, Susana's eyes turned to the watermelon pressed on Chela's lap.

Susana wrested the watermelon off the girl; Chela let out a deep sigh.

Susana then walked a little, and stopped. With great care, she placed the watermelon on her head and slowly removed her hand. The watermelon wobbled a little, threatening to fall into a splatter of green, red and black on the sidewalk. Susana steadied it again, then let it go. She took a few steps. This time the watermelon stood balanced, as if by magic, straight up on her head.

Chela looked at her mother — horrified.

Then Susana danced.

A crowd gathered around as Susana glided past the Broadway stores, immigration legal offices, and clothes and record stands. Merchants stepped out of their businesses, preachers stopped their exhortations and people at bus-stops strained their necks to see.

Horns beeped, hands waved and some people simply got out of the way.

Susana swayed and weaved to a *cumbia* beat blaring out of an appliance store. She laughed and others laughed with her. Chela stepped aside and observed in amazement. Mama's crazy, she thought, while shaking her head.

"Ahhhiiii," Susana yelled.

She had not looked as happy in a long time, there amid the bustling stranglehold of the central city, among her people, dancing in the shadows of a tall Victorian building, while she recalled a direct and simple life on a *rancho* in Nayarit.

INSIDIOUS DISEASE

Lucha Corpi

Little Michael David Cisneros had been identified by his mother and father, Lillian and Michael Cisneros, about six hours after Luisa and I found him. His maternal grandmother, Otilia Juarez who had reported him missing at 2:45 that afternoon, claimed that he'd been taken from the porch of her house on Alma Avenue, about three blocks from Laguna Park.

We had found him less than two miles from Otilia Juarez's house, approximately the length of the area swept by the police during the riot, as they forced the crowd from the park back toward Atlantic Park where the march had originated.

Joel had insisted on going back with me to that spot. Michael David's body was there, still with no more company than Luisa and the flies. I knelt down to fan them away so that Joel could take pictures of the scene. He didn't seem to have the same reaction I'd had when I first looked at the body, but his hands shook as he snapped photo after photo.

Luisa assured me that nothing had been disturbed. No one had passed by, for the area was quite isolated. A building rose to a height of about three floors, on the side of the street where we stood, one of those windowless low-budget plaster fortresses where unwanted memories are stored and sometimes forgotten. Across the street, a number of small neighborhood stores had been closed because of the disturbance. Even under ordinary circumstances this was an out-of-the way street, a good ten blocks from the main thoroughfare.

Suddenly I saw a Chicano teenager standing at the corner, smoking a cigarette and glancing furtively in our direction. He was wearing a red bandana, folded twice and tied around his head, a black leather vest, no shirt, and black pants. Just then, he turned around and I noticed a haloed skull and the word "Santos" painted on the back of his vest. He seemed no older than 18, most likely a "home boy" — a member of a youth gang. What was he doing there, I wondered.

Luisa told us she'd seen him cross that intersection twice since she'd been there. It was obvious the young man didn't seem disturbed by our surveillance, and after a few minutes he began to walk in our direction. Luisa instinctively retreated behind me, and I, behind Joel. Finding himself suddenly cast in the role of defender, Joel put his camera in its case, and began searching in his pockets for something to use as a weapon.

Two years before, after a couple of attempted rapes of students at Cal State Bayward, Luisa and I had taken a self-defense course for women, and as a reward for our good performance, we had received a small container of mace, a permit to carry it, and a whistle. I reached for the whistle and Luisa grabbed her mace from her purse. Joel gave out a sigh of relief, but his eyes didn't show fear. Instead, he frowned.

"Is this guy someone you know?" I asked Joel. He shook his head.

With a slow stride, the young man approached, then stopped few feet away from us.

"Soy Mando," he said and looked straight at Joel, but his eyes took in everything between the wall and the opposite sidewalk. He threw a quick glance at the body, then at me. "El chavalito este. Es tuyo?"

"No," I replied, "it's not my child." This Mando was much younger than he'd seemed from a distance, not quite 15. Not a bad young man I sensed, and relaxed a little.

"The dude who brought the chavalito here dropped this." Mando handed me a folded newspaper clipping, which had turned yellow and was already showing signs of wear at the creases. No doubt it had been kept for a long time in a wallet.

My heart beat wildly and my hands shook as I reached for the clipping. Almost automatically, I closed my eyes. I suddenly sensed the presence of a man, saw his shadow, then a small house surrounded by tall trees. Somewhere in the area children were laughing. The scene passed and I felt nauseous, but I managed to overcome the desire to vomit. Still I had to hold on to Luisa.

My strange behavior disconcerted her, but Mando didn't seem to notice it at all. Perhaps he had witnessed stranger things, seen a lot of pain or wanton cruelty in his short life. I doubted there was much left in this world that would shake him, except perhaps the death of the child. Why had he decided to give *us* the clipping? And why did I trust him? Instinctively I had felt that he had nothing to do with the death of the child.

"Did you see the person who did this? Can you tell us what he looked like?" Joel took a small memo pad and pencil from his shirt pocket, flipping for a blank page. Like my husband, who was also left-handed, Joel held the memo pad in the hollow of his right hand, across his chest.

"I didn't see nothing. Understand? *Nada.*" Mando looked at Joel's hand, put his palms out, and took a couple of steps back.

"How do we know it wasn't you who killed this *chicanito?*" There was a double edge of contempt and defiance in Joel's voice, which surprised both Luisa and me.

Mando stood his ground. His eyes moved rapidly from Joel's face to his torso and arms, locking on the camera hanging from his neck. A wry smile began to form on Mando's lips. He spat on the ground, wiped his mouth with the back of his hand. "Later, *vato,*" he said, waving a finger at Joel.

"*Cuando quieras,*" Joel answered back, accepting the challenge. "Any time," he repeated.

Irritated with their childish confrontation, Luisa commanded, "Stop it! Both of you!" She looked at Joel, then added, "A child is dead. That's why we're here."

Joel's face flushed with anger, but he remained quiet. Mando turned slightly to the left, cocking his head. The only noise was the distant clattering of the waning riot. Mando jumped over little Michael's body and stood beside me. With his face close to mine, he whispered in my ear, "The dude — the one who brought the *chavalito*? He wasn't a *Santo*. I know 'cause he was wearing a wig. *Era gabacho*. He had a scar — a *media luna* — a half-moon, and a birthmark under his right arm."

Looking over his right shoulder, Mando began moving swiftly down the street, every muscle in his body ready for either attack or defense. I was fascinated, yet sad. A mother would be crying for him sooner than later, I thought. Not many gang members live long enough to bury their mothers.

"I'll see if I can get some more information from him," Joel said. He ran off in pursuit of Mando, who was already turning the corner when Matthew Kenyon's unmarked car stopped with a screech beside us.

Why is it that cops and tough men — young or old — have to brake or start up a car with a screech, I wondered. Do they think they are establishing turf, like moose or sea elephants?

I looked toward the corner. How had Mando known the cops were on their way? I had a feeling I would never have a chance to ask him.

So I gave my full attention to Kenyon. He was a lanky man, six feet tall, with very short red hair already graying and a pallid, freckled face. Everything seems to be fading in this man, I thought, as I focused on his Roman nose, his only feature that seemed atypical.

With Kenyon was another man who answered to the name of Todd, obviously from the crime lab since he was already marking the place where the body lay. A third man, driving a car marked with the seal of the Los Angeles County Coroner's Office, pulled up behind Kenyon's car. He, too, got out and began to examine the body.

Before questioning us, Kenyon helped Todd cordon off the area. Actually, he hardly paid any attention to us at all until Todd referred to the vomit on the sidewalk and I claimed it as mine.

"Ah, yes. Gloria Damasco?" Kenyon said. It amazed me that anyone besides Marlon Brando and Humphrey Bogart could speak without moving his upper lip in the slightest. True, it is easier to do that in English than in Spanish, because of the closeness in quality of English vowels; but Kenyon's case, next to Brando's and Bogie's, was definitely one for the books. He had soulful, expressive eyes, and perhaps because of that I expected his voice to reveal much more emotion.

"Yes," I said, "I'm Gloria Damasco." I asked Luisa for the clipping Mando had given us and was about to hand it to Kenyon when I was seized by the same kind of fear I had felt when I had tried to take it from Mando. Again, I saw the house, but this time I saw the word "park" carved into a board next to it. In my haste to get rid of the clipping before I became nauseated again, I threw it at the policeman. "Here. I think the murderer might have dropped this."

"So much for fingerprints," Todd muttered, shaking his head.

"I told you not to disturb anything." Despite his perfectly controlled tone, Kenyon's eyes showed anger, but I didn't care since I was more preoccupied with the realization that I was experiencing something out of the ordinary every time I touched that clipping. Perhaps it was only the product of what my grandmother called my "impressionable mind," her term for an imagination that could easily develop a morbid curiosity for the forbidden or the dark side of nature. Even a liking for death. These possibilities distressed me.

I must have looked pretty distraught, because Kenyon invited Luisa and me to wait in his car. Since he had already taken note of our names and addresses, perhaps he simply wanted us out of the way until he had time to question us, I thought.

We got into the back seat and I lowered the window so I could hear what Todd and the Coroner were telling Kenyon, who was now putting Michael David's body on the stretcher and covering him with a cloth. "Well, Dr. D., was he strangled?"

Dr. D. — whose full name, according to his tag, was Donald Dewey — nodded, then shook his head, making the detective raise an eyebrow. "Whoever did this wanted to be extra sure that the boy would die. So the boy was drugged. I'm almost sure. This is all preliminary, you understand. I'll have more for you in the morning."

"That soon?" Kenyon smiled. "They're putting the others in the deep freeze, huh?" He flipped the pages in his notebook and read aloud: "Ruben Salazar, Angel Diaz and Lynn Ward."

"Looks that way." Donald Dewey picked up his equipment and headed toward the coroner's wagon. "Just buying time, I suppose. They got themselves into a real jug of jalapeno this time." I wondered if "they" referred to the police or to the demonstrators. Dr. Dewey came back after putting everything in the vehicle, then called Kenyon aside.

Trying not to be too conspicuous, I stuck my head out the window, but I could hear only fragments of the conversation because both men were speaking in a low voice. "...Second opinion. You never know. You'll have to tell them...soon."

Dewey patted Kenyon on the shoulder.

"Maybe Joel was right," I concluded. "Maybe it was a mistake to call the cops."

"Someone was going to do it anyway," Luisa said in a reassuring tone.

Todd and Kenyon picked up the stretcher and headed toward the wagon.

"Before I forget," Kenyon said to the coroner. "Will you find out as much as you can about the fecal matter?"

"Try my best," Dewey answered. "Need about two weeks though." He shook his head. "Real backlog and two lab boys just went on vacation."

Kenyon nodded and waved at the coroner.

I made the sign of the cross, closed my eyes and said a silent prayer for little Michael. My eyes were burning inside my lids. I opened them again and looked at my watch. It was now 5:15. The sun was still beating down on the streets and the sirens of ambulances and patrol cars were still wailing in the distance.

I had aged years in ten hours. By sundown, I would be as old as Mando.

For Ruben Salazar, Angel Gilberto Diaz, and Lynn Ward there was no going home, and the horror that would make the living toss and turn for many nights was of little consequence to them now. They were lying on autopsy slabs, side by side, waiting for their bodies to be opened and drained of blood, their insides emptied, then studied and tested to determine the exact cause of their deaths.

In time, perhaps someone would admit to the *real* cause of what happened that day. But perhaps we already knew the name of the insidious disease that had claimed three — perhaps four — more lives that late August afternoon.

More than ever before, I wanted to go home, to hold my daughter and seek the comfort of Dario's arms. But the spirit of little Michael had taken hold of me and I would not again be able to go about my life without my feeling his presence in me.

THE GHOST OF JOHN WAYNE

Ray González

Tony Marin read about it in the *San Antonio Light* Sunday magazine and couldn't believe it. A reporter hired a local psychic to find out if the ghost of John Wayne haunted The Alamo. For years, it had been some kind of local joke that John Wayne couldn't stay away from his beloved shrine, so somebody finally pulled this stunt. After wandering around the tourist crowded shrine in the middle of downtown San Antonio, the psychic discovered the restless spirits of several Mexican soldiers. He was able to communicate with one who told him the ghost of John Wayne came to The Alamo, every now and then, but never communicated with the soldiers.

The psychic told the *Light* reporter the soldiers were two brothers, José and Anselmo Vargas, who were conscripted into Santa Ana's army by force and died together in the famous battle. Their spirits are trapped in one of the rooms in the chapel and there is no way they can find eternal peace because of the way they died.

Tony reread the article and was amazed at how serious the reporter was in writing a story about how a Hollywood actor, who made a third-rate film about the battle, was haunting the Texas icon. Did people really believe this shit? Was this some kind of joke? He could tell the reporter, John Andrews, was skeptical. After reading the story a second time, Tony sensed the psychic, Bill Benson, was telling the truth about making contact with the frustrated spirits of the Mexican soldiers. He wondered how many hundreds of souls were trapped forever under the endless lines of tourists who came from all over the world to see The Alamo. That part of the story he could believe. He could see how historical events left their mark forever with the spirits of the dead who created those famous events. Plus, he had read enough about Santa Ana and the Mexican army to know thousands of young men were forced to join and die for the dictator's dreams of glory. If he despised the Mexican general's way of thinking, Tony could only imagine what deeper darkness the Texans carried to their graves.

He read the article a third time and knew he believed it, though he admitted to himself that he knew nothing about psychic phenomenon and had never encountered any ghosts or spirits. He found Bill Benson's number in the phone book and called him two days after the article came out. An answering machine took messages. Tony wondered if Benson had gotten many calls after the article.

He tried to reach Benson for several days, until he gave up and decided to go to The Alamo, a place he dreaded and had not visited in years. What he hated most was the Texas Ranger at the door whose job was to make sure no one entered the sacred shrine with a hat on.

"Please remove your hat. Please remove your hat." The Texas Ranger stood by the entrance and checked every tourist who entered. No man or woman with a hat on their head could gain entry without removing it first.

Tony watched the line of tourists move slowly into the chapel, and he hesitated from getting in step. As a writer, he had always been interested in how the history of Texas was written and portrayed and how Chicanos, Mexicans, and Native Americans had been left out of the picture. He had been working on a book of essays about Texas when the article appeared in the *Light*.

Now, as the line moved closer to the wooden doors of the shrine, he wondered what this had to do with what he was writing. He entered the cool interior of The Alamo. For a moment, it reminded him of his childhood days of going to church with his mother and *abuela* every Sunday, but The Alamo had been stripped of any religious mood long ago, the main chapel filled instead with artifacts and mementos from the famous battle, a museum for Texas pride that was surreal in its eternal nature.

Tony walked around the crowded room and inspected the glass cases that contained old rifles, flags, Jim Bowie's knife, and spent several minutes studying the intricate miniature replica of the mission and the surrounding fort, walls and buildings that were now gone, replaced by the paved streets and car exhausts of a busy city.

He stopped at one of the tiny rooms to the left side of the chapel, cell-like chambers that were closed to the public with black bars covering the doorways. Benson told the reporter that he made contact with the spirits of the Mexican soldiers in one of these rooms where many had died. The spirits communicated to Benson that John Wayne's ghost would stand in the doorway and stare at the trapped men. The spirits never felt threatened by Wayne, who just stared without speaking. Tony wondered if Wayne was checking the Mexicans out to see if they were authentic enough for casting in his movie.

As he stood and did his own staring at the brick walls of the cells, Tony was pushed by an elderly woman who crowded next to him to get a better view of the room. He moved out of her way when she grabbed the bars, pushed her face against them, and peered intently into the empty chamber. He stood before a plaque on the floor that marked the spot where several human bones had been uncovered decades ago. He wondered why the spot had been marked when this whole killing floor must cover thousands of remains that would never be unearthed.

Tony felt a chill and left the chapel by the exit door. He glided through a crowd of people who were headed for the tourist shop in the next building, the place where the Daughters of the Republic of Texas made sure you left a generous donation by purchasing Alamo t-shirts, hats, coffee mugs, books, posters, whatever.

Tony didn't go in, but turned and sat under the huge tree in the courtyard, a famous cottonwood whose massive limbs reached out in all directions to hover above the tourists as they wandered around the area. He watched people from all over the world and still didn't know why he had called Benson, or why he had come to The Alamo.

He went home and forgot about his visit to the shrine for a couple of weeks. One night, while working at his desk, the phone rang and it was Benson. When he first answered, Tony didn't recall who it was, until Benson said he was the psychic returning his phone call.

"Oh, yes," Tony perked up, surprised he called. "I tried to get a hold of you after the article came out. I thought you would be busy, or not taking calls about The Alamo."

"You are the only one who called about the article," Benson said in a calm, but bored voice.

"Really? I thought you would get many people wanting to find out more about John Wayne's spirit."

"John Wayne's ghost," Benson corrected him.

"Ghost? What's the difference?" Tony asked and reached for a notebook and pen.

"The spirits of the Mexican soldiers are in The Alamo," Benson explained, "but when I encountered them, they communicate that it is the ghost of John Wayne, not his spirit. His ghost comes around in a very neutral state with no sense of being trapped, or wanting to resolve his state, so he can go on. The Mexican spirits are trapped. They want out of there, to be laid to rest. Ghosts are usually satisfied with that neutral state. Spirits want to transform themselves toward..."

Silence.

Tony waited. "Toward what?"

"I don't know," Benson said in a low voice. "I'm not even sure why I am telling you this. I don't know you. Are you a reporter, too?"

"No, just a writer. I teach English and Chicano Studies, but I'm working on a book of essays about Texas. I was hoping you could tell me more about The Alamo."

"Why do you want to know?" Benson asked. "Isn't the story enough, or do you think it's all too phony?"

Tony noticed Benson was defensive, but he was fascinated that he had bothered to call back. "No, I don't think it's phony. I wouldn't have called you if I did."

"I think the reason you are the only one who called is because everybody else who may have read the story found it sacrilegious that John Wayne would come around to that holy place." His sarcasm made Tony feel at ease.

"I'm surprised you didn't get any threats from The Daughters of the Republic of Texas," Tony said.

Benson laughed for the first time. "Actually, I think they are delighted that an American like John Wayne would haunt The Alamo. It's probably the purists who sent me the letter."

"What letter?" Tony stopped taking notes.

Benson was silent for several seconds. "We haven't met. I need to get back to work. I can't talk anymore."

"Why did you return my call?" Tony asked more carefully. "Can we meet and talk some more?"

Benson did not hesitate. "Okay. I'm free tomorrow at two p.m. Where would you like to meet?"

"The flower garden behind The Alamo."

"Okay. How will I know you?"

Tony smiled. "I'll recognize you by your picture in the paper."

"I'll see you tomorrow." Benson hung up.

Tony sat in the lush garden behind The Alamo and hoped Benson would show up. In the early afternoon, several dozen tourists wandered around the finely kept gardens with the landscaped plots of bluebonnets and other bright flowers. Several of them stood over the *acequia* and watched the huge orange and white fish that filled the waters. As he sat and waited, Tony took in the peaceful scene and wondered what lay beneath the healthy green grass and the attractive acres within the ancient walls.

He recognized Benson right away, but was surprised at how thin and meek he seemed to look. Benson was fifty-eight, with a grey, balding head. He wore a white tennis shirt and faded blue

Levis. He looked like a retired professor, but there was something about him that Tony couldn't figure out as he approached.

"Hi, I'm Tony." They shook hands. Benson carried a large manila envelope in his left hand.

They sat on the bench by the coke machines that were set near the bathrooms, not the quietest place in The Alamo compound to talk. "Should we walk around?" Tony started to rise.

"No, this is fine," Benson squinted and placed a pair of sunglasses on his pale face.

"Thanks for agreeing to meet me. Do you get lots of demands on your time?"

"Not really," Benson looked out across the peaceful gardens. "I don't do much of this anymore."

"Much of what?"

"Find ghosts."

"Is that what you think this is? I thought you said spirits?"

Benson looked at Tony. "I used to make good money helping the police find missing persons. We solved quite a few cases. That kind of work was always easier than doing this."

"Does it bother you to come here?"

"Yes." Benson looked around to see if any tourists were listening.

"Why did you agree to do it for the *Light* reporter?"

"They paid me good money. They wanted a story."

Tony looked toward The Alamo and thought back to what Benson had stated in the article. He told the reporter that he couldn't stay inside the mission for very long because there were too many trapped spirits.

"I don't have any money to offer you, but I was wondering if you could tell me, or I guess show me, about the spirits of the soldiers?" Tony felt uncomfortable saying it.

Benson's eyebrows perked up. "You mean you don't want to find John Wayne?"

"Not really. I want to know more about the twin brothers who died in the battle."

"Don't you believe me about John Wayne? If you read the article carefully, the Mexicans acknowledge contact with Wayne. I certainly didn't find him."

"I know," Tony answered. "I read it carefully."

"Not everyone did." Benson waved the envelope in his hand.

"What's that?"

"A letter I got after the article came out," Benson explained. "I was rather surprised at the lack of mail on this one, but this letter is very interesting. Texas, I guess."

He handed the envelope to Tony, who opened it and read the scratchy handwriting, "You are a lunatic to say those things about The Alamo. You are crazy to insult us by saying those dumb Mexicans are still in there. John Wayne was right. Don't ever talk about The Alamo like that in public, or we are going to haunt you ourselves." There was no signature.

"Have you contacted the police?"

"No," Benson laughed. "I did enough work with them to convince them I am crazy. They won't pay attention to any threats against me."

"Are you scared? Who do you think wrote this?"

"I don't know," Benson shrugged and placed the letter back in the envelope. "A Texas history buff. Who knows? Its not the first time I've been threatened."

"Really?" Tony looked around, apprehensive for the first time. It had never occurred to him that some people could be this fanatical about the image of The Alamo.

"So, why do you want to make contact with the Mexican soldiers?" Benson changed the subject.

"I don't know if contact is what I want," Tony said carefully. "I just need to know that there is some way to come to terms with what happened here."

Benson sat up. "Look around you. The Alamo is right there in the middle of downtown San Antonio, surrounded by shopping malls, traffic lights, buses, and All Right parking lots. Millions of people come from all over the world. We have come to terms with what happened."

"I think you know there is more to it than that," Tony looked at him, suddenly liking Benson more.

Benson stood up slowly. "Yeah, I've always found that there is more. That is why I shouldn't be doing this anymore."

Tony stood with him. "Are we going inside?"

"Yes. This is a good time of day. It's not as crowded. Come on."

Tony's brief excitement turned to a strange fear. He wouldn't know what to do if Benson made contact with whatever, or whomever was really inside The Alamo. They walked through the quiet gardens and passed a Japanese couple giggling and shooting pictures of each other among the flowers.

As they got closer to The Alamo, Benson slowed down, his shoulders seeming to droop lower on his thin frame. Tony noticed a change on Benson's face as a nervous twitch perked his eyes and his cheeks seemed to turn a slight red.

The line was not real long, and they managed to get inside within five minutes. As soon as they entered, Benson folded his arms over his chest and walked carefully, as if he didn't want to touch anything in the enclosed walls. They walked around the museum casually, neither one of them saying a word, Tony wondering what to do, concerned that Benson might change his mind and leave. They stood in front of the table that held the miniature replica of the original mission and fort compound, the tiny soldiers and cannon enclosed in the glass.

Tony looked at the display, even though he had studied it several times in the past, and waited for Benson to say or whisper something to him.

Three tourists wandered over to the table, and Benson quickly stepped away from them and went to one of the tiny cells that lined the room. He put one hand on the black iron bars and peered into the room. Tony watched the look on Benson's face and was amazed at the trancelike glaze in his weary eyes. He stood a few feet away and hoped people would not crowd around Benson or notice what he might be doing.

Tony wanted to say something to Benson, but watched as he carefully leaned into the bars and rested his forehead on them.

Tony looked behind him and noticed the Texas Ranger making his rounds. He looked back at Benson and was shocked at the terror on his face — a strong force seemed to push Benson's cheeks inward and he closed his eyes. Tony stared as Benson's grey hair stood for an instant, as if someone was combing it.

Benson opened his eyes wide, whispered something Tony couldn't hear, then quickly walked out of The Alamo by the side exit. Tony hurried after him and had to push aside a young kid who blocked the door.

"Sorry," Tony muttered and ran after Benson. He was relieved that he was walking back to the bench in the garden and did not seem to be leaving the grounds.

Benson sat down, his chest heaving slowly, his breath short and raspy. "Are you alright?" Tony asked him as he sat down next to him, feeling guilty.

"Yes, I'll be okay," Benson said. "I need a drink of water."

Tony watched him drink at the water fountain near the bathrooms, then slowly return. They sat together for several minutes without saying anything to each other. More people streamed out of The Alamo and into the tourist shop, the afternoon drawing an endless stream of visitors.

As he waited, Tony wondered if he had made a mistake, but was also fascinated that Benson came upon the request of someone he didn't know. Was he this available with the special gift he had?

"Can you talk?" Tony finally asked quietly.

"Yes."

"What happened?"

"I found others I didn't know the first time."

"The twin brothers?"

"No. They weren't there. It is rare to encounter the same spirits twice. They were other Mexican soldiers, all of them very young, who are all trapped in there. There are at least sixty or seventy in that one tiny caged room."

Tony didn't say a word.

"I was surprised so many answered me." Benson said.

"What do you mean?"

"I didn't find that many the first time I came with the reporter. I think someone like me will find more and more with each visit."

"Does that bother you?"

"I don't know. There may be too many to handle it all."

"How long were you in there with the reporter?"

Benson shrugged. "About fifteen minutes. Time enough to make contact with the twin brothers and have them tell me about John Wayne."

"Why do you bring up John Wayne?" Tony asked. "Aren't there more important things in there?"

"Yes, but when I think I am crazy, I think about spirits talking to me about some movie actor. Who the hell is going to believe that? How do you know I didn't make this up about the twin brothers encountering John Wayne's ghost?"

Tony looked at Benson and felt sorry for him. Why were they here? Was this worth writing about? "I don't think you would make anything up, but I don't know what to do now. It seems too painful for you to go in there. Perhaps, this is enough."

"No, it isn't," Benson answered defiantly.

"Huh?"

"I need to go back in there, again."

"Why?" Tony sat up.

"Even though we were only in there a few minutes, I saw something. Someone showed me something."

"What was it?"

"I'm not sure. There was too much agony, too many voices, too many of them trying to reach out, but one of them showed me something. I need to go back in there in a few minutes."

Tony looked around and noticed a man standing about twenty feet away near the bed of blue bonnets. He would have dismissed him as just another tourist, but the man stood very still and stared at both of them as if he knew what was going on.

Tony bowed his head as he spoke. "Don't look up when I say this, but I think there's a man watching us. He's over there by those flowers."

Benson sat back casually and was able to scan the garden without much effort. "So, what about him? Are you getting paranoid?"

"He looks like he's watching us very carefully. I may have seen him inside when we were in there."

"So? There are many strange people downtown, and I'm sure lots of them go into the damn place all the time. Don't pay attention."

"Do you want me to go in with you?"

Benson looked surprised. "Of course. Why do you think we are here?"

Tony shrugged without a word and followed Benson to the end of the line, their second effort making Tony feel like he had done the wrong thing when he called Benson. He realized no psychic was ever going to change people's perceptions of The Alamo and how its myth and power would always preserve its status among Texan nationalists and history buffs. As he stood in line with Benson, Tony thought about the writing he was trying to do and wondered where all this fit. How could a sensitive person like Benson help him with answers to the questions Tony encountered in trying to write about the real history of Texas?

They entered, again, and Benson took his time getting to the room where he encountered something. They strolled around the front part of the museum, looked at a Bowie knife in one of the cases, and then found themselves in front of the barred room.

As Tony waited, Benson moved back in front of the entrance, but was unable to stand near the bars because five tourists were blocking his view. An elderly couple and their three daughters looked into the cell, the fascination and awe on their faces the common expression for so many visitors.

Benson waited patiently and closed his eyes, his arms folded over his chest. Tony looked around at the growing crowd and spotted the same man he had seen outside. He leaned against one of the display cases and stared at Benson. When the tourists moved from the entrance to the room, Benson quickly went to the bars and placed both hands on them.

Tony moved farther back to keep a better eye on the strange man who was obviously watching them. Tony heard Benson gasp and turned to look. Benson gripped the bars and stared intently into the room. Tony knew there was a Texas flag inside, but could never figure out why the tiny rooms were barred from the public. Benson muttered something to himself, let go of the bars, and gazed intently into the room, the initial agony or shock gone from his face.

Tony's anxiety eased a bit when he saw Benson's face relax, but he was concerned the stranger would do something. When Benson waved to Tony to approach the room., Tony hesitated, but Benson kept signaling.

Without a word, Tony stood next to him. Peering into the room, all he could see was the flag on its stand.

"The two brothers," Benson whispered.

"What?" Tony whispered back.

"I heard them. They want to go, but I'm afraid there is no way I can help them. They showed me what I knew I saw earlier." The sweat ran down Benson's forehead. Tony saw his face was turning pale.

"Are you okay?" Tony whispered.

"Yes, but I see why I have been drawn here. Not just you or the reporter have sent me here. There is something here besides the spirits of the dead."

Tony waited, but Benson stood there with his eyes closed. Tony looked around for the stranger and saw him talking to one of the Texas Rangers. They both looked at Tony at the same time. The area was clear of tourists for a few minutes because another wave of them was just entering the mission.

As the Ranger started to move toward them, Tony asked Benson, "What do you see? I need to know." He tried to keep his voice down.

"There's a flag in there."

"Yeah, the Texas flag. So what?" Tony said impatiently. The Ranger's approach was blocked by eight or ten people streaming into the central room, some of them asking him questions.

"No," Benson hissed, agitated and sweating. "There's another flag in there. It is draped around the body of one of the brothers. His other brother has been trying to pull it off his body. It's a white flag."

"The Texans tried to surrender?" Tony was startled.

"I don't know. The brother is trying to speak to me and pull the flag away from his brother. I can't see clearly. Too many bodies, but the brother is saying that the white flag belongs to them."

"To the Mexican soldiers?" Tony asked, the Ranger just twenty feet away.

"Yes, I think so. The brother's spirit is fading. The white flag belonged to them because they died that way, trying to stop the battle."

"But, who was surrendering?" Tony kept asking.

The Ranger stood behind them. He was a tall man with a stone face and a crew-cut, the stereotype of any Texas Ranger.

"You folks need to keep moving along. We have many people who want to see the exhibits."

Benson turned to him without a word and started to leave. Tony was relieved the Ranger didn't ask more questions because the stranger stood a few feet away watching them.

They went outside and Benson walked around the gardens for a long time, Tony keeping his distance, leaving him to his own thoughts, wondering what it was like to be able to see those things. Whether it was a life of too much vulnerability, too much agony. Or, yet a gift that drew the attention of police, reporters, and people like Tony who had no idea why they wanted more answers.

They finally sat down and Tony waited. Before Benson could explain anything, Tony spotted the stranger walking aggressively toward them. "That's him," Tony said. "He put the Texas Ranger on us."

"What?" Benson asked, still trying to recover. Before he could look up, the husky man dressed in a grey shirt and dirty black jeans ran up to them.

"I know you!" he screamed at Benson.

"What are you doing?" Tony jumped up.

"You're the guy in the paper. You're the weirdo who said Mexicans are in there!" the guy hissed.

Benson sat without a word. He looked up at the man as if he had seen him before.

"Why don't you go away?" Tony stood his ground.

The guy pushed Tony back, down on the bench. Benson didn't move, but bowed his head at the man. "You weirdos are always trying to get in the paper. I'm telling you, we aren't going to put up with that crap about Mexicans still being in there!" The man pointed a pudgy finger at Benson and started to walk away, unconcerned that Tony had risen to his feet, fists clenched.

"Don't," Benson commanded him and raised a hand to restrain him. "Don't. Let him leave."

Tony swayed a bit, his face red, a few tourists in the garden standing and watching, no Ranger in sight. Tony sat back down. The two of them watched the stranger leave and disappear in the crowd.

"I'm sorry," Benson said.

"Why? I'm the one who brought us here," Tony said, breathless.

"I'm sorry the publicity has made so many people curious about this place. There is too much hidden to ever get people to understand, but I'm glad we met and came here," Benson said.

"What about that lunatic?"

"I've encountered people like him before. I told you that."

"Yeah, but I haven't," Tony explained. "I wanted to hit him when he said that about the Mexicans."

"It always comes back to that," Benson said. "But, we don't really know what happened. I saw too much today. It's never going to change. This place will stand forever, and the spirits will be inside forever."

"What about that white flag? What do you think it means?" Tony asked.

"It means too much. We are not suppose to really find out who waved that white flag. It would change history, and too many people are trying to change all the things we are supposed to see and believe."

"Like me," Tony added.

"I don't mean you. You have a right to want to know. We all do, but when we ask the wrong questions, it is too difficult to come here and get those answers."

They sat in silence. Tony wondered if it was time to say goodbye to Benson. Part of him felt like seeing him again. He also discovered the anxiety and loathing of coming to The Alamo meant he had to search on his own without exposing this vulnerable man to more than was fair.

Tony and Benson rose together, knowing it was time to leave. They walked through the gardens with no sight of the stranger. Benson paused over the *acequia* to watch the white and orange fish weave slowly through the water.

"I never asked you how you make a living? Can I pay you for coming today?" Tony asked him even though he didn't have any money.

"No, I don't want any money," Benson said. "I'm retired military."

"Really? The article never said that. How come?"

"You can imagine how difficult it might be for someone in the military to be as curious as I am. There is too much there we don't see, but I found ways to do my job for many years. It's okay."

They stopped on Alamo Street, in front of the whole complex. "Thanks for doing this," Tony said and shook Benson's hand. "You have been a great help."

"Thank you for being so patient," Benson said and crossed the street.

Tony started to walk to his car, feeling a bit sad, but decided to go back to The Alamo. He felt he knew exactly where to go after being with Benson. He entered the huge gift shop located in a separate building from the mission. The crowded store featured everything from Davy Crockett t-shirts and mugs to Texas flags and books on Texas history. It was packed with people who shopped and stood in the long lines by the cash registers.

He pushed his way through the crowd and stopped in front of the book section. Hundreds of books on the battle and its heroes lined the shelves. He gazed at the titles until he found a book about the history of Alamo films. A writer named Thomas Woods had written a series of essays about the few films made about The Alamo and how they were all obscure documentaries or poorly made movies. A major chapter was devoted to John Wayne's epic.

Tony took the book and stood in line, the knot in his stomach growing tighter because he sensed he was in the right place. He couldn't see clearly until he got closer to the counter. Three customers were ahead of him when he saw what he was looking for. The line moved closer to the register as Tony pulled cash out of his wallet.

He fought hard to keep a straight face and not smile or want to yell anything. It was his turn and he set the book down hard on the glass counter. The man looked up at him and recognized him, but there were too many people crowding around for either one of them to acknowledge the earlier encounter.

The man took Tony's twenty dollar bill, rang up the book, and glared at him as he gave him his change. He didn't hand him the money, but set it on the counter instead. As Tony picked it up and grabbed the book bag, the man moved away from the counter and whispered something to the woman clerk next to him. They both watched him in silence as he moved away from the counter, the smile on his face about to break into a nervous quiver as Tony gave them a final nod and walked out of the shop.

DAYS OF INVASION

Juan Felipe Herrera

Zeta Mendoza is dead. I left him doubled up in a small corn field in Panama, somewhere near the Costa Rican border. That's all there is to say about it. No one knows this except me.

Larkin Street San Francisco drink joint.
This is where it's at for the moment. Light up a cigarette, buddy, gaze at the descent of the match stick as it twists toward the floor. Look up at the bartender and then look away; remember the City back in the fifties, the way Zeta did.

Boy, he used to say —
> you couldn't sport a finer gabardine jacket with Daisy Robles going up to the Orpheum on Easter Sunday or the Black Hawk - listen to Cal Tjader on vibes and Desmond on sax. You see, everything was in the shape of a fancy sparkle: even the question mark by her telephone number in my pocket calendar or the last note scribbled on a table napkin. It was all personality, black coffee and music.

Black Hawk, I whisper —
and feverishly drink down the tiny glass of bitter syrup in my hand. I look around. Greasy smiles.

Electric peanuts in the sky — I laugh to myself.

Zeta used to say that about the lights above the Bay Bridge. Kill time. Say anything that comes to your mind, just make sure you forget Zeta's twisted body. In San Francisco, you'll forget.

I had just gotten off the Golden Gate bus half a block away. I was wired. December afternoon outside, wind cooling. Another drink at Tony's tavern on the corner of Larkin and Geary. Outside: downtown archways, stone alleys — a kid with french fries and sauce leaking through the bag jumps at the curb.

The mirror behind the bartender betrays me. I stroke my right ear; I feel awkward. I was never this thin, so bluish — maybe too much left back there in the crazy tropics. Take a bus to the beach just like when you were a downtown boy. Yeah.

As the bus left Market street, looking at the kid wind up a staircase to his apartment, I think of my mother still in her tiny room without an escape ladder on Mission Street. The extra-large jar of Jergen's night cream on her wicker basket altar. Saints she prays to, offerings she makes.

Muni-pier looms ahead. Walk up the concrete coil where Chinese women huddle by the cold benches rigging up crab net. Hook an eel with the pole.

§ § §

"Look, Lopez, there's a lot going on. The military are swarming all over the place. This government is out to get Noriega one way or another, he knows too much, you know — all the fucking hanky-panky these white ambassadors have been pulling for years in Central America. Buying women. Hauling coke. Arms and champagne. I was at the college meeting the other day and some of the people that got smuggled in last week across the border said everything is hot out there. You know what I mean, man.

I am fucking tired of just looking at people getting screwed one way or another. Can't sleep, can't paint. Can't even screw right. Gotta go out there, check it out; I don't know, you want to come?" He was serious.

"You're crazy, Zeta, in Central America if you are Indian-looking, young and carrying a book, you're dead meat! I can't even speak Spanish right, shit." He came back at me. "What's the problem, bro'?"

I smiled a wilted smile. Then his face darkened, his jaw seemed to shift, widen.

"Lopez, we gotta go. The scene here stinks. Everyone is out for your jugular. The murals I painted back in '79 are washed out. Nobody seriously reads anything — even if the paper is on fire, they'll just lay it down and walk away to their stucco houses. What am I supposed to do now — apply for a candy-assed grant to paint an alley like the rest of the so-called artists around here? My tag is up in every alley all the way to Oakland. Nobody's crossed it out. You know why? You wanna know? Because they ain't got no guts and no souls, man! This city is dead. The people are dead and everything they are doing right now this very minute is dead. Got it?"

"Yeah," I half-mumble. I look out to the Trans-continental tower jutting from the heart of Chinatown into the weak sky. On the shore, a few hunched lovers examine the sand for the first time, picking up shiny stones that will fade as soon as they dry. Yeah, right.

§ § §

Daisy — yes, Zeta wanted her; she was good to him and now she was gone. He liked to make up pictures of both of them, draw them for me in his beat-up sketch pad on the way south through

Tegucigalpa, Honduras: Think of a romantic movie in the fifties, rum-colored bandannas and jukeboxes —

In the middle of Dolores Park, I was the guy with baggy corduroys doing a tango. Me and Daisy and her Portuguese accent. She was the only real dancer at one hundred twenty-two degrees west longitude, baby.

Daisy was out of the picture now. The art scene in San Francisco was a billboard inferno. Everything from Haight Ashbury to Daly City had been whitewashed and glossed with glitter and New Age Asians and Hispanics running for office. Zeta used to say a crazy demolition team had come in overnight and left us with six-story parking lots, bad cars, the elegant bold type of murder on the daily periodicals, frenzy pills, cut-out military episodes from the Nam pasted over with apologia and mirror bank buildings.

One night, after his last art opening at the *Galeria de la Raza* on Bryant Street, Zeta came up to me, a drink in his hand: "Lopez, all we have is a little kit — a few things like soap and toothpaste, a pair of odd-matched socks; well-packed bundles under our shirts — pear-like shapes of rage, desire and lonesome dreams."

A *little kit* — I wasn't good with words like Zeta.

I can still hear Zeta. I can't get over it:

Remember my mom? Yeah, you remember, he said. Remember how she used to cook us *caldo de res* after a whole weekend of us carousing, reading poems, getting drunk and thinking we were being political. Come on, how she looked at us — as if we were young and strong, full of fresh smells, smiles and medals; ready to walk all the way downtown for a riot with the cops at the snap of a finger, a phone call, anything. That look she gave us, man. We were losing something. We were the old lost ones, weren't we?

§ § §

I decided to leave for Central America with Zeta. Sure did. I was better off in Panama, maybe. I always ended up doing whatever Zeta got into, anyway. At City College, he used to hang around the teachers after class talking about astrology, Sartre and French films. French films? Never even had French bread. So I went along. Never said a thing. Nothing. Just kinda smiled. One time even gave everyone a penny. Didn't know what to do or say. Just gave them a penny. Then, at school: *Thus Spoke Zarathustra* on my desk in Chemistry lab. My mom was scared; she thought I was getting into devil stuff. It all worked itself out, somehow. Follow Zeta, it's ok, it told me, this thin stuff here inside my gut. Zeta is right, it said.

"I'll tell you about the Marine thing later, man." Zeta was throwing his arms up, pulling at his goatee, swiveling his shoulders, loose, striding, as we stepped out of the wrinkled wagon-bus we had boarded in the open-air depot back in Guatemala City. Later: "They say Edgar hasn't been seen in weeks." Zeta looked concerned as he hung up the phone outside the main Plaza in Tegucigalpa. Edgar was a guy on the inside of things — an accountant by day, a sentry for the Left by night.

The white colonial towers bounced light through the trees. I was spinning. Heat thickened the fragrance of the budding flowers. In the plaza, a half-naked boy tumbled over a towel sprinkled with glass slivers. Another blew out fire from his mouth, eyeing the *turistas* rushing by, looking for hotels, cigarettes, taxis.

By nightfall, we had ended up in Panama City, stopped at a cafe. Zeta mumbled something about trekking 25 kilometers further south. We rested and smoked. Then he made a call and got directions to Edgar's place in the hills. Edgar would fill us in — we were close, he said.

In the morning we found Edgar barely alive in a small village.

§ § §

I thought about all this on the pier.

§ § §

Crawling through the smoking corn slush, pushing my boots down on the blackened sod, then Zeta found Edgar ahead of me. Bullets burned in his right thigh. A gaping hole by his shoulders. Edgar was dreamy and spurted words as best he could, pointing ahead to a river. The villagers had fled to the border river, he said. Old farmers, women and children shot down by American soldiers — Edgar kept on repeating this and pointed again; there had been helicopters. Zeta went further. He disappeared and then came up holding the hand of another body along the field.

It was raining — hard rain smashing the wide, red-flared plant leaves along the small roads. I could hear the mad ticking all around and inside of me. The sky lowered and then unraveled its dark knots that had been tightening since dusk and then, thunder. All the tiny things in the earth below were loosening with a music of their own — little bones in water letting go of their cargo suddenly; all around us, the corn fields whitened in a sharp, strange light, a pure light. Zeta! His arms come up, caught in a storm of flickering sheathes, little blazing shards, his face slowly going to the side and the torso — stretching, curling at the edges, the thousand brilliant translucent shells falling to his feet — in a millisecond, not far from me; I lost Zeta to this light. I ran to Edgar and told him I would come back with help.

§ § §

I can still hear the lightning.

I've been pacing every walkway in San Francisco for the last two weeks thinking about this. Been drinking too much Yukon Jack syrup. Yesterday, it took me two hours to get out of the house — lost the keys in my sweatshirt, left the door open, got back and thought my cassette player had been stolen. Then, remembered I had pawned it for more fast food, cigarettes and sweet drinks.

Standing.

Thinking in the middle of the street. Shotwell Avenue. Zeta's last mural. I look to the southern sky and try to make the connection between Zeta's crazy acrylics — the swirling elongations of arms, robes, the fleshy ochre whiteness, even the piety of the hands as they reach up towards something dark and unknown — and my last image of him.

There was nothing that could be done in Panama.

§ § §

I wandered back — caught buses. Bummed money from old pals in Mexico City. Made it to Mexicali to pick up the Chevy we had parked before catching a train. It was slouched over a ravine by the train station. The seats were littered with orange sandwich papers, diapers and soiled pillows. I dumped the papers and diapers and a knot of newspapers that was stuffed into the door to keep out the cold air. Filled up one of the tires with air and made it to Escondido, California. Bummed more gas money and a dinner from Gabby Vasquez, a good buddy of mine who is the only decent person I know that is happily married — three kids and a wife named Rosemary. In his house there was a filmy kind of stream making everything moist: the wood grain on the door, the television's blackish rubbery plastic molding. Even Rosemary. Her lips, porous, the hair on her arms longer, lighter — having another baby, going to name him Toño, she said. Gabby gets up early. Pulls out his jump-rope with a black ball at the end of each cord. Five hundred, he says. Five hundred. I open my hands to my side, tighten my fingers two or three times, then close them into a fist and leave to San Francisco in one straight drive, loop into downtown where the green and silver windows block out everything the sun gives except the abstract noise shooting up from the asphalt. I park the Chevy on Polk, walk away still seeing patches of the corn field in front of me uprooted in yellowish brown heaps and the waxy faces and shoulders falling out of the bloody slush. And the brilliant lights crashing on Zeta.

My mother once told me about what happened before we moved to San Francisco. I was a child and my father, Emilio, was working the tractor as a farmhand out on the edge of a town bordering Arizona. The immigration patrol had snared three Mexicans without papers. They were taunting them and from a large reserve can poured gasoline on one of the men. My father never told anyone else about it. The immigration officers would blame him, he said. He would rub his face hard when he said this, then turn away.

⌣

It was getting late. The streets were hurting me — pacing in squares and zigzags, leaning on little restaurant walls I had never visited. My face against the windows. See the thick coats hunched over a bowl of soup, the nervous hands flipping the basket for more French bread. A waitress chewing gum grimaces at a wino that steps in and shoves a menu into him like a knife. Couples with their tiny pink pastry boxes in a bag hang their coats and wait for a glass of water to wash things away. My stomach churns, I tap my cigarette pack against the fleshy part of my palm and light one, slowly eyeing the furniture specials on the street.

The furniture stores still put up the same old Christmas sale signs, I chuckle sourly.

I thought of Zeta and Edgar. There was nothing I could do about Edgar. I told the villagers to go for him. What more could I do?

Central America was always hot. We said it — over a wine cooler or at a poetry reading in the Mission District. None of us would even dare leave San Francisco. And any fire-play out there gave us more reason to stay put.

I couldn't get back into the city — no matter how much I tried to dig into the concrete. Just couldn't get back.

Days are at a standstill. Papers say Noriega lives in the Vatican embassy now — listens to heavy metal blasting from the Marine's speakers. He doesn't want to show his face.

§ § §

The old deli had a dim light on. It was a greenish two-story Victorian that stood on the corner facing a Bekins storage facility — maybe the last Bekins building in the Mission District; U-Haul was taking over. Further up, a closed beer brewery was being torn down. People said the City was going to build a school there later in the year. The rest of the block was boarded up except for a few smaller houses scattered here and there. It was very late now. What could I say to Zeta's mom?

I pushed the little button again and again. "It's me, Señora Mendoza." I heard a young man's voice with a funny accent. I tried to think where to start. "Victor?" I said hoping it was Zeta's brother as the door opened.

I wanted to say more but, I couldn't. Vic said nothing, as he limped ahead passing the black deli refrigerators towards the back room. I could see the *coquitos* on display by the juices —

we used to wrap them in cellophane on weekends so Zeta's dad could sell them to the Mexican candy stores in the District. I smelled candles, medicine and the coconut oil in the candy. The smell of burnt corn stumps came up. My stomach loosened. "Vic?" I peeped again.

"Victor?" I was louder this time. Nothing came back.

I only had seen him a few times, at dinner or going out with his friends. Now, he wasn't very big; he was frail, the box of his shoulders tight, tiny. Angular face, unshaven; a religious air. Before I could ask him anything, he opened the door to an amber-lit room and just said, "He's waiting for you."

Another silence.

Nothing came back from me this time. I was stopped by the odd breathing coming from the man sitting in a makeshift bed in front of me. "He's been waiting for you." I turned to an old woman at the end of the bed. She moved her lips without looking at me.

Zeta's dead. I left him in Panama. A mortar shell burned him alive. I saw it. All this balled up in my throat and left me speechless. I couldn't say this now. There was nothing I could say. Who was this man? Zeta's mother knelt at the foot of the crooked mattress. I turned to Vic standing by the door. But, he motioned with his thin hand, shooing me back.

Zeta's breath was swimming through his lungs. Remember? I thought to myself: the forehead gnarls, things flutter across his face. "Come on, Zeta," I said. Blinking fast, his eyes watered, glaring at mine. His mouth opened and closed, trying to make something inside speak. But he couldn't make it work. The tongue moved and pushed. All I could see were the damn blisters at the back, by the tonsils. And he closed his eyes, dropped his head.

What happened? The strange man spoke with an odd childlike swing to his voice.

"Yes?" I said, awkwardly. He glared. Zeta's mom nodded and stood up, propping one hand on the bedside, walked over to the dresser and handed me a letter.

I was sweating. Raised a hand and brushed my hair with my fingers. All this had already done something to alter her quiet poise. The envelope did more.

She stood far away and pointed the letter at me. I moved up to her, took the note and heard myself saying: "*Gracias, Señora Mendoza.*" A muffled fear trembled in the corners of her eyes. She was turning her eyes to the suited man, then to little Vic. Then to me. I stood there looking at her, there in the dark box burning with an old bulb on the high ceiling. I started to open the envelope.

"Not now, Lopez." I turned to the man. He was sullen. Serious.
"What do you mean, *not now?*"
"Not now," I said.
"Is this about Zeta?" I stammered. "I need to know what's in this letter."
"You never made it to Panama, ok?"

He brushed the stubble on his chin. I wanted to put it in my shirt pocket, but nothing moved.

"You went on a vacation, maybe Acapulco, an old buddy looked you up, maybe."
"What?"
"You saw nothing, punk." He says and he jumps up to me.

"You saw nothing, ok? Or maybe you were running cocaine for the military back there? Maybe you've been doing this for two years now. You and Mr. Zeta. What else could two college dropouts do to keep up with things in the city? And maybe you sold some to your artist friends, you know the ones that wear all those Apartheid and USA out of El Salvador buttons? I got it all here in my notes." He laughs, walking around the bed.

"And then you know what?" Pokes me. "Why don't you ask Mrs. Mendoza and Vicky boy? They're smart."

He reaches inside his coat behind his worn leather belt and pulls out a snub-nosed gun. Waving it in a short, nervous circle, planting it on my right temple.

"Let us say it was going pretty good for a while. You started making fine drug money, eating fine — better than hanging around Berkeley selling rings with the rest of the wierdos. Then you know what?"

He was getting louder. "Your buddy Zeta got an idea: more stuff. Right? But, he didn't have the connections. So you guys went south." He was breathing hard. "You saw nothing, Lopez." He stalled, backed off, stopped: he was sorting things out, shuffling his story into my story — how I smuggled stuff back to the streets and how he could prove it in one easy sweep; how I had seen the American military kill one of our own and how he would pin me so I would stay quiet — he glanced at Zeta's mom, then at me. He brought up the gun again and pointed me towards the little door.

He was pushing me out of the room with the gun at my back. I wanted to turn around and grab at something. Zeta's mom was stiffening, opening her mouth trying to push something out, wheezing, pulling up the bones in her shoulders. She ran up to the headboards and dropped next to the bed.

"Come on, get out, I don't need you," he closed the back door with his free hand. Then he picked up a sandwich by the refrigerator door and took a sumptuous bite. "You say something and I'll get her too, Señor Lopez." A hot bitter liquid came up my throat.

I wanted to turn back to the corn fields — run back through the wetness. The mass graves — up there by the corn fields — the American military had them dug in already, just waiting for the air attack on Panama City. A set-up. I was frozen.

He pushed me by the head out the front door onto the street. Something came over me. I jammed my arm through the closing edge of the door lock, grabbed it and pressed back. I was backing him up now.

"Come on, mister, shoot my brains out." I was talking fast.
"Get the hell outta here, Lopez."
"And then what you gonna do, shoot the candies?"
"Shut up!" He was moving further back. A bit more every time.
"You didn't see nothing!" I pushed him.

Zeta's mom was moaning in the closed room. "Blow me away, buddy." My voice was coming from deep down. "You want to know what that letter says?" he barked, shielding the door to the little room. "Go ahead, let's see it, pull it out — let's hear about your *vacation*." He waved his little gun again.

I held up a picture: a couple of guys with a woman in fancy clothes, snorting powder on the table — drinks, aperitifs, musicians in blue vested suits. "Who's going to believe this crap — this guy don't even look like me. Zeta had straight hair." I wanted to tear the photos, shred them, and fling the pieces at him. Didn't say a word, just stood there, dropped the glossies on the floor. Squinting and wiping the side of my face, turned around and didn't look back. Walked out. "You saw nothing," he whispered. "Don't come back, Lopez, I swear...." he went on as I shut the front door. It was around four in the morning. The steel street signs above me.

§ § §

Moving off down the curb, Zeta talks into my ear — how one day he couldn't sell his uncle's landscape paintings at the market. No one was buying them anymore. Right? All of a sudden nobody wanted bulls and gallant, lean young kids in shimmering bronze suits on their walls. Now, it was all about abstract portraits. Squares. Upside-down eyes.

ALLIGATOR PARK

Benjamin Alire Sáenz

In 1984 or maybe 1985, I don't remember the year; the years seem far away to me like they never happened, but they happened — I know they happened. Anyway, whatever year it was, I think 1985, we were living in Tecapan and I heard my mother and father talking about all the rumors — I was always listening to other people's conversations — the rumors about the guerrillas. My mother said there was talk, lots of talk about the guerrillas, and they were assassinating people. My father shook his head like he already knew it. My mother kept talking about how the guerrillas had begun to bother people and how they sometimes took them out of their houses and encouraged them to join up. It was true. They tried, the guerrillas, to convince lots of my friends to fight the government and after a while I didn't see some of them anymore, so I guess some of them did join. I don't know, it's confusing, but I do remember those things. I remember those things. I dream about them sometimes; I don't know what the dreams mean, but they scare me, and so now I don't pray.

I had a friend of mine, well, not a very good friend, but a friend, and he was my teacher at our school. I liked him real well because he liked my ideas and he was very good to us, but he always seemed a little sad even when he laughed. Me and another friend of mine were talking to him before school one day and that day six men came into the school courtyard. The men were all covered up and they had handkerchiefs on their faces and all I could see was their eyes, and the eyes weren't old and the eyes were soft. But they had weapons, maybe rifles, maybe guns — I can't remember — and the men shot *and killed our teacher right there in front of us. And the teacher was right in the middle, saying something, but I don't remember anymore what he was saying and I guess it doesn't matter because he just fell. It was the first time I ever saw blood and I saw a lot of it afterwards, so now I hate the color red, and the men, the men took some of the students, maybe six of them, all about my age, between ten and fourteen years old because those were the ages of the people who went to our school, and me and my friend, Arturo, ran and hid. What we did was run and hide and I remember thinking that I was going to be dead like my teacher, so I ran. Arturo was right behind me and all I could think of was bullets and the eyes of the men. We hid in some fields of a farm outside of our town and we sat there all day until night came and we never said a word.*

Jaime put down the notes he'd taken down that morning. He didn't feel like reading any of it, anymore. It bothered him. He thought of Franklin and the distant look on his face when he was telling him his story. He had explained to Franklin that political asylum cases weren't easy and that it would take a long time, and the first thing they had to do was write down his story.

"Can't I just tell the judge what I know, what I saw?" Franklin asked.

Jaime tried to explain that everything had to be on paper and Franklin answered that he couldn't even speak English, much less write it.

"I know," Jaime told him, "that's why you need me. You tell and I'll write everything down, and then I'll put it into English, and then we'll fix it all up and organize it so it will all make sense."

"None of it makes sense," Franklin said.

Jaime nodded. "We have to pretend it makes perfect sense. We think that way in the United States." Jaime laughed at his own answer. Franklin laughed, too. They laughed for different reasons.

"Why is your name Franklin?" Jaime asked.

"That's what my mother named me."

Jaime smiled at his answer. He was only a kid, fifteen years old, and already he had seen everything, but he still didn't know what was behind all the questions. "Yes, I know, but why did she name you that? It doesn't sound like a name from someone who comes from El Salvador. I mean, like my name: Jaime. My parents are Mexican so I have a common Spanish name — but 'Franklin'?"

Franklin nodded his head. "Well, my mother joined this new church in our town, a church the gringos started, and one of the elders said Franklin would be a good name when I was born, so my mother named me Franklin like the elder said, but I never went to my mother's church, but I liked my mother — and all I have left of her is the name she gave me." He paused. "If your mother was Mexican, and you were born in the United States, aren't you a U.S. citizen?"

"Yes," Jaime nodded, "I'm a U.S. citizen."

"Do you like that?"

Jaime popped his knuckles. "Yes," he said, "it's very nice."

Franklin smiled and nodded.

Jaime pictured Franklin as he had looked when he let him in the door that morning. His dark Indian features impressed him. He carried himself with ease, with grace, not at all with the awkwardness of his age — but when he spoke he almost apologized for speaking. He showed up at the door saying, "But you don't have to help me if you can't — I understand, it's just that someone said you might help me and they gave me your name and told me where you lived." Franklin had apologized several times before he had even walked in the house. Jaime offered him a cup of coffee and watched in amazement as he poured four spoons of sugar into the cup. He looked around the living room and asked: "Are you rich?"

Jaime thought a minute and said, "Yes, I'm rich. Not rich like the people who own banks, but rich enough." If anybody else had asked that question he would have laughed.

Franklin was immediately drawn to all the paintings on the walls. Jaime noticed him staring at them and asked him if he liked them.

Franklin nodded. "Yes, I like them. Did you pay a lot of money for them?"

"No, my brother gave them to me. He's an artist."

"Will he teach me how to paint?"

"I'll ask him if you want?"

"And how much do you charge for helping me?"

Jaime thought Franklin already knew there was no charge, since whoever told him to come had probably also told him his services were free. Perhaps he felt better if he asked the question. "Nothing, I don't charge you anything. You just have to come and sign all the papers and then when we're ready, my wife, who is a lawyer, will represent you in court and you can both go before the judge and the judge will decide whether you can stay or not. But once we put in your application you won't have to be hiding from the *Migra* anymore."

Jaime thought of their morning interview. He looked at the words he'd dictated on the yellow legal pad. He asked himself why he did this, and why he let people like Franklin interrupt his life. *Is that what he was? — an interruption?* He shook his head. He was tired of analyzing himself and he was sick of other people's insights into his motivations. His mother said he got involved because he was a good person — but she was his mother; his friends said he did those "things" because he wasn't working and needed to feel like he was doing something worthwhile; his brother told him he was guilt-ridden; and his sister said he had a need to keep up his leftist image — "you've been building that radical image since you were twelve." "What does it matter why I do what I do," he said aloud, "when I know I'm going to keep on doing them." He shook his head in disgust. "But they never let any of them stay legally — what's the use? They get shipped back like unwanted mail." He arched his back and stretched his arms out toward the ceiling. "Maybe this time, we'll win. Sometimes asylums *were* granted. Why shouldn't it be Franklin this time?"

Franklin should be out playing football, he thought, or discovering girls and sex or something like that. He should be doing all those things that fifteen-year-old boys do. Instead he's hiding from the green vans of the border patrol and coming to perfect strangers asking for help. He looked at the yellow legal pad and reread the first paragraph. He made notes on a separate sheet of paper. "I'll need some dates," he whispered to himself. "I'll have to make him remember the exact year, the maybe's won't do — he's going to have to remember the exact day his teacher was killed." He took a few more notes and then put the pad down. He fixed himself a cup of coffee and stared at his brother's paintings. The colors were soothing: Indian blues. He wished Franklin could live inside one of those paintings and live in peace. "Goddamnit! Why did they have to go and name him Franklin!" He took a sip of his coffee and fought the urge to have a cigarette. "What in the hell is a Quiche Indian with a gringo name doing in El Paso?"

§ § §

When Joanna walked in from work, Jaime had dinner on the table. She kissed him on the cheek and Jaime breathed in her smell. "Looks good," she said. "We even have candles tonight."

Jaime nodded. "Nothing special. Just felt like candles. I got caught up in a few things — we're just having steak and potatoes — and a salad. I didn't feel like cooking. Good old fashioned gringo food."

She laughed. "I adore gringo food."

"It's cultural," he said, "and we have a new case."

"We do? Who is it this time? Why don't you just go to law school or become a social worker?"

"Do we need the money? If we need the money, I'll go back to school or get a job. But if we don't need the money, forget it."

"It's not the money, Jaime, you're just going to wear me out. I mean — well — never mind. We have enough money. We have plenty of money. No, I don't want you to go back to work — I like coming home to a clean house and a man who does all the shopping — someone who presses all my clothes." She smiled. "Interesting case?"

Jaime nodded as he opened a bottle of Chardonay. "Another political asylum case."

She shook her head. "I was hoping it was a battered woman's case or something like that. At least we win those. Political asylum cases are virtually unwinnable."

"Not if you're from Cuba."

"Is he or she from Cuba?"

Jaime shook his head.

"I didn't think so. We won't win."

"You're no expert. Immigration law isn't even your field. And besides, we might win this one."

"How many cases have we gone to court with?" She took a sip of wine and nodded. "Good. An excellent selection, *mi amor*." She touched his cheek.

He served the salad. "We've had maybe twelve cases or so."

"Fifteen," she corrected, "which, by the way, makes me at least competent in the field of immigration law — if not an expert."

"Well argued, counselor."

"But back to my point," she continued, "how many of those cases have we actually won?"

"That's not the point, wife. I mean, some of them did get into Canada. And most of them still write to us." His finger flew out and pointed at her.

"So, husband, now we have pen pals." She played with her wine glass. "And put your finger away. You're hopeless, Jaime. You and I both know those good-for-nothing immigration judges don't give a nationally indebted dollar —"

"I like that expression. You just hear that one?"

"I just made it up."

"I bet you're good in a courtroom."

"Can I finish? You always use these tactics when I'm about to make a point you don't like."

"Maybe I should go to law school."

"Stay home and iron." She shook her head. "Those damned judges don't give a damn, Jaime. You know it, and I know it, and anyone who's ever been in their courtrooms knows it. Maybe there have been a couple of good ones — but they got out. To those guys, our clients are just faces and they shake their pathetically phallic faces at Central Americans as if they really believe all of them are trying to pull a fast one over on them. The law — the law, Jaime — is all screwed up. The judges are appointed, honey, and if they let too many people in they'll get unappointed." She dug her fork into her salad and tasted it. "Good. You do nice things with salad. How come you never put in any olives?"

"I hate olives. I won't compromise on olives."

"What's his name? I take it he's a man."

"If you want to call a fifteen-year-old a man."

"He's a minor, Jaime?"

"Age doesn't make any difference, does it?"

"It might complicate things."

"Anyway, I guess we'll have to figure something out. I think his parents are dead. I don't know any of the details — we haven't discussed it, but I asked him and he said something about them disappearing, which amounts to the same thing as getting blown away."

Joanna put her fork down. She stared at her empty plate. "Let's skip the steak," she said. "Did you put them on already?"

Jaime shook his head. "I'll put them back in the refrigerator, but the potatoes are baked. We'll have to eat them."

"Anyway, white wine doesn't go with steak."

"You don't miss a beat, do you?"

"The whole family disappeared?"

Jaime nodded. "The whole lot. Just disappeared. I doubt whether they'll ever show up. He's the only one that's left."

"How convenient." She took a big drink of her wine. Jaime poured them both some more. He walked into the kitchen, put the steaks back in the refrigerator, turned off the broiler, and brought in the baked potatoes.

"Franklin thinks I'm not really a man."

"His name's Franklin?"

"His mother belonged to some church started up by some nice Americans and they thought Franklin would be a nice name."

"Well, if we can't let them stay in our country, we can at least export our names. Why doesn't he think you're a man?"

"I make my wife work for a living while I stay home and do nothing."

"Did you tell him your hands are magic when it comes to cleaning toilet bowls? Did you tell him you could out-iron Beaver Cleaver's mother?"

"He doesn't know who Beaver Cleaver is. Oh, your mother called. She always calls during the day, even though she knows you're at work. She doesn't think I'm a man either."

"Stop it. You know how she is. Very East Coast. She thinks I threw away a brilliant career in Washington just so I could live with *that Hispanic* in El Paso. 'Sent you to Yale,' she says, 'just so you could do something with your life — something important.' What my mother forgets to remember is that she conveniently stopped paying for that precious education at Yale as soon as she found out I was having a relationship with a man who 'only got into Yale because he was a minority' — that's how she put it. Remember when I told her I was marrying you? All she said was that it could be much worse. By that I take it that you could have been Black or Jewish. Jaime, you know how she is. Ignore her. And anyway, she thinks the kinds of things you do for other people are very commendable."

"Yes, like a Peace Corps Volunteer. Isn't that nice? I can just picture her patting me on the head."

She reached for his hand and squeezed it. "Anyway, I don't care what my mother thinks and neither do you. And next time she calls I think I'll remind her yet again, that it was you who put me through law school — not her. She has amnesia."

"She's an American, isn't she? All Americans have amnesia." She laughed. "Anyway, Mother would probably think Franklin was a wonderful name for a Salvadoran."

Jaime stared at her and said nothing.

"What?"

"Nothing."

"You're staring at me, Jaime."

"I think a husband should be allowed to stare at his wife."

"Eat your baked potato."

"Wanna go out for a drink tonight?"

"Can't tonight. I have to go back to the office. Big case coming up."

"Ah, honey, there's always a big case."

"I'm sorry, Jaime, but I win those big cases. And it's because I win them that the firm lets me take our cases. The big cheese calls me the *pro bono* queen."

Jaime smiled as he shook his head. "O.K. — go. I hate it. Only can't we meet for a drink or something when you finish. I haven't been out of the house all day."

"I'll call you from the office. Maybe we can get in a drink if it doesn't get too late."

§ § §

Jaime kissed Joanna goodbye, put away the dishes after he washed them, and started at the clean kitchen. "I'm becoming neurotic about clean kitchens," he said to himself. He walked into the living room, put on a Joni Mitchell album, and took out the notes he'd taken down when Franklin began telling his story. He'd drawn a line where he'd stopped reading:

Well, anyway, I didn't go back to school for three days because I was afraid. They knew who I was, the guerrillas. I knew they knew because they had forced some of my teachers to tell them, and a messenger from the guerrillas came to my house and nobody answered, so he left a note that said if I didn't join them they were going to kill all my family — my three sisters and two little brothers too. They knew all about me. So me and my family moved to another town, not far away, where my uncle lived and where my father was working. We just left in the middle of the night and no one knew we were leaving. I remember that night — it was cool and peaceful outside, but I felt like I was burning inside and I wondered if the night would ever be peaceful. It was my mother who first read the note the guerrillas left and she was so worried she couldn't even think. She said maybe she did the wrong thing by leaving the Catholic Church, but I don't think it would have made any difference except I'd have a different name, and she was saying crazy things because she was so nervous. She was afraid I would be kidnapped or killed, so she sent word to my father through a relative that we were going to join him, and we tried to start a new life, but it didn't last. I knew it wouldn't last, but I said nothing.

When we got to the town where we were going and joined my father, he asked if anyone had seen us leave or if we had been followed. My mother told him no one knew except her friend who was her boss at the place where she worked and later her boss was killed, but I said nothing. They found her mutilated body and I remember hearing my parents talking about it. The guerrillas said the government killed her, and the government said the guerrillas killed her, and nobody knew anything except that she was dead and my mother was very upset, but she tried to smile when she found out about it because she thought it was the brave thing to do, and I don't know anything else about all that. My father said he was going to find out if I would be able to continue my studies at school without being discovered by the guerrillas. If not, he thought maybe I'd have to go to school in San Salvador. School was important to him. He said I was smart and that nothing should stop me from going to school.

My father didn't agree with the guerrillas and he was afraid of them, but he thought the government was just as bad — maybe even worse, and though he hardly ever said anything to me I would always hear him talking to my mother and he told her if the government wasn't so corrupt and ugly and violent then there wouldn't be any guerrillas. But he said maybe men were born to kill because he'd heard that in the United States people killed each other all the time, and there wasn't even a war on, but I don't know where he heard all those things because I haven't seen any killing since I've been here, but I have seen plenty of fights in the barrios of El Paso. My father felt the guerrillas were destructive because they ruined crops and did things that hurt a lot of people who just wanted to be left alone and live in peace, but he said the government forced them into all that violence, too. I think my father was confused. "Life is hard enough without all that killing," he said to my mother, "already we live in hell and here they are starting more fires as if we're not hot enough already." Most of the time the guerrillas hurt or killed people they didn't even know, and they kidnapped minors like me as recruits and if any parent tried to stop them they threatened them or did something awful to their property. Sometimes they planted mines in the campesinos' land, but there were rumors that the government was doing the same thing and blaming it on the guerrillas — it's impossible to know who was doing what, but what was for sure was that the campesinos' land became worthless because of the mines, so things were bad for them. My mother said things would always be bad for the campesinos and that it would always be that way. I saw people without legs or arms, and stuff like that, and all because of the mines. The government kept blaming the guerrillas for everything, that's what a friend of mine said, but he said that the government never did anything to help the people who were injured and he said the government just didn't care — my friend hated the government.

And the government, the government was forming Civil Defense Groups which every adult had to belong to — no one had a choice. What the guerrillas did to young men, the government did to older men. Every adult had to stand guard one night a week and I knew my father didn't like the idea, but he knew he couldn't do anything about it, so he would just tell my mother that he would do anything to protect his family because he was the kind of man who tried very hard to be good. I knew lots of my friends' fathers who were not like my father. My father was the kind of man who liked to talk to his children and I have this memory of him when he talked to my mother. Sometimes when he talked to her I knew he loved her very much, I could just tell, and my mother — she was kind of nervous about everything — my mother would calm down when he talked to her, and I liked watching my mother when she was listening to my father.

My father told me that the Civil Defense Groups were formed to protect the people in the neighborhoods but, in fact, it was the opposite. The Civil Defense Groups had a list of people that the comandante made up and the comandante had been a member of the guerrillas at one time in his life, but they killed his brother or *something — for I don't know what reason — so he joined the government and he became worse than the guerrillas ever dreamed of being. The comandante made up a list of people who were to be kidnapped or killed, so they could blame the guerrillas for those kinds of things. I knew some of them might have been guilty of something, but most of them were just like you and me. Like my cousin, Chato, who was killed by the Civil Defense Groups. He was about twenty-one, I think, or somewhere around that age. They assassinated him and the real reason they killed him was because he didn't get along with the comandante. So they blamed his death on the guerrillas. I remember my father talking about it and he said he couldn't do anything about it, but he wanted my mother to know the truth, so he told her about what was going on. Someone should know the truth, he told her.*

My father was very upset about the whole thing because he liked the idea behind the Civil Defense Groups and he hated what it had become. He wanted to quit, but he knew if he quit something very serious would happen to our family, so he stayed and said nothing.

Once I asked him how the Civil Defense Groups killed people. He looked at me real strange. "I know about it," I told him. "You must never talk about it to anyone," he said. But I told him I wanted to know everything and that I was a man so he should tell me. He nodded and he told me what was done. For example, the first thing they did was poke their eyes with pins, skinned them a little at a time, take off a finger one by one, cut off their legs, sometimes eventually chopping their heads off. Always, they died a hard death. They did this so it would appear that the guerrillas were torturing them for information. And after he told me these things, my father made the sign of the cross and told me that he did not do these things, but that he watched because he had to, and he pretended it did not bother him, and he said to me that God might not forgive him, but he wanted me to forgive him for these things, and I told him that I forgave him. And I felt real bad about this.

Jaime stopped. That was all they had covered in their first interview. It didn't sound so very different from some of the other cases, but it always made him sick to his stomach. But the others had been adults. This was the first time a little kid had come to him. He focused on Franklin's face and remembered he didn't repeat his story with a lot of emotion. The only time he seemed to feel anything at all was when he was trying to jar his memory. He knew that the very act of remembering for Franklin was like cutting himself open with a knife.

Tomorrow he would find out the rest of it. "Jesus," he whispered, "if anyone ever tortured Joanna that way I'd kill them." He laughed to himself. "Right, Jaime, a nice macho thought — who do you think would kill whom?"

The phone rang. He let it ring three times before answering it. "I'll be done in about half an hour. Wanna meet me for a drink?" Jaime half smiled at the sound of Joanna's voice.

"That would be great."

"Same place?"

"Same place," he said.

"And bring some money — I forgot my purse at home."

"Sure, hon," he paused, "Jo —"

"What?"

"Nothing — never mind. I'll see you in half an hour."

He hung up the phone. He thought of Franklin's case. "I hate this — What do I do? Call the cops? They don't come. Bomb the Pentagon — a lovely thought." He hated all of this — not just that it was happening, but it would keep happening. It would keep happening, and happening, and happening. "If I had any balls at all, I'd renounce my citizenship — the only moral thing. But where would I go?" Blood, and more blood, and more blood. The thought entered his mind that he should buy guns, and send them to the right people, and then he laughed at the stupidity of the thought. More blood. "But we're not going to lose this case, damnit — not this time. No way in hell."

§ § §

Franklin rang the door bell a few minutes before nine. "Am I too early?"

"Right on time," Jaime assured him. His notes and legal pad lay on the coffee table waiting for them to begin. Franklin

125

seemed more relaxed sitting on the chair than he had the day before. Jaime noticed that he looked older than fifteen. His eyes were tired, almost old, as if he never got enough sleep.

"You want some coffee?"

Franklin nodded and again Jaime watched him as he poured four spoons of sugar into the hot coffee.

"You don't drink coffee," Jaime told him, "you drink syrup."

"It takes away the bitterness," Franklin told him.

Jaime picked up the yellow pad, popped his knuckles, and threw a newly opened pack of cigarettes on the coffee table. "Just grab one whenever you want," he said putting one in his mouth but not lighting it. Franklin nodded and reached for the pack.

"You were telling me about your father and the Civil Defense Groups."

Franklin puffed on his cigarette and nodded. "My father worked nights, did I tell you that? He worked the night shift at this bakery. Anyway, he worked nights because that's when they did most of the baking, and he made great bread. When it was his turn to work for the Civil Defense Group, he had to miss work which was bad for our family because he didn't get paid for missing work. My father really didn't want to go because he hated doing other people's dirty work and he was tired of all that, but there was no way out for him because he knew too much about what they did and he knew they would never let him get out of the group because he might say something to the wrong person. He finally decided to stop going. I guess he figured if they killed him, well that was it. My cousin was a good friend of the comandante's, and he came and talked to my father about why he wasn't coming to do his duty and my father told him he wasn't going anymore, but he told him that if he ever told anybody anything about the Civil Defense Group then he wouldn't ever see the sun shine ever again. So my father seemed more at peace, at least for a while. And then that same year...."

Jaime put his hand out for him to slow down. "Wait," Jaime said. He put down the pen, lit the cigarette that was dangling from his mouth, and popped his knuckles.

Franklin stared at the scratch marks on the sheets of paper. "Is that what English looks like when it's written?"

Jaime laughed. "That's not English."

"It doesn't look like Spanish."

"It's a kind of shorthand."

Franklin nodded. "Are you writing down everything I say?"

"Yes, everything. Later, I'll go back over it, read it, and maybe we'll have to put it in some kind of order, but right now I'm writing everything down. Does it bother you?"

"No. Well, yes. Maybe a little. It's strange, it's like all my words — everything I say is being glued to a sheet of paper. It doesn't seem right. Words are supposed to be said not written. I mean words on a piece of paper aren't real like what comes out of my mouth."

"I know, but you see, a judge has to read the case over and think about it, you know?"

"It seems he only believes things if he can see them. You think if he sees the words we write down he'll believe me? I'm thinking he won't. If the judges in your country are like the judges in my country then maybe we should just forget about this. I don't know. You know better than me, I guess, but I've never trusted words that were written down. I like words better when I can hear them instead of see them."

Jaime nodded. "You like music?"

"Yes, I like music. Music is real."

"But music is written down first, and then somebody looks at the music and plays it."

"No. I know a lot or people in El Salvador who can't even read but they can sing — and they play guitars and flutes made out of wood, and all kinds of other instruments."

"But what about books? Don't you like books?"

"No. I don't think I like books very much. I read them at school. I didn't hate them, but, well, I don't know. They didn't have anything to do with my life, you know? No, I don't think I like books." He pointed to the television. "I like television."

Jaime smiled to himself. So he was a normal fifteen-year-old after all. "Why do you like television?"

"Because it's alive. Not like a book."

Jaime smiled. He wanted to tell him that television was bullshit. "Why is television alive?"

"It's so real that it makes you forget about everything."

"And books?"

"Books make you remember."

"I see," Jaime said.

Franklin was a little puzzled. "Don't you like television?"

"Well, I don't watch it very much. I like to watch the news. Sometimes, when I'm tired I can watch it for a long time."

"So why do you have one if you don't use it all the time?"

Jaime smiled and shrugged his shoulders. He picked up the pad again. Franklin lit another cigarette. "So your father got out of working for the Civil Defense Groups. Then what happened?"

"Well, sometime in early October, maybe November, anyway, just after my father stopped working with the Civil Defense Groups, the guerrillas attacked their headquarters. All night they fought a battle and we could hear everything because their headquarters were only a block away from our house. All night we could hear bullets and yelling, and it all went on until about six in the morning, and we stopped trying to sleep. My mother made coffee in the dark and we sat up listening to the bullets that filled up the night. And my little sister fell asleep on my lap."

"Were you scared?" Jaime was immediately embarrassed by the stupidity of his question, but it was too late to retrieve it.

"No. I don't know why. I should have been scared, I guess. I wasn't scared like when I ran from the school and hid in the fields with my friend. I don't know what I felt. I felt nothing, that's what I felt. My mother whispered that there was no more music in our country, no more dance — just bullets. And then she said something else that I never understood, but I remember it because she sounded tired. She said, 'I'm tired of being a woman. Their war,' she said, 'not ours — not mine.' And I didn't know exactly what she meant, but she did say she hated men and the only man in the world who was worth anything at all was my father. She sounded like she didn't want to live anymore. We just listened to the sounds of the machine guns till the sun came up, and almost like magic, with the light of the day, the shooting stopped. But I remember thinking how quiet it was, like the earth was dead or something. The guerrillas won the battle and killed about eight or nine men from the Civil Defense Groups. That day, the guerrillas began going from house to house looking for young men to join them. When they came to our house, I knew they were going to take me. My father and mother said nothing. There was a group of them, maybe six or so. My father started to say something, but I stopped him. I nodded at them, and looked at my parents for what seemed a long time because I wanted to memorize what they looked like. I wanted to remember them. One of them told me we had to go, and my mother reached over and touched me, and I told her I would remember her touch, and that I would come back — and I left. I never saw them again, and I know they're dead." Franklin bit his lip. His face seemed to turn heavy and still like an immutable stone. "I don't cry anymore, not since that day because I know when you cry you're beaten — and then it's all over. But I'm telling you that I hate those sons of bitches, and not just the guerrillas, but the goddamned government, too — mostly the government — so now I don't know what to think."

Franklin lit another cigarette, and Jaime stopped taking notes. Jaime said nothing.

"I have to go now," Franklin said. "I don't know if I'll be back, maybe I will. I have to think."

"I'd like it if you came back," Jaime said. "I can burn this if you want. You can just come and talk or watch television."

Franklin smiled at him. "You're a good man, I think. I've met a lot of good people since I've been here, but I haven't met too many good rich ones. Your eyes look something like my father's. But I don't think you'll ever understand."

Jaime said nothing. He just wanted to make him stay.

"Would you mind very much if I took some of your cigarettes?" Franklin asked. "I don't have any, and I'd like some."

"Take them all," Jaime said.

"Thank you," he said. He got up from the couch and headed for the door.

"I'd like it if you came back," Jaime said.

Franklin nodded and opened the door. "Thank you," he said again. And walked away.

§ § §

Jaime took a walk that afternoon and thought about his morning visit with Franklin. He sat down at a bench at San Jacinto Plaza and stared at the water coming down from the fountain. He stared at the Mexican tile, and shook his head. He remembered the times his grandfather used to bring him here to watch the alligators when he was a little boy. He loved the alligators. But some soldiers from Fort Bliss had gotten crazy drunk one night and they killed them — stabbed them, knifed them, cut them up. He hated thinking about the dead alligators and ever since then he'd never liked soldiers. Those poor alligators never had a chance. His grandfather had tried to console him by telling him that alligators didn't belong in El Paso anyway, and that they'd never been happy outside the swamps where they came from. "But Grandpa," he'd cried, "the poor alligators, the poor, poor alligators — killed by those mean soldiers." He thought of that little boy and he remembered how the park had changed after that. But the people still gathered here to catch their buses, or eat lunch, or just sit. And no one even remembered the alligators anymore. He noticed a border patrol officer ask a young man for his papers. The young man shook his head, and the green uniform took him by the shoulder and led him into the green van. "I hate this damned park," he whispered, and walked back home.

§ § §

"What, no dinner tonight?" Joanna asked as she walked in the door. "Sorry I'm late. But I have a new client, and — well, you know — you've heard it all before."

Jaime nodded. He was sitting in the rocking chair in the living room.

"You look preoccupied," she said.

He nodded.

"Talk to me," she said. "I hate your silences."

He got up from where he was sitting and held her. She said nothing. She gently pushed him back a little and put her hand on his cheek. "I love your eyes," she said. "And tonight they're dark and brooding just like the first time you kissed me."

"It was you who kissed me," he said softly.

"Well, I had to. I was afraid you were never going to get around to it."

"I'm slow," he whispered, "I've always been very slow."

"So do you want to tell me about it?"

He walked over to the coffee table and sat on the couch. Joanna followed him and sat down next to him. He read her the notes he'd taken from Franklin's two visits.

Joanna listened to his voice, not moving — her eyes glued to her husband's lips. He finished reading Franklin's words, and looked at her.

"We'll do everything we can, honey. You know we will."

"It won't be enough."

"So we should bring down the U.S. Government?"

"Yes, we should bring down the U.S. Government."

"Long live the revolution."

"Shh," he said, "let's not talk about it."

He lay down on the couch and pulled her on top of him. "Let's lie here and leave the lights off and pretend the world doesn't exist, and in the morning we'll get up swinging."

They fell asleep in the darkness.

§ § §

A week went by without a word from Franklin. Every day, Jaime hoped he would come back. He studied the notes he'd taken so far. He shook his head. He would have to put in the correct dates, the names of all the places. He would have to turn the run-on sentences into cleaner phrases. He would have to take out all the personal asides, and make Franklin's story into a document. He would make Franklin's affidavit nice and neat and type it out on nice white paper with a nice I.B.M. typewriter, and the judge would look at it and say "No."

"It won't happen this time," he repeated, "not this time."

He waited for Franklin to return.

One Monday morning he showed up at the door. "I'm going back to El Salvador," he said. "I've decided that I don't want to live here. This isn't my country, and I'm going back."

Jaime said nothing. He just looked at Franklin and finally spoke: "But you'll never find your parents."

"I know. That's not why I'm going back. They're dead — I know they're dead."

"And if you go back you might be dead too."

"But the judge might not let me stay anyway, and I'd rather go back on my own then be sent back."

"But we don't have to do this the legal way — you can just disappear into a big city and no one will ever find you. There are lots of ways of doing things, Franklin."

"I don't want you to break any laws — not for me anyway."

"I wouldn't be breaking the law for you, Franklin, I'd be breaking it for me. Do you understand?"

Franklin shook his head. "No. But it doesn't matter. You don't understand me either. But I want you to know that I *am* going back. I don't know what there is for me in my country, but it is my country, and I'm returning."

"So why did you come back to see me?"

"Because I wanted to finish telling you my story. I never finished telling you everything. I don't think that's right. I don't like being told half a story. When I was little, my grandmother used to tell me stories, but she was old and she'd forget sometimes, and never finish telling me the story — I hated that because I was always left wondering what happened. It doesn't seem right to begin something and then never finish. I want to finish, but I don't want you to write it down. I just want to tell you."

Jaime nodded.

"Where's my cigarettes?" Franklin asked.

Jaime laughed and pulled the pack from his shirt pocket and handed them to him.

"So anyway," he said, lighting his cigarette, "I was telling you how the guerrillas took me from my parents. I didn't know where they were taking us. I remember we stopped to rest about six hours after we left our village in a place I didn't recognize, but then I really didn't know very much about the different places in El Salvador because I never went anywhere, except one time I went to San Salvador with my father. So we took a short rest, and we kept walking until it got to be night, and finally we rested. They didn't give us anything to eat, but I did get a glass of water which tasted good. I still remember that.

"The next day they explained to us why they had taken us. It was sort of like a class at school. The leader, a comandante, seemed like a nice man — he didn't talk like a killer. He talked more like a poet, I think. I bet he could sing and I bet he even played the guitar, at least that's what I thought at the time. So he explained things to us and we all listened. One person asked what the fight was about and he told us we would discover that in the future, but I never have figured it out. I don't think even today that I have it all straight in my head. It's strange. Maybe I'm not as smart as my father thought I was, or maybe I'm smart, but I didn't go to school long enough to be able to figure out all these things, but anyway, that future the comandante spoke about never came.

"They said they would arm us with weapons when we were ready. They told us that it was our duty to fight and that we should be very proud to have the honor of fighting with them because they were fighting for the freedom of our people. He asked if any of us had ever joined the government forces which was a dumb question because if any of us ever had we weren't going to tell them, and anyway we weren't old enough. He explained that if we ever betrayed them, either we would be killed or our families would be slaughtered like pigs. I thought about my teacher. If you asked too many questions they would take you to a place called Calaveras which was a cave, at least that's what I heard, a cave where you were punished and I heard people talk about it. Later, I learned that the government liked to place spies in with the guerrillas, so everybody was kind of paranoid. There was lots of spying going on, and lots of betrayals all over the place.

"During our training, we had to learn how to use the particular gun, or rifle, or machine-gun they gave us. Everyone had to learn how to use a weapon. I guess our training was pretty much like that of any military organization — they gave you orders and you followed them, and they talked about the enemy and everybody became like brothers and maybe, I think, it was all a big lie — or am I wrong?"

Jaime nodded. "Are you sure you're just fifteen?"

"Well, I'm going to be sixteen soon," he said seriously, "and maybe I'll think about getting married like you."

"That's crazy, Franklin. Why would you want to get married?"

"Well, marriage is a good thing, isn't it?"

"Maybe. I didn't really want to get married — it's just that I wasn't stupid enough to let the best woman I ever met leave me. I married her because I loved her, not because I decided that I was supposed to get married. Do you see the difference?"

Franklin nodded, but Jaime didn't think he got the message. "Your wife must love you very much, otherwise she wouldn't support you."

Jaime laughed. "She does."

Franklin thought a minute. "Well, see, I don't have a family anymore, so I guess I'm just going to have to start a new one."

Jaime nodded. It was a bad idea, he thought, but it was hard to argue with his logic.

Franklin lit another cigarette. "Can I finish the story?"

Jaime nodded.

"The first time I was involved in a battle was when we were traveling to some place they called Primavera. We were resting when we were discovered by the military, so we fought. It was the first time I fired a rifle at a human being and I don't think I hit anyone, but I can't say for sure. About ten guerrillas were killed and three soldiers died stepping on mines. We fled towards the hills, and my ears were ringing like bells from the gun shots. The sound of bullets is a funny thing — it becomes something like a game. I don't know what made me think of that at the time, but that's what I thought. You lose yourself in the whole thing like when you're a kid and nothing exists but the game you're playing, you know?"

"Another time, we were near this place called Las Piedras when a plane was spying in the sky and they discovered our camp where we were training. We were training new recruits — they were young like me. I called them 'the stolen' and all of a sudden we were being hit from all sides. Out of the hundred and fifty of us about fifty of us were killed. I remember seeing leaves soaked in blood and wanting to throw up. We took the wounded with us to a clandestine hospital and many of them had to have their arms or legs amputated. The hospital was in a big underground fox hole and it was big enough to hold about thirty people. We had a few people that knew something about medicine and a doctor, at least I guess he was a doctor. We left the wounded there and the rest of us had to move on. We just left them there. Two weeks later we returned and most of the wounded were dead. We made graves and buried them. I hated that. I wanted to jump in those graves, too. I knew I wasn't alive anymore. No, I wasn't alive."

"Sometimes we used to engage in small battles lasting about two or three hours with the military. Sometimes we'd set up traps and ambush the military and escape into rural areas, but we moved around a lot. It wasn't good to stay in one place.

"About a month after I thought of jumping into all the graves, I decided I would escape from the guerrillas. It wasn't that I didn't like the men I was fighting with. I liked them. I don't know, I just didn't belong there. So one night we set up camp after having stolen some supplies and for once we had good food, or at least decent food and I knew this was the night, the night I would escape because I knew it was my turn to stand guard. There were three of us who decided to escape, but only two of us were scheduled to be on guard, so the third guy traded shifts with another guy as we ate supper. And we were ready. At about two in the morning, when everyone was asleep, we just took off, but someone had been keeping an eye on us and followed us. When he figured out we were betraying the cause he started shooting at us in the dark and we ran, but only two of us made it. The guy that was hit just yelled, 'Run! Run!' and that was the last thing he said. Last week, a bunch of us were playing soccer in an alleyway and somebody yelled at the guy with the ball: 'Run! Run!' and all of a sudden I got dizzy and had to drop out of the game. I got a friend of mine to buy me some beer and I got drunk for the first time in my life."

He lit another cigarette and his hands were shaking. "So I made my way back to my village, and when I got back to my house, the house was empty. I went to the bakery where my father worked, and my father's boss looked at me strangely and took me into his house above the bakery. He said I should leave. He told me in a mean voice that my parents were gone — that they disappeared and they would never be seen again. He said that he had been harassed and that he was in deep trouble — all because of my father. He said now that things were settling down he didn't want any more of all this trouble, so I should just go. He was yelling. I stared at him and started to walk out. He grabbed me by the shoulders. 'Wait,' he said. I thought he was going to hit me, so I got away from him. He came at me, so I raised my hands to cover my face. Then he just said real quietly, 'Stay here until night. I know someone who will take you to San Salvador. My son — my son will take you.' I waited there until night and before I left, the man put some money in my pocket — it was a lot, and he said, 'Your father — your father — he was my friend, and I'm running out of friends. Go. Leave this country — just go, and don't ever come back.'

"The baker's son took me to San Salvador and told me I should go to a certain house and they would let me live there until I decided what to do. I was there for a month, and one day in the streets of San Salvador I saw one of the guerrillas — one of the trainers — he saw me, too. I just ran. He ran after me, but I finally lost him. I knew then that I had to leave. The baker had given me enough money to leave the country, so I began making plans. I stopped going out, and two days later the baker's son turned up at the house and said the Civil Defense Groups had burned down his father's bakery, and that they had taken his father. He said he had also gotten a notice that he must now join the military, but he said, 'I won't kill my own people.' I told him all about what happened to me and the next day we left for the United States.

"So here I am. I thought that when I got here I would be free, but I wasn't thinking right. I'm not free — don't belong here — I don't feel right. This is your country, not mine, and I don't think it could ever be mine. Look at me, does it look like I belong here?"

"All of us come from different places, Franklin — all of us. My parents came from Mexico with their parents when they were small. And now they belong here."

"Mexico isn't fighting a war. I'm going back. If I stay here, I'll die — at least that's how I feel. If I have to feel dead I'd rather feel dead in my own country."

"But you're only fifteen, Franklin —"

Franklin laughed. "I know you think I'm just a kid, but I'm not."

Jaime nodded slowly. "How will you get back?"

Franklin shrugged his shoulders. "If I got here, it will be even easier to get back."

"Can I help you? Maybe I can take you. I have a car — I could take you back."

"No. You belong here with your wife. You don't belong in my country." Franklin shook Jaime's hand and started to leave. "I'm glad I got to talk to you," he said. "It was good for me to talk."

"Will you write to me when you get back?"

"If you want me to."

Jaime wrote down his address and handed it to him. He walked over to a clay jar where he kept some cash. He reached into his wallet and took out all the money in it. "Take this," he said, "you'll need it."

Franklin did not reach for the money.

"Please take it."

Franklin nodded.

Jaime tried to smile. "Write to me. Let me know you're all right."

Franklin touched Jaime's shoulder and left.

§ § §

Franklin wrote to Jaime when he got back to El Salvador. Jaime wrote back, and they continued to write to each other for almost a year. Jaime sent him a present for his sixteenth birthday. Soon after, Franklin stopped writing. Jaime sent three letters in a row without a response. He almost decided to go to El Salvador and look for him, but he thought about what Franklin had said: "You don't belong in my country." He re-read all of Franklin's letters and thought about how Franklin might have become a poet because of the way he saw things. He discovered that Franklin mentioned the names of the people he was living with. He wrote to them and asked them about Franklin. He finally got a letter from them telling him that Franklin had disappeared, but they had hopes that he was still alive. Jaime knew he wasn't.

Jaime called Joanna on the phone after he read the letter and asked her to meet him at Alligator Park.

"Where?" she asked.

"Alligator Park. You know, San Jacinto Plaza."

"I've never heard anyone call it that before. Why do they call it that?"

"They used to keep alligators there, but some drunk soldiers ripped their guts open. Just meet me there."

When Joanna got to the park, she found her husband sitting at one of the benches. She knew that look of his.

"I got a letter today," he said. "Franklin's disappeared." He clenched a fist. "Somebody mistook him for an alligator."

Joanna held on to his wrist until he unclenched his fist. She slipped her hand into his open palm. They sat in the park saying nothing all afternoon — the ghosts of the dead all around them.

THE MARIJUANA PARTY

Mary Helen Ponce

The September morning is exceptionally warm, with the promise of a California sunshiny day. A breeze from the nearby foothills rustles the leaves of the coral tree near the stucco house where Petra feverishly works.

Her husband has left for work; the household chores are done and the dog and cat, satiated with food, lie near the warm fireplace. Her daughters Becky and Maggie are in school and not expected home till three. The long day stretches before her. I'll take a bath, then sew a while, Petra decides, running a hand through her greying hair. She scurries around the house, her round body moves with characteristic speed. Soon the house shines brightly — clean.

Petra sits near the dying fire made early that morning by her husband Leandro, to listen to Radio KALI, home of Tex-Mex music and her favorite singer, Freddie Fender. She gazes into the fire as the newscaster gives the highlights of this September day. Suddenly her head jerks up. In one swift motion she turns up the radio, then sinks back into the plaid chair. Today is September 10th! My birthday! How could I have forgotten? Petra frowns, pulls wisps of hair off her face, then sits back to reflect.

Today is not just her birthday but her 40th birthday! That ominous cut-off date that will make her middle-aged. ¡Cuarenta! Petra's face feels hot, but she continues to sit and fume. ¡Me lleva el tren! she grumbles. How could I have forgotten what day this was? Dammit! I have to do something different, exciting!

This is an important day! No! She corrects herself, I want to do something dangerous, *prohibited.* 'Far out,' as my kids would say.

I could go shopping, she muses, but I did that yesterday. The week's wash is done as is all the ironing (Petra hates being behind in her work). The thing is: I want to do something I've never done! Dammit, what shall I do?

Maybe I'll call Tottie and ask her over to celebrate. And Emily too, although she is such a Goody Two Shoes. After all, she sighs, glancing into the tall mirror, I won't be forty again! I'll make some coffee and whip up a batch of something. The girls just love my pumpkin bread. *Pero primero,* I'll dust my bedroom furniture.

Petra goes into the bedroom and with a swift, deft motion of her wide arms, sweeps the feather duster over the brass bed frame, maple chest and dresser. She hums along with "Los Bukis," Mexico's leading pop group, and methodically dusts, then adjusts a tilted lampshade. She smoothes the flowered bedspread and is about to leave the room when she remembers to dust the knick-knacks atop the dresser: the music box won at a church, the silver crucifix blessed by the Los Angeles bishop, and her favorite piece, the ceramic pinbox given her by her husband, where she keeps loose change, stray buttons, and stuff picked up by the vacuum. She takes down the box, dusts, then opens it. Inside lie copper pennies, straight pins, loose buttons and a wrinkled, brown cigarette. She stares at the cigarette, trying to remember how it got there. She brings the cigarette to her pert nose and inhales. Marijuana! *Hijo mano!* Marijuana in my ceramic pinbox! Petra feels giddy; she breaks out in a grin. Well, what do you know? There's marijuana in my bedroom!

¿Pero dónde? Where did it come from? She rolls the cigarette between her stubby fingers, pressing the weedy tendrils tight, then suddenly remembers.

The weekend before, her nephew Jimmy, a musician with a local rock group, visited. He stayed late, pigging out on his aunt's homemade tamales (made with hot New Mexico chili sent to Petra by an old friend). Long after Petra went to bed he remained in the patio, strumming his trusty guitar. The next morning while sweeping the patio, Petra had found Jimmy's Zippo lighter — and the thin cigarette — and tossed it inside the pin box where it lay forgotten.

Well, thinks Petra, her eyes shining bright, I'll smoke pot for my birthday, that's what! I'll get high! *Me voy hacer una marijuana.* Better yet, I'll invite my friends. She shuts the pin box, sticks the wilted cigarette in her apron pocket, then heads for the phone.

"Tottie? It's me, Petey. You remembered? Well, thank you very much. No, not 39 anymore. Forty! I swear it! I'm officially middle-aged. Thanks, comadre. You don't look fifty either. *¿Qué?* Oh, I'm sorry! Five? I thought it was seven. *¡Ay no!* You still look...."

"Listen, I want you to come over. Today. I have a little surprise...no, I won't tell you. Wait till...yes, I'm gonna call Amalia, *la que nunca quiebra un plato.* Ha, ha! Yes, right now. I only hope that kid of hers doesn't answer the phone. The other day he threatened to hang up on me! No? He thrashed your Creeping Charley? No, not like *our* kids at that age. *¡Te digo!* I'll tell her to dump him. Well, let me hang up and...no, we won't have lunch. The stuff I have will stunt your appetite. What stuff? Wait. Wait and see."

"Amalia? Emily? Oh hi, Feefee, is your mother there? Oh, she's in the car? Why aren't you? Cause you're talking on the phone? What a smart kid! Well, of course I want to talk to her. That's why I'm.... Hello! Yes, I want you to call her. Yes right now. Yes, I want you to put down the phone and...NO, NO! Don't hang up! I'll wait while you go outside to...hello...hello...."

"Amalia? Hello! Oh, I didn't know people still warmed up cars! I never do! At PTA? What committee is this? Drug Abuse? My goodness, you practically live at school! What about later? The Girl Scouts? Catechism! No wonder you're always in the car! *Mira,* I called for a reason. Today is my fortieth birthday and...why thank you! Do you really think I do? That's what my kids say, but I don't believe them. 35? Really now! Well, thank you. Listen, I've decided to do something really different for this.... No, nothing illegal! What? You're now on the committee

to what? ¡No me digas! Do tell! You get more important by the
minute! What? Tell him to wait. Ay, Amalia, that kid of yours is
too spoiled! Last week he threatened to hang up on me.... Yes, I
know he's your baby but...listen, I've brought up five kids
and...the party? Oh! Well, not exactly a party but.... What time?
While the kids are in school. About noon.

"No, my kids never come home for lunch. No, nothing, just
bring yourself. Feefee? Well...this party's special. Try to get rid
of...I mean, leave him with the neighbor. What? She can't stand
him? I wonder why! Why, of course he's well-behaved! The last
time I sat him he only kicked the dog three times! Well, he
didn't mean to break it. Yes, I got the jam off the sofa.... Well,
try to.... ¡Sí! See you about noon."

Petra hangs up the phone. From the window she sees Manuel,
the mailman, go by. God, I hope he doesn't decide to stop by,
she hisses. I don't mind giving him a cup of coffee and listening
to his problems, but not today. No sir! She undresses, takes a
quick shower, then sits at the dressing table to 'repair the
damage' as she calls putting on makeup.

She stares into the oval mirror, runs a finger around her
brown eyes, and opens wide her mouth. ¡Éjole! I look like shit!
¡Parezco mierda! she grumbles. She slathers cold cream on her
face, splashes astringent onto a cotton ball, then rubs her face
clean. Hmmm, maybe I should tint my hair, she thinks, or cut my
bangs. Becky says bangs are out of style. But bangs make me
look younger. Like Mamie!

She spreads moisturizer on her lined face, adds a layer of
pink foundation, dots her cheeks with rouge, pencils in arched
eyebrows, then puckers her lips for lipstick. Satisfied with her
appearance, she throws on a clean blouse and black polyester
pants bought on sale at K-Mart. There, Petra sighs, now I feel
more like myself. She turns off the small lamp, fluffs the
vanity skirt, then goes into the kitchen to fix salsa and cool wine
for the party.

Promptly at noon the doorbell rings.

"No, of course you're not early. Come in, come in." Petra opens the door, a warm smile on her face. "*Éntrale*, Tottie, you look great, as always! A new blouse! How pretty!"

"K-Mart."

"Really? I would have thought Sears!"

"Happy birthday!"

"Thanks, old friend. Oh! you shouldn't have. You mean you already had...."

"I knew your birthday was sometime this week, so...."

"Well, thanks a lot. Shall I open it right now?"

"Sure."

"On second thought, I'll wait until I'm high."

"High?"

"Later, I mean."

"Let's go into the living room. And how are the kids? Have they got over the flu?" Petra follows Tottie into the squeaky-clean living room, then offers a glass of wine and chips with *salsa* from a tray on the coffee table. Tottie eases her tall, wiry body into the overstuffed plaid chair; one thin arm hangs to the side. They sit, thoroughly relaxed as only old friends can be.

"And when did Laura go back to school?"

"Yesterday. I was tired of having her at home, so I sent her off. I only hope the school nurse...."

"That bitch!"

"Uhhhh, I only hope they don't send her home. I mean, the scabs have healed and according to my medical book...."

"Don't tell me you still read that? Shit, after five kids you should write your own."

"Probably, but you know how the school nurse is. I don't see how Amalia gets along with her!"

"She has to. Did she tell you she's on some drug committee?"

"No! Is the PTA doing drug abuse?"

"We'll soon find out. Here she comes."

"Happy birthday to you, happy birthday to you, happy birthday, dear Petra, happy birthday to you. And many more!.....Hi! Ummmm, and what momentous moment in history are we celebrating?"

"*Ninguno*, except of course the birth of the biggest sexpot in history!"

"Rita Hayworth?"

"No."

"Marilyn Monroe?"

"*No, hombre*. It's my birthday that's what."

"Oh! You are *so* funny. Great sense of humor, huh, Teresa? I mean, Tottie. But tell me, Petra, what's the mystery? On the phone you made it sound as though we're meeting to mix our own nuclear bomb! What *are* you up to?"

"Have some *salsa* and chips first."

"Can't. I gotta keep my weight down. According to statistics, obesity among homemakers is on the rise."

"I could have told them that. Just look at me. I'm the best example of homemakers' obesity." Petra lifts up her blouse. "*Mira, aquí traigo la lonja.*"

"You are so gross. Cover yourself, Petra! Someone might go by and...."

"*¡Pues que me lo miren!* Now that I'm all of forty, they might not get another chance. Quick, before it wears out!"

"Ha, ha." From her chair Tottie laughed uncontrollably. "This is fun," she said in a merry, squeaky voice. "You guys are so funny, always squabbling."

"I'm *not* squabbling," Amalia insists, wiping her mouth on a napkin. She points at Petra, saying, "She's always making sexual allusions..."

"Illusions, you mean."

"I think I will have some *salsa*."

"*Andale, que te pique*. Being that nothing else will...."

"You see, Tottie. See how she is? Honestly, is that all you think of?"

"What else is there?"

"Did I tell you the PTA is forming a parents' group against drugs?" Emily munches on a chip, trying not to feel offended at Petra's remarks. She and Petra constantly argue about how to bring up kids, but for the most part get along famously. She sits on the sofa and continues, "I'm representing our area...this entire block. I'm going to set up meetings and...."

"Well, girls. It's time for the surprise," Petra interrupts, bored with Emily's incessant talk about PTA. "Are you ready?" Petra removes the chips and salsa, draws the drapes of the window facing the street, bolts the front door, then turns to the two women. "¡Adelante! Follow me to the bedroom."

"The bedroom? Honestly!" Amalia frowns, but follows Petra and Tottie.

"Well, where are the porno movies?" she asks, munching on a chip.

"How did you guess?" Petra leads the two to the rear of the house, and towards the bed on which atop a flowered bedspread lies a lone cigarette, matches and an ashtray.

"Miren, aquí está el surprise," giggles Petra, drawing the curtains close together.

"Where?" asked Tottie, her myopic eyes searching the room. Atop the dresser, a small vanity light cast a rosy light. "I can't see anything!"

"Well, put on your glasses. Honestly, Tottie! Anybody would think you were trying to...."

"Glasses make me look old!" sighs Tottie, rummaging through her plastic purse.

"So who gives a shit? But never mind, you won't need them after this." Petra sits on the bed, then motions to Tottie and Amalia to join her. "I'm trying to make life interesting, my friends. So quit griping!"

"What's this?" Amalia holds up the withered cigarette.

"What do you think?"

"I don't know. It looks like a cigarette, but..."

"Smell it."

"Ummmm. Nice fragrance. Is it vegetable, or clove?"

"Clove mierda! Ha, ha, ha!" Petra rocks back and forth atop the wide bed. "This, my friends, is a miracle drug from...."

"Lourdes?" Amalia smiles her approval.

"It's marijuana," cries Tottie from her perch. "I'll bet that's what it is!"

"Marijuana! Dammit, Petra, is this some kind of a game?"

"The game of life, Amalia!"

"And just what are we going to do with this here marijuana cigarette?" asks Amalia, hitching up her jeans.

"We're gonna smoke it, that's what!"

"What?"

"We're all three going to smoke one little cig...."

"Why not? We'll take turns puffing."

"Honestly, is this how we're celebrating?" Amalia pulls at her knit top, getting more agitated by the minute.

"Yup! We're celebrating *con pura marijuana.*"

"Next you'll be showing porno movies."

"How did you guess?"

"What? I don't believe it!"

"Believe it, Amalia. Tottie and I watch them all the time — *¿verdad, comadre?*"

"You watch porno flicks, Tottie? You're gonna get a heart attack watching those....

"I haven't yet," answers Tottie, smiling at the younger woman. "Actually, I'm the one who has the movies. My son or his friends forgot them in his car. And, since I always search it for contraband, I found them. The color is quite good!"

"Honestly, Tottie! And you so active in the church! How can you help with communion and be into filth?"

"At our age, honey, nothing is filth," interjects Petra. "I'm always willing to learn new pos...."

"I think I need wine," gasps Amalia. She heads towards the kitchen, then returns.

"It's time to begin!" announces Petra. She takes the cigarette, wets it with her tongue, rolls it back and forth in her hand, then strikes a match. She puffs, waiting for the cigarette to catch.

"Marijuana takes longer to ignite," says Amalia, as she sits atop the bed.

"And how do you know all this? *Tu tan inocente.* How could you possibly know?"

"From PTA! Watch out, it's gone out!"

"Here, let me," says Tottie, her eyes merry behind the bifocals. "Let me try it!"

"What? Since when do you...."

"I used to light my dad's cigars, Amalia."

"Oh! Sorry!"

Tottie holds the marijuana cigarette to her lined mouth, takes a puff, then hands it to Petra. "Here, you try it."

"It's against the law to smoke marijuana!" announces Amalia, her face flushed. "Jesus, Petra, we could be arrested and taken to jail."

"Over one cigarette. Come on!" Petra takes a drag from the cigarette, then hands it to Tottie.

"*Toma*, Tottie. Have some Colombian Gold!"

Amalia appears to gag. "You mean this is imported? How do you know?"

"Jimmy told me."

"Your nephew knows you smoke pot?"

"He gave it to me. It's my birthday present!"

"Watch out!" cries Tottie. "It's going out!" She strikes a match as Petra puffs on the limp cigarette. Just then the doorbell rings.

"Jesus, I hope it's not the cops," cries Amalia, running to the bathroom, "Quick, the spray!"

"Hide it, hide it!" squeals Tottie.

Petra walks to the door. "Who is it?" she asks, trying not to laugh aloud. "Who is it?"

"It's Manny. Manuel! The mailman."

"What do you want, Manny?"

"The usual, *comadre*."

"I'd better let him in," Petra tells the startled women. "If not, he'll come back. He only wants a cup of coffee. Wait in the bedroom, I'll get rid of him fast." She turns toward the door and shouts, "Just a minute! ¡Un momentito.!"

Satisfied that the two are safe in the bedroom, she opens the door to a short, husky man who heads toward the kitchen, pulls out a chair and sits down.

"Man, it sure is hot! I sure could use a nice cup of coffee, comadre. And how's your better half?"

"As good as ever."

"Did he get over his cold?"

"Sí. He was sleeping too close to the crack."

"Hummm. Good coffee. It should hold me until lunchtime. Say, is something burning? Seems to me I smell smoke...dry leaves, or something."

"I threw some twigs in the fireplace...to keep it going."

"Yeah? Ummm, sure has a fragrant smell. I could swear it smells like...."

"How about some warm pumpkin bread?"

"Ho ho, you know my weakness! Say, comadre, did I tell you I spotted some kids down the block smoking pot? It's getting closer to home, that's what I told my old lady. It's getting closer to home. I'm sure glad my kids...."

"Another piece."

"Just a tiny one. I don't want to.... Are you sure something isn't burning?" Manny gets up and walks toward the living room. He sniffs the air, then points towards the rear of the house. "It's coming from in here, " he says, "It's...."

"It's later than you think," says Petra, "and I have to...."

"Me too. Thanks a lot for the bread. And give my regards to my compadre."

Petra closes the door, adjusts the safety catch, then runs back to the bedroom. Tottie and Amalia are standing near an open window.

"Qué pasó?" she asks. "What did you guys do with the...."

"Your birthday present? It went out so we decided to wait until...."

"Well, let's have it."

"I'll be the lookout," volunteers Amalia. "Tottie, you're in charge of the Lysol. Keep spraying. I'll watch for the cops."

"Lookout for what, pendeja? Honestly! Do you think...."

"Jesus, a cop car just went by! Look, it's stopping!" Amalia peeks out the pink rayon drapes, her face pale and drawn.

"It's coming this way! Quick, Tottie, get the spray! Rinse your mouth! Petra, Petra, what if we're arrested and the PTA finds out? I'll never live it down. Jesus, Petra, do something!" Amalia's face is drenched with perspiration, her pony tail swings to and fro. They stand quietly in the warm living room waiting to be arrested. Just then the black and white car drives away.

"Wrong address," whispers Petra. "They always have the wrong address."

"Thank God!" Tottie adjusts her glasses, then serves herself a generous portion of wine. "I sure need this," she babbles to the two women. "I thought for sure...I mean, what would my grandkids say if their gramma went to jail?" She clasps her yellowed pearls, then sits back and takes a deep breath.

"Give me the damn cigarette," snaps Petra. "I'm going to smoke this if it's the last thing I do." She takes the cigarette from the ashtray, tucks pieces of dry weed inside the thin paper, strikes a match to the cigarette in her mouth, then inhales.

"Muuuuuum! Here Amalia, you try it."

"I shouldn't. I mean, I don't think it's right to...."

"A little puff won't kill you! *Andale*. Here."

Amalia holds the cigarette in her shaking hand, raises it to her prim mouth, inhales, then begins to gasp for air. "Water, water. I'm choking! Petey, Tottie, help me!"

Tottie smacks Amalia on the back while Petra holds a glass of water to her mouth.

"Uhhhh, that's better. O God, I was choking! I swallowed a piece of...." Amalia drops on the bed laughing hysterically. "I think I'm high already," she cries, "I'm getting high!"

"She's high!" squeals Tottie, adjusting her glasses, "she's high! Well, it's my turn now. *Oyes*, Petra, Petra..."

"Shhhh, someone's at the door!" Petra whispers to the two women lolling atop the bed. She kicks her shoes off, then tiptoes to the door. She presses her ear to the door and shouts, "Who's there? Who is it?"

"Becky."

"What do you want?"

"I live here."

"Becky?"

"Open the door."

"What are you doing home from school?" Petra's eyes blaze as she opens wide the solid oak door.

"Someone stole my lunch. And the office won't loan me any money. They say you still owe for last month. Well, are you gonna move out of my way or what?"

Becky pushes her way to the kitchen, and in one swift move grabs a banana and pops it in her mouth. She takes a thick slice of pumpkin bread and lathers it with butter, all the while glaring at her mother. Suddenly she wrinkles her nose, and asks, "What is that smell?"

"What smell?"

"Like old rags, or something burning." She runs to her room, yanks out a drawer from a maple chest then quickly scans the contents. "You better not be burning anything of mine!" She screams at her mother. "You better.... "

"Who's burning anything?" answers Petra, trying not to look toward the rear bedroom. "Honestly, Becky, have you ever known me to.... "

"I know you sneak into my things when I'm in school."

"No I don't."

"You took my *Playboy* magazines!"

"What magazines?"

"The ones I found in Jimmy's car. He knows you took them. I told him. God! It smells worse in the hall. Oh, hi, Nina Tottie! Hello, Amalia. What are you guys doing in my mother's bedroom?"

"Trying on a dress your mother made for me," answers a flustered Tottie.

"Yeah? Well it sure smells funny in here," grumbles Becky, eyeing the women. She stomps to the kitchen, grabs an orange, then walks to the door. "I gotta get back to school. Tell Laura to call me, huh, Nina?"

"Okay."

"*Me lleva el tren,*" hisses Petra. "What next? I swear! There are days when no one calls — or drops over — and today, the one damn day I want for myself, the world comes knocking at my door. At this rate we'll never get to finish." She puts away the pumpkin bread and butter knife left by Becky. "But, I'm not giving up. Come on, girls. One more time."

In the dim bedroom the three women sip wine as Petra attempts to relight what is left of the cigarette.

"We need a bobby pin."

"A bobby pin? What for?" asks Amalia, smoothing her hair.

"To hold it, see?"

"Hummm. Well give it to me when....."

"Aha! You do like it, Amalia! Ha, ha!"

"I didn't say I liked it! But if I'm gonna be on the Drug Abuse committee I should know at first hand the dangers of....."

"What dangers? Honestly!" Tottie fondles her pearl necklace and smiles at Amalia.

"Well, they say it's easy to get addicted."

"On one little cigarette?"

"Honestly, Petra, you make fun of everything I...."

"I'm not making.... Watch out, you'll burn the carpet!"

"Where's the ashtray? Here, give it to me!

"It's my turn, girls!"

"Why, Tottie, I do believe you're salivating! And you a gramma!"

"Come on, Emily, grammas do other things too, you know!"

"Really? Not my gramma! All she does is watch her favorite *telenovela*. This week it's *Yo Compro Esa Mujer.*"

"Ummmm, I sure feel mellow," sighs Petra, rolling her eyes. "This is the best birthday I've had in a while. Now if only my old man were here I could show him just how good I feel...."

"Honestly, Petra! All you think of is sex. S E X!"

"What else is there at my age? There's more to life than.... What's so funny, Tottie?"

"Nothing. Honestly, Emily, you're so uptight."

"I'm not uptight!"

"She's high! Here, have another drag!"

"Shhhh. Listen! Someone's at the back door!"

"It's the cops! Someone must've smelled the smoke — and called the cops! Oh my God! Quick through the window!"

"Calm down, Amalia! Honestly, do you think people have nothing to do but call the cops! Wait here, it might be my neighbor Greta. Let me see what she wants. Don't call out whatever you do."

"Oh Hi! Greta. No, I'm not doing anything. Well actually, I'm on the phone. Long distance to Texas, but...you have a problem that won't wait? Well, come in then for just a minute. But first let me hang up the...."

"It's them kids again! They have no respect for private property! I went outside to take out the garbage and there they are, as big as all get out. Lounging on my fence, smoking pot! I tell you! Why aren't they in school? Every day I pick up coke cans and their garbage. I hate living so close to the school."

"Gosh, I didn't know it was that bad. I hadn't seen any kids hanging around here."

"Well, they're here every day. And what's worse, some dope dealer comes around to...."

"Where?"

"I'm not sure, but my neighbor swears it's some guy in a blue car that's pushing drugs on them kids."

"A blue car?"

"Yeah. We're supposed to be on the lookout. I mean, call the cops if...."

"What does he look like?"

"Reddish hair, dark glasses. A redneck for sure."

"Hummmm."

"Well I really must go. Ummmm, what is that smell?"

"Smell?"

"Like burning leaves. Reminds me of Munich in the fall!"

"Well, come again. And let me know if you see that blue car."

Petra locks the kitchen door, pulls down the shade, then swiftly crosses to the bedroom — and to her birthday celebration.

"Golly Moses! What took you so long? We're almost finished with the.... Here take the last puff."

"Never fear, Tottie. There's more where that came from. I was just talking to Greta and she knows a dealer."

"Greta? The lady next door knows a dealer? My God! That must be how she cleared her arthritis!"

"Hey, Emily, what's so funny?"

"I feel so good! Ummmmm, it sure beats...."

"Girl Scouts? PTA?"

"Yeah! But, it's addicting. I mean, I could never do this again!"

"Me neither," giggles Tottie, adjusting her pearl earrings. "It's just too stressful. I mean, why not just sip wine and.... Here, Petey, take the last puff. It's almost burned down. But, if you hold it like this...."

"Well, listen to the expert!"

"Golly jeepers! It's almost two. I've gotta get to Catechism.... But I feel so good!"

"Dammit, not again. Shhhh. A car's pulling up in front. Quick, Tottie, see who it is while I rub toothpaste on my.... Hey, Emily, Amalia! Are you okay?"

"Ummmm. I'm just a little dizzy, that's all."

"Pssst, Tottie. Who is it? Is it the cops?"

"It sure is. Come see for yourself."

"*Esperaté*. Amalia, gimme the Lysol. No, *él de* Pine. Okay, Tottie, open the door."

"Good afternoon, ma'am. I'm Sergeant Cooper with the Neighborhood Watch. We're canvassing the neighborhood to alert them to...say, are you burning trash?"

"No, Captain! I mean Sergeant. Well, come to think of it, I put some old newspapers in the fireplace and...."

"Hummmm — mind if I take a look around?"

"Around where?"

"Well, uhhhh, I'm here to alert folks on New High Street about the rise in drug abuse among high school kids. The LAPD is asking folks to call if..... Ummmmm, you sure you're not burning leaves? It's against the law, you know. Incinerators were banned in 1958, or thereabouts."

"What were you saying about drugs?"

"Only that we want all concerned citizens to be on the watch for a blue car driven by a blond-haired man. He comes around during lunchtime...he's hustling school kids. Here, call the number on this card. We're determined to find...."

"So am I!"

"Well, thank you very much for...say, mind if I take a look around? I could almost swear I smell...."

"Officer, I just remembered something. About ten minutes ago I saw a blue car cruising by. The driver had red hair, but he sure looked suspicious!"

"Yeah?"

"And Captain! My neighbor told me some hoodlums smoke pot behind her house. Over there...the white house with the pine tree."

Petra waits while the policeman darts across the lawn towards Greta's, then re-enters the house.

"Are they gone?"

"Yeah. Dammit! All these interruptions! Well, girls, there's only one thing to do."

"What?"

"Watch the porno movies I borrowed from...."

"How long will they take?"

"My Emily! You sure recover fast! I thought you had passed out!"

"I don't really want to see them. I mean the last ones were so gross! Honestly! Three men and...."

"I enjoyed that one!"

"Tottie! Since when do you watch that stuff?"

"I don't. But I don't want to be rude! I'll stay if you do."

"Well, it's really not my thing. But it could help me evaluate...."

"What? Positions?"

"¡Ay, no! But I just joined Catholic Mothers Against Pornography and have to give a lecture on...."

"What do *they* do?"

"Picket porno shops. My sister's president."

"Hummmmm, must run in the family," grumbles Petra to Tottie. "But before we begin *el show*, promise to come back next week, okay?"

"Next week?"

"Yeah. Being that we had so many interruptions, I want to do this again. Let's make it Friday. At ten. And you, Emily, get rid of...uhhhhh, line up a sitter. Tottie, bring the Lysol spray and lots of bobby pins. And I'll be on the lookout for a blue car."

THE BLACKBIRD

Victoriano Martinez

When I was thirteen, except for a box of peaches from Old Man Tito's porch, I never stole anything. Mostly, I would say, this was because of my mother. The thought of anything not hers occupying a space of guilt inside our home, even if just a measly candy bar, had a genuine terror for her. I think she was afraid that this would open her up to rude invasions by police, or housing authorities, or people demanding the return of things she imagined they'd hang their own babies for. People only become dangerous, she'd say, when arguments boil around things they own, or around jealousy, which she said was like a glue that sticks to people.

Despite my mother's fear, my friends Albert and Benny Molina and I once lugged a box of peaches off Tito's front porch. I remember the peaches clearly because of Tito's blackbird. He claimed the bird could talk — although he wasn't really a talking bird — and since the bird's cage hung right by the porch window, and we could hear its wings spanking frantically on the wrought-iron bars, we thought surely the bird must have seen us.

The next day Tito began roaming the neighborhood telling everyone that his blackbird knew who stole his peaches. He said the bird needed to see the scoundrel's face, however, since birds weren't really good with names. "But he'll squawk, you better believe it, he'll squawk when he sees that thief eye to eye."

Tito said this in our kitchen as my mother and sister Rebecca served him coffee and a piece of glazed Mexican bread. "I'll

157

take my bird around the neighborhood until I find out who those *pinche* thieves are...oh excuse me, Señora Hernandez," he said, covering his mouth to hide his browning teeth. Then, as if from remorse, he shrugged his shoulders. "And I was planning to give you a bag of peaches, Señora." He meant it, too, because he always gave my mom little presents of fruit, like blush-ripe papayas and mangos, and filbert and brazil nuts from South America.

Tito then started reminiscing about how delicious his peaches were, how he had bought them fresh from a farmer in Lodi, how he planned to temper their skins by cooling them in the night air. I could hear him from the living room where I was reading my dad's Archie comic books. My dad didn't like anyone reading his comic books, but I had a deal with my mother that if I stacked them back neatly, without soiling one page, I could read them before he came home from work. I had just slid them down from the top shelf of his closet when Tito appeared at the door, hat in hand, to gossip with my mother.

Everyone, except my mother who felt sorry for him and actually liked hearing his wild stories, believed Tito crazy, as mad as his blackbird and almost as dark. My mother liked him because he wasn't a man who twisted words around, or played games of suggestion with her eyes. He had curlicues of raisin dark hair that twirled around his battered ears and a grapeknife scar under his left eye which gave that side of his face a wrinkly erosion. My dad said he too thought Tito screwy, but only because he was Puerto Rican — that was explanation enough for him. Mostly though, people believed Tito crazy because he was a bachelor and didn't have a woman to smooth down the rumples of his clothes and speech. My grandmother said "*solteros*" always lost their marbles. People are like seams in a quilt, she'd say; without others, they're only a thread dangling in the heart of a cloud.

Tito lived by himself in a clapboard house bought with money earned from working as a janitor. There was a time when he used to go to Puerto Rico to visit his mother and two sisters. One of his sisters was married to a cigar wrapper at a tobacco factory; the other was too young then to soil herself in the business of men. After his mother died, though, the stray sister married, and both sisters became buried inside family duties and household chores. To make matters worse, his sisters' husbands were jealous of him for choosing to live in the comfort of the States and for embarrassing them by sprinkling money around to their kids. Tito believed there wasn't much room for any kindness between them, and, over the years, fewer and fewer letters were mailed.

When Tito left, I heard my mother and Rebecca joking, saying he was such a crazy man, the craziest man they had ever met. "How could a bird tell him who stole the peaches?" my mother said in Spanish, as if this were a scandal in itself.

"It's ridiculous," my sister Rebecca snorted.

After she and Rebecca stayed quiet for awhile, my mom said, "Maybe Tito isn't so crazy, Becca. After all, a bird can recognize people. They can be *pretty* smart sometimes, no?"

"You're right, it isn't *so* crazy," my sister agreed.

Mother winked at me from the kitchen. She made a smirk with her lips as though planning to pull Becca's leg all the way to the reservoir and back. Rebecca, kneading dough and mulling over her own ideas, said that even if a bird can recognize a person, how is it going to know what stealing is?

My mother flipped over a tortilla on the stove, thought about this for a long while, then shifted the iron skillet to another burner. "Why *can't* a bird know what stealing is?" she said. "Don't they know when a cat comes and scavenges their nests? Can't they know what is theirs?"

"Sure...sure they can!" my sister exploded — a chisel of truth had hit her square on the forehead. Her outburst let the air out of both their doubts, and they predicted Tito's bird would soon recognize the thief and the hands of the police laid upon him. They both laughed like crazy blackbirds themselves.

Listening from the living room, I felt my jaws stiffen, a sudden blurring of my eyes. My brain was spinning around inside my head like a stone, grinding against the walls of my skull. Only by squeezing the blood from my fists could I keep it balanced. But the thought of Tito entering through the door with the blackbird perched on his arm, fluttering its wings and squawking accusations at me, tightened the arteries in my neck and, from what seemed like a hub between my temples, the stone unhinged and began to wobble, flashing sparks of alarm all over the room. Quickly, and not too neatly, I put my dad's comic books away and ducked out through a broken slat in the backyard fence, heading for Albert's house.

Albert thought we should kill the bird. He was in his front yard, hosing water on his mother's roses. "We got to," he said, "I don't want to go to no Juvy. My uncle says the cops beat you up there because they know you're Mexican and can't do nothing."

"Can't we give him back the peaches?"

"We can't," he said. "Me and Benny ate mosta 'em. And besides, I threw the rest away."

"You threw the rest away!"

"Hey, my mother almos' smelt 'em under the bed! Boy, if she woulda found 'em, I'd be dead, real dead, and you too!"

"What do you mean — me too?" I said, indignant but not too surprised that he'd snitch on me.

"You know my mother," Albert said. He went to turn off the faucet. "She'd tell your mother in a second, and do you think she wouldn't ask you about 'em? Knowing you, you'd probably squeal on me and Benny."

"No, I wouldn't. You're the damn squealer!" I said.

Albert didn't say anything, just gazed at the hose he'd rolled over his arm, biting his fingernail. He was a nail-biting fiend, Albert was. At school, he'd chew pencil erasers down to the metal brace. After a while he waved his finger reflectively, "Do you remember what happened to Tony?"

A month before, the police had dragged Tony Montez out of his house. They had his legs pulled back and were wrestling to pin his arms so they could handcuff him. Tony was stretching and squirming, begging for somebody to please help him. Nobody did. Everyone was afraid of the police. Even Tony's dad who hugged Tony's mom to quiet her hysterics. She had tried grabbing at one of the officer's arms, but the officer looked at

Tony's dad as if to say he better do something about his wife quick, or else. Besides, everyone believed Tony must have done something wrong. Otherwise, why would the police come?

"Yeah...." I said, frightened at the thought of being dragged out of my own home in the naked glare of family and neighbors. "Do you think they'll do us the same?"

"Not if we kill that frickin' bird," Albert said.

I figured any way of killing the bird would be messy. I remember my mother once taking a kitchen knife, and after scratching a cross on the dirt, grinding the blade through a chicken's neck. The head scrinched right off. She let the wings flop in her hand, and a few gulps of blood puddled on the ground. Finally she tossed the chicken on the cross. It lay there pumping small, sudden twitches; then it was lifeless. My mom said this was because of the mercy of the cross. There was nothing to it, for her. But the thought of holding a chicken's doomed neck in my hand blazed the back of my own neck with goose pimples.

"We could poison it, stupid," Albert said, after seeing my face sour with thoughts of slaughter. "What do you think we're gonna do, chop its head off?" He laughed, but it was a serious laugh. He was thinking hard about the bird now. "We could feed it Clorox or some rat poison. Whatja think? Does your dad have any rat poison?"

"No, we don't have any rats," I said. "Only mice." For a crazy second I thought about how we could put a mousetrap loaded with a thimbleful of seed inside the cage and smash the bird to smithereens. That would be too obvious. Tito would know somebody killed his bird and why, and knowing Tito, even if he died twenty years later, his ghost would probably go around searching for whoever killed his bird. The thought of Tito's dark eyes and eroded cheek roving over me from beyond the grave scared me to death.

"What the hell are you thinking, anyway?" Albert broke in. "Every time I look at you, you're like twenty miles away. What the hell's the matter with you?"

"I'm just thinking," I said, hissing annoyance. But I couldn't melt the icicles grating inside my blood.

"Well, think about that goddamned bird, willya."

We thought about it, but there really wasn't any way that we could see. Tito kept the bird locked behind his door, and his porch was visible from almost any window on our block. To make matters worse, Tito had bought a glass doorknob at the supply store down the street and every day, when the afternoon sun angled over his roof ledge, the glass slithered light on almost every maple tree on our street. It attracted curious gazes and sometimes, while walking by it, a shard of light entered your eyes. We were lucky to have stolen Tito's peaches on a night when the moon was empty.

Another thought, definitely the most important, was that to enter Tito's porch when he was asleep was one thing, another was to enter his house, asleep or not. Rumors had it that he kept beside his bed a banana machete brought back from Puerto Rico. The thought of him lopping off sugarcane stalks and cutting through green coconuts with one swacking blow frightened our imaginations to a frenzy. We went limp over the possible wounds he could gap in our arms and chests, the slash he could rip across our navels, spilling our guts like wet blankets to the floor. No, there was nothing we could do.

"When I see that blackbird," Albert said with crazy bravado, "I'm gonna look him straight in the eye."

"I'm gonna spit in his eye," I said, stoking up my own courage.

Albert stabbed the air with two forked fingers. "I'm gonna poke his eyes, like the Three Stooges."

All the same, we went rushing to Bernardo at the first hint of Tito rounding the corner.

Bernardo, my older brother, was lying on his bed reading a Spiderman comic book. He elbowed up and listened. He was keen for scandal almost as much as my mom. He rubbed his chin worriedly for about a minute, then pointed a scolding finger at us for being stupid enough to steal from a neighbor. He never said it was wrong or that we should feel guilty, but that it was stupid — absolutely stupid! — a feat he claimed only we three geniuses were capable of. "I won't put it past Benny," he said. "That thief would steal from his own mother. But you guys!"

"Yeah, yeah, it was Benny. He's the one who told us it'd be all right," Albert edged in.

"Yeah...sure," Bernardo said. He dressed down Albert from the corner of his eye. Then he looked dead at me with deep disappointment. "Well," he said finally, "the way I see it, you both have got to keep away from Tito — and I mean *away* from him — because he'll find out, you can bet on that, he'll find out."

I went away believing that this was the most stupid thing I had ever done. It wasn't like we had stolen gold bars from Fort Knox. My dad's face would probably flush with pride if I'd pulled off something spectacular like that. It'd be a sign that at least one of his sons had ambition. But stealing big from a government didn't mean the same as stealing small from a neighbor. The smudge I'd make on his reputation among his friends would probably stick on him for life.

Now my mom. I knew her faith in me would shrivel like a cactus in a winter freeze. How would she explain it to all her *comadres* around the neighborhood who were already jealous of her for having kids who didn't get into as much trouble?

For a week then, I stayed away from Tito. Some days I lay paralyzed on my bed, listening for his tap on our door. On Tuesday I bit back the cold and took out the trash early, knowing that on that day he, too, put out the trash. Whenever he came toward me on the street, I ducked behind a corner or turned and greeted people I hardly knew. I felt as if even the people I spoke to during these embarrassing asides knew what I had done, knew that I was hiding to avoid capture. I hated myself for praying that maybe Tito would suffer an injury at work or that one of his sisters would die tragically in Puerto Rico — this, so that his box of peaches could shift further back in his mind.

Then one day, as I was putting on my white shirt in front of the mirror, Albert's moist face appeared at my window. He looked happy, anxiously pulling at the collar of his lapel, searching for the right words to spill his excitement. I took the screen off the window and let him climb in.

"Manny! Manny!" he said, catching his breath. "I saw the bird! I saw it!" He was raising his arms up and down as though spurring on a cheering audience. "Tito's blackbird. It saw *me!*"

"What...it *saw* you?"

"Yeah, and you know what?" he said, slumping down on my bed like a flattened balloon. "It didn't recognize me. That damned bird is as blind as a bat." All of Albert's energy saved to come and tell me this revelation now seemed exhausted. He groped around tiredly on the bed.

"What the hell are you talking about?"

"I'm talking about me and Benny going over Tito's to help him move his refrigerator," he said, catching his breath again. "My dad ordered us to go. We figured there was no way out of it. You know how my dad is, he don't take no excuses."

"And you guys went?" I said, grabbing his arm.

"I was tired, Manny. I just wanted to get the thing over with. Me and Benny figured, 'What the hell, we'd promise to buy him some more frickin' peaches.'"

"Benny too!" I said. I couldn't believe that Benny, being older, would give in to the same fears that were scouring us.

"Yeah...Benny too. Anyway, when we got there, Tito was sitting on his porch eating a can of pork and beans. The bird was in its cage. And you know what?" he said, rising up again, "for a minute I thought it recognized us. It started to squawk like we had hatchets in our hands or something. Tito couldn't understand what was going on. He said the bird was blind or almos' blind...been that way for a year."

Albert lay back, smiling like some damp heavy fog had lifted from his body. He began to finger out a loose thread from the quilt my grandmother had sewn for me the winter before. I stood there not knowing what to think, watching him as he pulled one thread out of its seam and flicked it with his finger.

I realized then that I'd been freed. The fear of getting caught and dragged off to Juvenile Hall, where I'd heard of Mexican boys crying and breaking down from the beatings, had been lifted. I remember my heart lurching, then emptying of any feelings in the whole affair.

I looked at Albert slouched on the bed, and thought about Tito sitting there on his porch eating out of a can of pork and beans, his spoon clanking against the tin sides. I wondered why he told everybody his bird could see when his bird was blind. Maybe he knew, and just wanted to scare us.

Maybe he was just a natural liar. Then it hit me, right there as I was watching Albert pull another thread loose from the quilt, it hit me. The reason why Tito said his bird could talk when he knew it couldn't wasn't because he wanted to scare us but because he wanted people to marvel at his stories, no matter if they believed him crazy. Tito wanted people to recognize him. I knew how he felt, because I was the same. Only I wanted people to approve of me. He was lonely, but I was afraid. And I knew that it was me, and not Tito, who was really the crazy one.

SUBTITLES

Ana Castillo

i have lived my life in a foreign film. Black and white mostly. Fassbinderish, i think. Having spoken one language in the five-room-flat secluded world of my grandmother until the age of six when i was sent to foreign film school —

hushhhh, i whispered the new language in fragmented sentences that jutted out of my mouth like broken glass caught in my throat. The first day when my older sister left me there, startled by the sudden appearance of subtitles at my feet, i ran out of the classroom.

i did enormously better than others back then, however, i have come to realize, when exchanging these early foreign film stories. Better than my old friend, Juana, who was sent to the class for the hearing-impaired for being unable to handle the subtitles. She did not learn the new language, she tells me. But she did become quite adept at signing.

In my school, however, there would have been no such luck. There was one alternative class alone, where all children who challenged their teachers for reasons not restricted to language difficulties were banished until they were old enough to drop out of school, six-year-olds with sixteen-year-olds: The Dumb Bell Room.

i, on the other hand, was not a foreigner — i was living in a foreign film. Typecast at times, especially during those formative years in the vast expanse of the inner-city — caught between African-American children with Mississippi accents

166

and gypsy adult-like children who simply had no use for school at all after the second grade.

Miscast during what may have been the bloom of my womanhood, except for the fact that a renegade does not bloom so much as explode.

But later, oh finally, much later, i ascended with tenacity and confidence to the illustrious heights of stardom. And a star can be anything she wants.

So here i am. New casting. This is not a set. We are filming this scene on location. Spare no expense. And who would have ever thought...?

Passing through the music department. i am not six in this scene but thirty-eight now. The students, the professors are all foreign, of course. Yet, what is beautiful about all this, what was once so tormenting and now is the very source for my celebrity EVERYWHERE i go is that i am the one who is cast forever foreign. There is Mozart playing in the halls and the women are natural blonds. They appraise my Chichicastenango *huipil*. i smile at their naked stares. My dark fingers, rimmed with gold, reach up to my collarbone to rub the Virgen de Guadalupe/Tonantzin talisman medal that hangs from a thin gold chain.

i live, you understand, in a foreign film.

i have cultivated a disturbing but sensuous foreign accent

[handwritten: Stereotypes of Clothes]

like Ingrid Bergman's.

i don't always wear *huipiles* from Chichicastenango, Xela, or Mitla. i usually show off spandex pants embroidered with silver roses, or a silk raincoat or Djuna Barnes red lipstick and wide brimmed hat or Marlene Dietrich waves or Kathryn Hepburn shoulders or a Greta Garbo cleft and i don't mean on the chin.

It is so hard to be
original.

Maria Sabina, Oaxacan shamaness peyote spell-caster suits my "type" best. If you can't be original, at least you can be complex. *[handwritten: Stereotype]*

167

i never disappoint my devoted public.

Traveling, not with *bruja* wings but on trains and jets to places Maria Sabina would not go, i find myself led to a place of foreignness of greater proportions than those created by the original script.

Behind a closed door at the end of the hall i recognize *Don Giovanni* on the piano. It is the only opera I have ever attended. A fortunate coincidence for me who can now turn casually to my host and smile: "Ah, *Don Giovanni!*" And he smiles back because the bridge i made by composition recognition makes him less uneasy with this unsolicited confrontation with otherness.

We reach the reception salon.

A dried flower arrangement at the center of the table. Domestic champagne. Platters of fruit and cheese. The usual.

Someone introduces herself and whispers in my ear. i throw my head back, laughing, a thousand rays of light radiate from the center of my being, à la Maria Sabina.

The cinematographer moves in for a close-up.

i have no lover. Neither on location nor back at the studios where my life is usually filmed. Another detail to note. It is certain to be relevant to the development of the plot.

Someone says in that pseudo-confident tone that ambitious people from general casting use in such scenes (nothing short of bad acting if you ask me), "*She's a lesbian, you know.*"

The other extra, the one who has become involuntarily privy to this new information, strains her neck a bit, scrutinizes the star to see if she can determine this for herself:

Beneath the *huipil*, sheer black stockings with seams.

Red manicured fingernails.

Have we entered Monika Treut territory?

The protagonist is still laughing. Definitely not "Seduction: The Cruel Woman" material, the observer concludes of the star who is still doing Maria Sabina with a little bit of Nastassia Kinski.

We are into something only marginally Hollywood here. More along the lines of the Canadian metis-feminist genre, if there is one. A cross between "Loyalties" and "Getting a Winter Tan," maybe.

Another nobody-extra offers: "Actually, if she takes off that costume, she has breasts."

Big breasts?

It is all a matter of perspective. The cinematographer's.

I like her earrings. Detail is the director's forte. They are gold, of course, tiny Mayan masks.

Clues to her origin or just more visual effect to dazzle the viewer, like the little espresso coffeepot earrings on that weirdly beautiful actress in Almodovar's *fabulously* successful *Woman on the Verge*....

Espresso is very European. Indian mask gold earrings are very American....

Indian from America. Where Columbus arrived, not where he was headed, but insisted that the inhabitants were Indian anyway.

Indigenous mask earrings cast from an original Mayan mold. You can count on that. Except that the originals were ear-plugs, going through the lobe in a much larger hole than the needle-thin one fashionable today. Holes were drilled into the teeth then as well, for adorning purposes. Embedded with precious gems. Trend setters those people were.

She is smiling gold and turquoise.

And starts to laugh again.

It is the domestic champagne. And the accent is getting thicker. Before you know it, she'll be speaking Mixtec.

She is not an actor.

She is not in costume.

She was born inside this film.

Her mother, who had birthed all her other children at home, was forced to a hospital with this last one. She gave her newborn daughter's name to the nun-nurse who immediately translated it. And thus, her career began.

Sometimes she cooks things, our star, but from no particular native cuisine. Yes, yes, she does mother-learned and grandmother-cherished recipes very well. She also does pesto and quiche with *molcajete* and *metate*. Very American, you know.

What isn't American these days with Gary Snyder declaring himself among the "New Indians of America"?

From across the room you can see that strange light emanating from her belly button.

What if she were Chinese? But, of course, not too tall.

Not too tall. What is it then?

She just isn't. Anyone can tell that. And you can't Anthony Quinn her into it, either.

She stops laughing, now sizing up the man with the full head of white hair and neatly trimmed beard, and assesses a potential development of the plot here. He could bring her gifts like St. Nick. Not just at Christmas.

Sometimes it's so hard to take her seriously.

She begins to fuss with her little Guatemalan change purse, the kind that is popular with Californian students these days, and pulls out two little photographs, passes them around. Everyone who examines them smiles politely, hands them to someone else. They are of a child who is a very small version of herself.

The child is away at school, she says.

Ah, of course.

Very bright, she says. Gets only the highest marks. Very sociable, too. Makes friends with everyone.

Of course.

He is going to be an artist when he grows up.

Oh? (Polite laughter here from those around her.)

Like his mother, she adds. And laughs again, putting the little photos that have been passed between index finger and thumb all around back into the little bag.

She has very thick, very black hair. It is natural.

Each time she laughs, either because of the champagne or because this is the only direction she has received so far in this scene, she runs her thin gold-rimmed fingers through the front of her hair. Gold with a pearl. Gold with black onyx. Gold and a diamond.

"You must catch the 19:04," someone alerts her. "The trains here are usually punctual."

"Yes, yes, don't worry!" she responds, almost flirtatiously although she didn't notice who in the crowd has spoken to her. It's certainly the champagne causing this sudden transformation of character. It doesn't make her giddy, but she would never smile

provocatively without the champagne, which is not a prop, but real.

The gathering is in her honor.

She is come to avenge the Conquest.

Don't make cheapshot Aztec jokes like: Will she cut any hearts out for an encore?

Of course, she will cut hearts out.

Just don't say it.

Don't ask if she will make it rain, either.

Maybe she will just do something mundane, like stare a bull down, later, in the scenes where she is resting in the countryside.

She reaches over to the table and with a silver pick helps herself to a piece of sheep cheese.

Cheap cheese?

Sheep cheese?

She repeats with her accent which, like the cheese, the locals have cultivated a certain taste for. The cheese is transported from Yugoslavia, unlike sheep milk which obviously sheep produce, to suckle baby sheep of course, and for Yugoslavs to produce cheese cheaply for export.

Enough of the cheese, and the strawberries too, cut into precise quarters to skirt the crystal platters.

Who will she sacrifice first?

The cast, for the most part, except for those cynics who would have guessed it, is unaware of her plan. Everyone is directed to move about the room, mingle cocktail party style, and assume that they have it all under control.

She is laughing a little again and you can see the ray of light from her center but cannot hear any sounds from her mouth. Kind of early Buñuel. Everyone appears oblivious and content.

Now, if she did have a lover, would it be a man lover?

The receptionists hold out their long-stemmed glasses to the new bottle of champagne (no, you cannot say receptionists for those attending a reception. They are guests, simply guests) and toast the Receiver. (She is not a Receiver, but the guest of honor.)

Translation is a vastly unappreciated artform.

If she does get a man lover on location or in this film at all, she wants him to have one of these strange names the people have here. They are ugly-sounding, actually, as if describing an organ transplant or a root-canal operation, or a food one wouldn't necessarily like to eat but surprisingly finds delicious, like cow brains or tongue.

But the men, apart from their names, are not necessarily ugly nor morbid in any apparent way, despite their Transylvanian accents, and she feels very certain that she could acquire a taste for one of them.

The women are much too tall for her liking, so they have all been dismissed. She doesn't see herself wearing Humphrey Bogart elevated shoes for the kissing scenes.

Engaging suddenly in an anarchy of mini-melodramas, the supporting cast has begun to drift off. "Try to remember why we are all here, people!" The director shouts through the megaphone, "At least *act* like you're interested!"

She is looking a little tired suddenly. Make-up! Make-up! Where the hell is that make-up person?

Full shot as she abruptly exits and hurries down the hall toward the lift.

Somebody stop her!

"i want to be alone," i say in a low tone.

"What? What did she say? What is it?"

"I'M GETTING MY PERIOD!" i shout. No one has directed me to say this, but i occasionally indulge my diva tendencies. Although with no-talent culture-appropriators like Madonna and Cher out there, what can you really do for shock effect these days, anyway? This, however, does freeze the cast, and the cinematographer and director for the moment let me go.

If you want to be alone, try living in an adobe in the desert. No one, with the exception of an occasional unwelcome rattlesnake or coyote, comes to visit, not even my child. My only human contact being when i go to the plaza to work out three times a week for two hours. Unlike celebrity sellouts, i cannot afford a private trainer and have to join the locals at the jazzercise class at the Y.M.C.A. It's hard to have a great body, Raquel Welch said recently, and she ought to know. While Rita Moreno, who made a big-time debut voluptuously dancing around to "I Want to be in America," now advertises her exercise video looking like a bulemic, along with the Klute radical, who seems to have started this all, forgoing international politics for staying in shape and making movies about foreigners. Victoria Principal, who looks foreign but is not, scammed a $300,000 advance for her exercise book and i suppose you could own your own trainer with that kind of money. But then, in a way not greatly advertised but brought out in a Barbara Walters interview for sure, she built a whole career based on scamming.

i do my own wax jobs, too.

Although there was a time when i definitely went *au naturel*. No, not in the 60s. Contrary to popular belief, i was not a flower child radical. In 1968 i was thirteen years old and playing an African American with a huge reddish-brown Afro wig, because the last thing i wanted to play then was hippy and white.

And Martin Luther King was an American Gandhi at my school.

But being neither black nor white invalidated my existence.

And even without the wig, back in "The Godfather Lounge" on the southside of Chicago where i used to sneak in with false IDs, people saw the long straight hair and would ask incidentally of my Black and Proud look, "Do you have a little Indian blood?"

A little?

East Indian, maybe? Barbados?
i am
Coatlicue.

But no, not then, not yet. Then i was only a neophyte stone fertility filth-eating goddess. Not when i left the long black hair on my legs and underarms either, although yes, there i was, being something hard to pinpoint again, Muslim-looking perhaps, with the nosepin and the occasional sari.

No one knew how to cast me then. i might have been up for a dozen Oscars but for the fact that exotic types were rarely appreciated for their acting. It was just assumed that i was doing what came naturally to being Other, and obedient to rote training — like Bonzo or Lassie. And to my knowledge neither of them was ever nominated either, despite the fact that one co-starred with a minor actor who became president of the country.

And how grateful i should have been, for the pats on the head, but no, surely my unrefined breeding had something to do with my Marlon Brando temperament, insufferable and sulking, a complete antisocial, not to mention fatality incarnate to anyone who attempted intimacy — back then.

i could not stand the very idea of anyone who belonged in the movie stealing the scene, feeling too comfortable with her or his part, assuming i would eventually be moved off the set, dismissed. And more than a few did more than assume. "Get rid of her!" they demanded of the director. "She's got no training! Doesn't know a damn thing about Shakespeare!"

But who was doing Shakespeare? Surely none of them. Cecil B. DeMille convinced no one that Charleton Heston parted the Red Sea, nor did Otto Preminger's fresh discovery Jean Seberg make much of a Joan of Arc — although ironically, she was burned at the stake in the movie of her life for being prophetic and unable to save her country, or rather, forbidden to do so, as happened to Joan.

In the desert i do not worry about honing my accent,
nor about my image. There isn't even a vague attempt at personal style. No make-up. Hair pulled back. In the plaza i look like any of the unemployed or underemployed women that

stock their family pantries with 89-cent 32-oz. colas, dried chili powder, and blue corn *atole* in a box, who drive a 4 x 4, and maintain a fifteen-year marriage to a man who wears a baseball cap to cover a receding hairline and has a name like Santiago.

i look like any of them, but i am not any of them.

i drive a red sports car with a license plate that reads: TOLTECA. i wear a gold-plated Gucci watch — sent to me by a secret admirer, of course — nouveaurichely to the supermarket where i buy my cola and *atole*. i drink brandy with supper and listen to Astor Piazolla on my tape player as i cruise up I-40.

It comes with the territory of being a self-made star.

i have earned a local unflattering reputation for snubbing would-be suitors of either gender and being very particular about friendships in general. Stars are tolerated around here but not the self-assurance that often comes with their renown. But snubbing is not exactly based on snobbery. i would snub even if i were not famous. i tolerate very few people, which is why i moved alone to the desert, but cannot have enough of the world — whether it is the opera or

this desert, with its dust and tumbleweeds. The constant drone of the cicadas. The sweat cupped beneath my breasts when i sit perfectly still in the shade. The sound of the hard rain at night.

In a foreign film everything, inanimate and otherwise, is an object, a prop. But in the desert, especially at night with the rain, no one directs me to throw back my head and laugh. No one is intimidated by the light that radiates from my center. No one knows what i dream when i lie in the middle of an empty room on a futon and close my eyes to the spider webs that connect between *vigas* on the ceiling. The dreams are yet another film, less foreign than the one i live in out there, that you, dear public, need only spend an hour or so viewing, while i must continue inventing and reinventing my roles until death, for the sake of your entertainment.

LA LUZ

Jack Lopez

The first thing you do when joisting a house is mark layout. Put marks on the top plate where the joist will lie. You do this before you spread material, while the walls are clear of lumber. Marking layout is a tricky business. You're balanced on a two-by-four, which is actually three and-one-half inches wide, sixteen feet in the air, and you bend at the waist, and in essence touch your toes. Not literally, but you make a mark on the plate, in between your feet, and you have to walk *backwards*, not looking, with your tape measure hooked on the far wall, telling you layout. That's what's tricky. The walking backwards. If there are any booby traps, nails sticking up, let-in brace not flush with the plate, plate not nailed, *sayonara* joister.

As I started laying out the various second-story rooms that I would roll, I heard the cutoff saw far off in the distance begin its high-pitched whine, and felt the dull steady drone of the plasterers' hopper kick in. And I soon became immersed in my task, forgetting about how cold my hands and feet were, and how frosty my throat felt with each breath I took.

When the first flake fell I'd almost laid out the entire house. It descended slowly, like a lost feather out of a down pillow, its form probably magic. We didn't get snow this far south in California. But there it was, a solitary snowflake, changing form before my eyes, turning from a frozen crystal into a wet imprint on the wood.

I looked up. Everything was gray, and I could see my breath exploding before me in small puffs. Saws were going on other slabs, guys framing. I could smell the aromatic scent of wet fir being sliced over and over as we fashioned three dimensional puzzles in space, and I could smell the wild, pungent fragrance from the surrounding fields, even now smell the oranges from the grove. The trees drooped, laden with fruit, orange Christmas decorations sparkling against dusty leaves, glowing in the dreary gloominess of another workday. Putting my keel back in my bag, I saw the snowflake half-disappeared into the two-by-four on which I'd made my last layout mark.

From out of the orange grove, farther down the dirt street where only the bottoms were framed, came two *paisanos*. I couldn't say wetbacks. Certainly not illegal aliens. Everyone working around me was from somewhere else, many of them here illegitimately. At first I thought the two strangers were men. But as they got closer I could see that one was a woman. She carried a small, faded-brown overnight satchel with both hands clutching the leather handle, and she had dark hair tied in a ponytail, yet thin strands had come undone and moved about her face as she walked.

A woman out here was odd. We didn't have them, except for the ones who drove catering trucks. This was Little League in the old days, Pop Warner, topless bars, and the Baja 500 all rolled into one male mindset. Maybe she was labor like the rest of us, I thought, watching them enter our outpost before Saddleback Mountain.

The man was tall and wore dark slacks with a fleece-lined jacket. He even had black ski gloves. The woman wore Levi's that weren't yet too faded, but they were well worn. Through the jeans her legs looked solid and strong. She only wore on top a white blouse covered by a thin red and blue blanket-shawl that crisscrossed her chest, and hung almost over her arms. On her feet she wore white sandals with thick gray socks.

The man would forge ahead, leaving the woman behind, and then he would turn, pulling her up even with him, but she continued to slow down, as if she were very tired or very willful. I knew there was a trail from the border through the backside of the Cleveland Forest, which we were on the west edge of, so I figured maybe the woman had walked that trail. She appeared exhausted.

They marched past me, the man in the lead, the woman following, up to the landscapers' fire, which was surrounded by old and crummy cars. Most of the landscapers were from the other side, *el otro lado*, and they worked for four dollars an hour. There were still some men around this fire, heating coffee and eating. The man and woman had words for a moment, seeming to strongly disagree over something. After they stopped yelling the man in the fleece-lined jacket approached the circle of men. He pointed to the woman and spoke, which brought laughter from the men. The woman turned her back on them, staring up to the sky. Our gazes locked for just a second. Then she quickly looked away out into the fields.

I looked out there too. Tracts of houses were springing up all around us, sort of like a gold rush or something. Scrapers and earth movers graded other quadrants for more houses; shopping centers would follow. Looking back at the landscapers' fire, I saw that the man in the fleece-lined jacket now had a beer. The woman had put her suitcase on the ground and cupped a steaming drink in her hands, sipping from it, yet nodding and then waking with a quick jerk. Someone else, another man, guided her to the fire. Her brown satchel remained outside the circle of men, looking lost and dingy, and so alone.

As I scanned the entire tract I felt a feeling of peace and familiarity. There was a sense of humanity here. The new arrivals were welcomed. Some of us, a few, were from here. Most everyone else came from far away: the east coast, the midwest, Asia, Europe, Latin America. But we were bonded in work as we gave it our all in fields that would soon become neighborhoods. None of the workers would ever be able to live in these instant affluent communities. Yet that was okay.

These houses were a huge contradiction. Casterbridge Estates, phase III. They would start at a quarter million. And that would be for the few single stories. The 3 Plan, the one I was rolling second-story ceiling joist for — what we framers called doing "tops" — would sell for half a million. And a lot of the labor lived in the hills, walking to work, sleeping in the brush, making do with plywood and cardboard lean-tos, or else sleeping in their cars, like Johnny Fasthorse, the guy who built all the kitchen soffits. Lots of guys in the trades were living on the job.

I looked at my last layout mark. No more snowflake, only a wet dab. Saddleback was lost in mist. Everything was pressed down, the way I felt most of the time since my divorce. So carry on. Don't stop moving. Not when you're in the air, for if you think, then you look down, and if you look down, you fall.

And the incredible thing about the fall is how fast the ground comes up to meet you. Thirty-two feet per second squared. It's one of a few completely fair systems, the same for everyone. You think you'll have time to think things through, but you don't. No way. It's too fast. You and the ground will meet. It's just a matter of time.

No more snowflakes fell, but they stuck in my mind, the same way the woman did. And as I made my way back to the load I now became aware of another level of stimulus. It seemed as if all at once and instantaneously I could hear music. Country from Waylon Willie, valium rock across the street, *rancheras* from the cleanup crew, and heavy metal from the Gold Dust Twins.

So I started spreading, taking the first boards, which if the loads were built correctly, would be the ones I needed, to the farthest end of the house. Somehow you walk on top of that three-and-one-half inch plate, your toes gripping as much as they can through your tennis shoes, with that joist, an eighteen foot long two-by-six, balanced in your arms so that it has equal weight on either side of your body, making you a bit like the tightrope walker, except he has that pole. Not looking down you walk: one foot over the other, a game of balance, all the way to the edge of the building. On the perpendicular wall set one end of the joist down, while still holding the other end cradled underneath your arm. Then wiggle the board across the wall until it has spanned the room. Lay it on its side and go back for another. The next will be easier as will the one following — for you can balance just a second in between the boards. After you've spread the room you have a bunch of sagging joist ready to be rolled.

You pick up each board, sight it to find the crown, which is the curve on the edge of the board from milling, and place the crown up, on the layout mark. All boards have crowns and all crowns go up. So after you sight, you roll, and then nail the board on the top plate, one nail going, two coming back.

And that was what I did all day. Mark layout, spread material, roll, block, and cut specials. Since Christmas was almost here, I wasn't going to work a full day because we were having a party. Efren, one of the stackers, the guys who build roof structures, was across the street, stirring *carnitas* in his big copper vat, using a rowboat oar to jostle the meat. Even from my high vantage point I could hear the crackle of the fire underneath the vat, smell hot food wafting up toward me. I supposed that *carnitas* from Efren was as close as we'd get to a Christmas party, which was okay by me because I hated parties.

Behind Efren some laborers had tacked up black paper over the studs of a framed house to darken the room and keep out the breeze. They had a television and a video inside and they were going to show porno films, as they'd done last party. A rumor had been spreading that claimed the superintendent was going to hire strippers to dance later. Both of these prospects made me sad. People handing out business cards had the same effect and so did children's voices at the playground. The tether ball chain clanking against its pole was about the loneliest sound I could imagine — I lived not far from a school.

After I'd rolled the upstairs master bedroom, the second bedroom, and the upstairs den, all I had left were the front two bedrooms. Usually I like to finish a house while I'm on it rather than setting up again. But I was excited about the food and the gathering so I figured if I pushed to finish this house the work would diminish, qualitywise. And I hated that. So I worked alone, hand-nailing. No compressor and nail gun, no partners, no illegal slave labor. Just my bags and saw and cord. That was it.

Light and quick. Agile. Accurate. I took responsibility for my work. I took pride in it, never leaving a house until it was done to my satisfaction. The only way to make progress in this world, I felt.

§ § §

"I saw a snowflake," I said, passing the sack to Al. He was the foreman.

"It's cold enough to snow," Grizzly growled.

"More money!" Julio shrieked from the porno room. He'd been decorated in Vietnam.

Al took a nice slow drink from the sack. He liked to watch people.

"Who are all them other guys?" Little Magua asked.

I watched Efren take a full platter into the house as guys from the other trades milled about. Plasterers by the sliding glass opening, wearing their splattered whites with down jackets over them, drinking beer; roofers out by a duollie sharing their own bottle; drywallers, their hands that chalky white from handling board all day, in the garage next door, smoking pot; plumbers, their hands permanently stained from the flux, drinking by one of the coolers filled with beer; and even a bunch of landscapers had returned to the fire next to the grove, yet the woman wasn't with them.

"They paid their ten bucks," Spot said, "so who cares?"

"More money for the craps game," the older of the Dust Twins added.

After eating there would be gambling, a lot of cash would be floating around, especially with fifty-sixty guys getting paid green, plus Christmas bonuses, if there were any. When the gambling started, the stakes sometimes got pretty high.

"More money!" Julio yelled again.

The Owner had arrived and was handing out envelopes. He glided effortlessly between plasterers, shaking his head in reaction to the taunt from Julio.

"The baby needs milk," Spot chimed in.

"As long as the eagle shits," Efren yelled from across the way.

"I've got your money," the Owner said, reaching into his breast pocket, stretching his camel hair coat tightly so you could see the bulge of his pistol.

I used to run work, even had my own company, employing fifteen guys, and I used to pay in cash too. But packing a gun was the one thing I refused to do. What was the point? I didn't want to shoot anyone.

"You guys working tomorrow?" the Owner asked. "You, Jesse?" He smelled like Aqua Velva after-shave.

He knew I always did. I didn't like to be alone on Saturdays.

"It's Christmas, man," Julio said.

"Not yet." The Owner had a quick rebuttal.

"Week off, paid," Grizzly said.

The Owner guffawed.

"Bonus?" a Dust Twin asked.

"You want a bonus?" the Owner said, not looking at his questioner.

"You bet," the Dust Twin answered.

"Bend over!" the Owner said, laughing heartily and showing his rotten, tobacco-stained teeth. He thought this so funny he could barely hand out envelopes.

"Come on, you guys!" Efren yelled, "nobody's eating."

After the Owner gave me my envelope I cracked the seal and counted my money. Ten one hundred dollar bills, which included a bonus. Cool. Then I too began drifting over toward the food with the rest of the guys.

Inside the house that was wrapped with black paper a table, complete with plastic floral tablecloth, had been set and all sorts of wifely dishes covered this table. But after looking at it closely, I could see that it was just a piece of plywood with two-by-four legs, slapped together in a hurry, like everything else around here. On the alleged table were potato salad, corn and flour *tortillas*, baked beans, Mexican style beans, pasta salad, green salad, crab salad, bean dip, shrimp dip, clam dip, onion dip, *salsa fresca*, potato chips, *tortilla* chips, bagel chips, plastic knives and forks, and paper plates. No napkins.

I didn't get it. Was this summer? Were we on diets? If this was Christmas what about fudge and cookies and rum cake and brownies and *pan dulce* and ham and turkey and *tamales* and egg nog and brandy?

I loaded my paper plate, slowly passing through a long line. Some of the landscapers and the man in the fleece-lined jacket were leaving the room, plates overflowing. The line culminated with Efren's brother giving out *carnitas*. He had a cutting board and a large hunting knife with which he expertly diced the steaming meat. I remembered the last time we'd had a party Efren had cooked *chivo*. He'd buried the entire goat in the ground, covering it with coals and letting it simmer overnight.

Just then a Martian, one of a clan of over ten guys who were all related, came stomping out of the porno room bare-chested and shouted, "Where's the women?"

I ignored him, taking a plate outside where the Owner had opened a bottle of Chivas. He was still on his work rap, but nobody really wanted to hear it. Yet he needed confirmation that we would work over the holidays. What else would we do? He handed me the slightly rounded bottle.

"What did you do with the purple bag?" the Cowboy Nazi asked. He had swastika tattoos and wore western clothes.

"What purple bag?" the Owner said.

"It comes with Crown Royal, asshole." Julio was Chicano, and he had no patience with rednecks.

"Say what?" The Cowboy Nazi said, staring menacingly at Julio.

Efren pulled hot *tortillas* off a skillet, quickly handing them around. I grabbed some and went to work on the *carnitas*, scooping them in small shovel pieces of *tortilla*, and then adding *jalepeño* on top. The *chiles* were hot, but that was a good thing. Besides, you could wash them down with beer.

We talked and ate and told stories, and a couple of mangy tract dogs fought for just a second, so they were put in separate trucks, and the time floated by. Lesser Martians began building a backstop for craps, while Big Martian started a fire right on the garage slab, which would discolor the newly poured concrete, but neither the Owner or Al said anything. The wind picked up briefly, breaking the clouds that clung to the mountain peaks. The mountain was covered with snow! But a huge black storm front was approaching.

The Martians did siding, and Big Martian kept importing his relatives from Florida to work for him, until he had an entire baseball team operating as support system. These Martians were thieves, and they loved money, and they would try to get it from you any way they could.

The Martian without a shirt dropped to his knees on the garage slab and yelled to the afternoon sky, "Come to papa, yeah!" and he rolled the dice. Snake eyes. The loser as bait. It worked.

A drywall man stepped up with green in his hand and said, "Let's go, baby."

They rolled. And the clinks of the dice were compounded by the cold, drawing everybody into a tight circle.

Out front Efren was cooking the last batch of *carnitas*, talking to a few latecomers. The porno moaning kept a steady beat, highlighted by sporadic yelling from the garage slab as the craps game gathered momentum.

The Gold Dust Twins had invited Johnny Fasthorse out to their lowered El Camino and were snorting coke. Grizzly and Waylon Willie were out by a brand new duollie smoking pot and drinking whiskey. The landscapers were heating handmade *tortillas* and making *tacos* out of the *carnitas*. The man in the fleece-lined jacket and the woman had been at the very same fire.

While I gawked at the mountaintop and the approaching snowstorm, suddenly applause and shouts filled the air. A lot of guys who had been out at their trucks were running toward the garage slab, joining the bulging crowd. Their bodies pushed in and then fell away like a tidal surge against sea rocks.

At first I thought a fight had started, although in all my years working I'd never actually seen one. But they did occur.

Yet this thought was quickly displaced when I heard the unmistakable gravelly voice of Big Martian yell, "You can buy a woman!" Upon hearing such a strange idea, I too hustled over to the side of the garage, behind where the backboard had been set up, and pushed my way through the studs onto the slab.

And there, much to my dismay, stood the woman I had seen earlier, for sale.

"Fifty ain't enough for liver," Big Martian said. "Who wants a *woman?*"

"She ain't even awake," Spot said.

And she wasn't. The man in the fleece-lined jacket propped her up. Yet in spite of her unconscious state she still clutched her small suitcase.

"You can't buy and sell people," I said.

The Owner said, "I'm history." He split.

"This guy wants to sell her," Big Martian said.

We all looked at the man in the fleece-lined jacket. He stood behind the woman, holding her steady, saying something in Spanish that I couldn't quite hear because of all the commotion.

Efren translated: "He says, 'She's very tired.'"

No shit. But there was something more. There always was.

"I'll give a hundred," a drywall man shouted.

"The strippers will be here soon." Al was trying to divert attention.

"They're not coming," Grizzly guffawed.

Come to think of it, I hadn't seen the super all day. Either he was unable to get dancers, or he was actually getting them. Who knew?

"I think I'll buy her and fuck her to death," Waylon Willie said.

"Easy," Al cajoled.

"Let's all chip in and buy her and then we can have a train," Spot said.

"Shut up," I said to Spot.

"I wouldn't fuck it," the Cowboy Nazi said. "Who knows what diseases it gots."

"Shut the fuck up, you moron," I snapped at Cowboy Nazi.

The man in the fleece-lined jacket spoke with Efren, who then announced that only one man could buy her.

"What gives him the right to sell her," I said quietly.

"He's her husband," Efren said for the benefit of everyone.

That quieted some of the meaner ones in the crowd. Even they knew something serious was happening.

I came back with, "So?"

Efren shot me a funny look.

"I'll get her alone, then," Grizzly barked. "One hundred-fifty."

"Gash!" someone yelled.

"Is this guy serious?" I asked Efren.

"I think so."

Al threw his hands up and said, "Forget it." He left the garage slab.

"Two hundred," Little Magua said.

Grizzly chanted two-fifty.

A roofer chimed in with three hundred.

The bidding was serious, everyone wanting to see how far it would go. This wasn't a joke.

"That's too much for a fucking Spic," Grizzly said.

"Hey, white trash," Efren said to Grizzly.

"Knock it off," Julio said in his deepest voice. He was big, almost as large as Grizzly, and he separated Efren and Grizzly. "No fighting on the job."

"Three-fifty," a plasterer said.

"Five hundred," Little Magua, the prick, said. That was his whole check.

"He don't want her no more," the Cowboy Nazi said gleefully.

Trying to get eye contact with anybody, I said, "You've got to stop this shit."

The woman moaned. Everybody looked at her. She brushed back a wisp of hair that had come undone from her ponytail.

A yell from the back claimed six hundred.

"You can stop it with *money*," Big Martian hissed to me.

I don't know why, but I thought of my own life and of all the times I'd acted wrongly, or even worse, the times I'd not acted at all. So without realizing the implications of my words, I said, "One thousand."

At first a ripple of "whoas" passed through the crowd. And everything seemed more immediate, colder, clearer, slower.

"Are you serious?" Big Martian asked.

I showed him my envelope and bared my teeth in a mock smile. I had a plan. I figured if we could end this auction then maybe some sense could be talked into these people.

"Don't be an asshole," Grizzly shouted.

"Mind your own business," I snapped at Grizzly.

"You pussy," he said.

Big Martian asked, "Any other bids?" Nobody answered. To me he said, "You bought yourself a woman."

"I've seen this in Peru, but never here," Fermín said.

Big Martian grabbed my envelope. Instantly he had green in his hands.

"Enema!" the Cowboy Nazi yelled.

"Helmut, yeah!" Waylon Willie added.

"Hand it over," I said to Big Martian.

Julio snatched my money from Big Martian and said, "Let's finalize this thing."

"Anal," somebody yelled.

"Let's shoot some fucking craps," Grizzly said at last.

§ § §

Al leaned against his truck. "Now what?"

We had moved out front by Efren's smoldering fire, away from all the men, off the garage slab.

"I'll get my money back," I said. "Thanks for your help."

Al shrugged.

"It is not done that way," Efren said in Spanish.

Efren, Efren's brother, Al, and Johnny Fasthorse surrounded Julio and me. The woman was trying to speak with her husband, but her words were slurred, and he would have nothing to do with her.

"He's right," Julio said. "A deal's a deal."

"I don't want to buy a person."

"You did."

"C'mon, Al, do something. Help me out here."

"Can't. You opened your big mouth."

"What should I have done? Let Grizzly get her?"

"You're the one that got involved," Julio said.

"She's good-looking," Efren said.

We all looked at her. I hadn't before noticed the angular high set of her cheeks or her full and bushy eyebrows. She looked to be in her mid-twenties. Her hair was still tied in a ponytail, but much of it had escaped so that small wisps bumped about her face as she moved. She was trying to get her valise back from the man in the fleece-lined jacket.

A huge roar erupted from the craps game. The clouds that had been moving over the countryside from the north now darkened what sun we'd had, making the light almost feel dusk-like, even though it wasn't yet sunset.

"I didn't know you were like that," Efren's brother said to me.

"Like what?"

"Get the copper pot," Efren said to his brother. "I want to split before them rednecks really get going." He was watching the craps game.

Oh, shit, I thought. "Look, Julio, I want my money back."

"No can do. This man put her up in good faith." He gestured to the man in the fleece-lined jacket. "Now you want to break the deal. Where would we be without our word?"

I didn't want a treatise about military code or any such bullshit. "You know in your heart that it's wrong for one person to sell another."

"No, it's not."

"We had a war over it. The Civil Fucking War." I looked at Al for verification. He nodded approval.

"That war don't mean shit to me," Efren said.

"But these guys aren't Americans." Julio had me on that one.

"But we are."

"Maybe you could sell her for a profit," Efren said. "Clean her up, know what I mean?"

"I used to think you were okay, Efren," I said.

"Little Magua will give you five hundred," Efren's brother said. He closed the back flap on Efren's yuppie nature vehicle.

"Why?" I yelled at the husband. "¿Por qué?"

He snickered and said, "Aquella es malvada."

"How bad can she be?" I asked everyone, anyone.

"She ain't bad," Efren said, starting his rig. He revved the engine. "She's evil," he said, smiling. His rear tires crunched a two-by-four as he pulled away.

"Don't start that shit," I complained.

"Why so glum?" Julio asked. "You've got a woman."
He handed my money to the man in the fleece-lined jacket.

"Don't," I said. Julio positioned himself between me and the man in the fleece-lined jacket.

"Got to," Julio answered.

"Have fun," Al said. He started his truck.

"Wait."

"What do you want me to do?"

"I don't want to be a party to this."

"You already are. Butch it out."

"Christmas is coming up," I said, as if that, somehow, made any difference.

"You want me to take her home? My wife would just love that."

"Why not?"

Al shook his head. "Have fun," he said again, driving off.

When I looked for the man in the fleece-lined jacket I caught a glimpse of him running toward the orange grove. Julio and Johnny Fasthorse both restrained me as I started after him.

Fermín walked out to us from the craps game and said, "I've got some Spanish love poems in my car."

"Shut up, Fermín."

"No, man, she'll like them."

"Get lost." I shook myself free from Julio and Johnny Fasthorse.

Johnny threw up his arms, said, "Ciao," and walked off.

I heard a car start up, heard the uneven lop of a racing cam, and then saw a trail of dust leaving the orange grove. Shit.

"You shouldn't have got involved," Julio said. He made for his truck, got in, started it, and drove off down the dirt street.

So there we were, the woman and I, standing in the dirt, with the sun almost gone and the air colder and meaner than I'd ever felt. The yells from the craps game now had an urgency to them as the losers exposed themselves. I looked at her. Was she a loser? Was I?

This was it. What we called civilization. Humanity. A few snowflakes drifted past my face in an unhurried decline to the ground. Then more fell, swirling about the woman and me, obscuring the men involved in the craps game, though their yells continued. The wind seemed to die down and a light muted snow began falling. Suddenly everything was strangely silent.

"Let's go," I said, gently.

She yawned and looked at me with dark eyes and said, "*Soy Luz.*"

You are Luz I said back and knew why I'd done it, knew that everything previous in my life was leading to this one moment and saw everything clearly for once.

OF COLOR AND LIGHT

Rafael Jesús González

When he was five, some neighbors, moving away, left Ramón and his little brother Antonio a dog house with a peaked roof and a door rounded on top and a square window. It was a large, sturdy, dog house and if he stood in the middle there was even a little room to spare.

Ramón's father was often away. José Filiberto Gómez made the family living by selling brilliantine, pomade, olive oil, threads and other notions and novelties in distant little places called Canutillo, Deming, Fabens, Fresnillo, Mesilla, Mimbres, Santa Rita, and Silver City. He called himself J. F. Gómez & Co. The company part, Ramón concluded, were his mother Clara, his grandmother and grandfather and aunts and uncles who affixed the labels on the little bottles of brilliantine, red (scented with roses) and yellow (scented with jasmine).

There were always bottles about the house: the flat, fluted bottles used for the brilliantine, the slender bottles with a bulb at the top and a bulb at the bottom used for the olive oil, and others of more or less interesting shapes. Ramón loved these bottles sometimes more but never less than he did his large box of Crayolas whose fine points he jealously guarded and which smelled like no blessed church candle ever could. His father even built him shelves in the dog house so Ramón could arrange his favorite bottles.

One of those god-inspired days of the desert just after Easter when the sun is an alloy of silver and gold, Ramón snuck from the house while his brother and mother slept the siesta. He took with him some bright crepe-paper flowers his mother had given him and some egg-coloring tablets he'd hoarded from the Holy Saturday past. Another treasure, these egg-coloring pills, large and glued to a sheet of paper with instructions, in English so he could not make out even one word. But he knew anyway. He loved the infusions they made and their smell in water and vinegar and how they stained the white china cups in which the eggs were dipped. And he always objected when his mother or father insisted on emptying them into the kitchen sink, careful not to splatter the white porcelain.

Ramón filled all his bottles with water from the back yard hose and forced crumbs of egg-coloring and pellets of crepe-paper down their tight throats. Some he was careful to keep pure of contamination one by another. With some he experimented, though he knew some things to avoid. (He had learned he must keep the egg-colors he hoarded dry, for if water got into them, strange things happened: some lovely strange as when green was touched with blue, but some just plain boring strange like when purple ran into yellow.)

After he finished, he arranged all his bottles (with the years they grew to hundreds) on the shelves his father had made him and he stood back near the far corner by the dog house door. And time stopped. As we know it does on god-inspired days. And the light came in just right. As it does when light is an epiphany. And it poured through all those colors in the bottles and he knew them to be more pure than the stained glass windows at 11:00 o'clock mass.

Later this became a measure for happiness mixed up with other things: the happiest moments with his father, his mother, his brothers; his grandmother's laugh; a stolen moment of drunkenness in the Navy hospital X-ray room with his best friend; cutting psychology class with his love Genoveva (Genny to their gringo friends); the tea ceremony, years later, with his other love Doris.

And with his ambitions. He would be a painter and in his fifteenth year, on a pilgrimage to the Basílica de Guadalupe, drunk on murals, he promised her a painting for one of her side-altars. But, no, his mother and father gave him to understand, this was not realistic. Okay, he said, pharmacy, thinking that it was chemistry that drew him. But it was probably the flasks, vials, alembics, retorts filled with potions, infusions, syrups, tinctures, elixirs, each differently colored, to be arranged on the drugstore shelves. He confused the healing for the color and after high school decided pharmacy was not ambitious enough so he set out to become a doctor — and perhaps a priest to boot. After the navy, college completed, when he was accepted to medical school he decided instead to teach — and to write.

And it took many, many years later for him to suspect that at the roots of his being a poet was the patience of cramming pastilles and bits of crepe-paper into the narrow mouths of brilliantine bottles full of water so that the precise and diffuse colors would bleed against the light.

Chapter One from
THE PINK ROSARY

Ricardo Means Ybarra

"When did it come?"

"What?"

"The telegram? Phone call?" His voice, as tightly wound as an empty pack of cigarettes, sailed past the old Indian out the window and into the kicked-up dust of the road. Another mystery of the Utah desert, he asked himself, or was it the sacred wisdom of Indians? And why don't I know the answer since the old man does? Beto pushed his boots hard against the floorboard of the pickup and kept them there. He always stiffened up when the old man was driving, his long legs bent at the knees. He didn't wonder how the old man got his license or even if he had one: Robert "Beto" Reynolds came from L.A., Silver Lake, to be exact, the edge of downtown and driving. He figured that like the DMV, Indian pacification under the guise of the Department of the Interior, hands out licenses so we'd all feel like citizens, privileged. But it wasn't this Utah canyon bottom they were in or the hills and valleys of Silver Lake and Echo Park that stiffened his legs; it was the other drivers. He looked at the old man driving, two hands high on the wheel. Beto was sure that he knew all about other drivers; after all, he had survived thirty-one years of life in L.A., although he wouldn't think of it as survival. It was more like getting around, knowing how to react on Glendale Boulevard and the intersection of Effie and Alvarado, what streets to take when the

194 *have to react who and act to the environment, it shapes who we are*

Dodger game let out, which nationality tended not to signal before turning. Silver Lake was full of lousy drivers. It was on the border of Echo Park. Some prof at L.A. City College in a night class he'd once taken had called these places microcosms. That was a laugh. He had, in fact, laughed out loud in class. The guy obviously didn't know anything. Microcosms. Beto knew other drivers because he knew where they came from. Take the professor, for example. He was a paddy, he'd obey the laws. And he'd shown him, hadn't he, got an A in Anthropology and didn't do a thing but take the prof on a cruise. Of course he'd borrowed Ray's ride. Beto smiled, realized he was stiff, that his arms were as locked in place as the old man's hands. Ray had made it happen for him, hadn't he? Ramon Cruz. Ray had lent him his '58, but not just any '58. This '58 was Chevy as art. Impala. And Ray was an artist of the power sprayer and lacquer, an auto body man.

The old Indian eased down a slight grade and over the round rocks of a river bed as dry as everything else in Utah summer. He drove so diligently that Beto felt every rock, every round grumble under the slowness of the truck. He tightened his legs so hard now he could feel the veins in his groin extend. "Oh shit," he muttered under his breath. The old man floored the relic of a Utah ranch Ford as the front wheels hit the opposite bank leading out of the river bottom. Beto felt the front bumper plowing into silt and sand, the rear wheels bouncing. Rocks, stones, even boulders, he imagined, were clanging off the bottom of the pickup. He thought of Ray. Wondered if style would have helped as he wished the truck over the top. Instead, what he felt were wheels, rear wheels, digging in.

"Sweet Jesus, old man, cut it," he yelled. It wasn't a weak shout; he knew the old man could hear him but the Indian, a picture of calmness with both hands on the wheel, gazed forward, laid it on, and the powers of Detroit, those lovers of the hidden V, this man's machine, and the Indian's zen-like application of the accelerator were the combination to sink the differential into a layer of pre-Anasazi silt.

"Jesus, Jesus, Jeezuus," he pounded at the metal dashboard.

195

"We're stuck," the old man said as he turned the motor off, replacing all the noise with a silence that hammered at the metal cab over Beto's head. Beto looked out his window; he wouldn't look at the old man. He felt that if he just stared out the open window the boring calmness of pink rocks and sandstone would release him. The old man was obviously unconcerned as he reached into his pocket for a tightly crumpled package of Red Man. Beto listened to the deliberate unwrappping, the spreading of foil, the fingers in a tight place, and grabbed the old man by the arm before he could bite off a plug, turning him so they were eye to eye in the dry river bed and asked him, "How do you know it's for me?"

"Buchanan had to go to town."

"It's a telegram, then." He released the arm and sat back. The old man bit off a chunk but didn't start to chew: he'd suck on it awhile 'til the juices got thick and filled his jaw. He didn't suck quietly; he was slurping, the sound a kid makes with a straw in a nearly empty glass. Beto listened to the tick of the cooling engine, the settling of rubber into sand, the old man's tongue warbling over tobacco, and decided he'd try it again since now he might be getting through. He'd try not to rush the old man, naked women couldn't rush him anyway, but Beto was in a hurry. He'd been in a hurry ever since this morning when the old man came out to the Gulch, and now it was more than a hurry, it was a rush, a rush to get somewhere, get out of here, go. He'd ask him anyway because he couldn't stop himself.

"How do you know the telegram's for me, old man?"

"Who else could it be for?"

Beto rolled his eyes skyward in a mock gesture and prayed, knowing that God had his own speed and that it never was the same as his, not when he was in a hurry. "God, please let it be for me," he said to the roof of the cab under his breath slowly, so as not to rush Him. "Please, let it be for me. A novena, no, I promise a novena and the stations of the cross and mass three Sundays of the month if it's for me." He touched his hands together hoping the message was slow enough to get through. He turned to the old man again before he got carried away and promised too much. The Indian was looking at him and smiling, the left side of his face round with Red Man.

"Who were you talking to?"

Beto ignored the question, asking, "Why did you wait so long to tell me?"

"You were praying, weren't you?" The Indian was grinning and talking and sucking, all at the same time so that his voice came out warbled and lopsided, the sound a car makes with a flat tire on the side of the road. "I thought you knew," he added, chuckling. The tire flapped against the fender now.

"How could I possibly know? You come out first thing in the morning and tell me there's an important message for me, that's all. How would I know something came for me?"

"Talk to your God."

Beto didn't want to discuss it. Anyway, he was concerned about talking to God since the old man had his own crazy ideas about rocks and birds and everything else and he didn't want God to act slow, to debate his request or wonder about the rocks. "I wasn't praying."

The old man grinned even wider than Beto thought possible with that much chew in his jaw. "That's good. Keep your mind open, son," the old man warbled.

He sounds just like my grandmother, Beto thought. Dolores, sweet vicious little Dolores Maria Bernadette Rivera Reynolds. That's just like something she would say while slurping her coffee. It struck him that she was everywhere, but would she send a telegram? Who else would send him a telegram? Ray? And if Dolores had sent it, then it couldn't be good news, could it? The old man's grin extended past his eyes into the soft bill of the Giants baseball cap he never went anywhere without as he continued speaking.

"A telegram is like a dream; it comes from somewhere else, doesn't it? And a dream must have a messenger. I saw the dream, son, and came for you."

Beto wasn't too surprised. The old man openly delivered messages from the universe, read his mind and possibly his soul as well. He'd long ago decided that this was coincidence, or peyote, which he was sure the old man chewed along with his Red Man. And Dolores would use a dream, wouldn't she? The old man and Dolores, what a pair: she dreams and he hears her. Dolores floated past the window, all 4 feet 11 inches of her standing in the kitchen, wrapped in her stained yellow housecoat, thinking of messages to give him through the old man. She can follow me anywhere, he thought with horror. And what could he do? He couldn't rid himself of her: she'd find him; she'd found the old man, hadn't she?

If the telegram was from the old lady, then was she the answer to his prayers? It was too much. His eyes glazed and he felt his body go slack, but his legs remained stiff, rigored, tight in his boots.

The old man hopped carefully out of the ridiculously sloping vehicle. He surveyed the truck, squatting to get a better look at it, stood up and spit into the river bed. He grinned and joyfully, if not lustily, shouted into the cab loudly enough to shake Beto, "We're gonna have to dig her out, Slim.

Beto muttered, "Of course we have to dig her out," but he continued to look through the windshield. At 7:00 a.m. the Utah sky seen through the dusty windshield of a Ford pickup tilting upward looked as blue as the ice in the bottom of an empty glass. "Dreams, messengers, goddamn right we have to dig." He relaxed his legs and hopped out of the truck.

"Here, give me that." Beto took the shovel roughly, rubbed the handle down, eyed the buried tires, the truck resting backwards, indecently comfortable. "You didn't see the telegram or even talk to Buchanan, did you? There might not be a telegram, old man." He forgot dreams, God and Dolores. The pleasure of smoking the old man out for once made Beto revere the beauty of the curved face filling with sand. "Maybe Buchanan just had to go to town early," he added, exuberantly flinging the full shovel so that sand and pebbles clattered like a rusty tailpipe. The old man smiled all the more and spit out a healthy slug that even the dry rocks couldn't immediately absorb.

"Whatever you say, Slim. I'll get brush for the wheels."

"Yeah, you do that," Beto muttered as he stripped off his t-shirt. "But I'm driving us out of here."

The old man laughed and spit. He watched as Beto dug faster than a pothunter in the middle of the night with the batteries going low. Ol' Slim, skinny and lean, he thought, back and arms and legs as thin as any deer leaping a fence, lean as could be, except for his head. Slim had a head of hair that was thick and curly and dark. A good-looking young man, easily the most handsome man around, a thought which made the old man laugh because they were in one of the least populated areas of Utah. They'd be out in no time, he knew, just as he never doubted the arrival of the telegram, and just as six months earlier he knew that Beto would arrive, and it would snow a hailstorm in May, and that Mrs. Halloway, finally fertile after ten years of marriage, would give birth to twins. He didn't wonder about it since there was nothing he could do about the things he saw, not that they were visions exactly; they were more like feelings. It was his hands that could see. Part of old age, he figured. Hands still good for something.

Beto laid down the shovel and surveyed the two paths he had dug like runways leading back and under the rear bumper. He had already dug out the rear bumper which had been partially buried in the river bed like the half-exposed femur of a dinosaur. As he worked he had thought about the telegram. It had to have come from Dolores. She had tracked him down, but then, he had always known she would find him. He'd been here six months. Of course, he thought, he might be ready to move on; it was getting old playing cowboy and the summer was already over, but he didn't know how to leave. What would he say to the Buchanans, friendly enough to take him in. And then he wasn't sure if he really wanted to leave, but he knew that he was leaving now and she had caused it, he knew that it was Lulu. He called Dolores "Lulu" when he wanted to infuriate her. He used it often. He used it now, but it didn't work any magic; it never worked really. He knew he couldn't win with her, not against that mind, "the reptilian brain," he called it, no guilt, all selective memory. "Lulu," he swore at the bumper; damn it,

199

wasn't it her fault that he was digging this relic out and that he was even in Utah in the first place? He'd shown her: he'd had a job for six months and could have stayed longer except for her.

He thought of dreams and messengers again, but what he needed now was brush. He stuffed the brush and weeds the old man had piled next to him under a jacked-up tire. He let the jack down, hurried over to the other side and jacked up that wheel, loading the hole underneath. I'll bet the telegram was at the Buchanans'; the old man heard about it in the morning, he told himself. He stepped back and checked both runways for straightness. He didn't care if his work looked good or was right, just that it was efficient enough. He'd already decided that the bank was too steep to go at it from here, that what they needed was a running start, that their chances were better to reverse out and have a try at it again. That was why he had dug the runways. "Hey you, supervisor, help me load some of these rocks in the back," Beto yelled at the old man.

"You want to get some weight over the wheels, huh?"

"Yeah, that's the idea."

"Right. Good idea, son." The old man either called him "Slim" or "Son," but he couldn't determine if they had any significance. Started with "S" is all he could figure. He'd given up on being called Beto, the name Ray had dropped on him when they were kids, the nickname for Robert that made him feel like a Mex, his L.A. *apodo* that Dolores wouldn't use. The old man had his quirks, and even the Buchanans called him "son" at times, which seemed okay because they were old and married, but they usually called him "Bobby" which reminded him again of Dolores. She'd like that.

"I'll sit on the tailgate, then."

Beto looked at the wiry old man who couldn't weigh more than one-forty in his bib overalls and said, "I don't think you should do that."

"Don't worry, Slim, I have excellent balance. Did I ever tell you that I was a champion bronc buster?"

"Many times, old man," Beto said tiredly, looking up into a sky that was starting to spread out under yellow oil.

"I haven't ridden something wild in years, but you know, you never forget." The old man was perched happily on the tailgate, his skinny fingers not yet on the metal, the left side of his jaw quiet for a moment. Calls me Slim, Beto thought, looking carefully at the old man who was dressed in bib overalls and a red cotton lumberjack shirt buttoned to the collar. Loose white long johns the color of sandstone poked out at the wrists, curling back on vein-thin wrists. He always dressed the same, whatever the weather, and sweat the same, no matter if they were down in some oven like this canyon or up on Boulder Mountain where it could get as cold as Christmas in August. He wore the same hat too, not a cowboy hat or a black Navajo hat, but a pulled-down-tight, washed-out San Francisco Giants baseball cap with no definition left past the brim, just round and soft. He imagined the old man had found it in a campground; an Indian could pick up a lot of things Beto'd never expect to find out here. Where had he been? What had he seen? Beto couldn't imagine him out in the world, the real world out past these canyons and mesas. They said he was an Indian. "Half Indian," they sometimes said, which made him an Indian to Beto because who's half of anything? Just like you can't be half Mexican or half white. Who'd believe that in L.A., he thought; your nationality just depends on who you're talking to. The old man was the only Indian he knew, but then he'd never seen any Indians in Utah, around here at least. The only Indians he'd ever seen were down near the Grand Canyon in that shitty town he'd passed through and they were mostly heavy and wanted to drink, but the old man never drank; he bit a little chaw, like the ranchers, who never could clean off the sides of their trucks for all the spit they slugged. And of course he had that nose, a nose like that Indian on the nickel, so thin and beaked it could wedge a seasoned round of wood. Thin face, thin all over, but not scrawny. The old man was sinewy, strong; Beto knew he could work all day whatever his age. Half Indian, hell, if he was half Indian then Beto could be half Mexican. It just hinged on who was looking at you. He looked at the old man once more, looking at eyes shaded under the floppy brim, eyes as dark as a burned clay pot. "Ready?" he yelled from the cab, engine running, the flies swarming around the smell of oil on his skin.

"Ready," the old man shouted back, but Beto hopped out of the cab and stood with his hand on the door until the old man turned around. "I don't like it."

The old man smiled. "Son, don't worry so much. If you worry too much when you're young you'll have a back like a curved woman."

"Oh Christ," Beto muttered and got back into the truck. He gunned the engine and turned in the seat so his right arm lay along the back under the window, his head cockeyed so he could look out at the rear of the truck and the old man on the tailgate. He knew the old man was grinning, the old fool. "Calls me an old woman; next thing he'll say I'm like Dolores."

"Here goes," Beto shouted and eased down on the gas. The wheels spun slowly for a second, caught in the brush, and then they were out and on the runways he'd dug, the front wheels bouncing in the holes made by the rear tires, and then they were clear. The old man let out a whoop and Beto grinned.

"You did it, old man, now come on up here in front."

"Go on, give it the horses, I'm riding it over the top," the old Indian shouted back.

Beto was out of the cab, stumbling in the river bed rocks and sand. "Goddamn it now, get offa there."

"Go on, I can handle it." The old man didn't look at all concerned when Beto rattled the tailgate. He felt the top of his cap, rubbed his jaw once and smiled. Beto kicked at a rock and called him a crazy mother and a crazy fuckin' injun, but it didn't change the look on the old man's face. "See any visions, like landing on your head?" he asked as he got back into the cab, but all the old man did was shout, "Give her the guns!" rather exuberantly. "Fuck'im," Beto muttered as he gunned the engine and took off slow and steady so as not to bury the front bumper again. When they had cleared the front, he goosed it, and they were over with a bounce, the rear wheels still spinning. He heard the "yahoo" over the engine noise and the clanging of the beat-up pickup, and he felt excited in spite of himself, but when he looked in the rear-view mirror, the tailgate was empty. He slammed on the brakes and ran. He ran back to the old man flat on the road, flat as spilled milk on asphalt, flat as dust waiting for rain, or a frog that hadn't made it across a highway. He scooped him up, wondered that he didn't weigh much, thought the old man was light as a feather, but told himself to stop it. The old Indian might be dead and what would he tell the Buchanans? Shouldn't have let him sucker me, he thought. I always let people sucker me. He tried to get him into the front seat on the driver's side, saw that it was useless, and started around to the other door. He couldn't see the old man's eyes because of the cap; must be some kind of miracle that it was still on, like water that you spin in a pail. He was having a hard time with the door handle and couldn't decide whether he should put the old man down into the pickup bed or on the road again.

"You gonna carry me over the threshold, handsome?" the old man whispered and then let out a whooping laugh.

"Oh sweet *Madre de Dios*," Beto said, and carried him over to the side of the truck. He propped him up above the wheel-well even though he felt like pitching him in the back where he could ride the rest of the way in.

"What a ride," the old man howled. "You should have seen your face. You were as puckered up as a cow flop. Didn't think I'd make it, did you?" He smiled and spit out a good one. Beto watched it hit the dust, amazed that the old man hadn't swallowed it. At least he could've choked a bit.

"Damn. Smells like brakes burning."

"Your brains," Beto replied. He watched as the old man pulled off his cap and rubbed his head. He looked closer; the old man had plenty of hair left, silver grey, but with a large bump showing.

"We'd better get you home." He realized he was worried for the old man. That was some bump.

"The Giants saved me," the old man said as his hands navigated the soft spot, "but I almost made it. I would have, too, but she kicked up her heels there and me with it." He rubbed his hands slowly. "I could've ridden her 'til the bell, but the hands, the hands ain't what they used to be." He was still rubbing them, then he fisted his Giants cap and put it right, carefully.

"You did all right, old man; you showed 'em." But Beto couldn't stop thinking about the old man. What if he'd broken a leg or arm or worse? He remembered when he and his friends had found a bum in the weeds of their hidden valley where the streetcars used to run. Finding bums had been easy at the tracks. Bums, sleeping off a drunk under the eucalyptus trees. They did what they always did when they were together, a bunch of them, a gang, but too young to be a real gang. Goddamn lazy bum. Sleeping in the daytime in their place, their special place. Wake him up. Kick him in the leg, hit him with a dirt clod. And Beto, crazy Beto wanted his hat, wanted the tired old fedora that maybe once had held a feather. Beto had advanced slowly, but the bum was waiting, he wasn't sleeping; he grabbed Beto by the leg and let out a frightened scream that turned the valley that was their own secret place into a long hallway with no doors. And how could he have known that the dirt clod in his fist held a stone until he saw the blood through the dirt that showered the side of the bum's face. Then he was sprinting for home; they were all running, but he ran past being tired so he couldn't feel the tiredness as he ran more. "You hurt him," Ray had said. "Damn right," Beto had answered, "he would've killed me. You saw him; he had it coming to him." But Beto had seen the blood on the old skin, pouring out of the weathered flesh, blood on old skin; it didn't look right. It didn't look good, blood on old skin, and an hour later when he had snuck back, and hid in the bushes under the eucalyptus, he had heard the bum groaning still.

He touched the side of the truck and then the arm of the old man. "You drive, okay?" Beto said and leaned through the passenger's side to flip the key off. "When you're ready to go," Beto added when he was next to the old man again.

"Hey, I'm ok, feel fine. I'll be a little sore in the morning is all." They were both quiet for a moment in the morning heat.

The dust had settled and it was still early enough that the pink and rust of the Gulch hadn't whitened under the press of the sun.

"You know, I almost did a complete flip. I forgot to tuck my chin is all. First thing a horse teaches you, tuck your chin." The old man rambled and Beto only half listened. He was staring at the cliff walls, imagining that he was climbing until he found a cave, a hidden overhang. In this overhang were artifacts left behind by the Anasazi: corn, a *mano* and *metate*, bow and arrow, blankets, drawings on the wall, a earthen jug of clear water, paperbacks by King and Ludlum, an Indian maiden in a doeskin bikini. He shook his head.

"I would've stayed on in the circuit." The old man was still talking.

"What circuit?" Beto asked, but he realized after he said it that he should have known.

"Rodeo, but it wasn't much in those days, not like it is now. The Four Corners was all we knew about." The old man leaped off the side of the truck as if he were a much younger man and rummaged under the seat of the cab. He came back with a rumpled, dust-covered but fresh package of Red Man, the chief on the package cover looking just as serene and somber as when he was behind the shelf in Hall's store in Boulder.

"There's a bottle of Jack Daniels. You wanta snort?" the old man asked.

"I know where to find it." Buchanan, a Jack Mormon, hid bottles everywhere. He didn't like Mrs. Buchanan to know, but everyone in Boulder knew where Buchanan's bottles were, including the missus. There was one inside the rear tire that lay flat in the back of the bed under a piece of rock, and there was always one under the seat, or in the dash. Every evening Buchanan would check on the horses. He'd make an announcement, but he wasn't asking for help and no one offered.

"Did I ever show you that buckle I won?"

"For what?"

"Rodeo, bronc bustin'."

"No, you never showed it to me." He waited, and the old man waited. Finally he asked. "Really, when was that?"

"1947, I was All Indian. I never showed you that buckle?"

Beto wasn't interested, but he didn't want to hurt the old man's feelings. Besides, he wasn't in such a hurry anymore, and he was more than relieved that there wasn't any blood showing on the old man. Still, he wasn't sure that he could care less about what the old man was rattling on about and he thought rodeos were boring anyway. "No, whatya mean All Indian?"

"Well, there was All Cowboy and there was All Indian. That was the way they did it in those days. But that was a ride." The old man chuckled and grinned, but didn't make a move to get inside the truck. Instead, he leaned against the side of the pickup with one foot on the running board and propped his arms on the truck bed just like they do at rodeos, and he chewed and spoke, but not in Beto's particular direction.

"That was a ride. I drew a pinto; they called him Paint, of course. Mean crafty pinto, small like a pinto, too, but I mean to tell you that horse knew his business."

"You mean he didn't like to have his *huevos* cinched up."

"They didn't need to do that with some horses, not the pinto. No, he was a horse made for the rodeo, knew exactly what to do, and that pinto didn't like to lose. Best ride of my life and he knowed it." The old man continued to stare wistfully at the rim of the Gulch and the pinion pines that had latched onto the edge.

"Yah, I'll bet, All Indian. What about Mrs. Buchanan, didn't she say anything?"

"She wasn't there."

"Christ, not in '47. I'm talking about this morning."

"I knew what you were talking about." He was fondling his cheek real good now, ready to spit a healthy one. How could he talk with that stuff, Beto wondered. Maybe that was why he always spoke so slowly. He wondered if the old man chewed when he was talking to all the spirits he said were everywhere.

"Come on, let's get going. Here, you drive. I asked you already."

"I don't want to drive. What's the matter with you! You need a drink."

"I don't need a drink and I don't want to drive. Understand, ol' man?"

"Yeah, but I ain't driving."

"Ohhhh," Beto blew out so hard his lips rumbled. He tilted his head back and rotated it. "All right, hop in. I'm driving," he said finally.

Beto drove fast, in third gear when he could, driving like the old man wouldn't.

"You didn't see her, huh?" Beto asked.

"Too early."

"She was hunting eggs?"

"Maybe."

A covey of quail scuttled across the road, topknots angled high, like Prussian cavalrymen at a gallup. Beto didn't brake or ease off the gas; quail were quick. They heard a thud. The quail exploded into the sagebrush, wings leaving a tattoo of air inside the cab.

"Hit one," Beto shouted, his head out the window, foot off the gas.

"A cicada," the old man said. Beto leaned back in and looked at the windshield, saw juice like tobacco spread on the glass, thin fingers reaching for an edge, the black rubber strip.

"Out already."

"Be a day for deerflies too," the old man added.

"Yeah, one helluva hot beautiful day." He looked over. The old man wasn't chomping or sucking now, but a thin line of dribble was seeping down the side of his chin.

"You tired?" the old man asked.

"I didn't sleep well last night."

"The Gulch is too warm for sleep. Coyotes?"

"Naw, I was just thinking too much."

"The owl came to you."

"It wasn't a dream that kept me up. I haven't gotten any telegrams yet, old man." That set the old man to chuckling.

"You don't like your dreams."

207

"Don't give me that Indian bullshit, sound just like my...."
He stopped. Just saying her name worked up a connection and
there were too many connections going on here. You know what
you know and you treat it accordingly, don't you? That was the
way to get by. But the old man saw things, said there were these
other levels, other lives. Horseshit and premonitions. Dolores
had premonitions and guilt. Catholic guilt. Lighting her candles
in the alcove to St. Teresa at the church. She could have won the
state lottery with all the quarters she spent there. And she
sucked it all up, didn't she? St. Teresa, the martyr. Premonitions
and connections. Take the old man on the tailgate. Shouldn't he
have known, felt it in his hands, like he always said? He drove
faster; better to drive than to think. Besides, he'd have to see that
telegram to believe anything.

They could see the boundaries of Deer Creek Canyon now,
a wide stretch where they would cross. A year-round stream and
plenty of cottonwoods and then sandstone behind them. That
was what they saw from the road: the tops of cottonwoods and
the sandstone.

"We're almost there now."

"You don't remember your dreams much, do you?" the old
man asked.

"No. It's because I don't dream much and I don't believe in
them. It's called the subconscious, things you've seen before. The
owl," he added sarcastically. The old man hopped right in.

"Sure you've seen them, in many lives you've seen them, and
not all in the past either."

"Say, you'd better put something on that bump on your head.
Rodeo's no place for an old man." He didn't respond, which
suited Beto fine. This crazy conversation was getting to him.

They crossed the wooden bridge over Deer Creek which
flowed slowly in the summer. Beto downshifted into second
gear.

"Any trout left in the pool?" he asked. There was a wide
pool where the flat sandstone had lipped up, not worn away
yet, downstream from the bridge. The pool was better for
floating than fishing, but there were trout hiding in the cattails

that ringed one side of the pool. They both saw the family at the same time, camping, breakfast smoke low over the fire, a dull green tent, and the father casting into the pool.

"The old one's in there," the old man said.

"He won't catch him."

"Yeah, but he'll see him."

"That'll drive him crazy, and in two more hours his kids will be splashing."

"He's a wise old trout, that one."

"That's the one whose belly you rub?"

"That's the one."

Madre, he thought, they don't come any crazier than this old man. If he were in Echo Park he'd be sleeping in the weeds at the Lake. Rub his hands and he's got a trout, and owls, and pickup trucks like horses. Connections. He's got a world of them.

Beto asked loudly, "why don't you keep a nice fat old trout like that?"

"Noooooo." The old man chuckled softly, and then spit out the window. "You don't keep a trout like that one."

"You don't?"

"No. Besides, he tells me where the young sweet ones are hiding."

"Good God," Beto snorted out of his nose. "I got to tell you, old man, where I come from they can tell stories, all bullshit. Good stories, but none of them are as crazy as yours, and I've heard some great ones." He noticed that the old man was looking at him intently, hands folded on his lap, back straight, cap on right, tight, and smiling, a gold-filling smile, his eyes almost closing. Beto wondered if the old man's hands were telling him something now, and then he thought of how he'd like to get his own hands on something nice and warm and suckable in L.A., where he'd be riding in style. He leaned back in the seat, one hand on the wheel. Ray's '58. Cruise the Strip, slow like, hit the clubs and listen to some real music: salsa, Los Lobos, a little funk — no more of this cowboy-shit and ride around the Lake and chat up the *chavas*. He saw Echo Park Lake floating in the sandstone before him, the fountain shooting straight up, blowing spray on the lovers, the grandfathers with kids in the paddle boats, the pushcart popsicle vendors, the mothers feeding the ducks. He saw cars slowing, young girls hanging out, the Hollywood Freeway crossing the mesa up ahead, trucks blowing smoke as they hit their brakes. Echo Park Lake disappeared and they were between the two long mesas that ran up to Boulder Town and Boulder Mountain. White sandstone now, like a bleached lava flow, the red behind them in the canyons.

"You ever see the ocean, old man?" He spoke out the window at the cooler air that-was blowing over his arm. He shifted into third even though the road was rougher from here on into Boulder, a washboard. He lightly touched the top of the door with his left hand, noticed the cicada had dried and sloughed off; only a brown stain remained. He waited for the old man to reply, not wanting to rush him.

"Sure. I was in San Francisco, you know, and I saw the Colorado before the dam." He used some kind of Indian name for the Colorado.

Beto spoke. "Well, the Colorado's not the same; you can't see the other side of the ocean." Beto reflected on the Colorado for a moment. "What I was going to tell you was that this is what the bottom of the oceans must look like. You know those shells we find all the time?"

"Yes, I know." Beto felt confused; he couldn't remember why he had brought up the subject of the ocean. Something he wanted to tell the old man.

"You knew this was an ocean?"

"Sure. Covered with water, filled up bigger than a lake." A lake, something he wanted to tell him, but the old man couldn't see the Lake, could he, sewer pit of Echo Park. What was he thinking of? Pine appeared, wedged in cracked sandstone, roots slithering over the smooth surface. Sugar pines and ponderosas. A big ponderosa was around the next bend. As they climbed to the higher altitude of Boulder and the sandstone broke up there would be stands of them. Which came first, old man, he thought to ask him. The cracks or the seeds?

"Who's gonna bring in the herd now that you picked me up?"

"I am."

"You're gonna have to bring them back from the Henry's and up over Boulder Mountain through the Waterpocket Fold. They won't like it."

"I know the way."

"Yeah, hell, any cow could find her way. Hey, wipe your chin. You want my maps? You're not swallowing that stuff, are you?"

"I don't need any maps."

"Well, I'll go back out if there isn't anything for me. Buchanan'll like that. You and me together. Didn't you talk to Buchanan?"

"Buchanan had to go to town." Right, Beto thought, he didn't dream anything; he saw Buchanan leave for Escalante early; only one reason to go to Escalante that early. A telegram. What a wily old fox. They were near Boulder now, the first ranch coming up on their right. With the ranch came the sudden green fields and the stringed wire and cedar poles every eight feet to hold the desert out.

"Morgan bring his herd in?" Beto asked.

"Too early, he'll wait until fall hits." They looked out at forty to fifty browsing cattle behind the wire.

"Why'd he bring these in?"

"The new fella's renting his field."

"What'll Morgan do for winter feed?"

"He mowed his fields twice already."

"Someone better tell the new guy how to run cattle."

"He'll figure it out this winter."

"He won't make it then and you know it." Beto was quiet. Ranchers are strange, he thought, only eight ranches here and yet they'd stand back and let a guy run his ranch into the ground. They were distant, but they'd help out any time you needed, always there in an emergency. "He'll figure it out," the old man had said. So that was the way it was: you either figure it out or get the hell out. Let it run its course. Sounded cold, but nothing he could do about it.

"He could run them in the canyons. Deer Creek and the Gulch are warm enough and there's plenty of grazing."

"The ranchers don't like the canyons; they lose cattle and it's too dry in the summer."

"But they're not all dry, for crissakes. You know those cows know where the streams and waterholes are better than we do. Besides, I was talking about the winter not the summer, right? No one in Boulder has ever run a herd down in the canyons in winter, have they? Have they?" Beto didn't wait for a response since he was talking too fast. "No one's tried it, but the new guy should, and no one will tell him not to. Buchanan won't say a word. You know why they don't like the canyons. They're afraid of them." The old man didn't look surprised. Then again, he rarely acted surprised.

"Well?" Beto asked.

"Why would they be afraid of the canyons?"

"I'm not sure." Beto was still talking fast. "But I think they're afraid of those little people down there.

"You mean the Anasazi?"

"Not the Anasazi. I thought they were dead and gone? No, not them, you know — the little people, cause all the mischief."

"The Mokis. I thought you didn't believe in them?"

"Of course I don't. You think I believe in the evil eye too, blessings and all that bruja shit. The Church is crazy enough. I don't believe it, but maybe they're superstitious. They're Mormons, aren't they? You don't understand them, do you? Jesus, even my grandmother is superstitious. She covers all the bases." Beto thought that maybe the old man hadn't understood the point he was trying to make. He knew that he wasn't making much sense to himself either.

"Well, I'll tell you, the canyons are better digs than the mountain any day," he said in order to ease himself out of the situation.

"So you're getting ready to leave us?"

Beto was shocked at the old man's question. "I never said that; depends on what I've got back at Buchanans'."

"You don't have to leave."

"What are you talking about? You don't know nothing yet, old man, and I was just talking about the canyons and mountains."

"Well, you don't have to leave. If you like it so much, why don't you stay?"

"Where? In the canyons?"

"Yes, for you, the canyons."

"Oh, for chrissakes. What are you talking about? Just because your people used to live in them."

"They still do." Beto turned and looked hard at him. He knew he was serious and that didn't surprise him, but why did the old Indian have to figure him out now. Why couldn't the old man just let him slip away as if it were out of his control, and why all this talk about the canyons? When he next spoke it came out mocking, sarcastic. "Old ones. You mean like you. All Indian. You're the only Indian I've ever seen around here and you're a half-breed, old man."

The old man didn't get upset. He could have, but then he decided that this was not the time for it. Besides, he felt too much anger in the young man, anger much of the time. He wished that he could help, but he couldn't ask. Asking would not be the right way. If Beto would just tell him why he must return, that might be the source of his anger, the old man thought. Hopefully, time would work on Slim, run its course, and then there would either be the anger that would eat him up, or there would be the new man. That was the way it worked. He looked at his own hands, knobby, the broken knuckles that hurt in the cold. He remembered when he would wrap those hands around a bottle, and the fists they would make, grabbing, prodding, senseless hands once. He felt his hands grow now as if he were a part of the blood in every vein, as if he were the very life under the thin covering of dust and stained fingernails.

"Someday, son," he said, facing Beto, "you'll meet them, the old ones. They're still here, everywhere I look, like the smoke around a campfire."

Beto snorted through his nose again and, stretching slowly, touched the old man on the shoulder. "You do that, old man, bring 'em to the Lake too. They'll have a great time, fit right in." He smiled, but he was still angry, angry that the old man could possibly have guessed that he might want to leave, that he was driving over this road in hot dust under a sun that hadn't even gotten hot yet, angry about the cows and this business with the canyons. He floated on the hostility like the paddle boats floated on oily water at the edge of Echo Park Lake with no hull visible under the water, and then they were at the ranch. He made the left turn hard onto a road smoothed by long use and yearly applications of crushed rock. He turned with one hand. The road into the Buchanan ranch was long and narrow, the house set far off, the driveway bordered by cedar fencing and corrals. He stopped under a cottonwood that dwarfed the house and the barn. Mrs. Buchanan had started coming out of the house when they turned up the road and she was talking before he shut the engine down.

"Bobby, your grandmother took a fall and broke her hip; she's laid up in a hospital. 'Queen of Angels,' it says." She paused. "I'm sorry to tell you this, son." Beto didn't see her. He heard wind, doors closing in the trees, a horse rubbing its neck over a strand of barbed wire, the rain on the mountain noisy as a spider's web in the birch and aspens. He touched his neck and felt wetness: the ocean? spray from the fountain in the middle of Echo Park Lake?

"What?" he asked stupidly.

Mrs. Buchanan dusted her hands, rounded, work-thick hands. The apron billowed flour dust, filled up the open edge of the sky and the flat fields and the old man in the corner of his eyes, almost to the barn. He wished the old man had stuck around, lean old man in shadows at the barn door. He didn't want to talk about her.

"When did it come, Mrs. Buchanan?"

She answered slowly, like everyone from around here did. Beto wondered if that was because they listened to what each other said or because they didn't say much. He never spoke that slow. "This morning. Bill got a call from Escalante (she said 'Escahlahnt') late last night. He was gonna send Sam for the telegram, but went hisself. Sam was gone anyway, took the ol' red pickup 'fore the sun rose." Beto imagined that the old man had talked to Buchanan in the dark before morning while Mrs. Buchanan was rising; the old man was always up before the sun anyway. Mrs. Buchanan continued speaking. "Sam took off 'fore we could talk to him."

It was a coincidence, Beto decided. He remembered back to the morning, kicking embers with his toes into the rekindled fire. He had been awake for a long time, half the night, the last half. Then, when he had heard the pickup from a long way off grinding down the grade into the Gulch, he was so tired that he hadn't been very surprised. He had known it was the old man coming as soon as he heard the unmistakable sound of the truck. Not that it was something he had felt before it happened; he didn't believe in that. Wasn't life like a car drive anyway? Anything could happen, what with all the other drivers.

"The old man must have known something was up."

"Yes, I suppose so." Her voice didn't carry acknowledgement or surprise. She was direct and friendly, not too surprised by anything after sixty-five years on ranches. He looked at her, saw a round face under a coil of grey, no glasses, a long-wearing dress, brown shoes, and immense breasts that didn't curve her back any.

"Bill says to pay you up to the end of the month and tell you to take as much time as you need, of course. We're both concerned." Did she say that knowing what he was thinking, knowing that he might not be back, that he might be glad to leave. He looked down at the ground, at a red and black ant working his way over the boot and up to the tongue. He suddenly wanted to get out from under this huge cottonwood, get away from these people who were supposed to be cold and aloof. There were too many people reading his mind and letting him go. He knew Dolores had caused all of this. She couldn't let him be happy. Dolores had to have him back.

"Bill told me to tell you he'd've been here hisself but they was at that auction over in Tropic, that you've got a job here if you come back. Don't worry none about that. Sam'll take care of things as best he can." She knew, but there were no questions. He began to feel the guilt attacking the corners of his eyes. He brushed at the ant with his other boot, pushing it into the laces.

"Thanks, Mrs. Buchanan. You mind if I make a call?"

"Lord, no." She patted her apron down hard. "And don't thank me. You just holler if there's any thing we can do. Get in that house and call the hospital."

Beto wasn't going to call the hospital. He didn't want to talk to her in a hospital bed, hear her complain about the room, the nurses she called "negras," the doctors, and how no one understood the pain she had. He didn't want to hear her voice. He'd call Ray. Ray would talk to her. Ray was patient. He even called her "abuela," respectfully. Of course, maybe he should; he'd spent almost as much time at Beto's grandmother's when they were kids as at his own home.

"I'm packing a dinner for you right now. You need it. I don't want your grandmother to think we don't feed you, and son, you're as skinny as Sam."

"You don't have to make anything for me, Mrs. Buchanan." He wasn't hungry, but it wouldn't stop her from wrapping the chicken and sandwiches, the huge slice of homemade pie or cookies that she always packed whenever any trip was made.

"Hush. How old is she?" He wouldn't get away without talking.

"Seventy-nine this February."

"Oh my, and it's her hip. Is she healthy?"

He saw Dolores climbing the long stairs at the front of the house on the hillside, Thanksgiving dinners, planting flowers, picking oranges and complaining. "She's a healthy old goat. I mean, uh, yes, she's healthy alright." And tougher than the venison jerky the old man always brought on round-ups, he thought.

Mrs. Buchanan let his comment pass. She didn't surprise too easily. Besides, she was curious. "Is there anyone who can take care of her besides you?" Funny how they saw things. L.A. was full of people, but there wouldn't be anyone there to watch over her.

"She'll be fine. There's plenty of family to care for her," he lied. "We're an awfully tight family," he lied again. Mrs. Buchanan looked at him pleasantly as if he'd just told her the sun was up in August.

"Uh huh, she'll be glad to have her grandson back, tho'."

"Right." He was backing up now, moving to the kitchen door of the house. He felt the ant in his pant leg. He stopped and shook his pants and then his leg, but it didn't do any good.

"Let's get you into the house now so you can make that call. I'm holding you up rattling on like this." She started walking briskly to the house, not looking back, expecting him to follow. Beto followed. He passed Mrs. Buchanan in the kitchen, almost kicking one of the sacks of bread she had left in the black garbage bags on the floor, and went into the living room to make his call. He wished then that the old man had never come out for him, that he was back in the canyons. But the old man was in on it. He was as much to blame as she was. Goddamn old lady had to fall and break her hip. It was the old man's fault too. Dolores had found him and he had listened.

An hour later as he stood hunched over, leaning into the short oval door of the trailer he had bunked in, an eight by twelve aluminum teardrop painted bright yellow once, he wanted to talk to the old man. He hadn't seen him since they had pulled into the ranch, and now he could see that the truck was gone, so the old man had already left to go back out to the Gulch. He wanted to remind the old man to take the Waterpocket Fold at night because of the lack of water. He wanted to tell him to take some of Mrs. Buchanan's fresh bread, that there was one calf and mother that liked to lay back behind the rest and then wander off, that you could see the Henry's on the blackest nights. That's what he'd like to tell him. Just tell him because they worked together and he wanted to help. That's what they did, help each other out, even when it really wasn't important or needed, and the other guy would nod and say thanks. Hell, he knew he didn't need to give the old man directions to where he was going. He knew the old man could take a pack of winos through the Kalahari if he wanted to. He remembered his first trip, only five months ago, right after he first arrived. It was his first trip across the Fold to the Henry's. The old man had woken him up at three in the morning under a sky as black as a cat's balls.

"See the Henry's. Right over there," he had said. "Always keep your eyes on them; head that way and you'll never get lost in the Fold." He hadn't seen them that night, not until he had walked into them, sure that this old man was crazy. But he did on his next trip. Black islands. The fountain in the Lake. How could he not have seen them before? He didn't need to tell the old man a thing, but he wanted to tell him all the same. Crazy old Indian riding tailgates.

He gathered up his two bags and ducked to get out the door. He stood in the heat and thick light of noonday Utah, an inch under six feet tall, in a Laker's championship t-shirt tucked into black Levis, and high-topped leather tennis shoes. He kicked the stick away from the door and shut it solidly, then stopped to look around quickly as if he'd felt a movement in the air like when a swarm of gnats hit, but there weren't any gnats. He picked up the bags and headed over to the shed on the west side of the barn, threw his bags into the back seat of the Camaro and touched the pocket of his Levis to feel the wad he had. Seven hundred bucks he'd saved, not bad, including this month's pay, but then there hadn't been much to spend it on either. He thought about driving out and harvesting the weed patch he'd planted up Deer Creek, up from the bridge, but he dropped the idea as a waste of time. Besides, he had two fat joints in the other pocket and he'd worry about money after he'd blown what he had. It was time to go. He got in the car, saw the key in the ignition, started it up and let it idle. The old man was a stickler about idling engines, so he let it idle. He looked at the grocery bag of food Mrs. Buchanan had packed for him, hungry now already, about to open it and search for a bag of cookies when a dull glint on the seat next to the bag caught his eye. He thought it must be a tool the old man had left behind when he'd tuned the Camaro for him. He picked it up and immediately noticed the heaviness, felt the supple leather. He dangled it in front of him for a second in the direct light coming through the shed doors that made it hard to see the big oval buckle that swung crazy for a moment until the light hit the rearing horse and 'Santa Fe 1947.' "That sonuvabitch," he swore.

AGUA BENDITA
(HOLY WATER)

Rich Yañez

—*para Polo y Chuy*

Apolonio stood in the courtyard of the Pebble Creek Nursing Home for a short while before he noticed the cement fountain. In its center there was a statue of an angel-faced boy holding a pitcher where water once poured. The fountain was not working, and judging from the boy's chipped limbs and the condition of the round base — drowned with leaves and dirt — it had seemingly been abandoned for years.

Taking a needed break from his third daily visit with his wife, Apolonio, a man who had seen more people die than any one person should have to, looked long at the figure in the fountain. He mumbled something in Spanish, a few words of sadness, and imagined a happier boy — if water would only come out of his *jarra*.

Apolonio went back inside the carpeted hallway that had led him out to the courtyard, past storage closets full of sheets and towels and rooms forty-two through forty-six, two hospital beds to each room. He entered the room near the entrance of the main building only to hear Mrs. Mercedes calling for Eva.

Esta mujer está loca, he thought. He wasn't being mean. It's just that he knew from personal experience what this place with such a beautiful name could do to one's mind. He wanted to go over next to the bed of the Mexican woman and tell her that

Eva, her only daughter, had left hours ago after feeding her lunch, but decided he'd better not or risk having to listen to many questions for which he didn't have answers.

In the other side of the room, Jesusita slept, or so it seemed. It was hard to tell, since Apolonio's wife hadn't spoken or moved voluntarily for many months now.

Apolonio took Jesusita's well-lotioned hands in his, rubbing his large fingers over them. He started to move her fingers like the young therapist had shown him, but something made him stop. He looked into a face he better recognized in years-old photographs and, almost methodically, he shut his eyes and started praying the rosary, picking up where he'd left off before walking out into the courtyard:

"*Dios te salve, María*
— *llena eres de gracia,*
— *el Señor es contigo,*
— *bendita tu eres entre todas las mujeres....*"

Pulling a watch without a band from his pocket, Apolonio realized that he was late for early evening mass at Our Lady of Fatima. He could attend the six-thirty mass if he hurried to Cristo Rey, but he decided to say another rosary for Jesusita at home instead. He'd be up a little after dawn and after feeding his *gatitos* — some his and others strays from around *la loma* — morning mass with Padre Yermo would put him back on schedule again.

Before he left, Apolonio made sure Jesusita was well under the sheets and blue *cobija* he'd brought from home that first night she was taken to Pebble Creek from Vista Hills Hospital. Hope it doesn't get too cold, he thought, putting dirty Kleenex, his Spanish *Reader's Digest* and an empty jar used for holding holy water in a plastic Big 8 Supermarket bag.

He inched his way towards the door, trying to make little noise. It didn't work. Mrs. Mercedes' eyes opened and in what was just above a whisper, she called for Eva again.

"*Venga, mijita, ayúdame.*" She repeated this several times, while managing to bravely raise one of her puny arms in Apolonio's direction. "*Eva, hija...ayúdame.*" Her archaic words sounded like they came from a scratched-up phonograph record.

Apolonio knew she'd keep on if if he didn't do something to comfort the noisy woman. He reached into his pocket, took out his black rosary and placed it in the woman's bony hand. As if she were a baby and the string of blessed beads a pacifier, Mrs. Mercedes' otherwise-blank face grew a gentle smile. Apolonio decided that if he wanted Jesusita to get some sleep tonight her roommate would need to be quiet. He left the rosary, which Jesusita had given him one day long ago.

The business-like nurses would remove it with much difficulty in the morning among their changing of soiled sheets and sponge baths. They wouldn't care if the scared, lonely woman cried for Eva — or God, for that matter. Mrs. Mercedes was just one bed-ridden body among the hundred-plus at Pebble Creek, so they would stick something in her contorted mouth if she made too much of a fuss. Apolonio never forgot his fear when one morning he found a sock tied around Mrs. Mercedes' mouth. In a way he didn't understand, he was almost glad Jesusita couldn't speak. Or else she'd also be exposed to nurses who harbored ill feelings from long hours of underpaid work.

Pebble Creek's superintendent, a Mrs. Hennessey, smiled in disbelief and surprise when Apolonio mentioned fixing the fountain in the building's courtyard. After getting her consent, he went to his truck for his tool box, flashlight and a long coil — *la víbora negra,* as his grandson, Dicky, called it — which he used for clearing the drain.

In his worn army-green overalls, Apolonio crouched over — his shrunken size held together by a life of labor — and put his hand into the pipe leading out behind the building. From the way it felt, the fountain's drainage pipe hadn't been cleaned in a long while. And if his experience with the plumbing of other newly-built buildings was any indication, Apolonio knew that the cheapest, worst materials had been used. The retired plumber would rely on his twenty-eight years with Escondido County Maintenance to complete the arduous task.

Apolonio felt good to be working on the fountain. Finally, after what seemed like forever of being an involuntary witness to Jesusita's demise, he faced something he could fix. The longer he spent straining to get the pipes cleared, replacing all the corroded fittings and hauling heavy pipes and tubings from the back of his truck, the more absorbed he became in his work. Padre Yermo would ask him later in the week why he hadn't visited with him lately, not knowing that Apolonio had taken a vow outside of church.

After a dawn-to-dusk day of work under Escondido's angry sun, Apolonio went home from Pebble Creek content for the first time in a long while. Tired and achy, he didn't look in on Jesusita before he left. He had not checked on her since the late morning. Not that she'd be any different, he sadly thought, a crooked, glassy-eyed image of her former self.

Though his thoughts driving home were of Jesusita, the fountain was still the priority for tomorrow. First thing in the morning, Apolonio would drive to Alamo Plumbing on Alameda Street and get some more materials he needed to complete the job on the fountain. Rafael, his best friend from his days with the County, always had the right supplies for any job Apolonio took on. It would be good for Apolonio to see an old friend again, regaining contact with someone who didn't feel sorry for him because of one thing or another.

Apolonio went to sleep that night and, unlike other nights, he didn't ask God why He had not just taken his wife that April afternoon, rather than prolong her ascent for a total of a year-and-a-half. Instead, after praying on his knees in front of his dresser — which with lit *velas* and a large print of *La Virgen* looked like a church altar — he fell asleep and dreamt of the boy from the fountain visiting him. The boy carried a clay pitcher full of water. Apolonio smiled at his visitor and drank. He was content to keep on sleeping not feeling too alone, and for quite some time after that night, Apolonio awoke without being thirsty for answers.

It was a few days before news of the working fountain made its way around to every room of Pebble Creek. No longer were the Home's residents satisfied with being placed in front of a talk-show-happy television set in the facility's lobby. Even ones that couldn't or wouldn't speak somehow managed to communicate to the nurses that they'd rather be outside in the courtyard. Mrs. Mercedes, for one, had Eva wheel her out every morning and evening to see the fountain, or else she'd refuse to eat.

The courtyard's centerpiece was not the only thing that was resurrected. Encouraged by Apolonio's success, Mrs. Hennessey put some staff people to work on the landscape: some flowers from the Home's front lawn were transplanted, plump bushes were trimmed into matching shapes, and, in a few weeks, the grass would be alive again with color.

Inside the faded bare walls of room forty-seven, Apolonio only hoped that Jesusita could imagine the courtyard from his simple descriptions in Spanish. But numerous doctors and specialists were not even sure if Jesusita heard or saw anything and, if she did, could her brain understand it? The stroke, along with her already weak heart and chronic diabetes, had completely wrecked one side of her brain. When Apolonio tried to speak with his wife or get her to move, he thought of a blink as a cruel settlement.

To make it easier for Apolonio to understand, a member of the Vista Hills Emergency Room's staff, who happened to be the son of a friend, explained Jesusita's predicament in terms Apolonio might recognize. The male nurse told him in Spanish that his wife had suffered a stroke which is like when a machine short-circuits, causing its malfunction. Apolonio, staring at Jesusita's lifeless face, remembered thinking back then at Vista Hills that if the stroke Jesusita suffered was like a machine breaking down, then there must be someone who would provide repair. The next eighteen months changed how Apolonio's own mind understood and registered things — a person in his wife's condition cannot be fixed, no matter how much she is needed and loved.

Apolonio heard Eva push Mrs. Mercedes in a wheel chair into the other side of the room. The younger woman was dressed for work in a dark outfit. She lifted her mother without much effort into the hospital bed. Greeting Apolonio, "*Buenos días, señor,*" Eva left in a rush. She and her mother had just returned from visiting the fountain. Apolonio looked at Mrs. Mercedes. There was a serene look on the old woman's face. Apolonio smiled in Mrs. Mercedes' direction and made a mental note to visit the fountain later that day.

He put a new box of Kleenex and a jar from home on the table next to Jesusita's bed. He opened the jar, put his fingers in the water and made the sign of the cross on Jesusita's forehead, then did the same for himself.

He prayed.

ESMERALDA

Roberta Fernández

Solamente una vez
Amé en la vida
...
Una vez, nada más,
Se entrega el alma
con la dulce y total
renunciación.
— Popular Mexican Song

every three minutes
every five minutes
every ten minutes
every day
women's bodies are found
in alleys & bedrooms/
at the top of the stairs
— Ntozake Shange

I

Esmeralda was the name they gave her, and for a long time
no one seemed to care who she really might be. She had
become a public figure of sorts, sitting for hours each day inside
her rounded glass house. The crowds who routinely exchanged
their coins for a new encounter with fantasy presumed she
would be flattered by the exoticism they projected on her.
Santiago Flores had been the first to refer to her as
"*Esmeralda*." In his daily flamboyant chronicle of local customs
he had called attention to the "green-eyed beauty who greets the
public at the Palace between one and six." For three days in a
row he made reference to her, each time more exaggerated than
before. "A beautiful jewel on display, one befitting the Museo
de Oro which I had the pleasure of visiting on my recent trip to
Lima." Finally, he had called her "*Una esmeralda brillante.
'Esmeralda!'* No name becomes her more." From then on the
public assumed a flattery that was more self-indulgent than

well-intentioned towards the silent, bewildered young woman inside the glass enclosure. Throughout all the commotion she did not speak to anyone unless she was first persuaded that her reticence was actually a form of rudeness, a trait she had been trained to avoid at all cost.

II

When Verónica first started to work at the Palace Theater, before Santiago Flores had created the furor about her, she had walked home by herself in the early evening. Then the situation changed, and Amanda and Leonor had wondered if I would pass by the box office after my dancing class so that Verónica could be accompanied on her way home. After that it was assumed I would meet her at the theater every evening promptly at six.

Verónica was five years older than I was; but, of the two, I had always moved about with more freedom. So, I was surprised she had gotten a job that required such direct contact with a large public. She surprised me further by explaining that the job had been her mother's idea. Since she was taking only morning classes to complete the credits she needed to graduate, her mother had suggested that she now get a full-time job in the afternoons. On the first day she looked for work, she immediately got hired at the theater.

In a sense, Verónica had always been working. Six years before, she had been brought to Leonor's house in a rather mysterious manner. At that time, the twelve-year-old girl had appeared unannounced at the door, accompanied by Isela — her mother — and her grandmother, Cristina Luna. I was sent home as soon as they arrived but from across the street I had watched as the driver of the pickup truck brought in several suitcases. Soon after, he drove off. I waited a while, then was about to head on home when the truck pulled up again. This time Amanda stepped out and hurried inside. The next day I found out that after Cristina and Isela had consulted for a few hours with the other two Luna sisters, Verónica had been left behind. From then on she stayed with Leonor and Hugo, and each day after school she helped Amanda with her work.

From the beginning I sensed that Amanda made a special effort to insure I was never alone with her grand-niece. Several times after Verónica arrived I also noticed that my mother and my aunt Zulema would cut off their conversation whenever any of us children were within hearing distance. So, even though I did not know anything about the new girl's background, I surmised there was something different about her and I withheld all my questions.

Verónica was soon under the tutelage of Amanda and Leonor. Amanda taught her to embroider with beads, and in no time Verónica assisted her with most of her creations. Leonor too spent many hours teaching her about the herbs and flowers in her garden and even though Verónica was not given to conversation she seemed to take in everything the aunts taught her. A little older than the rest of the children in the neighborhood, she was not paired off with anyone and spent most of her time alone, silently sewing glass beads onto Amanda's creations.

Often Amanda's customers remarked on Verónica's beauty. "*Cara de ángel* with a personality to match," was how several of them described her. I did not disagree with their evaluation; still, I wondered if her desire to remain unobtrusive played a role in how they viewed her. Why, I wondered, did she feel she had to be so obliging? What most perplexed me during all those years of observation was that she never ever went home. Even more intriguing was the fact that she did not seem to have the slightest interest in going back to Alfredo's ranch, a place she had called home for many years.

III

"*Verde, que te quiero verde!*" Orión recited in an insinuating tone the minute Verónica and I got back from the theater.

"Orión, quit that," Leonor told him.

At the same time Verónica murmured, "Orión, that's mean. You have no idea how humiliated I am by what's happened."

"Come on," Orión insisted. "Secretly you're enjoying all the attention. You just don't want to admit it. This afternoon I passed by the theater and watched you for a while. These two guys — the Mondragones — were trying to get a smile out of you. But there you were, high and mighty. Completely poker-faced. Come on, Ronnie, loosen up a bit. They just thought you were pretty and wanted to catch your eye. It was their way of complimenting you."

"I know who you mean and they don't strike me as harmless," Verónica replied. Suddenly, she began to cry, softly at first, then uncontrollably.

"Ronnie, you're exaggerating. What is the matter with you?" Orión asked in disbelief.

"Orión, I've already told you to hush up. Leave the room immediately. I want to talk with Verónica in private."

As Orión was swaggering out of the room, I started to go with him but Leonor called me back. "No, Nenita, you don't have to leave. The three of us are going to have a long talk."

I looked at Leonor rather doubtfully but she signaled for me to sit next to her. She then wove her fingers through mine and embraced Verónica with her other arm. I waited for someone to say something. Giving Verónica an uncertain sideways glance, I was relieved to see she had gotten hold of herself.

"Nenita, even though you're only thirteen," Leonor said, "you are much older than your years. I know, already you've had some unhappy experiences but you're really a strong girl." Leonor paused, then went on. "You and I are now going to help Verónica take control of a situation that has made her quite unhappy." Leonor took a deep breath before she turned to Verónica.

"Tomorrow you're not going back to work. I'll talk to the manager myself. I'm also going to give Santiago Flores a piece of my mind. *Lo siento*, Verónica. We should have made you quit your job as soon as the very first statement appeared in the paper. Like Orión just said, these men think they are doing women a favor by showering them with so-called compliments.

Piropos. They think we should be grateful for the attention they give us whether we want it or not. It's really self-indulgence on their part."

Leonor squeezed my hand. "Nenita, when Verónica was about your age, she had a problem. Something happened at Iris's and Alfredo's ranch where Verónica and her mother lived for eight years."

Leonor paused, then looked at Verónica. "Let's see. Your father died in France. In 1943, when you were five. That's when you and Isela went to live at the ranch with Iris. Why don't you tell us what happened at the ranch five years ago? I've only heard other people's version of things. Cristina of course has told me about it. Isela always stuck up for you. So did Iris. That's why she sent her four children to live with Hugo and me shortly after you came."

For a long time no one said anything. Then, Verónica inhaled deeply.

"His name was Omar," she began.

I looked at her as her eyes filled with tears once again.

"*Se llamaba Omar,*" she repeated and looked straight out, trying to give shape to images she must have been struggling to forget in her recent past.

"He was from close by, from Sabinas Hidalgo. At the time he was seventeen. Slender. Like cinnamon tea with milk and sugar. *Dulce. Muy dulce.* I didn't notice him at first but he made me take notice of him. Every night he would leave a present outside my window sill. The first time he left something wrapped in newspaper. I opened it up and found a fresh prickly pear. The following morning I found another one, neatly sliced. It was ripe and sweet. That afternoon I was sitting on the porch. He came towards me. I didn't know who he was but then he extended his open hand, offering me half an orange and a slice of prickly pear. I smiled at him and accepted his gift. He disappeared without a word. The next morning I found a scarlet flower of the *ocotillo* on my sill. Then, a nocturnal blossom of the tall *saguaro.* Every night for two weeks he left something."

"One morning I saw him heading to town with some of the other workers. I waited by the road for their return. Finally I saw the truck coming back. I pretended I was out for a stroll and waved as the truck passed by me. Then, I turned back towards the gate. As I had hoped, he was standing there, waiting for me. I told him I also had a present for him, then I took off my locket and gave it to him. He opened it up, looked at the tiny picture inside, then read my name inscribed in the back. 'Ve-ró-ni-ca,' he said, almost to himself."

"Every night after that I waited up for him by the window. He continued bringing me his usual presents and we would talk for about an hour, then he'd be on his way. One time I asked him to join me on the porch at dusk. He did, but Iris passed by and made him go away. 'You shouldn't be so friendly with the workers,' she said. Then she added, 'Besides, you're too young. People will start to talk.'"

"From then on I wanted to be with Omar all the time. But we couldn't figure out where we could meet during the day without being seen. Then, one night as we were talking through the screen, I suggested that on the following night we wait until everyone was asleep and then meet on the porch. If we were very quiet no one would hear us."

"The next night we carried out our plan. Omar brought me another lovely cactus flower and we sat under the stars, smelling the pink jasmine, continuing to tell each other our life stories. We talked for a long time. Then I said I'd better go in. He put his arm around me and kissed me, softly, on my lips."

Verónica paused, then went on.

"I never found out where he came from. We had not heard him at all. But suddenly Alfredo was yanking at us, screaming obscenities. 'En mi casa no tolero puterías,' he yelled at me. Then he slapped Omar over and over and threw him off the porch. By then all the lights in the house had gone on. There was a lot of confusion and all I remember is my mother taking me to her room. Alfredo was right behind us. 'If she's going to act that way with my workers, why should I wait my turn? Get your *huila*-daughter out of my house at once or from now on I'll take her anytime I want,' he shouted at my mother."

"*Pobre mamá*. She slammed the door behind us, then tried to calm me down. It was about midnight but she called Mamá Cristina who sent someone to pick us up. We packed quickly. By the time the car arrived we were ready. I was terrified for Omar and wanted to see what had happened to him, but mother shoved me into the car ahead of her. Only when we were on our way, out of the ranch did she begin to scold me. I was not trustworthy she kept saying. She'd have to figure out what to do with me. Now she'd need to get a job and think about where we were going to live. Mamá Cristina did not have room for two more people."

"You know the rest," she turned to Leonor. Mama Cristina thought you might be able to keep me for a while."

"What happened to Omar?" I asked.

"I'm not sure. I never saw him again," Verónica replied. "I think Alfredo had him killed. Mother said Iris was unable to give her any definite information."

"*Mira. Verónica*," Leonor said very seriously. "Alfredo may be given to bouts of violence but he'd never have anyone killed. I understand he called the *migra* and had Omar deported."

"How come Alfredo interfered in Verónica's life?" I asked. "She wasn't doing anything wrong."

Leonor sighed. "*Así es*." A moment later she added, "*Mi pobre Iris*. She refuses to leave Alfredo. At least she had the good sense to get the children out of the house."

"You got the five of us because of him."

"I have no complaints as far as that goes." Leonor touched Verónica's cheek to reassure her.

"It's nice of you to say that, Leonor. Makes me feel better. As a matter-of-fact I think I won't quit my job. I'm really being a big baby reacting to harmless comments like I have. Please don't call Santiago Flores either. I'll be able to handle things from now on."

"Are you sure?"

"Positive."

IV

The mystery around Verónica was gone. For the first time since I had met her I felt I no longer needed to be on my guard as we chatted on our way home together. Instead, I thought about the shame she must have felt, being exposed the way she had been, dragged from house to house. And for no reason at all. I was particularly preoccupied with the way she had lost Omar.

"Do you ever think about him?"

"All the time. But I'll never see him again. He was so different from Orion's and Orso's friends. They're always showing off, trying to outdo each other in everything. Omar was a gentle, giving person. It hurt me so much every time I thought about the way Alfredo hit him. Even now it hurts me. Some day I hope to meet someone else like him. But who knows what will happen?"

"It sounds like you're never going to be rid of him. You know my neighbor, Filomena, don't you? She's told me that her husband Martín will always be with her. She says if you lose the person you love when you're still in love, you never get rid of him. That's kind of nice, isn't it? Your mother probably feels the same way about your father."

"Probably. I've never thought about it before."

Verónica got very quiet. Then she looked at me. "I wonder what happens to a person like Iris. Why does she stay with Alfredo? She couldn't possibly love him anymore. I have the impression he hits her too."

"Aura says he does. She hates her father. He got violent with each one of the kids. My father's not like that at all. He's very good with me and I love him very much."

"You're lucky. I barely remember my father. After he died I used to pretend my *osito* was my father and I always made him promise to watch over me. After the incident with Alfredo I realized I didn't have anyone to protect me. In the long run that was probably as bad as losing Omar, for it made me feel very vulnerable."

233

"So we'll all have to take care of you."

After a moment of silence, I turned to her. "But you have to protect yourself too. Especially if you feel so vulnerable as you say you do."

V

Violeta Aguilera, my dance teacher, had kept us rehearsing much later than usual. So when we were finally finished I did not even attempt to change out of my leotard but simply slipped on my pants and ran. When I finally got to the ticket booth the person on the evening shift told me Verónica had already headed on home. "She'll probably be very glad to see you. Hurry," the woman said. "Hurry."

I followed our usual path. When I turned the third corner I spotted Verónica about two blocks up ahead. I ran up one block, then noticed that a white Chevy with big wings was inching along behind her. As I got closer I heard the two guys in the car cat-calling her, "*Esmeralda! Esmeralda!*" Verónica was pretending not to pay attention. I ran faster and got to her side as the two were getting out of the car.

"It's the same *imbéciles* Orión mentioned the other day, she whispered. "I told him they weren't harmless."

"Well, come on. Let's get out of here," I told her just as one of the guys grabbed her and started to drag her to the car. I hit him with my duffle bag and heard the cracking of the castanets against his ear. The other guy reached out for me but my foot hit him exactly at the spot where I had aimed at. He bent over, mumbling, "*Híjole.*" By then the first creep had pushed Verónica into the car. It was obvious they weren't concerned with me. The second one got in the car and they took off.

The street was deserted. I decided I was close enough to Leonor's to run there for help. When I burst in through the door I found Orso and Orión in the living room. "They took her. They took her," I said as I tried to catch my breath.

"What are you talking about?"

"Those guys you said you watched at the theater the other afternoon. Remember you told Verónica they were just trying to give her a compliment. Those guys." I pleaded with Orión. "They dragged her into a brand new white Chevy and zoomed off with her."

"*Los Mondragón*. Come on, Orso. Let's go after them."

As the twins took off, I started to pick up the phone.

"What are you doing?"

I turned and saw Leonor and Hugo. They had been in the dining room all the time.

"I'm going to report a kidnapping to the police."

"No," Hugo said. "The police won't do anything. Let the boys take care of business."

VI

The next day Santiago Flores's column contained the following cryptic statement: "Last night one of my favorite jewels was stolen, then shattered. The perpetrators of the crime were brought to justice but the damage they have committed will be long-lasting. I am sorry for any negligence on my part which may have contributed to what so unexpectedly happened."

VII

For the next several weeks everyone took care of Verónica. Leonor meandered through her herbal patch, carefully selecting sprigs of different properties to prepare into teas and ointments. Blending either *verba del oso* or *maravilla* with baby oil she'd pass the ointment on to Isela who would rub it for hours into her daughter's skin, inducing her to sleep profoundly for long stretches of time. After Verónica woke up, Cristina would soak her in hot minted baths, mixed with either *romerillo* or *pegapega*. Amanda insisted on stating simply that "Verónica had experienced a great freight, *un gran susto*." To alleviate its effects, she ran palm leaves up and down Verónica's body, then burned creosote in clay urns next to her bed.

235

One Sunday morning I stopped by to see Leonor and she insisted I visit with Verónica. "It'll do her good to see you. All this time she's only been seeing us old ladies. Three weeks ago she was in a daze but all the massages and affection we've given her have paid off. She needs to start living again. In fact, Hugo thinks we should have a small dinner party soon. He's going to invite one or two of his colleagues from the college. It'll only be us, and Aura and Marina. You know the boys have gone to stay at the ranch for a while. You are most welcomed to join us. *Andale.* Go in there and perk her up a bit. *Anímala.*"

VIII

Verónica was sitting on a rocking chair looking out the window, her long dark hair and tawny skin glistening with the sunlight. I was surprised she looked as well as she did and told her so.

"Ay, Nenita. Every day Mamá and Leonor, and Mamá Cristina and Amanda have scrubbed me up and down. They've wrung me out, smoked me through, sprayed me from head to toe with so many different perfumes and ointments that I feel like Cleopatra. All day long they've all forced me to concentrate on the moment. On the present. In the beginning they made me tell them in detail what happened that night, first to one, then to the other. I cried and cried with each telling. And they cried with me. In fact, one afternoon Leonor said we were all going to cry for the sorrows of all the women in the family. A wailing session she called it. *Lloronas, todas.* She went first. She talked about Iris. Her favorite child, she said. Yet, there was nothing she could do to help Iris out except care for her children. Since all of us had experienced a run-in with Alfredo at one time or another, we all felt we could empathize with Iris. Later we prayed for her to face up to her situation and to do something about it.

"Then Mamá Cristina spoke. Everyone else seemed to be aware of her affair but for me all this was a revelation. Apparently a lot of people know her 'secret,' but it's better if you don't mention this to anyone. It seems she was never married and my mother was born out of wedlock. She would only refer to the man she loved — my grandfather I guess — as Victor X. She said she was engaged to him, then he went away to fight in the war. Victor X. eventually came back the year before my mother was born. Mamá Cristina claims she was madly in love with him and had her first real passionate experience with him. He didn't bother to inform her he had gotten married to someone else until she told him she was pregnant. Later, when her condition was becoming obvious, her brothers sent her to one of the aunts in another city. For many years, though, she continued seeing Victor X. Then one day he took his other family up north and Mamá Cristina never heard from him again. When she came back, my mother was already six and Mamá Cristina did not try to explain her to anyone. The Luna brothers took care of the two for years and years. In fact, they are still supporting my grandmother.

"Mamá Cristina said she had no regrets for herself and she did not want any sympathy on her behalf. But she did want us to lament for my mother. 'Isela,' she said, 'a child orphaned from a father who had not yet reached the Stygian shore.'"

"My mother took her turn next. She started by emphasizing that wars are waged by men for dominance over other men. But their innocent victims turn out to be women and children. More specifically, she asked us to recall how one particular war, the Second World War, had left its mark on her, robbing her of a husband, a lover, a friend. Making her a widow and the mother of another kind of fatherless child."

Verónica finally paused. "I hadn't realized my mother felt as fragile and confused as she seemed to be that afternoon. It made me think I should help her somehow. But it also made me realize I don't ever want to get like her. Hearing her gave me the courage to take control of my own situation. So when my turn came I spoke in the name of all the women and girls who had experienced a sexual violation on the same day I did. On my own behalf, though, I insisted that the wailing stop. 'I do not want to become a victim', I said and the others cried for me with relief. 'In the end, that is how I hoped you would feel,' Leonor said to me."

"Mamá Cristina raised her hands in triumph, saying we needed to switch moods altogether. It was time to describe sheer happiness, she said, 'even *picardía*, our own or someone else's.'"

"This time she insisted on going first. She told us that a few years after Victor had abandoned her she had thrown all caution to the wind and had gotten involved with someone else. To this day she considers herself in love with the same person. The confession seemed to take my aunts by surprise and they wanted more specific details. But she refused to tell us her lover's name and would only smile mischievously. 'But you never even go out,' Amanda told her. 'The only person you ever go out with is your *comadre* Celia Ortiz. Do you each have a secret lover somewhere? Oh, no! Don't tell me you're sharing a lover. Well, are you?' Mamá Cristina laughed so hard we completely forgot the sad mood we had worked so hard to get ourselves into. So then we told the good stories."

Verónica paused. "The private ones," she finally said.

"Aren't you going to tell me any of them?" I asked, feeling I had been teased, then cheated of the bait.

"No. I'm not. We promised each other we wouldn't repeat those."

"Well, what was your own story?"

"You've heard it already. The one about Omar. But why am I the only one who gets to tell you both my own story and the stories I heard from the others? It's your turn to say something."

I paused for a moment.

Finally, I said, "Okay, I'm ready. Just remember, Verónica, you refused to tell me your good stories. I've got a *pícara* story for you. First I have to ask you a few questions though. What's a *foca?*"

"A seal," Verónica replied rather puzzled.

"What's a *foco?*"

"A lightbulb."

"Right! But remember you've just told me a *foca* is a seal. Let's just say a *foca* is a female seal and a *foco* is a male seal."

Verónica was giving me a dubious look.

I kept my eyes on her all the time I spoke.

"One morning Mrs. Foca was late to work. She waddled into her office half an hour late, swaying to her desk. All her friends noticed how clumsily she was moving but they pretended not to notice. Finally, when she was on her third cup of coffee her office mate turned to her."

"'What's the matter, Foca? It looks like you didn't get much sleep last night.'"

"'That's right, Carmina. I was so tired when I got up this morning.'"

"'*Caray!* Don't tell me you were working till late?'"

"'No it wasn't that. You're not going to believe me, *pero anoche me pasé la noche entera con el Foco prendido.*'"*

Verónica burst out laughing as she grabbed a pillow and hit me on the head with it. Then she put her arms around me, squeezing me tightly.

"Nenita, it's been a long time since I've laughed like this," she managed to say.

IX

Leonor explained to me that David Baca was Hugo's only colleague who could come for dinner on Wednesday.

David was new in town. A recent graduate from Houston, he was now associated with the program on international business at the local college. "David is teaching some business courses but his real love is *norteña* music. That's what really brought him here," Hugo said as he introduced the young man to us. "In his spare time he's making the rounds, recording *conjuntos* on both sides of the border."

"Do you play a musical instrument yourself, David?" Leonor asked as we sat down to eat.

---

* but last night I spent the entire night with the light on/with Mr. Foco lit.

"Just the guitar. I like to sing the old songs and to strum along as I go."

David turned to Verónica. "What about you? Do you like music?"

"All kinds," she said. "But I don't sing or play an instrument."

"Verónica is an artist of a different sort," Leonor quickly chimed in. "Her embroidery is matched only by my sister's. And there's no one who's better at it than my sister Amanda."

"Will you show me some of your work?" David asked.

It was obvious that throughout dinner, with subtle coaching from Hugo and Leonor, David made special efforts to involve Verónica in the conversation. Later, as he was about to leave, he thanked Hugo and Leonor for the invitation. "It's the first time I've had a chance to meet a local family," he said. Then, he added, "I think your niece Verónica is quite lovely."

"Well, David, why don't you ask her to accompany you the next time you go listen to music?" Hugo encouraged him, "I'm sure she'd love to join you. In fact, Flaco Jiménez will be in town tomorrow. Why don't you two go take in his concert?"

X

David and Verónica went out every night after that. Since I was busy with school and dancing classes in the afternoons and Verónica was out in the evenings with David, several weeks passed by without our seeing each other. It was not until almost a month later, when Leonor invited me to join the entire family for a *merienda* in the garden, that I got to see Verónica. At first I thought she looked quite tired but soon she was all smiles, as Leonor said Isela had an announcement to make. The following week, Isela stated, Verónica and David would be getting married in a small, private ceremony; after that they would be going to Acapulco for a brief honeymoon.

The announcement did not come as a surprise, and everyone managed to look cheerful and to wish the couple well. When I finally got a chance to get close to Verónica, I asked her outright, "How do you feel about all this?"

"I'd like to think I'm happy," she replied.

XI

When the baby was born, Leonor claimed that Verónica had been lucky to have had such a healthy premature baby. "A bouncing six and a quarter-pounder," she told me when I went to see Verónica at the hospital.

"Let's go take a look at her," David suggested as he, Leonor and I headed to the nursery. "See if you can pick her out."

"That might get you into trouble," Leonor chuckled. Then she pointed to the infant in the third crib. "There she is. Verónica's little Destino."

"Is that going to be her name?" I asked in surprise.

"Veronica insists on naming her Destino Dulce," Leonor said softly.

"She is pretty set on calling her that." David smiled. Then he added, "A girl named Destiny. I guess I'll just have to call her my little DeeDee."

He really thinks Destino is his baby, I thought. Suddenly, a strange feeling crept over me as I watched David. I realized then that he was very naive and I wondered what disappointments, if any, lay ahead for all three of them. Looking at the tiny baby, I considered whether Verónica had willingly stepped inside an invisible, but nonetheless binding, wall of self-delusion.

XII

Last night I dreamed I was inside a green glass prison, holding Destino on my lap. Strangers were peering at us, waving bits of paper in their hands, their mouths forming sounds I could not hear. I looked at one face after another impassively, wondering who those people were, amazed that they felt compelled to convey a message, a wish perhaps, to Destino and me. Suddenly a space opened up among the crowd and

Verónica was making her way through the path. As she crashed through the glass to get to us, the voice of the crowd rang out in a booming sound, "*Esmeralda! Esmeralda!*"

"I'm taking my Destino with me," Verónica whispered. "From now on, she will always be by my side," she said as she picked up the baby, then made her way outside again. The crowds pushed against her but one way or another she made her way through them. Once she was out in the open, someone shouted, "She's gone!" And the masses ran after Verónica, trying in vain to catch up with her. "*Esmeralda!*" they called. "Don't leave us, *Esmeralda*. What will we do without you?"

Alone at last, inside the glass house, I was fascinated with the walls which slowly began to disintegrate in kaleidoscopic fashion. In place of the green glass, images of flowers and gems flashed past me. Before my eyes, sprigs of dazzling dahlias glided through rubied milk, and saffron-colored sunflowers twirled by on minted teas. I saw clusters of crape myrtle floating on melted jade; and slowly all traces of the glass prison disappeared. I found myself, instead, inside a house made of golden raffia and in the darkness, a topaz presence began to glow. Sunbursts of volcanic warmth emanated from its center and all around me, *copal* and *creosote* burned in clay urns. Humming softly as nocturnal blossoms of the tall *saguaro* filled the room, I gave myself up to the energy of a powerful essence which began to breathe on me. Suddenly, a winsome face emerged out of the darkness and a cinnamon-colored stranger smiled at me as he offered me half an orange and a handful of freshly-cut cactus fruits. I smiled back, reaching out for his gifts.

FIREWORKS

Danny Romero

All morning long the two of them sat in the attic atop a ladder, looking out towards the park through a hole cut in the roof. By the picnic benches stood gangsters, smoking cigarettes and drinking cans of Schlitz. Dressed in muscle shirts and Levis, some of them wore dark glasses and the sleeves of their Pendletons rolled all the way down. Dark-skinned and dark-haired for the most part, they gathered around a fire in a trash can. Their women close by, they stood with a lean, slouched over with hands in pockets. Flashes of blue light broke through the fire as they tossed cherry bombs into the can. Some stood off to the side, throwing bombs and firecrackers at each other. They screamed and laughed, throwing things and wrestling, passing a pipe in a circle.

"Did you see that, Raymond, you see that?" one boy asked the other, pointing and nearly falling from his perch.

"Where, Manuel? Where?" he answered, crowding for some space, sticking his head further out of the hole. They both smiled at the sounds that came from the park.

Descending the ladder, the two sat on boxes in the dusty darkness. A light film of sweat covered both their bodies. "S, s, s, s, s, pop, pop, pop, pop, pop," said Raymond to the other. He threw a red package at his brother. The brother picked it up.

"When do you think he'll bring 'em?" Manuel asked.

"He said before dark," came the answer. Manuel tore the picture of a peacock off the package and carefully placed it in his pocket. He crumpled up the paper, letting it drop, then began separating the firecrackers.

"He said he'd bring us twenty packs," said Raymond. His brother handed him eight, keeping the same number for himself. They stood, stuffing their pockets, making sure they had matches. Below them they could hear their parents in the kitchen. The two walked on planks spread about for a floor; sometimes, hearing a cracking sound, they held onto boxes or the beams. "What the fuck are they doing up there?" they heard their father saying. The two stepped carefully over wires and made sure to stay on the lighted path. At the door, they stood for a moment, looking off into the darkest corner at a pile of straw and wondered if it really was a rat's nest like their cousin Tony had told them. They switched off the light and closed the door behind them.

"What time'd your brother say he'd be home?" the father asked. He was reaching into the refrigerator for a beer. He opened it, closed the door, and took a drink. The mother stood, her back to the boys, washing dishes in the sink. One of their sisters warmed a *tortilla* on the stove. The father sat down at the table, foam on his moustache.

"He said before dark, Daddy," said Manuel. He went and stood near his father, putting his elbow on the man's knee. Raymond looked into the sink, just tall enough to see his mother's hands working. He stuck his hand into the water, playing with the suds. "Don't play with the water," the mother said, swatting his hand away. "Why don't you go watch television or go outside."

"Gigantor's coming on," said the sister. She was spreading butter on the now warm *tortilla*, the butter easily melting.

"Gi-gan-tor. Gi-gan-an-an-tor," began Manuel. His sister joined him singing as they left the room. The father followed, the two children walking stiff-legged with their arms stretched out in front of them. "Gi-gan-tor. Gi-gan-an-an-tor. Gigantor's a great big robot, robot, robot...."

"I'm going outside," Raymond told his mother.

In the yard the boy picked up avocados which had fallen on the ground from the tree. He made sure he only picked up the green ones as they were still hard. With a screwdriver he made holes where the stems had been, and inserted firecrackers. Having gathered and made bombs out of the eight he had, he set them down on the porch. Grabbing a hold of one of them and striking a match against the fence pole, he threw it into the sky. It exploded with a burst of blue smoke and sound, the bits of avocado raining down into the yard and on the boy.

He tossed another one into the air and watched it smoke and fizzle out. He ran towards the back of the yard, looking for it among the ivy at the fence. He poked his head through a hole in the ivy, looking into the park. Here he got a closer look at the gangsters and could hear their talk. "Give me another *colorada*," one with dark glasses asked his friend, taking a drink from his beer and wiping his mouth. "*Orale* homes, check out the *ruca*," said another, while two over to the side said, "Fuck those niggers, *ese*, they're just talkin' out their assholes." Raymond backed away, fearing they would see him, and from a little ways back watched a couple kissing against the wall of the pool, the girl's tits squashed in the other's hands, their lower bodies grinding into each other's.

Raymond stepped out of the clearing and walked towards the avocado tree, trudging through the foot high weeds. At the tree he hoisted his body up by his arms to the first perch. From there he climbed higher, walking carefully on the limbs and hoisting himself up further until he came to a spot twenty feet above the ground. He reached into his pocket, sitting on a large branch. He lit a firecracker half whose gunpowder had burned away and tried to smoke it like a cigarette. He remembered his father used to smoke and sometimes saw his cousin smoking while he walked down the street. He knew it wouldn't be the same, but tried it nonetheless. He climbed down after coughing from the smoke, hoping he didn't smell like it, but figuring he could always say it was because he had been popping firecrackers that his breath smelled like smoke.

When dinner time came, he went back into the house where his brother and sisters already sat eating fried chicken and drinking Mother's Pride root beer. The two parents had gone out earlier and bought the food for the holiday. All six of them sat in the living room, the father sitting behind a T.V. table, the mother beside him on the couch, and the children on the floor. "Will you kids be quiet," said the father, "I'm trying to watch the news." On the screen the newscaster reported on other celebrations across the nation.

"Daddy, can we see the fireworks?" asked Raymond.

"No, just wait until dark," said the younger of the sisters.

"You shut up," said Raymond. "Daddy, can we see the fireworks?"

"Will you stop bothering your father?" said the mother.

"Yeah, but can we..." said Raymond.

"Will you hold on," said the father, standing and walking out of the room. He came back carrying a small bag. "Here," he said, handing his sons some firecrackers. The two boys looked at him, wondering where he had got them.

"I bought them at work," he said, "You wanna hear one of these?" He showed his sons a cherry bomb he held in his hand. The boys agreed, following him out onto the front porch. In the yard, the father set the bomb underneath a plastic dump truck of theirs. The two boys covered their ears, big grins on their faces, and standing as close as they could without their father yelling at them to "get the fuck away from there, you stupid apes!" The father lit the fuse and they all stepped back, the mother and two daughters watching from behind the screen door as the truck blew into pieces and the parts flew thirty feet into the air.

"Whoooooooooooo," both Manuel and Raymond said at the explosion, running into the cloud of smoke, their arms raised above their heads, smiling and jumping around. They chased the parts that flew about and rounded them up, taking them to their mother and sisters to show them the force of the explosion. "Look at this, look at this," they said, holding up a half-burned plastic wheel and the scarred remains of the cab. They put all the pieces on the porch to show their brother and cousin when they came home. The family walked back into the house.

Their brother showed up just before it got dark, saying, "Here you go," and handing the two their firecrackers, but only coming home with ten packs and a couple of cherry bombs. The two looked at each other and could almost have cried, but didn't, not bothering to ask where the rest of their money had gone. The entire family came out to watch the fireworks and bombs go off.

"Be careful with the cars," the mother said to the three boys standing at the curb, throwing firecrackers into the street. "I don't want any of you blowing off a hand either," she continued.

"Ah, mama, nothing's gonna happen to us," the older boy turned and said. His younger brothers agreed in silence, barely able to control their excitement. The two sisters stood in the yard, twirling sparklers in their hands.

"Eh, you little monkeys," the father yelled at them when they threw the sparklers into the air, threatening to kick their asses if the house or any of the trees caught on fire. He stood drinking beers and setting off the larger cones, the smoking log cabin and Piccolo Pete's. "You need a punk, punk," he would say when asking his children if they wanted him to light their sparklers with a punk from the fireworks package.

"You want to hold the California Candle?" the father asked the older boy. He agreed, feeling old and important, standing on one of the ledges of the porch, his father poised to light the fuse. With the fuse lit sparks began pouring out of it and in a panic the son held it over his head, the sparks falling down on him, with a big smile, dancing about from the burns of the sparks. "Give me that, you fool!" the father said, wrenching the candle away from him and holding it away from his body with an extended arm. "This is how you should have done it," he said.

From time to time the father would go inside the house and watch the television fireworks from the coliseum on KTLA Channel 5. He would watch it with some pride, having been a Marine during the war. "Daddy, come out and see the bomb," Manuel said through the screen door. "In a minute," said the father, thinking for a second about the gangsters in the park and the kids not caring less if it was the nation's birthday, only knowing it was a day to make noise, eat hamburgers and fried chicken, watch fireworks and party. And already getting drunk he would start throwing firecrackers in the house, the kids laughing and smiling at the door, looking in, and the mother complaining.

"Don't do another one," the mother said, and the husband set off two more.

"I'm not kidding. Go outside and do that, come on now...." And the father lit a whole pack, the kids at the door laughing and smiling.

At ten o' clock the fireworks were all gone and the girls were inside. The three boys still stood outside, watching the sky for rockets flying overhead. "Hey, hey, look at that one!" they'd say, pointing to the flying sparks and colors before they disappeared, just as soon as they had come into sight. They also searched in the dark for firecrackers that hadn't gone off. They'd crack them in half, sprinkle a little gunpowder and lay the pieces in it. One would crouch down and light the powder while another stomped on it.

"Eh, what are you guys doing?" said the cousin, walking over to them from out of the darkness, alcohol on his breath and his hands in the pockets of his coat, a cigarette in his mouth.

"You got any firecrackers?" said the oldest brother.

"Yeah, I got some," he said, pulling out a few packs and some cherry bombs. He put them down on the porch. Everyone helped themselves.

"Hey, these are loooouuuud," said Raymond and Manuel. "Ay *Dios mio*. You have more," said the mother from the screen door. She had her fingers in her ears.

"Yeah, *tía*," the cousin said, "I brought some home with me." Afterwards, thinking no one was watching, the cousin walked over to the side and took a drink from a beer he had in a bag. They'd all turn around just before he saw them looking. "Eh, get out of the way," the cousin said, lighting a cherry bomb with the cigarette in his mouth, "watch this." He threw the bomb and it rolled by the tree in front of the house, going off with a loud bang and a flash of light.

"You got anymore?" they all asked each other after a while. They walked into the back yard, climbed the roof of the garage and looked over towards the park and railroad tracks. There they saw groups of flashes followed by loud explosions in the dark. "That was a motherfuckin' loud one," said the cousin. They all agreed, the older boy saying, "Yeah, those bloods over there have a bunch of stuff, huh?"

Later they climbed down and stood in the open yard, looking up into the sky. They grabbed bricks from the broken-down incinerator in the yard and pretended they still had fireworks and bombs left, throwing them against the already weakening side of the garage, imagining the sound they made against the wood was in fact a loud explosion following a bright flash. And when they tired of that, they all went inside, it already going to be midnight and the day almost over. And the two youngest would always take the longest to fall asleep, their cousin snoring loudly from the booze. And the two would listen to the sounds that still went on without them, imagining they could still see the flashes and colors in the dark sky, and hoping the year would pass quickly.

LA PUERTA

José Antonio Burciaga

It had rained in thundering sheets every afternoon that summer. A dog-tired Sinesio returned home from his job in a mattress sweat shop. With a weary step from the *autobús*, Sinesio gathered the last of his strength and darted across the busy *avenida* into the ramshackle *colonia* where children played in the meandering pathways that would soon turn into a noisy *arroyo* of rushing water. The rain drops striking the *barrio's* tin, wooden and cardboard roofs would soon become a sheet of water from heaven.

Every afternoon Sinesio's muffled knock on their two-room shack was answered by Faustina, his wife. She would unlatch the door and return to iron more shirts and dresses of people who could afford the luxury. When thunder clapped, a frightened Faustina would quickly pull the electric cord, believing it would attract lightning. Then she would occupy herself with preparing dinner. Their three children would not arrive home for another hour.

On this day Sinesio laid down his tattered lunch bag, a lottery ticket and his week's wages on the oily tablecloth. Faustina threw a glance at the lottery ticket.

Sinesio's silent arrival always angered Faustina so she glared back at the lottery ticket, "Throwing money away! Buying paper dreams! We can't afford dreams, and you buy them!"

Sinesio ignored her anger. From the table, he picked up a letter, smelled it, studied the U.S. stamp, and with the emphatic opening of the envelope sat down at the table and slowly read aloud the letter from his brother Aurelio as the rain beat against the half tin, half wooden rooftop.

Dear Sinesio,

I write to you from this country of abundance, the first letter I write from los Estados Unidos. After two weeks of nerves and frustration I finally have a job at a canning factory. It took me that long only because I did not have the necessary social security number. It's amazing how much money one can make, but just as amazing how fast it goes. I had to pay for the social security number, two weeks of rent, food, and a pair of shoes. The good pair you gave me wore out on our journey across the border. From the border we crossed two mountains, and the desert in between.

I will get ahead because I'm a better worker than the rest of my countrymen. I can see that already and so does the "boss." Coming here will be hard for you, leaving Faustina and the children. It was hard enough for me and I'm single without a worry in life. But at least you will have me here if you come and I'm sure I can get you a job. All you've heard about the crossing is true. Even the lies are true. "Saludos" from your "compadres" Silvio and Ramiro. They are doing fine. They're already bothering me for the bet you made against the Dodgers.

Next time we get together I will relate my adventures and those of my "compañeros"...things to laugh and cry about.

Aurelio signed the letter *Saludos y abrazo.* Sinesio looked off into space and imagined himself there already. But this dreaming was interrupted by the pelting rain and Faustina's knife dicing *nopal,* cactus, on the wooden board.

¿Qué crees? — "What do you think?" Faustina asked Sinesio.

¡No sé! — "I don't know," Sinesio responded with annoyance.

"But you do know, Sinesio. How could you not know? There's no choice. We have turned this over and around a thousand times. That miserable mattress factory will never pay you enough to eat with. We can't even afford the mattresses you make!"

Sinesio's heart sank as if he was being pushed out or had already left his home. She would join her *comadres* as another undocumented widow. Already he missed his three children, Celso, Jenaro, and Natasia his eldest, a joy every time he saw her. "An absence in the heart is an empty pain," he thought.

Faustina reminded Sinesio of the inevitable trip with subtle statements and proverbs that went straight to the heart of the matter. "Necessity knows no frontiers," she would say. The dicing of the *nopal* and onions took on the fast clip of the rain. Faustina looked up to momentarily study a trickle of water that had begun to run on the inside of a heavily patched glass on the door. It bothered her, but unable to fix it at the moment she went back to her cooking.

Sinesio accepted the answer to a question he wished he had never asked. The decision was made. There was no turning back. "I will leave for *el norte* in two weeks," he said gruffly and with authority.

Faustina's heart sank as she continued to make dinner. After the rain, Sinesio went out to help his *compadre* widen a ditch to keep the water from flooding in front of his door. The children came home, and it became Faustina's job to inform them that *Papá* would have to leave for a while. None of them said anything. Jenaro refused to eat. They had expected and accepted the news. From their friends, they knew exactly what it meant. Many of their friends' fathers had already left and many more would follow.

Throughout the following days, Sinesio continued the same drudgery at work but as his departure date approached he began to miss even that. He secured his family and home, made all the essential home repairs he had put off and asked his creditors for patience and trust. He asked his sisters, cousins and neighbors to check on his family. Another *compadre* lent him money for the trip and the coyote. Sinesio did not know when he would return but told everyone "One year, no more. Save enough money, buy things to sell here and open up a *negocio*, a small business the family can help with."

The last trip home from work was no different except for the going-away gift, a bottle of *mezcal*, and the promise of his job when he returned. As usual, the *autobús* was packed. And as usual, the only ones to talk were two loud young men, *sinvergüenzas* — without shame.

The two young men talked about the *Lotería Nacional* and a lottery prize that had gone unclaimed for a week. "*¡Cien millones de pesos!* — One hundred million pesos! *¡Carajo!*" one of them kept repeating as he slapped the folded newspaper on his knees again and again. "Maybe the fool that bought it doesn't even know!"

"Or can't read!" answered the other. And they laughed with open mouths.

This caught Sinesio's attention. Two weeks earlier he had bought a lottery ticket. "Could...? No!" he thought. But he felt a slight flush of blood rush to his face. Maybe this was his lucky day. The one day out of the thousands that he had lived in poverty.

The two jumped off the bus, and Sinesio reached for the newspaper they had left behind. There on the front page, was the winning number. At the end of the article was the deadline to claim the prize: 8 that night.

Sinesio did not have the faintest idea if his ticket matched the winning number. So he swung from the highest of hopes and dreams to resigned despair as he wondered if he had won one hundred million pesos.

Jumping off the bus, he ran home, at times slowing to a walk to catch his breath. The times he jogged, his heart pounded, the newspaper clutched in his hand, the heavy grey clouds ready to pour down.

Faustina heard his desperate knock and swung the door open.

"*¿Dónde está?*" Sinesio pleaded. "Where is the lottery ticket I bought?" He said it slowly and clearly so he wouldn't have to repeat himself.

Faustina was confused, "What lottery ticket?"

Sinesio searched the table, under the green, oily cloth, on top of the dresser and through his papers, all the while with the jabbing question, "What did you do with the *boleto de lotería?*"

Thunder clapped. Faustina quit searching and unplugged the iron. Sinesio sounded off about no one respecting his papers and how no one could find anything in that house. *¿Dónde está el boleto de lotería?* — Where is the lottery ticket?

They both stopped to think. The rain splashed into a downpour against the door. Faustina looked at the door to see if she had fixed the hole in the glass.

¡La puerta! — "The door!" blurted Faustina, "I put it on the door to keep the rain from coming in!"

Sinesio turned to see the ticket glued on the broken window pane. It was light blue with red numbers and the letters *"Loteria Nacional."* Sinesio brought the newspaper up to the glued lottery ticket and with his wife compared the numbers off one by one — *Seis - tres - cuatro - uno - ocho - nueve - uno - ¡SIETE-DOS!* — Sinesio yelled.

"¡No!" trembled a disbelieving and frightened Sinesio, "One hundred million pesos!" His heart pounded afraid this was all a mistake, a bad joke. They checked it again and again only to confirm the matching numbers.

Sinesio then tried to peel the ticket off. His fingernail slid off the cold, glued lottery ticket. Faustina looked at Sinesio's stubby fingernails and moved in. But Faustina's thinner fingernails also slid off the lottery ticket. Sinesio walked around the kitchen table looking, thinking, trying to remain calm.

Then he grew frustrated and angry. "What time is it?"

"A quarter to seven," Faustina said looking at the alarm clock above the dresser. They tried hot water and a razor blade with no success. Sinesio then lashed out at Faustina in anger, "You! I never answered your mockery! Your lack of faith in me! I played the lottery because I knew this day would come! *"¡Por Dios Santo!"* and he swore and kissed his crossed thumb and forefinger. "And now? Look what you have done to me, to us, to your children!"

"We can get something at the *farmacia!* The doctor would surely have something to unglue the ticket."

"¡Sí! ¡O sí!" mocked Sinesio. "Sure! We have time to go there."

Time runs faster when there is a deadline. The last bus downtown was due in a few minutes. They tried to take the broken glass pane off the door but he was afraid the ticket would tear more. Sinesios fear and anger mounted with each glance at the clock.

In frustration, he pushed the door out into the downpour and swung it back into the house, cracking the molding and the inside hinges. One more swing, pulling, twisting, splintering, and Sinesio broke the door completely off.

Faustina stood back with hands over her mouth as she recited a litany to all the *santos* and virgins in heaven as the rain blew into their home and splashed her face wet.

Sinesio's face was also drenched. But Faustina could not tell if it was from the rain or tears of anger, as he put the door over his head and ran down the streaming pathway to catch the *autobús*.

BROWN HAIR

Ana Baca

His thick, straight hair was parted neatly on the side, the brownness of it matching the color of chocolate. He clutched his gray felt hat in one hand and closed the door behind him as he called to his wife, "Theresa, I'm home. Come here. What do you think?" He held his hat to his chest, placed one fist at his waist, and smiled a toothless grin. "See. I finally went to the barbershop today. What do you think?"

Theresa slowly trudged to the doorway of the kitchen, wiping her hands on her apron which was spotted with various sizes and colors of stains. "What do you want now, *viejo*? Can't you see I'm busy. Oh my God!" Theresa suddenly gasped, staring wide-eyed at her smiling husband. "*¡Ave María Purísima!* What in the name of God have you done to yourself, Leonisimo?"

"What? Don't you think I look younger? Twenty years younger, at least." Leonisimo turned, opened the closet door, and grinned at himself in the mirror. He pressed the long, bony fingers of his right hand over both cheekbones, stretching the skin under his eyes. "Except for these wrinkles." Then he turned back around, left the closet wide open, and stepped over to his wife, quickly sashaying his wet lips over her nose.

"Stop it, *viejo*. You look like a...." Theresa paused, staring intensely at her husband. She shook her head from side to side, knitted her eyebrows and suddenly let out a booming laugh. "You fool, Leonisimo. You fool, that's all I can say." Theresa turned to resume her chores in the kitchen and then stopped in mid-stride. She stood with her back to her husband and paused for several seconds. She rolled her eyes, closed them for a brief moment, and without turning to her husband, she whispered, "And all, just for a woman."

Leonisimo stood shocked. He wasn't exactly sure if he had correctly heard his wife's words or not. He nervously ran one hand through his hair, scratched his stomach, and slowly rocked back and forth on his short, bowed legs. Leonisimo stopped, walked toward the potbellied stove and absentmindedly released his hat from his sweaty fingers onto the wooden rocking chair. He briefly bent his head as if in deep thought and then darted into the kitchen.

"What do you say we go dancing tonight, *mi vieja querida?* Tonight they're holding a dance at the hall in Los Jarros." The tiny man danced around his wife, humming a *ranchera*. "*Andale,* what do you say, Theresita? Let's go, yes?" He grabbed her hand which was covered with a film of flour, lifted it into the air and danced under it.

"No, I shall say not, *viejo tapado,*" Leonisimo's wife replied in a tone that could only be interpreted as scorn. She snatched her hand from her husband's, swung her shoulders back toward the counter, and began violently kneading her dough.

Leonisimo's smile vanished from his lined, olive-complexioned face. He took a few steps back away from his wife, braced himself against the white-washed wall behind him, and shoved his hands down into the deep pockets of his khaki trousers, readying himself for the coming onslaught.

Except for Theresa's heavy breathing and the echoes of punching that her reddened knuckles made against the mound of *masa*, silence passed between the couple. Leonisimo sighed and methodically raised his eyes from the wood floor up to the ruddied face of his fleshy wife.

"What do you know about dances in Los Jarros anyway, Leonisimo? Have you been running around with those shiftless people?" Theresa eyed her husband as she blurted this out between punches.

"Eh? What do you mean?" Leonisimo asked suspiciously. "Not everyone from Los Jarros is lazy," he suddenly pronounced, his mind made up to take on the cause of defending the people from the poorer area of town.

"Oh? And how would you know, Leonisimo? Have many friends from Los Jarros, do you?" Theresa asked her husband sarcastically.

Leonisimo stepped away from his harbor against the wall. "What are you talking about, *vieja*? Just because you live in this warm house, and are *güera*, and your father was a rich sheepman doesn't give you the...." Leonisimo stopped and rethought his tone. "Do all those things give you the right to look down on them?"

"Ay, what's this, Leonisimo, suddenly the Savior? You planning to run for office like Senator Cha-viz," Theresa quipped. She stared at her husband unbelieving, the furrows on her high forehead intensifying. "You know well and good what I'm talking about, *viejo asqueroso*," Leonisimo's stalwart wife frowned at her husband.

"What? What, Theresa? What do you want me to say when I don't know what you're talking about? You don't make sense!" Leonisimo raised his voice, attempting to draw out the charade.

"Okay!" Theresa pounded the table in one last exasperated effort to pry the truth from her husband. "Okay," she said more softly as she turned toward him. "Leonisimo, Martha tells me she saw you...."

"Saw me where? What did that gossip say?"

"She saw you in the *plaza* with...." Theresa waited, turned again toward the counter and lowered her eyes. "With that woman. Again."

Leonisimo shook his head from side to side and scowled. "That damned Martha, always carrying stories. Doesn't she have anything better to do? Doesn't she have work to do? Where's her husband? Letting her roam the streets."

"How dare you, Leonisimo?" Theresa's watery gaze flew from the countertop to her husband's drawn face. "You've done it. Now you can't even take responsibility for your actions and you blame wrongdoing on Martha. How dare you, *viejo asqueroso*. I really can't trust you, now."

"What? What did I do wrong?" Leonisimo looked at his distraught wife. He breathed deeply and finally exclaimed, "Okay. Okay. I may be an old man, but no *estoy muerto*. I still enjoy the company of beautiful women. Okay? Maria Ríos just brought me a plate of *empanadas de ciruela*. She told me they were right out of the oven, so I bent to smell one she held in her fingers. I couldn't help it if my nose nuzzled her hand. Is that a crime? Is that what you wanted to hear — a confession?"

Theresa stared blankfaced at her husband of fifty years. She thought of their life together: her long-awaited but troubled courtship in which her father's stubborn refusal to allow their marriage incited her husband's deep resentment; the feud between her father and husband which lasted until her father's death; their eight children; the burial of two; the loss of acres and acres of land to the *rancheros*. It had been a difficult life. But why then, could they both still smile? Theresa's face suddenly jerked as if she had been awakened from a restless sleep. She glanced over at her husband's bent figure.

Why was it, Theresa wondered, that her father could never accept Leonisimo? He was kind and hardworking and always joking just like her father. Her mother liked her husband, even though she didn't always show it, especially in front of her own husband. How was it that her mother displayed nothing but loyal devotion to her father? She thought about her mother's never-ending patience, her understanding and even her willingness, it seemed, to be second fiddle to her father's work. Theresa wondered about her own battles with her husband which seemed to be ongoing. If it wasn't this, it was that, and now it was this woman. Leonisimo was no saint, and her father must have detected this years ago.

"Okay, if you want a confession, you'll get a confession, Theresa." Leonisimo fell to his knees, closed his eyes, and folded his hands. "Forgive me, father, no mother, for I have sinned. It's been two days since my last...."

"Oh, Leonisimo, get up, get up. And stop it. Shame on you." She raised her eyes to the ceiling and softly said, "He doesn't mean to jest. Forgive him." She lowered her eyes down to her husband's crouching body. "Be serious, Leonisimo. It's no joke. You always make a joke out of everything."

"What joke, Theresa?" he said breathlessly as he began to lift himself off the cold floor. "Ay," he uttered as he stood with his back bent and his hands on his tailbone. "My old bones just aren't what they used to be. *Ay, que dolor.*"

Theresa watched her husband out of the corner of her eye, but instead of helping him up, she stepped to the wood stove, bent to rekindle the hot ashes, scooped a tablespoon of *manteca pura* out of a tin, and smeared it into several bread pans.

"If you can't laugh, why live, Theresita?" Leonisimo moved behind his wife and gently reached up to touch her on the shoulder. He squeezed it softly and then slowly ran his hand down her arm and placed his hand on top of his wife's. She stopped greasing the sheet and stood still.

"When I was fifteen, Theresita, I found out something. Something important. Very important." Leonisimo moved one hand up to the base of his wife's neck and gently smoothed the dark wisps of Theresa's hair. He tilted his head upward and whispered, "This tongue wasn't for tasting *chile.*" Leonisimo breathed into the back of his wife's neck. "Or fresh *brel,* or wine." He stood on the point of his boots as he touched her neck with the tip of his tongue. "You're the one I care for, *querida.*"

"Leonisimo, stop! You behave like a dog in heat," Theresa swirled around to face her husband, knocking him back on his unsteady feet. "You won't talk to me, will you? What is it with you men that you're either clowning, or hiding something, or eating, or trying to have more children? Why can't you ever sit and talk to me? You're getting more and more like my father, Leonisimo."

"Your father? Please, Theresa. He had no time for either you or your mother. After he provided your mother with children, that was it. *Se fue al rancho.*"

"What do you know about my father? At least he was out there working to make our livelihood better while you're out there searching for women who will make you forget. Forget that you have gray hair, not brown." Theresa searched her husband's eyes for a response, but there was none. Leonisimo stared without expression at his wife. And then he turned, left the kitchen, walked through the entrance hall out through the door.

FAMILY THANKSGIVING

Nash Candelaria

I never understood why Mama insisted on living in that little adobe house in the country that was left to her by her mother. I do know that when Papa died, she sold their house in town because it was haunted by too many sad memories. She also needed the money to pay medical bills. At the same time, her widowed mother, my Grandma Sanchez, was alone and starting to fade. Grandma's chickens were bones and feathers because she sometimes forgot to feed them. The nanny goat's udders had gone dry, and she was only fit to barbecue — if you could stand ribs without much meat on them. While the vegetable garden had been overrun by a ragtag army of weeds.

I had a suspicion that Mama felt compelled to be a nurse, although she complained about Grandma Sanchez the same way she complained about working in an office in town. Yet when I told her I'd help pay for a part-time housekeeper, she blew up.

"I'm going to do my duty to my mother, Irene," she said. "And I don't care what you think." I was just part of an entire generation of selfish young people, she raved on. She didn't have to read about the "me" generation in the newspapers to know. All she had to do was look at her own children.

"Fine," I said. "Do you complain because you overwork? Or do you overwork so you can complain?" For an instant I thought she was going to smack me.

Instead she said that she liked the New Mexico country. It reminded her of when she was a girl. Quiet and slow. Peaceful. A retreat from the crazy city life people lived today. She could look at the house and take pride that her father and uncles had built it adobe brick by adobe brick almost fifty years ago. It connected her to her roots. Adobe was cool in the summer and warm in the winter. Her garden was a constant delight, both to work in and to harvest. Besides, where better for her children and grandchildren to gather on important occasions? Like Thanksgiving.

Of course she didn't reckon with the families of her two sons-in-law and one daughter-in-law. As far as Mama was concerned, other families were a supporting cast back in the shadows. But I could hear my sisters' husbands grousing to my brother, Dan, that they had to spend Christmas with their parents this year. Dan was the only one not drinking beer. He had to go on duty right after dinner. His neatly pressed police officer's uniform was hanging in Mama's bedroom closet.

"Hey, big sister Reeny," Dan said when I carried out a stack of plates to the living room. He and little brother Sammy had lugged the plastic-top table from the kitchen to where things were being set up buffet style. "What's this I hear about you defending those Commies?"

"What Commies?" I said. I knew damn well what he meant: the Sanctuary defendants.

"The wetback smugglers," he said.

"What smugglers?" I answered.

"All right, be that way," he said. He cast an envious glance at his brothers-in-law's beer cans, ignoring the silly grins on their faces. I didn't. They were waiting for me to pop off and start the show.

"Reeny," Dan went on. "Why didn't you stay with the District Attorney's office? How come you became a public defender for that low-life you deal with in court? Jesus!"

I couldn't stand it. Members of your family really know where to get you. I set the plates on the table and shot my right arm straight out in a salute. "Heil, Hitler!" I said.

The goofball brothers-in-law started to snicker. Dan glowered at them. Then he turned back to me. "I ought to know better than to ask," he said.

Little Sammy, bless his heart, started to recite some lines from the play he was rehearsing. He did the voices of all the characters, starting out with Jacob Marley, answering as the Ghost of Christmas Past, and ending as Tiny Tim blessing everyone.

I retreated to the kitchen to keep from giving Dan another shot, the ingrate. When I had been with the D.A.'s office, I had helped tutor him for his police exam. Obviously, I hadn't tutored him well enough about innocent until proven guilty.

Mama had gone next door to borrow a cup of something or other. If I know her, she was probably spreading it on pretty thick about her loving family that was with her this holiday. Especially if it was old lady Cordova, whose children didn't even speak to her anymore.

My youngest sister, Lisa, was basting the turkey. "Where's Marta?" I asked.

"Cleaning up after the kids." Since Marta had three children, Lisa two, and Dan and Helen only one, I guess child messes were more Marta's problem. "If one more little brat spills anything on the floor, I think I'll scream," Lisa said. The spoon in her hand was shaking.

"Here. Let me do that," I said.

What I wanted to tell her was to have a beer or a glass of the Chablis that Sammy had brought. Sammy was the one in the family with a little class. But even when she wasn't uptight, Lisa wouldn't take a drink. She figured if she did, her husband would have an excuse to be like his father and drink even more, although a couple of beers on holidays was no big deal as far as I was concerned.

Her arms were folded across her chest as she watched me. "Are you taking Mother to mass this Christmas?" There was a hard edge to her voice. It was an unnecessary question, since she already knew the answer. She was probably pissed off because her husband was having a good time watching the football game on TV and laughing and scratching with the other changos.

I closed the oven door and put the spoon on the counter. "I think the turkey's almost ready," I said.

"Are you?" she insisted.

Oh, Lord, I thought. What is it about me that brings out the worst in my family? Is it because I'm the oldest? Am I so different? Was I born into the wrong tribe?

Luckily Marta and Helen came in just then. "I sent them all out," Marta said. "Little Maria's in charge. Nobody gets back in before dinner unless they're bleeding." She picked an open beer can off the counter and drained it as she eyed us. "What's with you two?"

"Nothing," I said.

"Hmm."

"I think we should heat up the chili rellenos," I said. They were Mama's special. The old-fashioned kind with green chili and beef ground really fine, garnished with raisins, and shaped like short, fat Chinese egg rolls. Mama always heated Log Cabin syrup to pour over them for a Southwestern sweet and hot that was really a treat.

"She's not taking Mother to mass again this Christmas," Lisa said.

"Why don't *you* then?" Marta said. Then she looked at me with a mischievous smile on her face. "Tell me, Reeny. Are you going to marry Robert?"

Robert was a student counselor at the local high school. Marta's husband, Leo, who was a teacher at the same school, had accidentally-on-purpose invited Robert over one night when I came for dinner. I used to think that it was only unhappily married relatives who couldn't stand to see one of their kin single. Especially divorced older sisters who were pushing forty. But Marta and Leo were a pretty good match, which disproved that theory.

"Are you kidding?" I said. Helen suddenly got busy carrying the good stainless flatware to the living room. I figured she and Dan had been over that subject more than a few times.

"He's hot to marry you. He even told Mama when she was over one night." Well, goody-goody, I thought. It's none of Mama's business. Marta had a funny expression on her face. Maybe she had read my mind. "Has he ever asked you?"

265

"Oh, yeah."

That look was still on her face. She popped open a fresh beer can and took a swallow. "Has he ever been married?" I shook my head. "God," she said, "he's got to be almost forty. Is — is he — normal? You know what I mean. Not —"

I almost laughed. "He's just an old-fashioned boy. When his papa died, he promised to take care of his mama the rest of her life. The old bag is going to live to be a hundred."

"You sure he's not — you know — gay?"

"You're not worried about Leo are you?" I said.

Marta hooted. "Oh, really!" Lisa said indignantly. Helen, who had come back, looked shocked.

All three of them were watching me closely, eager to know what was none of their business. "Well," I said, "one night we went out to dinner and he asked me to marry him. I told him he didn't have to marry me if all he wanted was to go to bed."

"This is disgusting," Lisa said, and stomped into the living room.

"He'd just have to ask me some night when I wasn't exhausted from work," I continued. "He almost choked on his steak. His face got red right up to the roots of his hair." Marta was laughing. Helen's mouth fell open. "Have you ever seen Dan blush?" I asked Helen.

She shook her head slowly, staring at me like I was the kind of woman her sweet old mother had warned her about.

"I don't think my brother can," I said. "Not even if his pants dropped to his ankles in the middle of mass."

Marta was having a fit by now; there were tears in her eyes from laughing so hard.

Dan came in with that cocky streetwalk of his that I call the Aztec strut. "What're you hens cackling about?"

"Oh, go back with the boys and play with your drumstick," I said.

Marta and I looked at each other and started to giggle like when we were girls. Helen looked from us to her husband as if she didn't know what to do.

The screen door creaked open and Mama came up the back steps into the kitchen. Her eyes were shiny like she had just seen an apparition of the Virgin in the backyard, and she was smiling. The large bowl in her hand was full of ice cubes.

"It's such a blessing to see my family having such a good time," Mama said.

"Hey, give me that," Dan said, taking the bowl and putting it into the refrigerator. "You should have told me you wanted ice. I could have gone to the liquor store for a bag."

"You children always had such a good time together," Mama said. "Never a fuss. Never a harsh word."

Marta and I exchanged glances like when we were children and Mama insisted that there really was a Santa Claus even after we had snooped all over the house and finally found the presents in the broom closet.

"I put the rellenos on to heat," I said. "The turkey is ready to come out."

"Everything's ready out here," Lisa hollered from the front room.

"All right," Mama said. "I guess it's time. Don't forget to turn off the stove," she said to Marta. "And call the children," she said to Helen.

We went into the front room and gathered around the niche with the plaster statue of Jesus pointing to his sacred heart. It was across the room from the niche with the photo of Papa in his army uniform. Lisa hissed at the men to get rid of their beer cans.

Mama lit the two votives as we shuffled restlessly in a cluster, leaving enough room for her and the kids to kneel. The rest of us stood. "All right, Daniel," she said. "You can begin now."

Lisa stared at my motionless right hand as she made a sign of the cross. Dan began to recite a prayer out loud, and the others joined in. He ended saying grace, and I joined this time. Then the line formed at the end of the loaded table. Dan began to carve the turkey while Sammy turned up the sound on the TV.

I got out of the way of the stampede and went out the front door to get some fresh air and wait for the line to shorten. Marta sneaked out after me. We picked our way through the chickens away from the house.

"Did you really say that to Robert?" she asked in a low voice. "About going to bed?" I just smiled without answering. After all, I had my reputation to uphold. "You're just teasing, aren't you?" she said. "You're always teasing."

"How come you're not inside feeding the kids?"

"It's Lisa's turn," she said.

From inside, her oldest daughter Maria's voice sang out, "Rub-a-dub-dub. Thanks for the grub. Yea, God!"

I looked at Marta. Well, I thought. Now there'll be hell to pay. They'll probably blame that on me too. But it didn't bother Marta at all. She sort of squinted and stared into my eyes as if she was trying to see inside me. "Are you going to marry Robert?" she asked.

I put a hand on her arm. "No," I said. "He's a lovely man, but there's just nothing there. If there's no spark, why bother?"

"Mama will have a conniption," she said. "She practically had the wedding planned."

"Maybe we should fix her up with Robert, "I said. "Older women and younger men are in these days."

Marta wasn't sure whether or not to take me seriously. When I smiled, she started to giggle. Then Lisa pushed open the screen door. I half expected her to say something about little Maria, but all she said was, "Come and get it!"

Be thankful for little things, I thought. Now all I needed was Dan to rush out with a plate in his hand saying that he was late for work and that we would argue about my Commie clients some other time. If I had really believed in prayer I would have prayed for that right then. But all that came to me was: Rub-a-dub-dub. Thanks for the grub. Yea —

CARDINAL RED

Natalia Treviño

"'Mi'ja,' she said, 'when I die, I want you to fix my hair and make-up...I want you to be the one to do it. You know how I like it, the curls to the sides, and not the back, you know. I wanna look pretty when I see your Daddy.' And I told her...I said, "Mamá, don't talk like that.' But she kept going on, Pera. She said, 'Tell me you will, Mi'ja,' so I told her I would. I promised her, really. I mean, what could I say, Pera? 'No'?"

Pera's hands covered her face. Her fingers looked old and angry. "But...I can't believe you really want.... How can you go in that that, room and...ay. It's bad enough! Mamá is dead, and you're talking like..."

Melana watched her sister in silence and looked out the open window at the blooming Chinese tallow outside. She could hear the bees' hum coming from it. Melana remembered how every spring it was the bees that brought the back yard to life.

Their mother had died the day before. It had not been a complete shock to her children, since she had been sick with pneumonia for over two months. And now, the Cardenales children had no father and no mother. They were drawn to the oldest sister Pera's house to stay the night together.

Melana stood up and said, "This hurts all of us, not just you, Pera. The only way is if we — si la familia se ayuda." Pera would not look back at her. Melana turned to leave, "I have to get ready," she said. She stepped over four sleeping children strewn on the floor as she walked toward the bathroom.

She needed a shower before she went to the funeral home.
She had called earlier to make the arrangements to fix her
mother's hair, but Mr. Valdez had said it was "absolutely
inadmissible to allow any family to prepare a body for viewing
at a rosary." As she turned the hot water knob, she mumbled to
herself, "Don't tell me what's admissible." Melana imagined
Pera going on and on about how she was blowing this out of
proportion. She sat down in the middle of the tub, and began to
shave her legs. As she tried to picture the reactions of her
brothers and sisters, she felt a sting under her kneecap; the
sharp razor had cut into her. "Damn it," she said, and she set her
chin on the wounded knee, watching the pinkish stream of blood
and water flow down her leg onto the white porcelain tub, and
stream into the drain. She let out a heavy sigh and got herself
up.

Melana reached for a towel to dry her hair, and looked
down at her toes. She had her mother's feet, but unlike her
mother's, Melana's toe nails weren't painted. Her mother had
always told her, "At least keep your toe nails painted. If
nothing else, pretty toe nails make a woman feel put together."
Melana looked for some of her sister's nail polish, opening and
closing and slamming the cupboards in the bathroom, and she
found an old bottle of light pink nail-polish. She tried to open
the bottle, but it would not give. She kept wringing her hands
around the lid of the bottle, gritting her teeth, and hardly
letting a breath escape from her lips. "Damn," she said, and she
sat down on the toilet seat, letting the bottle drop to the floor.
She cried, holding her face in her reddened fingers.

When she came out of the bathroom, her younger sister
Tatia was waiting for her at the door. "I'll go with you if you
want me to."

"You will?"

"I think you might need me...there, I mean someone
to...well..."

"Yes," and Melana wrapped her small hands around her
sister's. "And God, it would help...it would be for her, you
know? I mean we'd be doing this for her. It would help. We

need to see the mortician first. He told me on the phone that he won't let me do it."

"Why?"

"I don't know why, but if I talk to him in person..."

"He'll have to let us."

§ § §

As they drove to the funeral home, Tatia was fidgeting in her seat, trying to adjust the seat belt in Melana's car. Melana thought that her sister was too quiet. She broke the heavy silence, "It's because of Daddy. You probably don't remember this... what were you? Four? After he died, I had these awful nightmares for about...God, I'd say two weeks. I'd be in this maze-like place, running from this man in a...white suit. And I thought he wanted to kill me, but every time I ran in a different direction, you know? I'd end up in the same place, and he came closer each time. It got to the point where I was so afraid to go to sleep.... And then Mamá let me fall asleep in her bed."

"And then?"

"That night, I dreamt that he got me. All he did was look at me, into my face, and it was okay. I looked back at him and saw who he was." She looked at her sister waiting for a reaction, "The dreams stopped."

After a moment, Tatia said, "How long did you have to sleep with her, with Mamá?"

"Just that one night." Melana bit her thumb nail and looked at the center of her steering wheel, "Isn't that something?"

"That's why you have to do this? Because you let the guy catch you? Who was he?"

"He let me go. Daddy let me go."

§ § §

Back in the car, after convincing Mr. Valdez to let them do the make-up and hair, the two sisters were flushed with excitement over their triumph. Tatia giggled, "I can't believe it. I mean he wasn't going to let us do it! 'Against the policy of this establishment,'" she mocked.

Melana agreed, "these guys take themselves so seriously, don't they? 'Oh yes sir, forgive me for getting into *your* territory. Of course, Mr. Dogface, you have the legal right to make our own mother look like shit at her own funeral...how had she gotten along without your beauty tips all these years?'" They both wiped their laughing tears as they pulled into the parking lot of the drug store.

Melana stepped out of the car, "I'll be right back; I only have to pick up one thing."

"Okay."

Melana ran straight to the cosmetics aisle. She only liked red fingernail polish, and she found one called Cardinal Red, "our name," she whispered. She grabbed it, and as she turned to leave, her eyes fell on a box of Miss Clairol, Medium-Ash-Brown. "Yes," she thought, "you wouldn't want your gray roots showing at your own funeral, Mamá...with everyone there. And you have to look good...for Daddy."

When she got back in the car, she dropped the paper sack in the middle of the seat. She felt relieved to get back into her warm seat; her stomach tight with excitement.

"What is this?" Tatia said, going through the sack.

"Miss Clairol. She would never buy it for herself, but I thought..."

"That'll be a mess! And no, Melana, it takes too long, we don't have to do that, no."

"It's not that much trouble. Come on — think of what she'd want... to look her best..."

"No! Melana. I...I really don't think you should do that. It...." Tatia shook her head and crossed her arms, looking out the window. Her eyes widened.

Tatia's silence dug into Melana, making her feel alone, thinking that she was always the one making everyone around her uncomfortable, always going too far. She looked down at the crumpled sack, and thought for a moment that it was pathetic and that she herself was pathetic, nail polish and hair color, driving from place to place. She felt a heavy, dull soreness at the bottom of her stomach.

"I won't do it," she said. "I won't use it."

Tatia was staring out the window. "It's just that you seem so, I don't know, unaffected. It scares me."

Melana was looking down, "All I can think is how I need to do this for her. Not me...all I can do is what she asked."

Tatia was quiet for a moment. "I wish I could be like you, but I can't." She started to cry lightly.

"That'll be fine. Just be there for me," and Melana drove to their mother's house to pick up the clothes and the make-up.

As they pulled slowly into the driveway, Melana turned to her sister. "Do you..."

"No. You go. I'll wait."

When Melana opened the door to the house, she could faintly smell her mother's perfume drifting in the air. Every time her mother was going somewhere, the house would smell like lavender. She'd be all dressed up, walking up and down the living room, filling every corner of the house with that smell, shoes and purse always matching perfectly.

Melana looked at the pictures of herself and her brothers and sisters on the wall at the entrance. There was that one picture of Melana and her mother. Her mother was standing next to her, displaying the hair-do that she had just finished. The child's hair was drawn up in a bun; two soft curls fell at each side of her little face. Melana remembered how beautiful she had felt. She remembered for the first time the familiar look of hope in her mother's eyes. It was as though at that moment she were saying, "My baby's going somewhere...look at her, and I helped her get ready."

In the sunlit bedroom, Melana looked for the dress that her mother had wanted to be buried in. It was the off-white with the deep neck that made her feel, as she had said, "Ah, Mi'ja me siento como una mujer." Melana pulled the dress out of the closet and noticed a light grease stain on the neckline of the dress, "Ay, Mamá, how did you, of all people...get this?" She went to get the make-up. "I want it to be my make-up — not that, that stage make-up they have, Melana. Mine."

Melana recalled each word her mother had said the day she had asked her. The words *"Blue Anis"* surfaced to her lips. She looked all over the bedroom for her mother's perfume, in cabinets, under some clothes, and then she remembered — the fridge. Melana let out a small smile, "Ah, *que Mamá.*"

As she got back into her car, she showed Tatia the stain on the dress: "Look at this."

Tatia studied the stain. "Oh no," she said, "I don't know if it will wash out. Put something over it...that scarf. Cover it with that pretty one she liked, Pera's scarf! Remember? *'Que bufanda tan linda,'* she'd say to Pera when she wore it. Ask Pera."

"You think?" Melana shook her head to herself, "Pera doesn't even think I should be doing this." She put the car into reverse, backing out of the cracked driveway. Her stomach felt as if someone was digging a messy hole inside her.

§ § §

When they arrived back at Pera's house, she was sitting at the kitchen table, smoking a cigarette. "So, are you going to do it?" she asked, flicking ashes into a crystal ashtray.

"Pera, she's doing the right thing," Tatia said. "You should come too; Melana needs both of us." Tatia's eyebrows made two even arcs over her round brown eyes, and the creases in her forehead looked soft and deep. Melana noticed that her sister had the same expression on her face that her mother had had years ago when she was telling Melana to have another baby. "You should have a son, *Mi'ja.* Every married woman should have a son, not only for her husband, but *por su vejez.* Since your daddy died, you don't know how much Miguel's helped me with — well, practical things. I mean like giving me financial help and dealing with insurance. It's just good to have a son of your own, *Mi'ja.* You should try to have another baby. A boy." When she heard her mother's voice this time, she didn't feel as angry as she had the day her mother had said it. She saw sense in the advice, remembering how her brothers took care of doctor appointments and how they dealt with the hospital when their mother was sick. The girls never worried about those things.

Pera's sharp voice interrupted, "Now you've got Tatia going along with you, Melana! Do you realize what you'll do to her — and to yourself! Look, I just want you to think!" Pera got up from the table, her face on fire, "I can't stand this! You two are going to go in there and prove what? That you're not bothered by Mamá's death? Because if you were, I don't see how you'd be able to go in there and fix her hair!"

Melana did not answer, and Pera went to her bedroom. Wiping muted tears, Melana walked out of the kitchen and saw her small daughter in the living room playing with her toy truck. She went to see her baby. "Hi, Angel," she said, stroking her child's hair. "Hey, what would you say if Mommy had another baby? You want a little brother?" her daughter tilted her head up and looked at her mother blankly.

"Do you know what Tommy said? That Grandma was going to go and see God today."

"Really?" Melana sank back on her knees, her stomach hot and shaking. "Well, yes, Tommy's right. She is."

"Can I go?" The dull pain sharpened, cutting through her.

"Uh...not today, honey, but you will...someday." The arcs over the child's eyes looked as deep as Tatia's had. "Promise?"

"Yes, Angelita, I promise. Now Mommy's going to help Grandma get dressed up to see him...God."

As the child rolled the truck back and forth, she said, "I like Grandma's pink shoes."

Pera appeared in the room with her mauve scarf in her hand, and she gave it to Melana. Taking Pera's hands in hers, Melana kissed them hard. Pera's voice calmed the burning in her stomach. "Just be back in time for all of us to go to the rosary together tonight, o.k.?"

"Of course."

§ § §

Mr. Valdez was waiting for them at the entrance to the funeral home. He had coal black hair and a porcelain complexion. An air of formality surrounded him as he greeted them with a light handshake. "*Buenos días,* Señora Cardenales." He adjusted his tie. "Your mother's body is ready. You only have to put her make-up on and do her hair, as you asked, Señora. We've made all the other preparations. I will put the dress on for you." She handed him the dress, and he walked through the swinging door.

While they waited in the lobby there was no sound. The air conditioners started abruptly, and Melana and Tatia jumped in their seats. They laughed nervously at themselves. Tatia was winding a strand of her light brown hair around her forefinger, letting it go and winding it up again. She was moving her left leg up and down, trying not to look around the room.

Mr. Valdez came back through the doorway. "You may come in now."

Tatia stood immediately. Melana noticed that Tatia's face had become completely ashen. She was taking short breaths, and her eyes were wide open, "I...have to go," she said, and she rushed to the ladies' room. Melana followed her, trying not to think about the trembling hole growing inside her.

When Melana walked into the bathroom, she saw her sister staring into the mirror, "I thought my face would be red, all flushed. I felt the blood come up...but no. It was gone — the blood out of my face." Tatia walked to one stall, sat, her face dropped to her hands. "I don't know what happened. I-I'm sorry Melana. I'm so...embarrassed."

"It's okay, Honey. Do you still want to go?"

"Um hmm."

They walked out of the bathroom holding hands, and Mr. Valdez was waiting outside for them. "Ladies," he said in a calming voice, "I know you've never done anything like this before, so I want you to listen." He punctuated his words with periodic nods of his head. "You need to control your emotions, or you won't be able to do it. You have to separate yourself somehow." He paused and held his hands together, finger to finger. "I know this is very personal and special to you, but we must separate ourselves in some way. Otherwise you won't be able to finish.... And I would say that could be very painful." He smiled reassuringly. "Okay?" They nodded in unison. He held the door open for both of them, letting the door swing closed.

§ § §

The body was under a sheet in a shampoo chair, half seated, half lying. Melana walked toward her mother. In a slow steady movement, she pulled the sheet off her mother's face. "Hi, Mamá," she whispered. The hole inside of her began to pulse with her heart and grow with each beat.

Tatia looked at her mother from the door. She did not get close. "I'm here," she said quietly. And then whispered, "She's grey." Melana turned and saw her sister gasp violently for air, her face white, stricken with anguish. "It's okay," Melana said. "You don't have to stay." Tatia ran out of the room, and Melana could hear her crying outside the door.

The white florescent lights only defined the emptiness of the room. The dull glint of the stainless steel counter wrapped itself around the walls. There was no sign that anyone had ever been there before. But her mother was there. And the smell of nothing lingered in the air.

The hole in Melana was gone. She was the hole, disappearing into the voided room. She was emptiness, bleached of feeling. A cold wet sensation came down her leg, the wound from shaving this morning. It surfaced. Deeper than she had imagined, it was bleeding again.

Instinctively, her hollow hand covered the wound, placing pressure on it. "Mi'ja, whenever you have a cut, all you have to do to make it stop bleeding is to press on it." She was sitting on the cold floor, crying. "It's nature, you see. Here, let me see it. Ay, Dios mío, that's deep, baby. Here, I'll get something; it'll feel better. Yes, isn't that better? Just remember, press on it. Don't cry, Mi'ja no, no. It'll go away, I promise, Angelita." Melana looked up at her mother, wiping her nose with the back of her hand, and tried to catch her breath.

She pulled herself up from the floor and looked inside the cosmetics bag. She found her mother's curling iron, plugged it into the outlet, and set it on the silver counter to heat. She found the mauve scarf and draped it over her mother's shoulders, the way Pera wore it. The bow was a blossom of color, adding softness to the stark room. No wonder you loved this scarf, she thought. "It's perfect for you, Mamá." She opened the bottle of Blue Anis, put three strokes of it at the base of her mother's neck, and the smell of her mother going somewhere filled the room. Then, she spread a dab of the perfume in the center of her mother's chest, over her heart. The lavender scent filled the room with her mother's hopeful smile.

She checked the curling iron and took a small handful of her mother's hair between two fingers. She picked up the curling iron, clasping it over the hair, rolling it in slowly. Gently. She could not see the hair clearly, and she realized that her eyes were full of rock-hard tears. She blinked, letting the water fall. She held the hair in the clasp. "Twelve seconds, Mi'ja," the voice staying with her. She remembered not to burn her mother's scalp, like she had countless other times. She took each strand with equal care, slowly. Gently. She sprayed the hair lightly, careful not to get it into her eyes, covering them with one hand, and spraying evenly with the other.

Make-up. She took out her mother's foundation, opened the bottle, and took a dab on her finger, "Start in the middle then spread out, Mi'ja; you know how." The skin did not feel like she thought it would. It was soft. As she spread the foundation on, she pulled the cheeks up, and made small smiles on her mother's face.

She tried to apply the mascara to the lashes, not knowing that the eyes, her mother's eyes had been sewn shut. She stopped. She pressed her hand on her own wet cheek, half over her eye, "It's o.k., Mi'ja; it didn't hurt, I promise."

Try again. Then she lined her mother's eyelid with a purple stoke of eyeliner. Beautiful, Mamá.

Lipstick. Melana had to angle herself in different ways to place the color on evenly. Lips sewn shut. "I didn't feel it, Mi'ja, don't worry." These lips that spoke to me, these lips that yelled at me and kissed me goodnight and checked my temperature, these lips, small, flat, soft. She stopped again, closed her eyes hard. Look good for your daddy.... Can I go with grandma? So I can look good for your daddy.... To see God? Melana evened out the color with her fingertips.

She put the last touches on the hair, lifting the front, patting down the sides. "Ay, Mi'ja, thank you! Oh how can I thank you? I knew you could do it. Knew you were the only one. I knew. I knew. Knew."

Melana looked in the cosmetic bag for the nail polish she had bought, Cardinal Red, and kicked off her sandals. She opened the bottle easily, and painted each of her toe nails with smooth, even strokes.

THE MAN WHO FOUND A PISTOL

Rudolfo Anaya

This was the man who found the pistol, Procopio said as he pushed the newspaper across the bar for me to read. Procopio has worked in the village cantina many years; he knows the stories of the village. He wiped the bar thoughtfully and placed my drink in front of me. When he begins a story, I listen. He doesn't embellish the story, he just tells it. If you listen, fine; if you don't, there's always another customer at the bar.

The story of the man who found the pistol reminded me of something that happened to me years ago. My wife and I were driving up in the Jemez mountains when we came to a stream. We stopped to eat lunch and enjoy the beauty. While my wife spread our picnic lunch, I walked along the bank of the stream, enjoying the beauty of the forest. I came to a place on the stream where I felt a presence.

There were no footprints, but I knew someone had been there. I looked around the clearing, but there was no one. Then I looked into the water. Submerged in the water lay a handsome double-bladed axe. Someone had left it there. Again I looked around, but there was no one in sight. Maybe one of the locals had forgotten it.

Why had he left it in the water? Perhaps he wanted the water to swell the wood so the axe head would not slip. But there was no camp nearby, and no logging in the area. There was no sign of life.

I took the axe out of the water and felt its weight. It was a well-used axe, and it fit snugly in my hands. I admired it, for I did not have such an axe. But as I held it, a strange feeling came over me. I felt I was being watched. Around me the forest grew very quiet. The mountain stream gurgled and a few birds cried, but the forest grew still and sullen. I thought of taking the axe, but I didn't. I put it back in the cold water where I had found it, and I hurried back and told my wife we should leave that place.

When I drove away, I felt I had come upon a mystery that was not for me. Many years later I still remembered the axe I found in the stream.

The man who found the pistol lived in the village of Corrales. He taught at the university, Procopio told me. In the afternoons he came to the cantina to drink a beer after his walk. He was a loner, Procopio continued, nobody in the village knew him well. He wasn't a talker. It was the man's wife who told Procopio's wife that her husband grew up in a ranch in Texas. When he was a boy, her husband was hunting rabbits with his brother: there was an accident. That's all she said.

What happened, I wondered. Procopio shrugged and shook his head.

Procopio never told a story all at once, he told it piece by piece. He would be relating the events in his quiet way, then new customers would come in and he would lumber off to serve them. I had to return to the bar from time to time to listen to the story.

I learned that the man who found the pistol used to go walking along the irrigation ditch in the afternoons. Tall grass covers the banks of the ditch. The fields and orchards in that part of the village are isolated. During his walk the man could enjoy the silence of the pastoral valley. That's why he had moved to Corrales, to be away from the city where he worked.

In the fields of the valley he could be alone with his thoughts. I began to understand that the man was much like me. I, too, enjoy being alone; I like the silence of mountains. One has to be alone to know oneself. I also realize that one must return to the circle of the family to stay in balance. But the way Procopio told it, the man spent most of his time alone. His wife did all the chores and took care of the house; the man only went to teach his classes, then returned to walk alone in the fields.

Hearing Procopio talk about the man who found the pistol made me curious about him. I drove by his home with the old weathered barns. The place looked deserted and haunted in the sharp January wind. Dark curtains covered the windows, and the banging of a loose tin on the barn roof made a lonely sound. Later, when I told Procopio this, he looked at me strangely. Let it go, he said.

I didn't let it go. The story of the man who found the pistol became an obsession with me.

One day I walked along the irrigation ditch where the man had walked, and standing in the open fields I could see what he had seen. He could look east and see the stately face of the Sandia mountain. The mountain reminds me of a giant turtle. When I was a boy I had killed a turtle, and when I look at the mountain I am sometimes reminded of that incident. This is the way of life: remembering one incident kindles another, and one doesn't know where the stampede of thoughts may lead.

Around him he could see the fields, winter bare now, but in the summer they were green and buzzing with life. Meadow larks called, black birds flew to the horse corrals, pheasants laid their eggs in the tall grass, and an occasional roadrunner scuttled in front of him. How could a man who had so much beauty around him do what he did?

Maybe Procopio knew more than he was telling. I found excuses to ask questions of other people in the village, but no one had known the man well. They knew he was a teacher; most said he kept to himself. He was always alone. The man who dug wells for a living had dug a well for the teacher. The well-digger told me something horrible had happened back in Texas. There was a hunting accident. That's all the teacher said, and he grew melancholy.

I stood in the field alone and thought about the man. Walking here, he would meet no one. Here he could be at peace with himself. In the winter he could feel the earth sleeping; in the spring he could breathe the fresh scent of apple blossoms from the orchards; and in summer he could see the green of the alfalfa fields.

Was he not happy in that silence of the valley? Had it become like the silence in his heart, a haunting silence? When one is alone, the hum of the earth becomes a mantra whose vibration works its way into the soul. Maybe the man was sucked deeper and deeper into that loneliness until there was no escape.

The day he found the pistol, Procopio said, he came to the bar, and he didn't order his usual beer — he drank a whiskey. His hands were trembling. "I found a pistol," he told us. There was only me and Primo in the bar, and Primo's nephew, the boy with the harelip. We looked at him. "What should I do?" he asked. "Don't give it to the sheriff," Primo said, "he will only keep it for himself." The boy with the harelip said, "You can shoot rabbits with it." I said, "Keep the pistol, you found it, it's yours."

"I have thought often of the man finding the pistol in the grass by the side of the ditch," Procopio said. "Maybe it belonged to a criminal who threw it there to get rid of it. Maybe he had killed someone with it. There is a curse on things you find. They can never be yours."

There it was, I thought, like a snake concealed in the grass, ready to strike, perhaps glistening in the sun. There was mud on it, perhaps the stain of blood. The man trembled when he stooped to pick it up. The hair along his neck stood on end; he felt a shiver. It isn't everyday a man finds a pistol. Should he dare to pick it up? Yes, he did, as I had picked up the axe. It fit into his hand.

Should I take it? the man thought. He weighed it in his hand and then looked around. He was alone; the fields were quiet. A cool breeze hissed as it swept across the grass. The man shivered. Many thoughts must have gone through his mind, memories of the past, things he knew he had to resolve. Aren't we all like that, haunted by memories of the past, the sights and sounds which come to overwhelm us? Maybe he knew this, and that's why he sighed when he slipped the pistol into his pocket.

"After that he came to drink every day," Procopio said. "He would drink whiskey, always alone. Once he asked me if anyone had reported the pistol as lost or stolen. No one in the village had mentioned the pistol. His hand was always in his pocket, as if he was making sure the pistol was still there."

"He had cleaned the pistol until it was shiny," Procopio said. "He bought bullets for it, but I think he was afraid to fire it."

I listened intently. There was something in the man's story which seemed to be my story. A word, a fragrance, the time of day can transport me into that depth of memory I know so well. The man's story was doing that to me, allowing me no rest.

I began to go into the bar every day, and when Procopio had time, the conversation would get around to the story of the man who found the pistol. My own work began to suffer; I was obsessed with the story. Why did this man find the pistol? Was it his destiny, his *destino* as we say in Spanish. Our tragic sense of life allied so closely to the emotions of memory.

"No one can escape el *destino*," Procopio said, as if reading my thoughts. "When your time comes, it comes." "Karma," I said, and we argued about the meaning of words.

That night I dreamed of the axe I had found in the mountain stream. I saw it submerged in the cold water of the stream, the steel as blue as the sky. I saw myself picking it up, and a voice in the dream saying no. The next day I drove to the mountain to look for the place, but it had been years, and I no longer recognized the road that led to the stream. I wondered how many times the man who found the pistol had gone to the spot where he found it. Why didn't he throw it away and break the chain of events that were his *destino*?

"Why are you so nervous?" my wife asked me. I could not answer. I needed to be alone, and so every day I drove, up to the mountains or along the back roads of the silent *mesas*. When I was alone, I felt the presence I had felt in the forest the day I found the axe. I was sure the man had felt the same, but he had decided to take the pistol anyway. Troubled by my thoughts, I found myself returning to Procopio's cantina to listen to the story of the man who found the pistol.

"Late in the summer, the wife left the man," Procopio said. "He had grown more moody and introverted. He didn't clean his place all summer, the weeds took over his fields. His milk cow got loose, and the people of the village complained, but he paid no attention. Perhaps they grew afraid of him. Maybe his wife became afraid also, and that's why she left."

Listening to Procopio, I thought I understood the man who found the pistol. He was like me, or like any other man who wonders how the past has shaped our destiny. He was a scholar, a sensitive man who thought of these questions. All those days alone in the fields, brooding over what he could tell no one. It was bound to catch up.

"He tried to get rid of the pistol," Procopio said. "He was drunk one night and he tried to give it to Primo, but Primo wouldn't take it. He begged Primo to take it, saying he was afraid something bad was going to happen. By then we knew there was a curse on the man. He always kept the pistol in his pocket, perhaps he slept with it. Now there was no peace for him in the silence of the valley. Even the mountain wore a stern, gray look as winter came."

Why? I asked myself. Late at night I thought of the man who found the pistol. Why did finding the pistol change the man's life? He had committed no crime. He was a good man, a teacher. Was it because he had taken the pistol, or was there a greater design, a destiny he had to fulfill? Was the pistol like the axe, something which came to sever the cord of life?

The past haunts us, and only the person who carries the sack knows how much it weighs, as the saying goes.

"Do you remember the day we found the axe in the stream?" I asked my wife. But she had forgotten. To me the time and place and the texture of the day and the stream were so clear I would never forget. But she had forgotten. It was that way with the man who found the pistol — he would never forget that time and place. Maybe he knew that by taking the pistol he would have to settle a score with the past.

Ghosts of the past come to haunt our lives. What ghost came to haunt this man? I felt I knew what the man thought when he sat up late at night and stared at the pistol at his bedside, or when he walked through the village with the pistol in his pocket. He knew why the people let him pass in silence.

"Then they found the man dead, "Procopio said softly. "Shot."

"Shot himself," I nodded. This is what I had assumed all along, but there was a new twist Procopio had not yet shared with me.

"No," Procopio shook his head. "That's what the paper said, but what do they know! I will tell you," he whispered. "You remember the boy with the harelip? He used to do odd jobs around the village?" I nodded.

"He was staying with the man, because the man had grown fearful of living alone. The boy slept in a small room near the front door. Late one night he heard someone knocking at the door. He got up and was going to open the door, but the man told him no. 'It is a ghost,' the man shouted. 'Don't open the door!'

"The man went to the door and listened. He shouted at the ghost to go away. The boy saw the man was terrified, and the boy too was full of fear. Both felt it was no ordinary person who came to knock at night.

"For weeks they were haunted by the knocking on the door. It was the feast of the Epiphany, and the night was cold. You remember, so cold it cracked some of the apple trees. Late at night the knocking came; the man went to the door. This time he held the pistol in his hand. This time he opened the door."

Procopio paused. I waited, my hands trembling. He poured me another shot, which I drank to calm myself.

"What?" I asked.

Procopio shrugged. "This is the strange part," he said. "The boy with the harelip swears that when the man opened the door he saw the man's double standing there. The man raised the pistol and fired at his image. A cold wind shook the house, and the boy with the harelip rushed forward to shut the door. The man who found the pistol was dead. The pistol was at his side. I don't know what made the boy grab the pistol and run away. Later he told me he had thrown it away. Somewhere in the fields."

Procopio wiped the glasses he was drying. He was sad, sad for the man who had found the pistol and for the boy who saw the death. "What was it?" I asked.

"Who knows?" Procopio said. "A ghost from the past. Maybe just the boy's imagination."

I nodded. So he had made his peace. I shivered. There are certain stories that touch us close to the heart. We listen to the tale and secretly whisper, "There but for the grace of God go I." Procopio had told me only sketches of the man, but I felt I knew the man as if he was my brother.

I rose and walked outside. The night was cold but the feel of spring was already in the air. What is the future, I thought, but a time which comes to swallow what we make of life.

SALVATION

Alexanna Padilla Heinemann

What is it that Tía Sarquita sees? It turns the townspeople's minds into a whirlwind of questions, scares them, yet they are drawn to her for inspiration and answers. They cannot deny her power as a *curandera*.

Tía Sarquita's house sits at the edge of the town of Truchas, so close to the Penitente *morada* that she can almost hear the secret chanting of this martyred brotherhood during Holy Week. The town is divided by the argument over who claimed that piece of land first: the Penitentes or Tía Sarquita's parents, the late Dolores and Estevan Alvarado. The townspeople like to imagine what a dramatic war it would have been between the solemn and holy Penitente brothers and the proud Alvarado family. Somewhere a truce had been drawn, a compromise made, but the people of Truchas never spoke about any agreement between the two property-holders. In the interest of preserving a mystery, of keeping a story alive in the air, they continue to puzzle over the originality of each tenant, talking only of possibilities, never solutions.

Despite the questions about the original owners of the property, one thing is true: Sarquita Alvarado has grown from a child to an old woman right next door to a building that houses the rituals of the oldest and most mysterious religious sect in New Mexico. The people of Truchas agree that Tía Sarquita's proximity to the *morada* has touched her.

The old men remember being young schoolmates with Sarquita and often recall the first time she inspired their awe.

Three of them — José Montaño, Teodoro Lucero, and Alejandro Marquez — feeling particularly reckless one day, surrounded little Sarquita in the playground. They gathered crooked sticks which they formed into crosses, and they circled Sarquita, dragging their crosses behind them, just as the Penitentes did when they paraded through town during Holy Week. "Tell us some holy lies, tell us some holy lies," the three chanted as they walked around her, dragging their mock burdens. But when they walked one way, Sarquita turned in the opposite direction. This was very annoying to the three boys, who placed great importance and hope in getting a frightened response from her. So, whichever direction Sarquita turned, they quickly altered their circle to follow her motion, and as soon as they were following her, she, of course, switched her direction. Soon, the three were involved in a competitive dusty dance that grew so frantic that even the crooked crosses were laid aside and forgotten.

Alejandro Marquez was the one who broke the rhythm by standing perfectly still and shouting, "Sarquita, maybe your father is a member of the secret Penitentes." After he said this, Alejandro looked to his two friends for support and approval. He was a boy made insecure by the fact that his face was too pretty and he often rubbed dirt on his cheeks to make himself look tough. José and Teodoro did not invent insults of their own but grunted in lame agreement with their sudden leader. Sarquita looked from José to Teodoro, then at Alejandro. Her eyes were such a light hazel that they shone almost amber against her olive skin, and Alejandro felt very small beneath their gaze.

"You will be very sorry," she said slowly and evenly, "that you said that about my father." Alejandro did not betray that he was disturbed by her defiance but valiantly stuck his tongue out in Sarquita's direction. But when he tried to pull it back into his mouth he was horrified to find that it would not move. Alejandro strained his body so hard that his eyeballs seemed to lie against his pretty cheeks but his tongue stayed stubbornly, stiffly outside of him. Sarquita watched Alejandro for a moment and a satisfied smile crossed her face before she turned and walked away from the three boys.

Sarquita could hear Alejandro's moans and panicked footsteps as he ran behind her. In his desperation, he pulled mightily on her long, thick braid. Sarquita reeled around to face him, and her eyes, suddenly dark with fury, met his, which were wet and pleading. Sarquita could see that the moment was in her hands.

"Are you prepared to apologize?" she asked, and Alejandro nodded and threw his hands up to her, folded, as if they were in prayer. "Then follow me," Sarquita said.

The trio followed Sarquita to her house where she instructed them to wait outside. They stared uneasily at the nearby *morada* until Sarquita returned. In her hands she held an onion, a knife, a salt shaker, and a small, clear bottle with a black top. She sliced a thick wedge out of the onion, then opened the little bottle and poured oil onto the wedge. After sprinkling the onion with salt, she placed it in Alejandro's hand. Sarquita looked at him, prepared to issue a harsh order on how to apply the cure, but her heart fell open when she saw Alejandro's tongue — it was so dry from the lack of saliva that it had started to crack and bleed. But when Sarquita saw that Alejandro had noticed her moment of softness she grabbed the onion from his hand and placed it firmly under his tongue. She took his fingers and laid them against the onion and said, "Hold it there until you forget how to say such foolish things. Only then will your tongue give way."

But now Sarquita is old, and the town long ago ceased to be awed by her strange powers. Instead, the townspeople entertain themselves by trying to solve the mystery of Tía Sarquita. She gives them a certain power because she can connect them with the things they need desperately but cannot explain or call for themselves. She has taught them that they do not need to fear death because spirits that have been long gone are awakened at Tía Sarquita's insistence. She acts as a telescope that allows them to see beyond the things they already understand.

Perfecta Alire needs Tía Sarquita now. The old woman can feel this, although the sad little girl has never asked for her help. One day, she instructs Pablo, the boy she hires to shop for her, to go to Perfecta's house and tell the girl that the town *curandera* requests her to come to her home.

"Today is your birthday," Sarquita says when the girl arrives, "and I can hear your sadness all the way across town."

Perfecta is frightened of this woman, whose light eyes seem to see all the secrets her heart contains. "Who told you about me?" Perfecta asks in a small voice, her eyes unable to raise above the *curandera's* feet.

"Your secrets are yours alone," Sarquita says, "but God has given me the power to heal, and I cannot ignore a child in pain. There is something you want and can't find, and it draws a shadow across your face every year on your birthday."

Perfecta's fingers twist around themselves, and she looks into the old woman's amber eyes, which are still as clear and alert as a child's. "I want to find my father's love. I want him to lose his pain so he can learn to love me." Sarquita nods slowly, and Perfecta knows she does not have to explain where her father's sadness has come from.

"Your father has lost his vision," Tía Sarquita says. "Your mother had his life folded in her hands and when she died giving birth to you, he was sure that she took his life also. He tries, but he can't always see that you are his new life. Serapio sees only the blackness of his own sorrow." Sarquita waits several minutes before she asks, "And Perfecta, why are you afraid of the night?"

Perfecta looks into the old woman's eyes and sees that this is the part she doesn't understand. "He is so alone," Perfecta begins, but looks down at Sarquita's feet again.

"Go on," Sarquita urges her.

"At night he forgets who I am, and he tries to bring the happiness back to himself," Perfecta says, and her heart grows numb and empty as the secret flies out of it.

"Perfecta," Sarquita asks firmly, "does he hurt you?"

"No," Perfecta says in a voice that is barely above a whisper. "He doesn't even touch me. He pulls the covers between us and falls into a deep sleep with half of his body on top of me. He doesn't move for the rest of the night."

But thinking of the night during the day makes Perfecta feel that there is nowhere left to hide and her body shakes with sobs. "His pain grows larger every year," she cries, "and it is just getting too heavy for me to bear."

Sarquita takes the girl in her arms and holds her until she is quiet. "I will help you," she says.

MRS. VARGAS
AND THE DEAD NATURALIST

Kathleen Alcalá

Mrs. Vargas had been cleaning the house for a week in anticipation of the visit, and the guest wasn't due for at least three more days. The hemp floormats had been beaten and aired out, the whitewashed walls had been scrubbed inside and out, and Mrs. Vargas was now spreading her best embroidered tablecloth on the big square table in the *sala* while admonishing her family not to spill anything on it for the next few days. When she heard the thump on the door, she thought it was a neighbor.

"*¡Entren!*" she said loudly. Mrs. Vargas, a short, sturdy woman, fluttered her hands over her hair as she started towards the door. The handle turned, and a dusty figure half-walked, half-fell into the front room. She had never seen him before.

"Dr. Ellis?" she said, "Dr. Ellis?" Receiving no answer, she helped him to a wicker chair. The Anglo was greenish-white, and a cold sweat stood on his forehead and upper lip. Panting heavily, he said nothing, but looked up at her with pleading eyes.

"*¡Agua!*" she yelled. "Just a minute, I'll bring you some water." And she patted him into the chair as though that would keep him from falling over while she went for cold water. Returning from the kitchen with her daughter, she could see that it was too late. He was slumped over and not breathing.

Nevertheless, she said, "Luz, go get the *curandera*, and you," she said to her other children, attracted by the commotion, "help me put him on the bed." A leather folder fell to the floor as they carried the dusty man to the guest bedroom and laid his body on the clean cotton bedspread.

As she had suspected, the naturalist was quite dead by the time help arrived.

"It was his heart," said the *curandera*. "Besides, he drank too much. That's why he's so yellow."

The man looked older than Mrs. Vargas had imagined, and was not well dressed. He wore a torn black raincoat completely unsuited to the Yucatec climate, a cheap cotton shirt, and polyester pants that were frayed at the cuffs. He wasn't at all what she had expected.

"Dear Claudia," the letter from her sister in Mérida had begun. "I have a favor to ask of you. A man my husband sometimes works for, a famous naturalist, would like to go to our village to study the *ikeek*, which the Americans call the 'rockbird.' Since there is no place to stay, I thought you might be able to accommodate him for a few days. I am sure that he would be very appreciative of the favor. Please let me know if this will be all right." Mrs. Vargas had quickly written back, mindful of the prestige which might result from having a famous naturalist as her guest in the village.

As the *curandera* was finishing up, the priest arrived.

"What happened?" he asked.

"He had a heart attack and died," said Mrs. Vargas. "I guess the journey was too much for him."

"Is it the scientist?" he asked.

"Well, he's an American. Who else would it be?" Then Mrs. Vargas remembered the portfolio. Finding it on the floor, she and the priest unzipped its stiff edges and looked inside. It contained colored pencils and drawings of tropical birds on very thin paper.

"But how did he get here?" asked the priest. "The bus doesn't come this far. And where is his luggage? His passport?"

No one knew the answers to these questions. By now, a crowd had gathered outside.

"We saw him walking up the road," said Saladino Chan, "as we were returning from the fields. He asked the way to Mrs. Vargas' house. He didn't have any luggage then, and he didn't look well."

"Maybe he walked from Napual, where the bus stops, and forgot his suitcase. Or maybe he was robbed." Yes, nodded everyone, or maybe he was having it sent later, with special scientific equipment. In any case, it would be of no help to him now.

Mrs. Vargas perched on a chair for a minute to collect her thoughts. She was upset by the death, but at the same time, the prone figure in the bedroom filled her with uneasiness. She wasn't sure just what sort of a guest he would have been, anyway.

After administering the last rites to Dr. Ellis, the priest returned to the front room and sat down opposite Mrs. Vargas. "We could take the body by truck to Napual, and put it on the bus back to Mérida," said the priest, "but it is very hot, and I'm afraid the body will deteriorate. I think we should bury him here."

"Yes — " said Mrs. Vargas, perking up a little, "at least we can give him a nice funeral."

So a black wooden coffin was prepared for the naturalist, and the stonemason carved his name on a slab of marble he'd been saving for something special. The next morning, the coffin was covered with the bright flowers of the hyacinth and the blossoms of the silkcotton tree. The coffin bearers sang the songs for the dead as they marched in procession to the cemetery, and the whole village turned out for the occasion.

"God respects those who respect his creations, and scientists who study birds and flowers, in their own way, respect and conserve God's work," said the priest. The people nodded, final prayers were said, and the coffin was lowered into the rocky grave. Everyone gave their condolences to Mrs. Vargas, since the naturalist had no family present.

After that, the men went off to the fields, and everyone agreed that it was the best funeral they'd had in a while. The bill for the headstone would be sent to the university.

Mrs. Vargas, still crying a little, hurried home to write to her sister and tell her the bad news. The cotton bedspread was washed, and her three younger boys, who had been sent to stay with cousins, moved back into the guest bedroom.

Three days later, a Toyota Land Cruiser roared into the village. An American asked directions to Mrs. Vargas' house, and drove on.

"It must be someone from the American consulate," said the villagers, finding an excuse to walk up the road that led to Mrs. Vargas' house.

The Land Cruiser stopped in front, and out jumped a trim, athletic man in his mid-thirties. He was not dressed like a diplomat, but instead wore a khaki shirt and trousers.

"Mrs. Vargas?" he asked, when she opened the door. "I'm Dr. Ellis, from the university," and he smiled his best American smile.

An expression between horror and ecstasy crossed her face and, with a little cry, Mrs. Vargas swooned into her daughter's arms. Luz, confused and scared, burst into tears while the naturalist stood in the doorway, unsure whether to try and help, shifting the strap to his expensive camera uncomfortably on his shoulder.

Finally, Mrs. Vargas blinked her eyes and, assuring the man that she was all right, offered him a chair and described the death of a few days before.

"What did he look like?" asked Dr. Ellis.

"An older man with yellow skin," she said, "and a black raincoat. He carried a leather envelope with pictures of birds."

"How strange," said Ellis. "I have no idea who that could have been. Didn't he have a passport or anything?"

"No," said Mrs. Vargas. "We found nothing in his pockets, and he had no luggage. All he brought were the drawings."

At her mother's bidding, Luz brought out the worn portfolio, and Ellis opened it. He carefully examined the drawings, which were unsigned, and turned the folder inside out looking for clues, but there was nothing. The colored pencils had been manufactured in Mexico, and were the sort commonly used by schoolchildren.

"I don't know what to tell you," said Ellis, "except that people sometimes write to the university, or call, if they think they've seen something unusual. He might have called after I left and found out I'd be here. But I don't know anything about him. I'm sorry."

Mrs. Vargas recalled the acrid smell of the dead man's skin, and her sense of foreboding returned. "I thought there was something odd about him. He didn't look right."

"I'm very sorry about the mixup," said Dr. Ellis. "If I can compensate you, or someone, for the burial expenses, I would like to do that. I guess someone should notify the authorities, if it hasn't been done. I would be happy to take care of it."

He waited for a response from Mrs. Vargas, who sat with her hands folded in her lap. She seemed to have forgotten him.

"Oh, yes," she said finally. "I'm sure it can be worked out." She realized that the young scientist was waiting to be invited to remain. "If the circumstances permit, I hope that you will stay and continue with your work."

"If that's all right," he answered. "After all the confusion, I hope it's not too much trouble."

"Not at all," she answered. "My house is your house."

So the three younger boys went out the back door to their cousins' again, while Dr. Ellis brought his suitcase and several six-packs of Orange Crush in the front door. He opened and gave a bottle to each of the remaining children, and they drank the warm soda right before dinner, much to Mrs. Vargas' consternation, but she said nothing.

At dinner, on the old tablecloth, since the good one had been soiled in the meantime, Dr. Ellis gave her a fancy silver salt and pepper set.

"I thought you might like these," he said. She thanked him profusely and placed them out on the table. She didn't tell him that she would never use them, since the high humidity made

297

salt stick together, and it would clog up the little holes in the shaker.

Dr. Ellis told them about his work. He taught ornithology at the university and studied the birds of southern Mexico and Guatemala. The rockbird was of interest because it is one of the few species of birds which maintains a *lek*, or dancing ground, which the male clears on the jungle floor in order to display his beautiful feathers and attract a mate.

"The reported sightings near your village," continued Dr. Ellis, "if confirmed, would make this the farthest north this type of bird has ever been found in the Americas. It would change the maps of ornithology!" The family nodded politely and ate their beans and tortillas. They didn't tell him that he would sleep that night where the dead man had lain.

The next morning, Dr. Ellis set out early to find the rockbird. Overtaking some farmers on the way to their fields, he asked if they had seen the small yellow bird.

"Oh, yes," they said nervously, "it has been seen. Out there. It lives out in the jungle." But no one seemed to know just where.

Late that afternoon, on his way back to the village, Ellis stopped by the cemetery to pay his respects, and saw the tombstone with his own name on it. He went into town to the cantina, found the stonemason, and offered to pay for the tombstone, if he would just take it down. After a few beers, and after ascertaining that the real occupant of the grave was penniless and unknown, the mason decided to reuse the stone on another occasion, and would put up a wooden cross instead. He was very grateful for the handsome pen and pencil set which the scientist gave to him.

Ellis noticed that, as he walked down the street, people shrank back to let him pass, and were careful not to let even their clothing touch him. Whispers followed him, and a few of the older women even crossed themselves. The next morning, walking out to the jungle with the farmers, he saw that the headstone with his name on it had been taken down, and additional, plain stones had been piled onto the already mounded grave.

"Why are there more stones on the grave?" he asked.

"Just to make sure," was the answer.

Again, he searched fruitlessly for any sign of the rockbird. The drawings in the portfolio had included one of a yellow bird, but it looked more like a glorified canary than anything else. Ellis suspected that it had been traced from another picture. Again, that evening, he asked the villagers if they had ever seen the bird, and instead of specific answers, received only vague, affirmative answers.

Finally, the *curandera* said to him, "We only see the *ikeek*, as we call it, when someone in the village is about to die. The bird waits to accompany the spirit back to the gates of heaven, so that it won't get lost."

After that, Ellis stopped asking the villagers for help, but continued to search the jungles on his own for two more days. He found a single yellow feather that could have belonged to any bird at all, but he took a picture of it, wrote down the location, and sealed it up in a little plastic envelope for further analysis.

Disappointed by his lack of findings, and put off by the villagers' superstitions, Dr. Ellis decided to return to Mérida. Mrs. Vargas was relieved to see him go, but cried in spite of herself. The children walked along behind the Land Cruiser as he slowly made his way back through the village towards the main road.

As Dr. Ellis headed for the highway north, the villagers wondered if his visit would bring them bad luck; the priest wondered if God had taken care of the dead man's soul, although all of the prayers had been said in Dr. Ellis' name; and Mrs. Vargas decided that her sister in Mérida owed her a big favor.

In the jungle, under the tangle of vines and fallen trees, the rockbird stomped and shook out its golden feathers on its carefully groomed square yard of bare ground, little knowing that it was the cause of so much trouble.

The mystery of the dead American was never solved. The mayor received a letter from the American consulate, saying that a representative would be sent to investigate, but no one ever came. Two or three people claimed to have seen the old man standing outside of the village at dusk in his tattered raincoat. It was an evil spirit all along, said some, come to stir up trouble in the village. If the coffin were to be opened, nothing would be found inside but corn husks. But Mrs. Vargas never doubted the reality of the man she had helped prepare for burial.

The night that Mrs. Vargas awoke with moonlight on the foot of the bed and heard a noise outside, she knew that the dead man had returned. A wind blew from the east, whistling around the edges of the house. A lonely dog was barking. Mrs. Vargas got up and walked barefoot into the front room in her long, cotton nightgown, her black and silver braids down her back. She knew what she had to do. Feeling for the worn leather portfolio which had taken up residence under the sofa, Mrs. Vargas then unlatched the front door.

Even in the moonlight, his complexion looked unhealthy, his coat dusty and torn. The wind made wisps of hair stand up on his head, then lie down again.

Not daring to speak, Mrs. Vargas threw the portfolio as far as she could away from the house, across the road into the waiting jungle. The man bowed slightly, a wistful look on his face, and turned away. Mrs. Vargas slammed the door, locked it, and returned to her bedroom. And all the living, and all the dead, were in place.

MR. MENDOZA'S PAINTBRUSH

Luis Alberto Urrea

When I remember my village, I remember the color green.
A green that is rich, perhaps too rich, and almost bubbling with
humidity and the smell of mangos. I remember heat, the sweet
sweat of young girls that collected on my upper lip as we
kissed behind the dance stand in the town square. I remember
days of nothing and rainstorms, dreaming of making love while
walking around the *plazuela*, admiring Mr. Mendoza's portraits
of the mayor and the police chief, and saying dashing things to
the girls. They, of course, walked in the opposite direction,
followed closely by their unsympathetic aunts, which was only
decent. Looking back, I wonder if perhaps saying those dashing
things was better than making love.

Mr. Mendoza wielded his paintbrush there for thirty years.
I can still remember the old women muttering bad things about
him on their way to market. This was nothing extraordinary. The
old women muttered bad things about most of us at one time or
another, especially when they were on their way to market at
dawn, double file, dark shawls pulled tight around their faces,
to buy pots of warm milk with the cows' hairs still floating in
them. Later in the day, after their cups of coffee with a bit of
this hairy milk (strained through an old cloth) and many
spoonfuls of sugar, only then did they begin to concede the
better points of the populace. Except for Mr. Mendoza.

Mr. Mendoza had taken the controversial position that he was the Graffiti King of All Mexico. But we didn't *want* a graffiti king.

My village is named El Rosario. Perhaps being named after a rosary was what gave us our sense of importance, a sense that we from Rosario were blessed among people, allowed certain dispensations. The name itself came from a Spanish monk — or was it a Spanish soldier — named Bonifacio Rojas who broke his rosary, and the beads cascaded over the ground. Kneeling to pick them up, he said a brief prayer asking the Good Lord to direct him to the beads. Like all good Catholics, he offered the Lord a deal: if you give me my beads back, I will give you a cathedral on the spot. The Good Lord sent down St. Elmo's fire, and directly beneath that, the beads. Bonifacio got a taste of the Lord's wit, however, when he found an endless river of silver directly beneath the beads. It happened in 1655, the third of August. A Saturday.

The church was built, obliterating the ruins of an Indian settlement, and Rosario became the center of the Chametla province. For some reason, the monks who followed Bonifacio took to burying each other in the cathedral's thick adobe walls. Some mysterious element in our soil mummifies monks, and they stood in the walls for five hundred years. Now that the walls are crumbling, though, monks pop out with dry grins about once a year.

When I was young, there was a two-year lull in the gradual revelation of monks. We were all certain that the hidden fathers had all been expelled from the walls. A thunderclap proved us wrong.

Our rainy season begins on the sixth of June, without fail. This year, however, the rain was a day late, and the resulting thunderclap that announced the storm was so explosive that windows cracked on our street. Burros on the outskirts kicked open their stalls and charged through town throwing kicks right and left. People near the river swore their chickens laid square eggs. The immense frightfulness of this celestial apocalypse was blamed years afterward for gout, diarrhea, birthmarks, drunkenness and those mysterious female aches nobody could define but everyone named "*dolencias.*" There was one other victim of the thunderclap — the remaining church tower split apart and dropped a fat slab of clay into the road. In the morning, my cousin Jaime and I were thrilled to find a mummified hand rising from the rubble, one saffron finger aimed at the sky.

"An evangelist," I said.

"Even in death," he said.

We moved around the pile to see the rest of him. We were startled to find a message painted on the monk's chest:

HOW DO YOU LIKE ME NOW!

DEFLATED! DEFLATE

YOUR POMP OR FLOAT

AWAY!

"Mr. Mendoza," I said.

"He's everywhere," Jaime said.

§ § §

On the road that runs north from Escuinapa to my village, there is a sign that says:

ROSARIO POP. 8000.

Below that, in Mr. Mendoza's meticulous scrawl:

NO INTELLIGENT LIFE FOR 100 KILOMETERS.

There is a very tall bridge at the edge of town that spans the Baluarte river. Once, my cousin Jaime said, a young man sat on the railing trading friendly insults with his friends. His sweetheart was a gentle girl from a nice family. She was wearing a white blouse that day. She ran up to him to give him a hug, but instead she knocked him from his perch, and he fell, arms and legs thrown open to the wind. They had to hold her back, or she would have joined him. He called her name all the way down, like a lost love letter spinning in the wind. No one ever found the body. They say she left town and married. She had seven sons, and each one was named after her dead lover.

Her husband left her. Near this fatal spot on the bridge, Mr. Mendoza suggested that we:

UPEND HYPOCRITES TODAY.

Across town from the bridge, there is a gray whorehouse next to the cemetery. This allows the good citizens of the village to avoid the subjects of death *and* sex at the same time. On the wall facing the street, the message:

TURN YOUR PRIDE ON ITS BACK
AND COUNT ITS WIGGLY FEET.

On the stone wall that grows out of the cobble street in front of the cemetery, a new announcement appeared:

MENDOZA NEVER SLEPT HERE.

What the hell did he mean by that? There was much debate in our bars over that one. Did Mr. Mendoza mean this literally — that he had never napped between the crumbling stones? Well, so what? Who would?

No, others argued. He meant it philosophically — that Mr. Mendoza was claiming he'd never die. This was most infuriating. Police Chief Reyes wanted to know, "Who does Mr. Mendoza think he is?"

Mr. Mendoza, skulking outside the door, called in, "I'll tell you! I think I'm Mendoza, that's who! But who — or what — are *you!*"

His feet could be heard trotting away in the dark.

§ § §

Mr. Mendoza never wrote obscenities. He was far too moral for that. In fact, he had been known to graffito malefactors as though they were road signs. Once, Mr. Mendoza's epochal paintbrush fell on me.

It was in summer, in the month of August, Bonifacio's month. August is hot in Rosario, so hot that snapping turtles have been cooked by sitting in shallow water. Their green flesh turns gray and peels away to float down the eternal Baluarte. I always intended to follow the Baluarte downstream, for it carried hundreds of interesting items during flood-times, and I was certain that somewhere farther down there was a resting place for it all. The river seemed, at times, to be on a mad shopping spree, taking from the land anything it fancied. Mundane things such as trees, chickens, cows, shot past regularly. But marvelous things floated there, too: a green De Soto with its lights on, a washing machine with a religious statue in it as though the saint were piloting a circular boat, a blond wig that looked like a giant squid, a mysterious star-shaped object barely visible under the surface.

The Baluarte held me in its sway. I swam in it, fished and caught turtles in it. I dreamed of the distant bend in the river where I could find all these floating things collected in neat stacks, and perhaps a galleon full of rubies, and perhaps a damp yet lovely fifteen-year-old girl in a red dress to rescue, and all of it speckled with little gray specks of turtle skin.

Sadly for me, I found out that the river only led to swamps that oozed out to the sea. All those treasures were lost forever, and I had to seek a new kind of magic from my river. Which is precisely where Mr. Mendoza found me, on the banks of the post-magical Baluarte, lying in the mud with Jaime, gazing through a stand of reeds at some new magic.

Girls. We had discovered girls. And a group of these recently discovered creatures was going from the preparatory school's sweltering rooms to the river for a bath. They had their spot, a shielded kink in the river bank that had a natural screen of trees and reeds and a sloping sandy bank. Jaime and I knew that we were about to make one of the greatest discoveries in recent history, and we'd be able to report to the men what we'd found out.

"Wait until they hear about this," I whispered.

"It's a new world," he replied.

We inserted ourselves in the reeds, ignoring the mud soaking our knees. We could barely contain our longing and emotion. When the girls began to strip off their uniforms, revealing slips, then bright white bras and big cotton underpants, I thought I would sob.

"I can't," I said, "believe it."

"History in the making," he said.

The bras came off. They dove in.

"Before us is everything we've always wanted," I said.

"Life itself," he said.

"Oh, you beautiful girls!" I whispered.

"Oh, you girls of my dreams!" said he, and Mr. Mendoza's claws sank into our shoulders.

We were dragged a hundred meters upriver, all the while being berated without mercy: "Tartars!" he shouted. "Peeping Toms! Flesh chasers! Disrespecters of privacy!"

I would have laughed if I had not seen Mr. Mendoza's awful paintbrush standing in a freshly opened can of black paint.

"Oh oh," I said.

"We're finished," said Jaime.

Mr. Mendoza threw me down and sat on me. The man was skinny. He was bony, yet I could not buck him off. I bounced like one of those thunderstruck burros, and he rode me with aplomb.

He attacked Jaime's face, painting:

I AM FILTHY.

He then peeled off Jaime's shirt and adorned his chest with:

I LIVE FOR SEX AND THRILLS.

He then yanked off Jaime's pants and decorated his rump with:

KICK ME HARD.

I was next.

On my face:

PERVERT.

On my chest:

MOTHER IS BLUE WITH SHAME.

On my rump:

THIS IS WHAT I AM.

I suddenly realized that the girls from the river had quickly dressed themselves and were giggling at me as I jumped around naked. It was unfair! Then, to make matters worse, Mr. Mendoza proceeded to chase us through town while people laughed at us and called out embarrassing weights and measures.

We plotted our revenge for two weeks, then forgot about it. In fact, Jaime's "I LIVE FOR SEX" made him somewhat of a celebrity, that phrase being very macho. He was often known after that day as "El Sexi." In fact, years later, he would marry one of the very girls we had been spying on.

There was only one satisfaction for me in the whole sad affair: the utter disappearance of the street of my naked humiliation.

§ § §

Years after Bonifacio built his church in Rosario, and after he had died and was safely tucked away in the church walls (until 1958, when he fell out on my uncle Jorge), the mines got established as a going concern. Each vein of silver seemed to lead to another. The whole area was a network of ore-bearing arteries.

Tunnels were dug and forgotten as each vein played out and forked off. Often, miners would break through a wall of rock only to find themselves in an abandoned mineshaft going in the other direction. Sometimes they'd find skeletons. Once they swore they'd encountered a giant spider that caught bats in its vast web. Many of these mine shafts filled with seepage from the river, forming underground lagoons that had fat white frogs in them and an albino alligator that floated in the dark water waiting for hapless miners to stumble and fall in.

Some of these tunnels snaked under the village. At times, with a whump, sections of Rosario vanished. Happily, I watched the street Mr. Mendoza had chased me down drop from sight after a quick shudder. A store and six houses dropped as one. I was particularly glad to see Antonia Borrego vanish with a startled look while sitting on her porch yelling insults at me. Her voice rose to a horrified screech that echoed loudly underground as she went down. When she was finally pulled out (by block and tackle, the sow), she was all wrinkled from the smelly water, and her hair was alive with squirming white pollywogs.

After the street vanished, my view of El Yauco was clear and unobstructed. El Yauco is the mountain that stands across the Baluarte from Rosario. The top of it looks like the profile of John F. Kennedy in repose. The only flaw in this geographic wonder is that the nose is upside-down.

Once, when Jaime and I had painfully struggled to the summit to investigate the nose, we found this message:

MOTHER NATURE HAS NO RESPECT FOR
YANQUI PRESIDENTS EITHER!

Nothing, though, could prepare us for the furor over his next series of messages. It began with a piglet running through town one Sunday. On its flanks, in perfect cursive script:

Mendoza Goes to Heaven on Tuesday.

On a fence:

MENDOZA ESCAPES THIS HELLHOLE.

On my father's car:

I'VE HAD ENOUGH!
I'M LEAVING!

Rumors flew. For some reason, the arguments were fierce, impassioned, and there were any number of fistfights over Mr. Mendoza's latest. Was he going to kill himself? Was he dying? Was he to be abducted by flying saucers or carried aloft by angels? The people who were convinced the old "MENDOZA NEVER SLEPT HERE" was a strictly philosophical text were convinced he was indeed going to commit suicide. There was a secret that showed in their faces — they were actually hoping he'd kill himself, just to maintain the *status quo*, just to ensure that everyone died.

Rumors about his health washed through town: cancer, madness (well, we all knew that), demonic possession, the evil eye, a black magic curse that included love potions and slow-acting poisons, and the dreaded syphilis. Some of the local smartalecks called the whorehouse "Heaven," but Mr. Mendoza was far too moral to even go in there, much less advertise it all over town.

I worked in Crispin's bar, taking orders and carrying trays of beer bottles. I heard every theory. The syphilis one really appealed to me because young fellows always love the gruesome and lurid, and it sounded so nasty, having to do, as it did, with the *nether regions*.

"Syphilis makes it fall off," Jaime explained.

I didn't want him to know I wasn't sure which "it" fell off, if it was *it,* or some other "it." To be macho, you must already know everything, know it so well that you're already bored by the knowledge.

"Yes," I said, wearily, "it certainly does."

"Right off," he marveled.

"To the street," I concluded.

Well, that very night, that night of the Heavenly Theories, Mr. Mendoza came into the bar. The men stopped all their arguing and immediately taunted him: "Oh look! Saint Mendoza is here!" "Hey, Mendoza! Seen any angels lately?" He only smirked. Then, squaring his slender shoulders, he walked, erect, to the bar.

"Boy," he said to me. "A beer."

As I handed him the bottle, I wanted to confess: *I will change my ways! I will never peep at girls again!*

He turned and faced the crowd and gulped down his beer, eı ʳtying the entire bottle without coming up for air. When the lasᴜ ᶜ the foam ran from its mouth, he slammed the bottle on the counter and said, "Ah!" Then he belched. Loudly. This greatly offended the gathered men, and they admonished him. But he ignored them, crying out, "What do you think of that! Eh? The belch is the cry of the water-buffalo, the hog. I give it to you because it is the only philosophy you can understand!"

More offended still, the crowd began to mumble.

Mr. Mendoza turned to me and said, "I see there are many wiggly feet present."

"The man's insane," said Crispin.

Mr. Mendoza continued: "Social change and the nipping at complacent buttocks was my calling on earth. Who among you can deny that I and my brush are a perfect marriage? Who among you can hope to do more with a brush than I?"

He pulled the brush from under his coat. Several men shied away.

"I tell you now," he said. "Here is the key to Heaven."

He nodded to me once, and strode toward the door. Just before he passed into the night, he said, "My work is finished."

§ § §

Tuesday morning we were up at dawn. Jaime had discovered a chink in fat Antonia's new roof. Through it, we could look down into her bedroom. We watched her dress. She moved in billows, like a meaty raincloud. "In a way," I whispered, "it has its charm."

"A bountiful harvest," Jaime said condescendingly.

After this ritual, we climbed down to the street. We heard the voices, saw people heading for the town square. Suddenly, we remembered. "Today!" we cried in unison.

The ever-growing throng was following Mr. Mendoza. His startling shock of white hair was bright against his dark skin. He wore a dusty black suit, his funeral suit. He walked into a corner of the square, knelt down and pried the lid off a fresh can of paint. He produced the paintbrush with a flourish and held it up for all to see. There was an appreciative mumble from the crowd, a smattering of applause. He turned to the can, dipped the brush in the paint. There was a hush. Mr. Mendoza painted a black swirl on the flagstones. He went around and around with the legendary brush, filling in the swirl until it was a solid black O. Then, with a grin, with a virtuoso's mastery, he jerked his brush straight up, leaving a solid, glistening pole of wet paint standing in the air. We gasped. We clapped. Mr. Mendoza painted a horizontal line, connected to the first at a ninety degree angle. We cheered. We whistled. He painted up, across, up, across, until he was reaching over his head. It was obvious soon enough. We applauded again, this time with feeling. Mr. Mendoza turned to look at us and waved once —

whether in farewell or terse dismissal we'll never know — then raised one foot and placed it on the first horizontal. *No,* we said. He stepped up. Fat Antonia fainted. The boys all tried to look up her dress when she fell, but Jaime and I were very macho because we'd seen it already. Still, Mr. Mendoza rose. He painted his way up, the angle of the stairway carrying him out of the *plazuela* and across town, over Bonifacio's crumbling church, over the cemetery where he had never slept and would apparently never sleep. Crispin did good business selling beers to the crowd. Mr. Mendoza, now small as a high-flying crow, climbed higher, over the Baluarte and its deadly bridge, over El Yauco's and Kennedy's inverted nose, almost out of sight. The stairway wavered like smoke in the breeze. People were getting bored, and they began to wander off, back to work, back to the rumors. That evening, Jaime and I went back to fat Antonia's roof.

It happened on June fifth of that year. That night, at midnight, the rains came. By morning, the paint had washed away.

THE LAST RITE

Alicia Gaspar de Alba

For sixty of her ninety-two years, Estrella González had been singing in her garden every evening before retiring. After her third prayer to the sun at sunset, she would roam among the herbs for a while, deepening the furrows around them, pinching off the dead leaves, pronouncing each of their names in Latin and invoking their essences to come out of the ground to revitalize her healing powers. Then, she would sing.

But on this October twilight, she felt tired again. She had already talked to the plants and fed the parrot and the rooster, but she still had to take Malinche, her mule, her nightly medicine. The poor mule was getting old, now, her eyes almost completely shrouded in cataracts, but she knew that Estrella still depended on her to carry her up and down the foothills to the village, and, once a year, to San Cristóbal de las Casas, for the yearly *curandera* gathering. As Estrella approached her singing place — a huge slab of lodestone that she had unearthed under the Adobe Room — she heard the parrot insulting the rooster inside the hut:

"*Pinche gallo!* Go to hell! Go to hell!"

Estrella shook her head and chuckled at her eccentric family of animals. The black stone rocked with her weight as she sat down. She dug her hand between her breasts and pulled out the small reed flute which she kept on a string. Her hand lingered a moment over the left nipple, now swollen more than ever before. She had stopped fomenting the blisters, and sometimes, especially on amethyst nights like this one with the October moon rising in Libra, she regretted knowing her destiny.

"Ay, Madre," she sighed, "I *am* getting too old, just like my Malinche." She could feel the tears creeping into her eyes like foxes, but tonight she would not weep, she could not forget who she was. "Estrella González!" she called aloud, "where is your faith?"

She put the flute to her lips, closing her eyes so that the music would run out of her like water, so that all she could see were the swirling stars at the back of her head. When she sang, her voice carried with it the baying of the foxes.

"Salías del templo un día, Llorona,
cuando al pasar yo te vi.
Hermoso huipil llevabas, Llorona,
que la virgen te creí."

The Ballad of La Llorona gave her the most comfort on these long nights of waiting, for it reminded her of Malintzin, mother of La Raza, and of Tonantzin and Coatlicue, mothers of the Earth and of the Night — the immortal memories in her blood. In six months, she would perform the greatest, the most difficult, of all her experiments, and she needed the Mothers to lend her more power.

"Ay de mí, Llorona,
Llorona de ayer y hoy.
Ayer maravilla fui, Llorona,
y ahora ni sombra soy."

Her voice faltered, now, in the middle of the song, and her notes on the flute were more like the whimpers of an old, indomitable longing. The music stopped and she got up heavily, pushing herself off the lodestone with a grunt.

"Six months," she mumbled, walking towards her hut, barely lifting her feet from the ground. She stroked the thunderbird on the *sarape* that served as her door, and remembered that she had to set out the jugs. It was going to rain later and she needed to collect the rainwater for her altar.

The hut felt cold. She hurried lighting the fire, then placed a kettle of water to boil for her tea. She would have the *palo azul* bark to strengthen her kidneys, orange blossoms to bring sleep, and cinnamon for spice.

"Strong kidneys give you a long life," she told the parrot, who had heard it all before and just preened under his turquoise-colored wings. "It's a wonder you haven't died with all the mezcal you drink!" she scolded.

"Go to hell!" the parrot squawked. "Go to hell!"

She tried to get the rooster to come out from behind the trunk, but he had still not recovered from her last experiment. He refused to crow in the mornings, and he didn't trust anything that she gave him to eat or drink. "*Pinche gallo!*" she said. The parrot echoed.

Estrella wasn't in the mood for her nightly ritual. She had become so vain since her ninetieth birthday, and had taken to smearing her body every night with a cream that she made herself, grinding the herbs in the *molcajete* and letting them steep in a bowl of grease that hardened in the two hours that it took to do her studying. But she didn't feel strong enough to study tonight, much less do any grinding. What if she used the fish oil that she reserved only for the Mothers' work?

"Just this once," she muttered. Surely there would be no harm if she just used a drop or two to ease the wrinkles in her face. She did feel so tired, and the thought of making anything other than her tea exhausted her even more. *Yes*, she thought, *just a drop or two can't hurt.*

She passed through another *sarape* at the back of the hut and into the Adobe Room. The smell of *copal* permeated her bones, and she knew that invisible eyes watched her in the penumbra as she made the sign of the five points before the altar.

"*Madres*," she whispered to the corn, straw, and clay figures on the altar, "guardians of this room and its implements, I beg you to forgive me for taking of this oil to soothe my withered flesh." She took a copper bowl that hung from a nail on the wall and poured into it a few drops of dark oil that gleamed like the melted wax of the candles. The smell of seaweed and fish cloyed her nostrils as she rubbed the first drop on her forehead. When she came out into the main room, her eyes were stung by the bright flames of the fire. She noticed that her water was boiling and took a few pieces of bark, a handful of dry petals, and a strip of cinnamon from their respective jars, and dropped everything into the kettle.

As she removed her blouse, her skirts, she hummed another tune of *La Llorona,* a tremulous humming, filled suddenly with the memory of her only child, a memory that she did not allow herself to indulge in, for she was too old and had Learned too much to regret anything. But the memory stayed, and she tried to defend herself against its accusations.

The little girl was dying in her care. Estrella's Learning took her away from the hut for days, and she would forget that the child was waiting for her, eating dirt and playing in chicken droppings. Estrella had not wanted to have a child. She had simply been experimenting with the egg, and had ended up using her body as the laboratory. Her pregnancy had not been the surprising thing; even at seventy she had been fertile, thanks to her teas. The truth is, she didn't expect the egg to have the effect that it did on the young man. He had just come to deliver the wood the villagers sent her once a week, and Estrella had offered him breakfast. The egg looked darker than he was accustomed to, but it was good, he said, especially with that spicy salsa on top. The next thing Estrella knew, the young man was on top of her, poking under her skirts. She had laughed through the whole thing, and for weeks afterwards, congratulating herself on the potent aphrodisiac she had created. And then her blood stopped. Her old breasts filled with milk.

She could have stopped the child. Could have taken *toloache* or punched herself in the belly, but she had wanted to see the results of the experiment. Maybe it would not be a child at all, but a monster born of an inhuman seed, a creature to dissect and investigate. But it had turned out to be human, after all. A girl with too much sugar in her blood.

Just after the girl's third birthday, the parrot brought her the rumor of a prediction in Mitla, the town — an old Zapotec ghost town that was more popular with the tourists than the ghosts —

that bordered the ancient Zapotec and Mixtec catacombs, three days north of La Subida. The prediction had been made by the same *curandero* whom Estrella had ousted from La Subida sixty years before. It was in this way that fate always worked for Estrella González. And so Malinche the mule took them north to Mitla, to leave the girl in the ruins where some *turista* would probably find her. Estrella never expected to see the girl again, but thirteen years later, she appeared, as miraculously as the Virgin whose name she'd been given, one afternoon in Estrella's garden, seeking a potion to give death to her own child. Estrella had never told the girl the truth. The truth was *her* burden. The girl had other crosses to carry.

"Y *aunque la vida me cueste, Llorona,*
no dejaré de quererte."

She sang softly, her head swaying with each word as she uncoiled her long braids. Once her hair was loosened and hung down her back, she stepped over to the fire and knelt down. Taking the copper bowl from the table, she held it over the flames, rotating it slowly between her palms. The fire licked at her bracelets as it warmed the dark green oil. She felt her pubic hair and her armpits grow damp. On his perch, the parrot rustled his wings at her, nearly losing his balance in the heat of the room.

The oil released a strong, salty odor, and Estrella felt herself getting dizzy as she set the bowl down next to her on the dirt floor. Rivulets of sweat ran down the middle of her spine and between her breasts. Eyes closed, she dipped three fingers of each hand into the bowl. She rubbed the warm oil over the loose skin of her neck, and could hear herself singing silently:

Dicen que no tengo duelo, Llorona,
por que no me ven llorar.
Hay muertos que no hacen ruido, Llorona,
y es más grande su penar.

As she continued to wet her fingers in the oil, dabbing it behind her earlobes, in the hollow of her throat, on each nipple, under the arms, and on the inside of each wrist and knee, she felt her body move from side to side, a rhythmic swaying that removed her fatigue. Head hanging back, hair trailing in the dirt, she started speaking her name in one of the first old languages that she had Learned, the Tzeltal word ululating out of her throat:

"'Ek'etik! 'Ek'etik! 'Ek'etik!"

Even with her eyes shut, she could see the room circling about her. The fire lapped at her in huge roaring flames, and she realized that her body had become very small, that she stood beneath a great cloud of flames, the Scorpion's nest, her arms reaching up to it, her fingers clawing the brilliant air. She could feel herself about to perform the Dance of the Scorpion Cross, the old fertility dance of the Tzeltales.

"Tsek, Scorpio!" she called, looking up at the fire cloud as the Scorpion arched its giant tail and stung her skull with its white light.

"Kurus'ek!" she cried, facing north as the Scorpion's tail injected the light into her lungs and heart. Fire shot down through her spine and formed a pillar of light in her body. Slowly, the Scorpion's great pincers pierced her belly.

"Sakubee ek'!" she wailed, facing east, "Yek' uljch' ultatik!" She faced west. The pincers gripped her ovaries, and the Cross of the Scorpion burned inside her as she whirled around the room. At the end of the dance, she cupped her breasts in her hands and milked the light out of her body.

When she awoke two hours later, she found herself lying naked on the ground next to the smoldering logs. The kettle she had set with water had turned over, drenching the fish skulls that she used as a border for her hearth. At first she did not remember the Dance of the Scorpion Cross. Her head throbbed and her whole body felt hot and cold at the same time. Her lips were covered with sand and she felt thirsty. She wiped her mouth with the back of her hand, closing her eyes as she tried to recall how much of the mezcal she had imbibed, cursing silently at her self-indulgence. She heard rain pattering on the tin roof.

"But I ran out of mezcal!" she cried out, sitting up quickly. The mezcal jug had been empty for days, now, just like the water jugs she had forgotten to set out. She remembered she had used the oil of the Mothers.

"Santa Madre!" she cried again as the image of the tail and pincers filtered out of her memory. How could she have been so stupid? This was a time of preparation. She could not allow the old rituals to mount her until she was stronger. If only she had made her usual cream. She got to her knees groggily, the pain slicing through her head with each movement, but she welcomed that pain, now, her fever and thirst, as well. Her punishments for being such a lazy weakling, such a lazy, crazy *vieja!*

"*¡Loca! ¡Loca!*" screeched the parrot.

Estrella felt like poisoning the bird. She groped around for her clothes and found one of her skirts near the table. She threw it over her head and pulled it down to her waist, wincing as the coarse fabric grazed her breasts. There! She had gone and infected the nipple again, lying in that dirt. Well, that's what she deserved for her foolishness. She lumbered up the ladder to the platform where she kept her most precious things: her books, the water-jugs, and her *morral* — the snakeskin medicine bag that held the sacred earth and thorns from the hill of Tepeyac.

It took her a long time to carry down all the jugs, and by the time she finished, the rain had abated. Her efforts had been useless. The rain would stop any minute, and it would not rain again for months. Her thirst became unbearable, and she knew that she had better allow herself at least a few drops of water, otherwise her fever would increase, and she would not be able to get up in the morning. She leaned against the hut, opened her mouth, and let the drizzle cool her parched tongue. She would not let the vision of the Scorpion Cross surface again, but standing out here, she could not help but contrast the burning light and the chilly darkness. Malinche brayed, once, reminding Estrella that she still had to make the salve that ate at the mule's cataracts.

Later, as she lay, exhausted, in her hammock, watching the Milky Way through the hole in the roof, she invoked the spirit of La Gran María, mother of the First Name, whom she only called upon when the doubts swelled like goiters. She had been so weak, lately, given to fits of rage and despair and outright sensuality. Just last year, she'd gathered all her herbs in a basket and cast them into the bay, and then, to the embarrassment of the villagers, she had stripped herself like a prostitute and waded into the sea, a fat old woman having a tantrum because her experiments weren't giving her the results she wanted. Since then, her cures hadn't been the same. The healings had become monotonous, and she found herself doubting her abilities more and more.

Tonight, she needed La Gran María to fortify her faith for this most vital of all her experiments. In her sixty years of experimentation, she had never inseminated anything other than chickens and ducks. If she allowed the doubts to root inside her, the egg would rot and the scorpion would kill her. The experiment for which she had been preparing her entire life, her mission as a *curandera*, would fail. If she failed, the one the Mothers were waiting for would not be born. Estrella González could have no doubts. Everything was ready. All she had to do was wait for the stranger who would call at her house in six months, a young man of the new breed bringing her word of another religion. After feeding him well and extracting his seed, Estrella would send him to her daughter in Mitla. Thus, the experiment would begin, and it would end on the night of the insemination.

"Six months," she sighed.

"Six months," the parrot repeated.

Just before her eyelids closed, Estrella heard the rooster come out of his hiding place behind the trunk, his talons scratching at the floor as he scurried out to the garden. When the rooster crowed, she knew that La Gran María was with her, a blood-fresh presence in the room.

"Madre," she spoke, "I know that the insemination will be my last rite, that, once it is finished, I will shed this old skin, and with it will go all my power as well as my illness. But will it work, Madre? Will the egg carry the memories?"

The egg is the name, Estrella González, the mother of the First Name answered. *Just as La Gran María evokes the gramarye of our kind, the name you choose must evoke the memories. If the ritual does not work, it will be because you have chosen the wrong name.*

The rooster crowed again, and Estrella González took her flute out and played another tune of the *Ballad of La Llorona.*

A SUBTLE PLAGUE

Alejandro Murguía

The president of Monumental Lawyers Title Corporation, John C. Shaker, stood on a crumbling farmhouse porch and looked over the last one-hundred-fifty acres of open land in the valley. On the landscape of orange trees dotting the soft rolling hills, he mentally airbrushed a sprawling shopping mall with a glass fountain bubbling in the center of a parking lot filled with cars. He imagined an imitation rain forest for the atrium, and three floors of elegant cafes, restaurants, and up-scale shops. So focused was Shaker on his future creation that he failed to notice the grain-like specks floating in the air around him. When he did glimpse the minute white specks clinging to the wool threads of his suit, he merely flicked them away. For an instant, he was reminded of the time ashes landed in town from a volcano explosion at Mt. Helena.

Shaker had long coveted this parcel of land of old man García's. Over the years, all the other citrus ranchers had sold out, one by one, to the Corporation. In the entire valley only José García had refused to sell. The old man stubbornly turned down all offers and continued working his ranch, sometimes hiring a day laborer to help him out. But the Corporation broke the ranch when they bought the packing house at the edge of town and turned it into condominiums. Without a packing house to handle his yearly crop, the old man's ranch went slowly under, until in the last few years before he died, García was never seen in town. People speculated he lived off what he grew in his garden and whatever wild game he hunted. The old man's body was not yet cold before the Corporation's lawyers huddled over his estate like white-skulled buzzards in dark suits. García left no will, and no one in town could remember the names of his relatives, or where they might be. Shaker moved quickly to get a probate judge to sell the ranch to the Corporation.

Now Shaker had what he wanted; the Rancho Maravilla was thoroughly his except for the red rays of the setting sun that darted through the rolling hills. The run-down house on the ranch was worthless, and he intended to tear it down tomorrow. It was a turn-of-the-century farmhouse, with a wrap-around porch that kind of settled in the middle, and white paint long faded and chipped down to the wood. In front of the farmhouse, a solitary palm kept a lonely vigil.

While standing on the porch admiring the site, Shaker noticed the overpowering army of smells assaulting him from within the house. The stink of pungent Mexican cigarettes permeated the walls; the smell of grease and *chiles* and jerked deer meat stormed from the kitchen, and emanating from the bedroom came the sad odor of loneliness and stale farts.

Shaker stepped off the porch and headed towards the rows of orange trees neatly spaced and well cared for. He'd gone about four trees in when a fine white dust covering the leaves drew his attention. He ran one fingertip along a leaf, then closely examined the glittering white powder. The dust was really minute, triangular-shaped white flies. He'd never seen anything so insignificant, so utterly pointless in the scheme of things. He rubbed his fingertips together grinding the flies into a fluffy ball. He looked down the rows of orange trees wondering at this sudden appearance of white flies. In the short time he'd been standing in the orchard, the flies had grown perceptibly thicker. A quarter-inch of powdery dust now covered all the trees and half the hillside. A soft wind swirled the white specks around him, and the flies settled softly on his eyebrows, drifted down into his eyes, and got clogged in his nose hairs. Shaker couldn't wipe them away fast enough from his forehead.

How strange, he thought, as he hurried towards the house. Where could they all be coming from? With each step he obliterated thousands of flies, and each time he lifted his shoe, he left behind a black print in the carpet of snow-like whiteness.

By the time he reached the house, the whiteness was piled thick on the window screens and the front door screens. As he hurried up the porch steps he saw his Cadillac half buried in a white-colored mound. A blinding flurry of flies greeted Shaker's face as he grabbed the screen door handle. He stumbled into the partial darkness of the old García house. The door slammed shut behind him. Fear, at first irrational, then controlled, twisted his gut and tightened his throat. His tongue, caked, dried in his mouth. The rafters of the old house creaked with the weight of half-a-ton of pressure bearing down on it.

Fighting panic, Shaker went looking through the old house for a telephone. There was none. He decided to stay there until daybreak. The house groaned with shadows. Shaker picked up the heavy scent of old man García's Mexican cigarettes. At the signing of the deed, one of the secretaries had joked about a deathbed curse that, supposedly, old José García had put on Shaker. Everyone in the room had laughed, including himself. Shaker was a graduate of the state's most prestigious MBA program, and he didn't believe in ghosts, in old men dying with curses on their lips, or in attaching emotions to profits. With a trembling hand, Shaker lit a Bic and held the flickering flame high above his head to get a good look around the house. Nothing but dead flies and cobwebs in the corners. A breeze from nowhere blew out his lighter. The wind whistled somewhere outside in the orchard.

Well after nightfall, Shaker pushed open the front door and looked upon a surreal moonlit landscape. The land, the orchard, his car, everything seemed to be covered by freshly fallen snow. Half a mile away he could see the headlights on the main road whizzing by. Seized by a sudden, irrational panic, Shaker made a desperate sprint for the main road. Five steps off the porch he sank knee-deep in the powdery white dust. By the time he reached his car, the white powder was up to his waist and the door handles were buried and impossible to reach. He flailed at the mounds of white but succeeded only in stirring up the flies. Turbulent clouds of white rose up against him and clogged his ears, blinded his eyes, choked his throat. Shaker stumbled through the moonlit orchards in a blind rage — howling, spitting, choking, and lost.

The next morning when the crew came with the tractor and trailer to demolish the old García house, they found Shaker lying in a mud puddle face down in the murky water. A grotesque, agonized expression of terror twisted his stiff features. The demolition was held back till the coroner arrived to inspect the body.

The five-man crew lolled near the tractor, smoking cigarettes, waiting all morning for word on what to do. A thin layer of white dust still covered the farmhouse roof, the tarp covered body of Shaker, and the Cadillac. By noon, a southern wind had swept away the last of the strange dust. Just before dark, long after the coroner had removed the plastic-draped body and a tow truck had taken the Cadillac, a messenger arrived from town. All projects of Monumental Lawyers Title Corporation were postponed indefinitely due to the tragic and unforeseen death of its president, John Shaker.

The five men loaded their crowbars and sledgehammers onto the small trailer by the light of a full moon that rose through a blue haze. A small, Indian-looking day laborer by the name of Ignacio rode alone with the tools, on top of the open trailer. Ignacio had once worked here for aged José García, and he had liked the old man. After work, García would often invite Ignacio to stay for a bowl of *pozole* and a cigarette. The old man smoked strong, unfiltered Mexican cigarettes that filled the ramshackle house with blue smoke.

The foreman started up the tractor. The peaked roof of the crumbling farmhouse, the solitary palm tree, and the neat rows of orange trees were painted with white, translucent moonlight.

Ignacio balanced himself on the toolbox as the tractor and trailer pulled away, swaying and pitching over the furrowed fields. Then he saw a hunched shadow, like that of José García, pass across the porch and the night suddenly filled with the pungent odor of strong Mexican cigarettes. Ignacio rubbed the goose bumps on his arms. When the crown of the palm tree was barely visible, Ignacio raised his hand in a sort of farewell benediction to the old farmhouse. "Sleep well, old man," he said, and arched a half-smoked cigarette at the burning ember of the moon.

BIOGRAPHICAL NOTES

KATHLEEN ALCALA is the author of a book of short stories, *Mrs. Vargas and the Dead Naturalist* (Calyx Books) and an editor at *The Seattle Review* at The University of Washington in Seattle, where she lives.

RUDOLFO ANAYA is the author of several novels, including the legendary Chicano novel, *Bless Me Ultima* (Quinto Sol Publications) and the forthcoming novel, *Albuquerque* (The University of New Mexico Press). He is the editor of *The Blue Mesa Review* and teaches in the English Department at The University of New Mexico in Albuquerque.

ANA BACA is a student at The University of New Mexico in Albuquerque. This is her first published story.

PATRICIA BLANCO is a native of Arizona. This is her first published short story. She lives in Tucson.

JOSE ANTONIO BURCIAGA received a Before Columbus American Book Award for his second book of poetry, *Undocumented Love* (Chusma House Publishers). He is also the author of an essay collection, *Weed the People* (Pan American University Press). He teaches at Stanford University in California.

NASH CANDELARIA is the author of four novels, including *Leonor Park* and *Inheritance of Strangers* (Bilingual Review Press) and a book of short fiction, *The Day the Cisco Kid Shot John Wayne*, also from Bilingual Review Press. He lives in Palo Alto, California.

ANA CASTILLO, in addition to being a widely published poet, is a novelist, essayist, translator, editor and teacher. She is the author of several books, *Women Are Not Roses* (Arte Publico Press), *My Father Was a Toltec* (West End Press), The Mixquiahuala Letters (Anchor/Doubleday), and *Sapogonia* (Bilingual Review Press) among them. A non-fiction work, *Massacre of the Dreamers: Reflections On Mexican-Indian Women in the U.S.*, will be published by the University of New Mexico in 1994; her new novel, *So Far From God*, is forthcoming in 1993 from W.W. Norton.

DENISE CHAVEZ is the author of numerous plays, works for children, and stories which have won several important literary awards. Her collection, *The Last of the Menu Girls* (Arte Publico Press), won the Puerto del Sol fiction award for 1985. She also tours the country with her one-woman performance piece, "Women in the State of Grace." Chávez holds a master's degree in Creative Writing from the University of New Mexico. She is a native of New Mexico and currently makes her home in Las Cruces where she is working on her new novel, *Face of an Angel.*

SANDRA CISNEROS was born in Chicago, the daughter of a Mexican father and a Mexican-American mother. She is the author of *The House on Mango Street* (Vintage), awarded the Before Columbus American Book Award for 1985, and *My Wicked Wicked Ways* (Third Woman Press/Turtle Bay Books) which will be published in hardcover by Turtle Bay Books in 1992. Her short story collection, *Woman Hollering Creek* (Vintage/Random House), published in 1991, received the Lannan Award for Fiction and the PEN Center West Award for Fiction. Her work has been translated into seven languages. Cisneros currently resides in San Antonio where she is at work on her novel, *Caramelo.*

LUCHA CORPI's books include a novel, *Delia's Song* (Arte Publico Press) and a book of poetry, *Variations on a Storm* (Third Woman Press). She teaches in the Neighborhood Centers Program for the Oakland, California public schools.

ROBERTA FERNANDEZ received a Multicultural Publishers Award for her first novel, *Intaglio* (Arte Publico Press). She is a senior editor at Arte Publico Press at The University of Houston, Texas.

ALICIA GASPAR DE ALBA is one of three Chicana poets in *Three Times a Woman*, an anthology of three full-length collections of poetry from Bilingual Review Press. Her collection in the anthology is entitled *Beggar on the Córdoba Bridge*. Alicia's first book of short fiction, *The Mystery of Survival and Other Stories*, is forthcoming from the same publisher in 1992. She is a doctoral student in American Studies at the University of New Mexico, and is currently a Chicana Dissertation Fellow at the University of California, Santa Barbara.

DAGOBERTO GILB is the author of *Winners on the Pass Line* (Cinco Puntos Press) and a forthcoming collection of stories from the University of New Mexico Press. His work appears frequently in *The Threepenny Review* and has been reprinted in several anthologies, including *The Pushcart Prize Stories* and *The Best of The West*. He is a 1992 recipient of a National Endowment for the Arts fellowship in fiction and lives in El Paso, Texas.

RAFAEL JESUS GONZALEZ was born and raised in the bilingual/bicultural setting of El Paso, Texas. He received his education at the University of Texas at El Paso, Universidad Nacional Autónoma de México and the University of Oregon. He is currently teaching creative writing and literature at Laney College in Oakland, California. Widely published in reviews and anthologies in the United States, Mexico and abroad, his collection of verse, *El Hacedor De Juegos / The Maker Of Games* (Casa Editorial, San Francisco), went into a second printing.

RAY GONZALEZ is the author of two books of poetry, including *Twilights and Chants* (James Andrews & Co.), winner of a 1987 Four Corners Book Award and the editor of eight anthologies, including *After Aztlan: Latino Poets in the Nineties* (David R. Godine) and *Without Discovery: A Native Response to Columbus* (Broken Moon Press). He lives in San Antonio, Texas.

ALEXANNA PADILLA HEINEMANN has published fiction in *Tonantzin* and other journals. She lives in Albuquerque, New Mexico.

JUAN FELIPE HERRERA received a Before Columbus American Book Award for *Facegames* (As Is, So and So Press), his second book of poetry. His *Selected Poems* is forthcoming from Broken Moon Press. He teaches in the Creative Writing Program at Southern Illinois University in Carbondale.

JACK LOPEZ has published short fiction in a number of journals throughout the country, including *Quarterly West, Saguaro,* and *Nuestro*. He teaches in the English Department at California State University in Northridge.

VICTORIANO MARTINEZ is the author of a book of poetry, *Caring for a House* (Chusma House Publications). He received a John MacCarron New Writing in Arts Award for a book of essays on Chicano artists and writers. He lives in San Francisco, California.

ALEJANDRO MURGUIA received a Before Columbus American Book Award for *Southern Front* (Bilingual Review Press), a book of short stories. He lives in San Francisco, California.

MARY HELEN PONCE is a highly regarded critic of Chicano literature whose reviews and scholarly work have been published in numerous journals and anthologies. She teaches at The University of California at Santa Cruz, California.

LEROY V. QUINTANA is the author of *Hijo del Pueblo: New Mexico Poems* (Puerto del Sol Press), *Sangre*, and *Five Poets of Aztlan*. He has two books of poetry forthcoming in 1992: *Interrogations* (poetry of Vietnam experience) from Viet Nam Generation/Burning Cities Press and *Now and Then, Often, Today* from Bilingual Review Press. He teaches at Mesa College in San Diego, California.

ALBERTO RIOS received the 1982 Walt Whitman Prize in Poetry for his first book, *Whispering to Fool the Wind* (Sheep Meadow Press). He received a Western States Book Award in fiction for his book of short stories, *The Iguana Killer* (Blue Moon Press). He teaches at Arizona State University in Tempe.

LUIS J. RODRIGUEZ is the author of two books of poetry, *Poems Across the Pavement* (Tía Chucha Press), which received a San Francisco State Poetry Center Prize, and *The Concrete River* (Curbstone Press), which received the 1991 PEN West/Josephine Miles Award for Literary Excellence. His book of memoirs, *Always Running*, is forthcoming from Curbstone Press in 1993. He is the publisher of Tía Chucha Press in Chicago, Illinois.

DANNY ROMERO's fiction and essays have appeared in numerous journals and in *West of the West, Imagining California* (North Point Press) and *California Childhood: Recollections of the Golden State* (Creative Arts Book Company). He was awarded a Future Faculty Fellowship at Temple University in Philadelphia, Pennsylvania.

BENJAMIN ALIRE SAENZ received a Before Columbus American Book Award for his first book of poetry, *Calendar of Dust* (Broken Moon Press). His book of short fiction, *Flowers for the Broken*, is forthcoming from the same publisher. He teaches in the bilingual MFA Writing Program at The University of Texas in El Paso.

NATALIA TREVIÑO teaches in the Poetry in the Schools Program in San Antonio, Texas. Her poetry and fiction has appeared in *Cactus Alley*, the student publication from The University of Texas in San Antonio.

LUIS ALBERTO URREA is the author of *Across the Wire: Life and Hard Times on the Mexican Border* (Doubleday/Anchor Books). His first book of poetry, *Ghost Sickness*, is forthcoming from March/Abrazo Press in 1993. He teaches at The University of Colorado in Boulder.

ALMA LUZ VILLANUEVA is a poet and fiction writer whose first novel, *The Ultraviolet Sky* (Bilingual Review Press) received a Before Columbus American Book Award and is scheduled for republication by Doubleday in 1993. Her second novel, *Naked Ladies*, as well as a new book of poetry, *Planet*, are forthcoming from Bilingual Review Press. She lives in Santa Cruz.

RICH YAÑEZ edited *The Rio Grande Review* at the University of Texas in El Paso and is a student in the bilingual MFA Writing Program at the University.

RICARDO MEANS YBARRA is the author of a novel, *The Pink Rosary*, forthcoming from Latin American Literary Review Press. He lives in Malibu, California.

Other Latino titles available from Curbstone

THE BLOOD THAT KEEPS SINGING
a bilingual selection of poetry by Clemente Soto Vélez
translated by Martín Espada and Camilo Pérez-Bustillo

"He works in the realm of pure poetry....as one reads these marvelous pieces, it is apparent that a social and political compassion contributes largely to their intelligence."—*Library Journal*

"...the English-speaking reader can discover at last this major writer whose poetry and passionate social vision are inseparable, a man for whom the poet must be 'light transformed into humanity.'"— *MultiCultural Review*
$9.95 paper, 0-915306-78-6

THE CONCRETE RIVER
poetry by Luis J. Rodriguez

This collection of poetry by the Chicano poet, journalist and publisher, Luis J. Rodriguez, received the 1991 PEN Oakland/Joesphine Miles Award for excellence in poetry.

"Rodriguez writes from the inside out, with great knowledge, passion, and compassion....Highly recommended for contemporary poetry and multicultural collections."—*Library Journal*

"In the highly emotional and oracular register of Whitman and Ginsberg, Rodriguez speaks for a silent generation of Mexicans who came north for economic freedom....For Rodriguez, poetry is a sacred act that can rescue the poet's past in order to instruct his community about his relationship to it and the world."—*The American Book Review*
$9.95 paper, 0-915306-42-5

REBELLION IS THE CIRCLE OF A LOVER'S HANDS
a bilingual edition of poetry by Martín Espada
translated by the author and Camilo Pérez-Bustillo
foreword by Amiri Baraka

About this powerful collection of poems, which received the 1989 PEN/Revson Award for poetry, the judges (Carolyn Forché, Daniel Halpern & Charles Simic) said: "Whoever in the future wishes to find out the truth about our age will have to read poets like Martín Espada....The greatness of Espada's art, like all great arts, is that it gives dignity to the insulted and the injured of the earth."
$9.95 paper, 0-915306-95-6

FOR A COMPLETE CATALOG, SEND YOUR REQUEST TO:
Curbstone Press, 321 Jackson Street, Willimantic, CT 06226